*For Kim,*
*But for whom, the inspiration for this book*
*would've been sausages*

# CHAPTER ONE

The old saddleback sow lifted her head and gazed across the yard at the livestock trailer.

Pigs are highly intelligent creatures, with enquiring, analytical minds. They're considerably smarter than we give them credit for. The only reason you don't get more pigs at Oxford, Cambridge, Harvard and the Sorbonne is that they're notoriously picky about the company they keep. Lacking binocular vision and opposable thumbs, they can't read or write; instead, they *think* – long, complicated, patient thoughts that often take years to mature. The old sow had thought long and hard about the trailer, the metal box on wheels into which her seven broods of piglets had gone, and from which they'd never returned.

Odd, she thought.

It always happened the same way. The men from the farm came up early in the morning and lured the piglets into the box with kind words and food; then, when all the little ones were inside, the ramp went up, and the men went back to the house. At that point, invariably, the farmer's wife came along with the sow's morning feed, which she put in the trough inside the concrete sty; and after the sow had eaten it, she always had to have a nap, which lasted till midday. When she came out again, the trailer would still be there in the corner of the yard, though (curiously) not in exactly the same place, and the sow would watch it carefully for many hours, to see if the piglets came out again. She'd observed that the trailer had only one means of entry and exit, the ramp that folded up and down, so it wasn't as though the piglets could sneak out unobserved. But when, shortly after the afternoon milking, the men opened the ramp and went into the trailer to wash it out with the hose, it was self-evidently empty. No piglets in there. Nothing but air and floorboards.

There had been a time when she'd suspected foul play; that the men did something bad to the piglets. But that quite obviously didn't compute. They looked after the piglets. They gave them food and water for eight months, mucked out the sty, even called the Healer if one of them fell ill. If the humans wanted to hurt them, even (the sow winced at the blasphemy) do away with them, why go to all that trouble over their welfare?

Accordingly, the sow reasoned, it was only logical to assume that, whatever the purpose that lay behind putting the piglets in the trailer, it had to be something beneficial. Well, it didn't take a genius to figure that out, let alone a pig. Nor did it have much bearing on the essential mystery of how a dozen squealing piglets could enter a box on wheels and simply disappear.

To get a better understanding of the factors at work in the mystery, the sow had, over the years, figured out the basic laws of physics: the law of conservation of matter, the laws of thermodynamics, the essential elements of gravity and relativity. Instead of clarifying, however, these conclusions only made the problem more obscure. According to these laws, it was physically impossible for the piglets to enter a box and never leave it. Frustrated, she abandoned scientific speculation and went back over the obvious things. Might there, for example, be a trapdoor in the bottom of the box, through which the piglets descended into an underground passage? No, because she could see the yard quite plainly, and the box (as previously

noted) did tend to move from time to time. She could categor-
ically state that there were no manholes or covers in the yard
that could possibly open into any sort of passageway or tunnel.
Was it possible, then, that the box with the piglets in it was at
some point taken out of the yard and emptied of piglets at some
other place? That one was easily answered. The box couldn't
possibly leave the yard, because it was too big to get through
the little gate, the one the men came in and out of; and the
big gate was impassable, firmly secured with a chain. Nothing
could get through that. She knew that for a fact. She'd tried
it herself, the time her sty door had been left open and she'd
got out into the yard. If her four hundredweight of determined
muscle and sinew hadn't been able to force the gate open, how
could weedy little creatures like the men possibly hope to get
the box through it? She was ashamed of herself for even considering it.

So, back to square one. She re-evaluated the physical universe and arrived at the conclusion that it was made up of
matter and energy. She went a step further and figured out
that it was entirely possible to convert matter into energy (the
equations were tricky; they'd taken her a whole morning) and
thereby achieve teleportation. Which would, of course, explain
everything. The piglets went into the trailer and were beamed
out to some destination unknown.

For a while, she was almost satisfied with that. Not, however,
for long. As she reflected on it, she realised that the power required to convert the piglets into a coherent stream of data
and energy was far beyond the capacity of the men from the
farm. Even if they'd worked out how to tame the potential of
matter/antimatter collision (the only means she could think of
whereby enough power could be generated; though, she was
humble enough to admit, she was only a pig, so what did she
know?), the vast array of plant and machinery required would
fill the yard ten times over; no way it could all be fitted inside
the little tin box on wheels and still leave room for a dozen

piglets. Reluctantly, she abandoned the teleportation hypothesis, and went back to rubbing her neck against the corner of the sty.

Twice, science had failed her. Clearly, then, she wasn't looking at it the right way. She was being too narrow-minded, too conventional and linear in her approach. She cleared her mind, ate a couple of turnips to help herself focus, and began to re-evaluate the basic world model on which all her assumptions had been based.

What if, she thought, what if this world, this universe that we perceive, is not the be all and end all of things? What if it's only one of a number, an infinite number of such worlds, such universes; not a universe in fact but one small facet of a multiverse, an infinite number of alternative realities all simultaneously occupying the same coordinates in space and time? And suppose the trailer was an access point to some kind of portal or vortex, whereby one could pass from one alternative into another, seeming in the process to disappear but in fact merely phasing into another dimension, another version of the story?

Over the next month or so she thought about that a lot, and even made some progress towards constructing a viable mathematical model of the phase shift process. Before she could complete the model, however, she was struck by a sudden, blinding moment of pure insight, as happens with pigs more often than you would think.

The men, she reasoned, look after the pigs, and the cows and the sheep and the turkeys and the chickens. That was a fact of everyday life; but *why* did they do it? Such a simple question, so easy to overlook. Once she'd formulated the question, however, the answer came with the force of complete inevitability. The men looked after the animals because they were part of a greater mechanism, a process or series of functions that ordered the entire universe, or multiverse. The men looked after the pigs because *that was what they were for*, and in that case it stood to reason that there existed in the hierarchy of functionality a greater force that looked after the men, fed them, watered them, mucked them out, replaced their straw, healed them when they were sick, ear-tagged them when the Ministry came to inspect; and it was that higher agency, that supremely powerful and benevolent entity, to whom all things must surely be possible, who descended on the trailer after the piglets had gone in and took them away, presumably to exist on some higher plane of being, in a moment of supreme rapture.

As soon as the thought had taken shape in her mind, she was certain she'd at last found the answer. Both logically and intuitively, she *knew*. There could be no other explanation. Once she'd reached that piercing instant of clarity, however, there was no going back. She barely slept or ate. She stopped rubbing her back against the rough edge of the breeze blocks, and could scarcely be bothered to kick over her water trough when the farmer's wife filled it each morning. Every molecule of her being was filled to bursting with the desire to get inside the trailer and experience the sublime perfection of the transfer.

And then, quite unexpectedly, she got her chance. The farmer's wife went away for a day or so, leaving her teenage daughter to look after the sow. The daughter, completely absorbed with talking to the little rectangle of plastic pressed to her ear, failed to shut the sty properly. The old sow waited until the daughter had gone away and seized her chance. Nudging the sty door open with her mighty nose, she charged out into the yard and trundled as fast as her legs could carry her towards the trailer. As she did so, she realised that she had no means of lowering the ramp but, incredibly, when she got there she noticed that the retaining pegs that locked it in place were loose, practically hanging out of their sockets. One precisely aimed blow of her snout, at just the right angle applied with just the right degree of force, would be enough to bounce them out, whereupon gravity would cause the ramp to swivel on its hinge and fall to the ground.

Feverishly, forcing herself to concentrate, she did the maths, calculating the angles in two planes, applying Sow's Constant (mass times velocity squared) to quantify exactly the force needed. At the last moment she closed her eyes and appealed to the Supreme Agency itself: *If I am worthy, let the ramp come down.*

She headbutted. The ramp came down. She lifted her head and, shaken but filled with wonder, walked slowly up the ramp.

Inside the trailer she stopped. For an instant she was flooded with disappointment, an agony of existential isolation and despair. The trailer was just a box: four metal walls, a metal roof, a wooden plank floor, a lingering smell of disinfectant. Then, as she lowered her head, a dazzling blue light exploded all around her, so that for a moment or so she was bathed from snout to tail in shimmering blue fire. And then the back wall of the trailer seemed to melt away, as though its atoms and molecules were the morning fog over the river, and beyond it she saw a flickering archway of golden light, and running under it a road that led to green pastures, softly rolling valleys and the distant cloud-blurred shape of purple hills.

"Oink," murmured the sow and walked through the arch, and was never seen in this dimension again.

Returning to her office after a swift visit to the lavatory, Polly found to her disgust that someone had drunk her coffee.

She picked up the mug and frowned at it, tilted it slightly towards her (just in case a quarter of a pint of coffee had found somewhere down the bottom of the mug to hide?), raised both eyebrows and put it down again. Odd and annoying. Not the first time, either.

Just to be sure, she replayed the sequence of events in her mind. Polly is working. Polly is thirsty. Polly reaches the point where thirst and caffeine addiction are screwing up her concentration. Polly gets up from her chair, leaves her office, walks down the corridor, through the printer room, up the half-flight of stairs, into the kitchen. Polly makes herself a coffee and takes it back to her desk. Coffee (black, no sugar) too hot to drink. Polly feels the call of nature, leaves her coffee, does the necessary. Polly comes back. Coffee gone.

Ridiculous, she decided. For starters, why bother? As she'd just demonstrated by experiment, getting hold of a coffee in the offices of Blue Remembered Hills Developments plc wasn't exactly difficult; the management offered all the hot drinks you could get down yourself, free of charge, any time of the working day. Besides, who'd want second-hand coffee, with the attendant risk of contamination from the previous owner's lipstick and drool?

She sat down and pulled a blue folder off the top of the pile. Sale of Plot 97, Attractive Drive, Norton St Edgar, Worcs. She yawned.

Two hypotheses.

One, she had an enemy. She dismissed that as unlikely. True, BRHD was an office like any other, saturated with petty suspicions, resentments, slights real and imaginary, and generating enough internal politics every week to keep a faculty of historians busy for a decade. But she'd only been there a month, and in that time she'd gone out of her way to be nice to everybody, or at least as nice as she could manage during office hours. She tried to think of anybody who'd displayed any material level of hostility, and failed.

Two, she had an admirer. Slightly more probable, and she could sort of get her head around the motivation, though she regretted letting that particular train of thought into her mind; but no, she didn't believe it for a moment. She shrugged and shooed the whole aggravating mystery out of her mind.

A month already. It hadn't, she cheerfully admitted to herself, seemed that long. Mostly, she guessed, because they'd kept her busy. Back at Enguerrand & Symes, where business had been slow, there'd been the endless, souls-in-torment afternoons when there'd been nothing to do, and she'd sat at her place in the vast, hangar-like conveyancing room, trying to pretend she was productively occupied, surrounded by two dozen others just like her – bored to death, scared stiff of being caught not working by one of the partners. The thought of it made her shudder, and she glanced round, just to make sure it was still there; an office all to herself, with a door. When she thought about it in those terms, the occasional stolen coffee was nothing.

She finished off the transfer on 97 Attractive Drive and opened the next file down the pile, 208 Green and Pleasant Crescent. She riffled through the tagged-up sheaf of papers, trying to gather exactly what still needed doing, but as far as she could tell it was complete: Land Registry forms, completion statement, PDs, the lot. She shrugged. Apparently her predecessor had been a bit slack about closing files when the job was done, because this wasn't the first such file she'd come across. She'd never have got away with that at Enguerrands, where failure to close completed files was a court-martial offence.

Next folder, routine pre-contract enquiries. As she worked her way through them, her mind began to drift, like a carelessly unmoored boat on a swift river. Attractive Drive, she thought, Green and Pleasant Crescent. She'd never seen an actual example of the houses BRHD built; she'd never been anywhere near the slab of Worcestershire in question. At the rate they were going, it wouldn't be long before the whole county was buried under BRHD concrete, aggregates and specially imported Polish garden topsoil, and the Norton St Edgar conurbation joined Los Angeles in having the dubious distinction of being visible from planetary orbit. Presumably when that happened, it'd be a good thing. After all, people had to live somewhere, and BRHD houses appeared to be quite good value for money. A lot of people thought so, anyway. None of her business, in other words. What mattered was that she had a job at a time when an alarming percentage of the bright, ambitious young people she'd been at law school with were flipping burgers, washing cars, answering phones in call centres or working for the Crown Prosecution Service. Gift horses' teeth, she thought. My goodness, gift horse, what great big teeth you've got. All the better to bite you with, my dear.

It was curious, she thought, that none of the world's major religions had ever adopted conveyancing as a spiritual exercise. Prayer, meditation, ganja, transcendental yoga are all very well, but it's only through the unparalleled tedium of conveyancing that you can attain the sublime separation of mind and body, allowing you to exist for a while as a creature of pure thought, no longer hawsered to earth by the distractions of the physical. The trick, of course, was to be able to maintain control, to surf the wave-tops of boredom-induced death of self and make them take you where you wanted to go. She had to admit she hadn't quite mastered it yet, but with thirty-two years to go before she retired...

So, who in their right mind would wander into someone else's office and drink their coffee? It made no sense. It offended her at the very core of her rational being. As an act of spite it was pretty low key. Someone who had it in for her would have poured the coffee over her keyboard or drenched a file with it. A caffeine addict who couldn't hold out long enough to get to the kitchen? In her mind's eye she mapped the floor plan. All but two of the offices on her floor were closer to the kitchen than she was; of those two, one belonged to Barry Tape, who only ever drank tea, and the other housed timid, cow-eyed Velma Hewitt, who jumped out of her skin if you coughed. All right then, someone with a warped sense of humour. But nobody on the second floor had any kind of sense of humour whatsoever.

Instinctively, she banked and wheeled away from the question, for fear that it might weigh her down and break the trance. The essence of a conveyancing high is its tentative fragility. You're a leaf floating in the wind, not a 747 battering its way through heavy turbulence over the north Atlantic. Pausing only to glance down at the sheet of paper on the desk in front of her ("Has the property ever been the subject of a Section 44 Order under the Domestic Properties Act 1972?" No, she answered. She had no idea what a Section 44 Order was. As far as she knew, nobody did. But they'd told her at law school that the correct answer to the question was No, so that's what she wrote) she launched herself back into the network of mental thermals and allowed them to take her weight.

All right, she told herself, so it was in-house. In-house lawyers, she knew, are basically inferior. Though all her friends had been terribly nice and understanding about it, there was still the unavoidable sense that she'd let herself down; that it was demeaning for a lawyer to work for mere civilians, shambling low-caste creatures without qualifications, who wouldn't know the rule in Rylands v. Fletcher if it sat on the end of their beds and glowed with a pale blue light. An in-house lawyer can never be an equity partner, a great tawny lion roaring in the long grass. She'd allowed herself to be fitted with a collar with a bell on it, issued with a bowl of milk and a blanket to sleep on – voluntary servitude in return for a little paltry security. Also rather shameful was how little she cared. Quite possibly she wasn't the great roaring tawny lion type. True, her job here was mindless slog, as fulfilling and socially useful as a hamburger box, but what the hell, it was only *work*, annoying stuff that had to be got through so she could...

Could what?

She pulled up out of that one in a hurry, before the spin turned into a nosedive. Not all conveyancing trips are good experiences. There's always the danger that you'll find yourself face to face with something scary or depressing, such as a mirror.

Now, she thought, would be a good time for the phone to ring. And, much to her surprise, it did.

The caller was a solicitor in Evesham, and for a moment her heart crumpled with envy. Evesham, garden of England, apple blossom and golden stone soaked for centuries in pale autumn sunlight – not that she'd ever been there, but she'd seen it once on the *Antiques Roadshow*, a programme she heartily loathed – but, she thought, he's just a solicitor like me. A mile from his office there may be orchards in bloom, but he spends his days doing this shit, same as I do. "Hello," she said cheerfully. "What can I do for you?"

It was all to do with some piece of paper, a damp-proof course inspection certificate or some such garbage. "You promised me you'd let me have it by the sixteenth," he said (his voice was high, reedy and annoying; she pictured him as five feet four and looking a bit like William Hague). "Sorry to make a fuss about it, but I do need it before I can get back to the mortgagee."

Well, fair enough. "Sure," she said. "I'll get it in the post to you tonight." And then she thought, Hold on. *You promised me*, but I've never heard of you before in my life.

"All right," he was saying. "But this time do please make sure. I'm in a chain here."

No, she thought, I'm not having that. "Just a moment," she said.

Not that she was after an apology, as such. But no, he insisted. He was adamant. He'd spoken to her the day before yesterday; no, not the receptionist, not a message while she was away from her desk. He had a note of the conversation on the file in front of him; *Phoned BRHD, re dpc inspection cert.* He distinctly recalled speaking to her.

"But that's not possible," she repeated. "I'm sure I've never talked to you before."

"Yes, you have. On Tuesday. You promised me that certificate. I know it was you. I remember your voice."

Her eyebrows shot up like ducks off a dew pond. "Really? Why?"

"It's a nice voice."

Which shut her up like a clam for the next four seconds,

a very long time in that context. "Thank you," she mumble-squeaked. "But honestly, I don't remember..."

Her voice (her nice voice) tailed away and died, and there was another silence, long enough for both of them to grow prize entries for the Chelsea Stalactite Show, and then she said, "I'll make sure it's in tonight's post," and he said, "Look, if you could possibly see your way to getting it in tonight's post," simultaneously. Then a slightly shorter pause, and she asked, "Anyway, how *is* Evesham? I mean, is it nice?" and he said it was all right, and somehow, by a gigantic joint effort of will, they managed to kill the phone call off before it could do any more damage.

Well, she thought, misunderstandings, misunderstandings. Obviously she hadn't talked to the wretched man; she'd have remembered *his* voice sure enough, it was what you'd get if Dr Dolittle taught air brakes how to speak. On the other hand, her nice voice. So, logically, she had spoken to him and then forgotten all about it. That was, she supposed, mildly worrying, or she could make it so if she tried hard enough. She could convince herself that it was the early stages of short-term memory loss, or, if this was a movie, it'd be a clue to alert her to a missing day, leading to a storyline involving drug-induced amnesia and the CIA. At other times she might have been tempted, but today she lacked the mental energy and couldn't be bothered. And anyway, she added to herself, I *have* got a nice voice, which is probably why people who meet me in the flesh for the first time always look so disappointed.

Even the best pre-contract enquiries can't be made to last for ever. She slung the finished form in her out tray and reached for the next file.

Maybe it was her nice voice (she thought, as she floated through Requisitions on Title on 12 Where the Heart Is Terrace) that had got her the job in the first place. Hard to think what else it could have been. Sure, she was competent, she could do the work. Being able to do the work wasn't the most stringent of criteria. But she knew for a fact that she'd been up against two dozen other applicants for the job, times being hard in the lawyering biz these days, and the specimens she'd met in the waiting room when she came in for interview had been vastly more impressive than her, at least in her opinion. Of course, a nice voice is a valuable asset. It can take you a long way – in radio, say, or when it comes to marrying a blind millionaire. True, a lot of her work was done over the phone, so it was probably just as well that the Voice of BRHD didn't sound like a ferret in a blender. She weighed the argument and found it wanting. Another mystery; and that was the Recs on Title done, and that's how we get through the day.

Another file. Oh God, she thought, I remember this one: 14 Amazing Road, the bloody awkward one with the drainage easement, the one she kept putting off because it needed thinking about.

Like a lion tamer armed with a fly whisk and a deckchair, she faced the problem and decided that today she'd be brave. It was, after all, only a matter of draughtsmanship, of finding the right combination of words to transfer a slab of territory subject to a few conditions. It couldn't bite her or bash her over the head. True, it could make her lose her job, but so could lots of other things. The world is a dangerous place, after all. She opened the file and found the lethal document.

She stared at it, then blinked and stared again. And thought, for the first time in years, of Terry Duckett.

A tall ash-blond young man with a face like a pig, Terry had made salaried partner by the time he was thirty by timing his annual holiday with micromillimetre-perfect precision. Every difficult thing, everything he'd screwed up on or didn't know how to do, he left to moulder quietly on the file, with a bare minimum of weeding and watering to ensure it didn't actually die or turn septic, but with an eye constantly fixed on the clock and the calendar, and then he'd book his two weeks in Ibiza at exactly the point when every toxic chicken in his filing cabinet was due to come home to roost simultaneously. Result: while he was away, his co-workers charged with minding the store had to cope with a year's backlog of poison, and Terry came back to his desk looking suitably tanned and dissipated with a squeaky-clean slate and a 100-per-cent record. Needless to say, everybody knew how he did it, but the sheer skill involved commanded unqualified respect and admiration. This man, the partners agreed, was born to delegate. We need him on the team.

She dismissed Terry Duckett from her mind and checked the front cover of the file, just to be sure. Then she reread the perfectly, actually quite brilliantly worded drainage easement in the draft contract for 14 Amazing Road and said quietly to her-self, *I didn't do that.*

The obvious temptation was to shrug, grin and get on with something else. There was, after all, an element of natural jus-tice about it all. Why, after all, should shoemakers have all the luck? Why shouldn't conveyancers also have kindly elves to help out with the daily chores? It was payback for all the times she'd been landed with Terry Duckett's files. It was com-pensation for half a dozen cups of undrunk coffee. It was the perverse inexplicability of the universe doing something nice for a change. Don't knock it. Put out a saucer of bread and milk, be grateful and move on.

My mind's going, she thought. In six months I'll be in a home, with battleship-grey paintwork and the TV on all the time in the day room. Maybe (she shuddered at the thought) it was me all along: I drank the coffee and then forgot I'd done it.

Thoughts don't come much scarier than that, and the mild euphoria of the conveyancing high was gone for good. It was of course absolutely impossible that a healthy twenty-seven-year-old like her should be suffering from some ghastly brain-eating disease. She was annoyed with herself simply for letting the thought amble across her mind. She wasn't like that, not one of those sad people who spend their time wishing all manner of unspeakable ailments on themselves and treating medical dictionaries like mail order catalogues. On the contrary. She was so relentlessly healthy it was practically unfair. She couldn't remember the last time she'd had a day off work for a cold or a sore throat or a sniffle.

The door opened. She looked up and was annoyed to see a short, turkey-throated young man standing in the doorway. Alan Stevens, her head of department. She found the desiccated shell of a smile and put it on.

"I thought you ought to know," said Mr Stevens gravely. "We have a darts team."

His tone of voice went far beyond gravity. To get the full impression, imagine that what he'd actually said was, "Houston, we have a darts team." Clearly there had to be more to it than that, and she waited patiently until he added, "We play in the London and Middlesex Young Lawyers' League. Fourth division."

She nodded. "How many divisions . . . ?"

"Four. It's a social activity," he explained. "We feel it fosters a sense of community and teamwork, and there are first-rate opportunities for networking and establishing contacts within the profession." He paused for a very long time, then added, "Can you play darts?"

"My parents run a pub," she replied. "Yes," she translated. "Actually, I'm pretty good."

"Ah." Mr Stevens frowned, giving the impression that dart-throwing ability wasn't his main selection criterion. "Only," he went on, "we're playing Thames Water tomorrow evening, and Leo Fineman's got an important meeting at half seven, so he's had to drop out."

"Ah. Tomorrow evening."

"You're busy, I'm sorry." The speed with which Mr Stevens spoke annoyed the hell out of her for some reason. If he was disappointed, it was in the same way that water is dry. Silly, she thought; if he didn't want her on the team, why'd he asked her in the first place? Answer: because she'd admitted to being good at the game, and it probably wouldn't go down well, from a networking and contact-establishing viewpoint, if Thames Water's star player got beaten by a girl. Not on my watch, his little piggy eyes were saying. In which case...

"Nothing I can't cancel," she said, perfectly truthfully as it happened. "Tell me where and when, and I'll be there."

Mr Stevens was wearing a wounded look, as though he'd just been tricked into doing something ghastly by someone he believed he could trust. "That's great," he said. "We'll meet up here at seven and go on together."

He left, looking very sad, and about thirty seconds after the door closed behind him she felt the another-fine-mess reaction that she knew so well. *Idiot,* she told herself. You could have lied. You could even have told the truth. But no. Instead, you volunteer to join the office darts team, just because an annoying man annoyed you. *Must* stop doing things like that.

She sighed. The world would be an OK sort of place if it wasn't for people. It was just as well, she thought, that she'd taken her I-don't-really-want-to-be-here party dress in to be cleaned the day before yesterday. It was the only garment she possessed which was anything like suitable for such an occasion. The thought of going to an office darts match in an article of clothing she actually liked was rather more than she could bear.

(And then she thought, Yes, but it's taken your mind off that other business, hasn't it? And now you've got over the panic you somehow contrived to whisk yourself up into, you don't really believe it any more. See? All for the best, really.)

The hell with it, she thought, and went to the kitchen for another coffee. She took it back to her office and put it down on her desk, where she could keep an eye on it while she was working. Then, after about five minutes, she deliberately got up and left the room.

In the corridor she ran into the boss. The great man himself, not a spokesman or a representative, not a lookalike hired to foil kidnappers. She knew it was him because his picture was everywhere: framed on walls, smiling gleaming-toothed from brochure covers and in-house newsletters. Actually meeting him was faintly surreal. *You're supposed to be flat, what are you doing in three dimensions?* Also, he wasn't smiling, Mr Huos was like the *Mona Lisa* and the Cheshire Cat. He *was* the smile.

She tried to slip past, but her personal invisibility field wasn't working. He noticed her. Worse, he spoke.

"Polly Mayer?"

Oh shit, she thought. "Yes, that's me."

"Ah, right. I was just coming to see you."

"Me?"

Slight frown. "Yes," he said. "Got a minute?"

This from the man who owned her daytimes. "Yes, of course. Um, come into my office."

Of course, it was his office really. Rumour had it that BRHD actually owned the freehold to this vast, centrally located castle of commerce. If true, it was a staggering display of reckless indulgence. She opened the door for him, but he didn't go in. There was an awkward pause while she wondered what the matter was.

"After you," he said.

She went in but didn't sit down. She couldn't figure out which chair to sit in. Normally, of course, she'd sit on the far side of the desk, in her chair, because it was her chair, in her room. But you couldn't very well expect the owner, master of all he surveyed, to park his bum in the visitor's chair (small, plastic, stacking) while she luxuriated in foam-backed swiveldom. It'd be like Captain Kirk taking the ops station while Chekov sat in the centre seat.

Get a *grip*, she ordered herself. "Please," she heard herself say, "sit down."

Mr Huos sat on the visitor's chair and smiled at her. Normality at least partially restored.

"Um," she said, perching on her chair (not sitting back and stretching the spring, just in case it broke), "what can I do for you?"

It turned out to be nothing more than routine enquiries about the progress of half a dozen ordinary, everyday sales. As she answered the questions, he nodded, frowning slightly. He looked ever so slightly worried, which scared the life out of her, but when the interrogation was over, he smiled again, thanked her politely and stood up as if to go.

"How are you settling in, by the way?" he asked.

If she'd been a cat, her ears would've been right back. She knew that question, or at least she knew the way in which he'd asked it. The Columbo technique: make 'em think they've got away with it and you're going, then at the last moment turn round and hit them with the real question, the one you can't answer without giving the game away.

"Fine," she said.

"Splendid." He frowned again. "No problems, then."

"No."

He nodded. "All the files in good order?"

She had to replay that a couple of times in her mind before she figured out what it meant. "Fine," she said.

"That's good. Only," he went on, and the frown deepened, "the girl who was here before you left in a bit of a hurry. I was afraid she might have left you with a bit of a mess."

"No, not at all. Everything's..." She ran out of words and did a goldfish impression.

"Fine?" he suggested.

"Yes."

"That's all right, then." A slight pause, during which he didn't leave the room. "Alan Stevens tells me he's recruited you for the darts team."

Now she was being a goldfish with a sore throat trying to do long division in its head. No words, not even a grunt. So she nodded.

"Great stuff," said Mr Huos. "Best of luck. I'll try and look in on the match if I've got time. When's kick-off?"

She heard herself mutter something about the team meeting up in the lobby about seven. It seemed to do the trick. He smiled, said, "Drink your coffee before it gets cold," and left, closing the door behind him.

She sat quite still for ninety seconds, then reached for the phone and dialled a number.

"What?" a man's voice snarled at the end of the line.

"Don."

"Sis?" A moment of bleary confusion followed by an explosion of righteous fury. "Sis, for crying out loud, it's the middle of the bloody night."

She sighed. "Draw the curtains," she said.

"What? Oh. Hold on." Short pause, whizzing noise offstage. Then, "What's the time?"

"It's a quarter to one, you idle sod. Don't tell me you're still in bed."

"Of course not," her brother replied haughtily. "I had to get up to answer the phone. What's up?"

She hesitated. "So, how's things?"

"What? Oh, fine. You didn't call me in the –" he paused "– in the early hours of the morning just to ask after my well-being. What's the matter?"

"How's it going?"

"Finished," he replied smugly. "Well, nearly. Just needs a final polish."

Her brother Donald composed jingles for radio stations, for which he got paid what Polly considered to be obscene amounts of money. It was ludicrous, she maintained, that he earned the equivalent of a quarter of her annual salary for juxtaposing seven musical notes. He rebutted her accusations by saying that compressing the very essence of a daily two-hour radio show, listened to by millions, into a mere seven notes was a work of genius, which should be remunerated accordingly.

*Just needs a final polish* probably meant he'd made up his mind to start work on it tomorrow. He was, in short, the most aggravating person she'd ever met: infuriatingly lazy, unforgivably talented, luckier than a shedful of cats. It wouldn't be so bad if he lived a life of reckless dissipation. But he didn't smoke or drink, he only ate organic vegetables, and he hadn't been on a date in three years. The last item, she had to concede, wasn't through choice. He wasn't so bad-looking, in a bony, unfinished sort of a way (seated, he tended to remind her of a dismantled tent); his problem was a total refusal to compromise for the sake of making himself agreeable. He didn't do small talk. If he was bored, he yawned or looked out of the window while scratching his ear, or (if the assignation was in a pub) leaned slightly sideways so he could see past her and watch the football on the big screen. He had all the social skills of a hand grenade; what was worse, he knew it and didn't seem to care.

He also knew her just a bit too well. "So," he said, "what's the matter?"

She knew she could tell Don anything. Even so, she hesitated. "I think I may be going crazy," she said.

"Mphm." Slight pause; then, "What makes you think that?"

So she told him. Another thing about Don that annoyed her (but not this time) was how he managed to stay calm, no matter what. Also, he was probably the only person in the world who took her entirely seriously.

"Well?" she demanded.

"I take your point," he said. "But I wouldn't start panicking quite yet."

Not exactly what she'd wanted to hear. "What's that supposed to mean?"

"It does look like there's something funny going on," Don replied, "but probably not what you think it is. What I mean is, unless there's other stuff you haven't told me about, that's not nearly enough to support a diagnosis of mildewed brains. What I mean is, it's just happening at the office, right?"

That hadn't occurred to her. "I guess so."

"Outside the office, no battier than usual?"

She took a moment to think. "No."

"Well, there you go then. Coffee going missing at work is one thing. If the same thing was happening in the silence of your lonely room, I'd say you had something to worry about."

For a moment she was overwhelmed by a flood of relief and sisterly affection. Then she said, "Well?"

"Well what?"

"What d'you think is going on?"

A sigh from the other end of the wire. "How the hell do I know?"

She smiled. "But Don," she said sweetly, "you know everything. You keep telling me so, all the time."

"True." Silence. She could hear him thinking. "Let me mull it over and I'll get back to you. Tell you what," he added (she could picture that quick, face-creasing frown that looked so ominous but only meant he was applying his mind). "Meet me tomorrow evening, say sevenish, at the—"

"Can't," she interrupted him. "Otherwise engaged. And before you say anything..."

"Me? I never—"

"It's a work thing, all right? Office darts team. *Don't laugh.*"

"There's nothing remotely amusing about an office darts team," Don replied gravely. "It's the sort of thing we all hoped mankind had outgrown in the twenty-first century, but apparently not." His voice sharpened a little as he added, "You didn't *volunteer*, did you?"

"No, of course not. Well," she amended, "yes, I did, but it wasn't voluntary volunteering, if you get me."

"That's what you get for going corporate," Don replied with toxic smugness. "The team ethic. Next it'll be baseball caps and compulsory t'ai chi on the roof before breakfast. Me," he added, "I go to work in my pyjamas, and my daily commute is five yards, from the bed to the desk. Be that," he added, as she started to say something vulgar about his life choices, "as it may, I'll certainly think over what you've told me, and I'll get back to you as soon as I've solved the mystery. If I don't speak to you before then, enjoy your night out."

He rang off before she could swear at him, which in her view was cheating.

At least her coffee was still there. It had gone cold, but she drank it anyway.

It was raining when she got off the bus. She had her umbrella, but it wouldn't open; its slim, fragile little spokes jammed as she pushed, leaving her with something that looked upsettingly like a crushed daddy-long-legs. She interred it quietly in the nearest bin and scuttled across the street to the dry cleaners, to pick up her party dress for the darts match.

It was fat rain, the big, ripe drops like water bombs that soak you to the skin before you know it. Accordingly, she didn't hang about. She lunged for the shop door, pushed it open and charged inside. A pleasant-faced middle-aged lady looked up from behind the counter and smiled at her.

"Hi," Polly said, fumbling in her pocket for the ticket. "I've got a dress to collect, please. Mayer."

The woman didn't frown, but her eyebrows twitched slightly. "Excuse me, please?"

"I've come for my dress," Polly said, trying not to sound impatient. "Here's the ticket. My name's..."

At which point she realised why the woman was looking at her like that. This wasn't the dry cleaners. Where the racks of polythene-sheathed clothes should have been, there were magazines. Instead of the big stainless-steel laundry machinery, there were shelves of instant coffee, crisps, pot noodles, biscuits. Oh, she thought.

"Sorry," she said. "Wrong shop."

"Excuse me, please?"

She bought a small jar of coffee and a bottle of washing

up liquid by way of an apology and went out again. In the street the yellow lamps turned the puddles into pools of honey. She looked up and down the small huddle of shops. Video library, mobile-phone shop, the corner shop she'd just come out of, hairdresser. No cleaners. No indication, furthermore, that there'd ever been a cleaners there at any time. She walked a few yards down the road until she was able to see the street name on the corner. Clevedon Road. Which was where her bus stop was, and the dry cleaners. Or not.

*Outside the office, no battier than usual.* Not any more, apparently.

Rain trickled down her nose and dripped on her chin. She dug her phone out of her pocket and stabbed in Don's number. A polite voice told her she was being transferred to voicemail. She recorded a short, shrill scream, then rang off.

# CHAPTER TWO

Always a pleasure to talk to his sister, he thought as he put the receiver back on its cradle. Hearing about her life always made him feel so good about his own. That kind of unsolicited affirmation is beyond price. He grinned as he looked around, caught sight of his trousers (they'd tried to burrow under a pile of discarded sheets, but they'd left a few square inches of grey corduroy sticking out, just like the proverbial ostrich), retrieved them and pulled them on over his pyjama bottoms. A new day.

When he'd told Polly he was just giving his current work-in-lack-of-progress a final polish, he'd been stretching the truth a little. He had five of the seven notes – they were locked in his mind like chunks of steel gripped in the toolmaker's vice, as good as money in the bank – but that still left two more to go, and as far as they were concerned he was standing on the flat plain looking up at the peaks of the Himalayas. He could see where he needed to get to, but...

*Dah*, he thought hopefully, then shook his head. No. Completely wrong.

He wandered into the kitchen, thinking about breakfast, looked up at the clock, converted breakfast into lunch, opened the fridge door. There was a yoghurt, but when he looked at the date on the foil lid, he decided against it. By now there was a better-than-average chance that the contents of the pot had evolved into an entirely new form of life, in which case the Prime Directive applied, and it'd be unethical to interfere in its natural course of development. There was a small slab of cheese, but on inspection it proved to be heritage cheese, and since it had lasted so long it would be a shame not to preserve it intact for future generations. There was a bread roll, which looked rather more hopeful. But when he tried to take it out, it slipped through his fingers, fell on the floor and shattered into a dozen pieces, which suggested it was probably a bit on the stale side. Shucks, he thought. I'll have to make do with pasta.

Donald Mayer could cook pasta. He was proud of this fact. You put water in a saucepan, you heat it till it starts surging and heaving about, then you get the plastic bag of little shrivelled yellow shapes—

Which proved to be empty. He frowned. No pasta. Also, while he was on the subject of negativity and things not going right for him, *dee* was just as unsuitable as *dah* had been, if not more so. Fine. He was hungry, there was no food and he was two notes short of a jingle. Nothing for it; he was going to have to go Out.

*One little room an everywhere.* He couldn't remember where the quotation came from, but it summed up his world view very neatly. He wasn't afraid of Out, as such. It didn't bite. That said, he found it hard to work up any enthusiasm for it. A fact of life, one of those things, and he didn't have to like it; it was just there. He sighed, found his shoes, remembered his keys and made for the door. *Something else*, whispered a voice in his ear. Ah yes. The dry cleaning. Must remember to pick up the dry cleaning. He found the ticket on the kitchen shelf (it had got inside the empty drinking chocolate tin, ingenious little devil) and headed out into the world.

Bright sunshine; he squinted. Why can't the sun be more like electric light, he often thought. He walked down the street, and as he went he felt the fog inside his mind thin and clear away. Say what you like about Out, it was bracing. A leftover from the cavemen, he supposed. Outside the cave you've got to be sharp, alert, or the sabre-toothed tigers'll get you.

*Derr*, he hummed. Yes, of course. Perfect. He stopped for a moment and beamed a huge smile at a fat woman pushing a pram, who stared at him.

*Six down*, he told himself as he walked on, just one to go. How difficult could one note be?

The length of Palmerston Crescent and into Harcourt Road. Streets named after dead politicians; he frowned at the thought. Who chose street names, anyway?

Pasta, milk, bread, cheese, a pizza or two, and don't forget to pick up the dry cleaning. Just one note to go, and then—

Of course, the last time he'd been stuck for just one note it had taken him six weeks to find it. That said, the note he'd finally come up with had been perfect, quite possibly the best note of his career so far, and radio listeners from Whitby to Penzance now had that jingle embedded deep in their minds, like a bullet lodged in a wound that can't be extracted without killing the patient. He contemplated *dumm*, then felt ashamed of himself for even considering it.

Down Evelyn Street into Clevedon Road, where the shops were. Into the corner shop – pasta, milk, bread, cheese, pizza and a special treat, a six-pack of toilet rolls – then the video library, but *Blood Frenzy IV* wasn't out yet, shame, and then the dry cleaners.

"Afternoon," he said to the woman behind the counter. "Overcoat and a pair of trousers, Mayer."

She nodded. "Got the ticket?"

"Yes," he replied proudly, and gave it to her. She looked at it, then turned to the rack and unhooked a shiny plastic-wrapped hanger. "That'll be twelve seventy-five, please," she said.

He paid, thanked her nicely and went home, just missing the rain.

The first thing he did was write down the newly captured note: dum de dee, diddle-derr. But no dice. Sometimes it worked like that: hum what you've already got, and the rest just happens. Not this time, however. He sighed and put his shopping in the fridge. Just one last lousy note and he could relax for a month. All in all, it was a good life, but he could really do without the pressure.

He fitted himself into his armchair, which long use had moulded to the contours of his body, and gave his mind to what Polly had told him. Intriguing. Obviously she wasn't really losing her marbles; he could rule that out straight away. His sister was a curious kind of life form in many ways – conventional, driven, insecure, plagued by a whole load of those nasty little Easter eggs programmed into human software to slow it down and screw it up. She cared about so many things that he simply couldn't imagine himself bothering about. But she was smart. You could hear it in her voice, a slight tension, as in a coiled spring or a bent bow. I'm way ahead of you, it signified, but I'm too polite to leave you behind, so please think faster. It had always been something of a mixed blessing. It impressed college tutors and prospective employers at interviews, scared off boyfriends, infuriated her contemporaries at school and was completely wasted on her parents, who hadn't listened to a word she said since she was six. If Polly was really losing it, he'd know. His musician's ear would pick it up in a fraction of a syllable.

He couldn't tell her that, of course. So, if he meant to do his fraternal duty and reassure her, he'd need something else, such as a rational explanation. He ran through the data, but nothing dropped into place. The only conclusion he felt sure about was that something funny was going on. What that something might be, he had no idea.

He glanced at his watch. A couple of supplementary

questions had occurred to him, but he knew she didn't like him ringing her at work. They'd keep till later. He got up and, in a frenzy of virtuous activity, put away the newly cleaned trousers in the suitcase under his bed. He had to sit on the lid to get it shut again.

The three bears, he thought. Who's been drinking my coffee, asked Baby Bear. All right, he told himself, let's go with that. Who's been drinking my coffee; who's been messing with my files; who's been sitting in my chair? He wandered into the bathroom and turned on the bath taps. Let us consider, he said to himself, the quality of the actions in question.

*You what?* he asked himself; the phrase had sort of presented itself, ready-formed and complete, abandoned on his mental doorstep like Paddington Bear. It was a good question, though. What sort of thing were these things that kept happening to his sister? Annoying and inexplicable, yes, but only in context. Drinking coffee, doing work, a tricky legal document drafted, a phone call taken, a promise made to mail a bit of paper to a fellow solicitor. Ordinary stuff, the sort of things people do all day in offices.

He hadn't solved the mystery, but he felt he was in a position to rule out a poltergeist. Having allowed himself to touch on the supernatural angle, he followed it up a little further. How about, he conjectured, the unquiet ghost of a solicitor, haunting her office, his soul burdened with the guilt of all the documents he hadn't drafted and bits of paper he hadn't sent on during his life? Well, he thought, it fits the known facts – possibly not the coffee; can ghosts drink coffee? Sure they can, if they're also capable of drawing up transfer documents and answering phones. No, belay that. A transfer document is information inserted into a computer, which then transmits it down the wire to a printer. A voice on a phone is just a series of electrical impulses. Coffee, on the other hand, needs a throat, lips, a bloodstream and a bladder. With a certain degree of relief, he ruled out the supernatural. He was pretty open-minded about such things, but he knew for a fact Polly wasn't.

*Dah?* For a moment he actually thought he'd got it, but no. Back to the drawing board.

While he was in the bath, the phone rang. He ignored it. As soon as the warmth of the water took hold and relaxed him, he slipped into that special bathtime mental state, part daze, part intense concentration. The note. He chased it through the maze of his subconscious mind, nearly managed to pounce on it half a dozen times. The mystery. Not a ghost, not an enemy, because enemies don't do your grotty jobs for you, not a friend either, because friends don't drink your coffee. Maybe she was going round the twist after all. Eventually he snapped out of it and realised the water was stone cold. He got out, looked for a towel, couldn't find one and dried himself off with the bath mat.

His newly cleaned overcoat was hanging behind the door, still in its plastic wrapping. He frowned at it. There was a case to be made, he knew, for saying he was in danger of degenerating into a slob. Sometimes he worried about that, which was why he'd bought the coat. It was smart (navy blue, 100-percent pure wool, dry clean only) and he wore it when he went out into the world for important meetings with clients, agents and other grown-ups. It made him look serious, and if he kept it buttoned up to the neck nobody need know that he still had his pyjama jacket on underneath. Hence the need to keep it maintained, in good order. Carefully he removed the polythene and ran his hands down it to smooth out any wrinkles. Two thirds of the way down, he paused. There was something in one of the pockets.

There hadn't been when he took it in to be cleaned. He was punctilious about that. Don't leave anything in your overcoat pocket – it was the only bit of advice his father had given him which he'd ever taken any notice of – it'll stretch the fabric and spoil it. Clearly the idiots at the cleaners didn't know that.

If they'd ruined his beautiful coat, they'd be hearing from his lawyers.

He reached down into the pocket, fumbled about and connected with something small, cold and heavy. He pulled it out and looked at it.

Odd, he thought. Why would somebody at the dry cleaners have put a pencil sharpener in his overcoat pocket?

And what a pencil sharpener it was too. Presumably it had come from one of those mail order catalogues, the sort that cater for people who can't live without genuine Russian army watches, occasional tables crafted from paddle-steamer gear wheels and handsomely mounted slivers of deck timber from the ruins of the *Cutty Sark*. Solid brass, orifices to accept a bewildering range of pencil sizes from ultra-slimline to scaffolding-pole calibre, tastefully engraved in a script he couldn't identify, possibly Cyrillic or maybe Klingon or Old Elvish. A gift idea for the man who has everything and whom you don't particularly like. It lay in the palm of his hand, and he shivered.

Well, he thought, I can't keep it of course; it doesn't belong to me. Probably I should take it back to them, but I can't be bothered to make a special journey. Next time I'm passing will do, and they'd better be grateful, not to mention apologetic for putting my best coat in jeopardy like that.

It's one of the basic laws of human nature that a man suddenly finding himself in possession of an unanticipated pencil sharpener will immediately proceed to sharpen all the pencils in his possession. Don had a lot of pencils. He acquired them without realising, in much the same way as he shed pens. It was, he knew, all to do with the essential equilibrium of the universe. Every time he found himself in Smith's he bought a bumper pack of ten or a dozen ballpoints, and every time he looked round for a pen, he couldn't find one. Instead, there'd be a pencil (broken or worn down to a stub), and he knew for a fact he hadn't bought a pencil since he'd left school. No matter.

Some part of the Great Machine required that surplus pens be transmuted into pencils, to maintain cosmic balance, and for some reason he'd been chosen to act as the instrument of Providence. It was, if anything, an honour, and he'd learned to live with it. It was just unfortunate that he happened to be on the heavy-handed side when writing.

Accordingly, it only took him a moment to put together a small heap of blunt, mutilated pencils. Then he set to work. It was one of those really fun sharpeners, the sort where you turn a handle, and a hidden mechanism feeds the pencil into the blades; if you keep on cranking away, you can reduce a pencil to a pile of feathery shavings in just over a minute, or you can exercise a little restraint and create a beautifully tapered, needle-pointed graphite spike that'll last just long enough to write one letter before going *ping*. As he worked, it did occur to him to wonder where all the shavings were going – usually there's a little transparent box underneath, but if this model had such a thing he couldn't identify it – but since it wasn't his property, and he didn't intend to keep it long enough to have to empty it, he didn't waste time and mental energy on the problem.

Eleven pencils later, he paused to rest his aching wrist and consider what he'd accomplished. Nothing like a freshly sharpened pencil to give a man a sense of purpose.

Sharp, he thought. Stay sharp, be sharp, see sharp—

*C sharp.*

Which is musician's secret code for *dah*.

His eyes widened and his jaw dropped. Well, of course. What else could it possibly be? He grinned and a moment later became the first of untold millions to hum *dum de dee, diddle-derr dah* under his breath.

He staggered back until his bum collided with the back of a chair, into which he flopped. It was, he recognised, one of those moments, a bathwater-spilling apple-on-head moment, a point of intersection between humanity and the Continuum. He sat unable to move for about five minutes. Then, scattering pencils like straws in the wind, he lunged at the phone and pecked in a number.

"Dennis?"

"Who is this?"

"Dennis, it's *me*. Listen."

"Don?"

He took a deep breath. "Dum de dee, diddle-der dah."

Long pause.

"Dennis? Are you still there?"

"Bloody hell." The voice at the other end of the line was hoarse with awe. "That's brilliant."

"Yes."

"Hum it again."

"Dum de dee—"

"Diddle-der dah. Don, that's perfect. It's amazing. Oh shit, I'm going to be stuck with that in my head for the rest of the week. That's—"

"I know," Don said. "I'll send an invoice."

He put the phone down, feeling vaguely but powerfully unsatisfied. The best work he'd ever done, quite probably the highlight of his career, the jingle he'd always be remembered for, the one he'd spend the rest of his working life vainly trying to equal – his Ninth Symphony, his *Enigma Variations*, his "Hound Dog," his "Paint It Black" – and what was he feeling? Nothing, apart from a tense, nervous buzz, a bit like a caffeine rush. *Is that all?* a little voice was muttering inside his head. *Call that a day's work?*

Well, no, he didn't. That was three months' work – completed, what was more, in record time. But the buzzy voice wasn't having that. *What's next then?* it was saying. *More work. Bring it on.*

Weird. Usually, when he'd just completed a major commission, it took him a week to recover from the strain. Then, if he was sure he was up to it, he'd start sketching out the broad outlines of the orchestration. A week after that, he'd consider bracing himself for the ordeal of putting on his posh coat and doing lunch with the sound mixers. Instead...

He glanced down at his right hand. There was a pencil in it, with which he'd drawn a few roughly sketched staves on the back of a gas bill. He narrowed his eyes and realised he'd just orchestrated the jingle: complete, job done, and very well too.

Maybe, he thought, Polly's not the only one around here who's going loopy. Maybe it's genetic, a sort of family curse, afflicting the female line with memory loss and the male side with exaggerated work ethic. No, probably not; his mother never forgot a birthday and Dad's contribution to the family business was drinking the profits. Besides, he didn't feel mad as such, just painfully on edge, listless, impatient to be getting on with something. But what?

He stood up and walked briskly across the room, noting as he went how small it was. Silly little room, no bigger than a rabbit hutch. What he needed to do was move to a decent-sized place, where he wouldn't be cramped up like a battery hen all the time. Somewhere with a bit of garden...

Jesus. Did I just think that?

He went into the bathroom and peered at his face in the mirror. Yes, he reassured himself, still me. The important thing was not to get overexcited and start panicking. Unfortunately, he wasn't entirely sure he could manage that, not without help.

He got the phone and rang Polly, tapping his fingernails impatiently on the tabletop while he waited for her to pick up.

"Don?" She sounded pleased to hear his voice. "Thanks for calling back. Listen, I..."

"Polly."

"...went to pick up my party dress from the dry cleaners and it wasn't there."

He frowned. This was no time for his sister to be babbling at him. "What?"

"It wasn't there. Gone. Not a trace."

"Well, it must've got lost, or the ticket fell off or something."

"Not the dress. The shop."

Preoccupied as he was, he couldn't help but realise there was something wrong there. "How do you mean, gone? Boarded up?"

"No, *gone*. Not gone," she amended. "More like it hadn't ever been there in the first place. Turned into a newsagenty-corner-shoppy sort of thing." There was a funny sound to her voice, a bit like when he used to play guitar, and he over-tightened a string. "And I know I didn't just go to the wrong street, because I looked, and it said it on a wall, Clevedon Road."

It was as though he'd just tried to walk through a plate-glass window. "The dry cleaners in Clevedon Road?"

"Yes. Why, do you know it?"

"Next door to the corner shop?"

"No, I mean yes. I mean, the corner shop *is* the dry bloody cleaners. I went in there before I'd realised, and this woman looked at me."

His throat was unaccountably lagged with wire wool. "When was this?"

"What? Oh, about six-ish, I suppose. Why?"

Calm, he thought. Rational explanations. "Because I was in there around lunchtime."

"Oh. Which one, the cleaners or the corner-shop place?"

"Both."

A long silence. Then Don said, "Have you still got the ticket?"

"The what?"

"The ticket," he said, rather louder than he'd intended. "The dry cleaning ticket, with your name and a number. And," he added firmly, "the name and address of the shop."

"Oh."

"Well?"

"Hold on." *Clunk.* She'd dropped the phone. A very long ninety seconds, then, "Yes, I've got it right here. It's green. It says forty-six, then Mayer in handwriting, and on the back..."

"Yes?"

"SpeediKleen, 16 Clevedon Road," she chirped triumphantly. "Oh, thank God for that. I was so worried..."

He closed his eyes. "But you're not now."

"Well, no, because it means I didn't just... I mean, I wasn't just imagining..."

"I see," he said grimly. "A dry cleaners vanishes into thin air, but you're not particularly fussed about that. Sort of thing that happens every day of the week, in fact."

"What it means," she replied sharply, "is I'm not going mad, like I thought I was. Sorry if my overwhelming relief offends you in any way."

"And the shop vanishing. That's all right, is it?"

"What? Oh, I'm sure there's a perfectly rational explanation, if only—"

"Such as?"

"I don't know, do I?" she replied irritably. "Presumably they closed down and someone else moved in. To be perfectly honest, I'm not all that interested."

He breathed out heavily through his nose before replying. "It was there at lunchtime," he said. "They must have worked bloody fast to have removed every last trace of it by six o'clock this evening."

"So they must," she said. "Polish shopfitters, probably. They don't hang about. Anyhow, that's none of my business. Thanks, Don. I'd got myself into a real state."

He realised he was starting to hyperventilate. "Quite all right," he muttered.

"That's what I like about you," she went on happily. "You're so calm about things. Honestly, I'd never have thought of the ticket. It's so obvious, but it just didn't occur to me. It must be marvellous to have a rational, unflappable mind like yours."

He made a sort of grunting noise.

"Anyhow," she went on, sounding much more relaxed, "how's everything otherwise? Got your jingle finished?"

Sarcastically said, so he took a certain small pleasure in replying, "Yes, actually."

"Wow. Quick work."

"A sudden flash of inspiration."

"Well, there you go. I guess you'd better go and lie down in complete darkness with an ice pack on your head. Can't risk your brain overheating."

A drop of moisture fell on the back of his hand. Sweat, from his forehead. "Ha ha," he said, "very funny. How about you? Looking forward to your darts match?"

Growling noise then, "Oh hell, I haven't got my dress. The one I was going to wear."

"Indeed."

"Damn," she said violently. "They've got no right to do that, close down the business when they've still got my stuff. Now what am I supposed to do?"

He felt a smile crawling over his face. "Search me," he said. "Doesn't it strike you as just a little bit odd, though?"

"Dunno about odd. Bloody annoying. That was an expensive dress. And I'm buggered if I'm going to waste time and money getting another one just for a stupid office darts match."

"Quite. Totally unreasonable, if you ask me."

"Oh, stop sounding so bloody magisterial. Look," she went on quickly, "you can't do me a favour, can you? Only I can't get away. Could you go round there, see if you can find out what happened to the dry cleaners and where my stuff could have got to? You could ask the people next door, they're bound to know. Or they could give you the name of the estate agent or the solicitors. Go on," she added, as he hesitated to reply. "You've got time on your hands, now you've finished your jingle."

"I don't know," he said, trying to sound like he meant it. "I've got a lot of other stuff on right now. I mean, there's a job for Radio West, I'm already late with that."

"That's OK," she said brightly. "You can hum to yourself while you're looking for my dress. Come on, Don, it's no big deal. And I can't go to this ridiculous darts thing in my office clothes, and I definitely can't wear anything nice, or they'll think I'm a complete loser. Please?"

He overdid the sigh a little. "All right. I'll go there in the morning and see what I can find out. No promises, mind."

"Thanks, Don. Call me at the office, not my mobile. See you."

He sighed for real as he put down the receiver. Just because he'd been given a second problem didn't necessarily mean the first one had been solved. On the other hand, this new mystery struck him as distinctly more interesting, not to mention rather less threatening than the possibility that there was something wrong with his head.

Vanishing dry cleaners. Disappearing coffee. Work that just sort of does itself – ghastly complicated transfer deeds and usually impossible seventh notes. Take five minutes or so out of your not particularly busy schedule and sort it all out, will you? Because, after all, you've got a clear, calm, rational mind that about three minutes ago was threatening to boil over and come frothing out through your ears.

We can't both be crazy, can we?

Jack Tedesci always insisted on driving, and he was one of those men who believes that paying for parking is like paying for sex, the mark of a loser. Accordingly, they'd been round the block six times, and now he was trying to edge his Mercedes convertible into a Fiesta-sized gap. He was a good slow-speed driver, but not nearly as good as he thought he was.

Mr Huos yawned. "There's a multi-storey about a hundred yards down," he said wistfully.

"I can get in here no problem," Jack replied through gritted teeth. "Just watch that side for me, will you?"

"Sure. You've got about an inch."

"Shit. I'll have to come out and go back in again."

Deep inside Mr Huos' soul something whimpered. *Make it*

*stop*, it begged. Briefly he considered grabbing the wheel and putting the handbrake on, but then Jack would be offended and he'd cancel the deal, and it'd take weeks of grinding effort and melodrama to get it back on course. Pleading wouldn't help; shouting might do the trick, but that would involve an outlay of mental energy he couldn't really justify right now. Which only left one option.

He closed his eyes.

He really didn't want to. For one thing, it always gave him heartburn. For another, there was always the chance that Jack, or somebody else, would notice, which could lead to complications he really didn't need. Also there were ethical considerations, though he wasn't too fussed about that side of things at the best of times. On the other hand, if he had to sit here and endure Jack's parking for another minute, his mental comfort would be seriously impaired. Oh well, he thought.

He visualised the road. In front a red Bedford van. Behind a blue Discovery. Between them a stretch of black tarmac with a stone kerb on one side.

Centre on that word *stretch*.

He dug the clawed fingers of his mind into the road surface, until they passed through and gave him a grip; then he compressed his mental chest and shoulder muscles and slowly began to heave. Gradually did it; too much force and he'd either rupture himself or tear a hole in the fabric of the Continuum, which really would bugger up his day. He felt the molecules of the tarmac begin to stretch, as time slowed, congealed, broke up and started to convert itself into energy, and then change from energy into space. Six inches. It doesn't sound much, but the effort involved was stupendous; he was, after all, shifting two thirds of a tectonic plate. Next time he was going to have to insist they got a taxi. He felt his strength draining away, and that made him rush the last six inches. He felt something give and immediately slackened off. A bit late, but it was only a tiny little fracture, no more than a sixteenth of an inch, if that. Even so, he felt embarrassed, and angry with himself for the error in judgement. One of these days he'd get it disastrously wrong, and God only knew what the upshot would be.

"There," Jack said. "Told you I'd get in."

He opened his eyes. It would, of course, have been far simpler just to shrink the car, not to mention far less dangerous, but he hadn't thought of that. He opened his door and got out, and found that his knees were wobbly.

"Jack," he said, "do you realise you've parked in a loading bay?"

"What? Oh snot. Hang on. I'll have to move it or I'll get a ticket, sure as eggs."

"Fine." Mr Huos sighed. "Tell you what, you carry on. I'll meet you back at the office. I've got a couple of things to do anyway."

What he couldn't understand, he mused as he watched Jack winkle the Merc back out again, was how it worked. He could stretch the road, he could shrink the car, but he couldn't get rid of the white paint letters that spelt out "Loading Bay"; it simply didn't work like that. Which was why, he reflected, he was justified in refusing to think of it as magic. If he could do magic, he'd be able to conjure away a few square inches of white paint. Since he couldn't, it plainly wasn't magic. On the whole, he was glad about that. He wasn't sure he'd be able to cope with a universe in which magic was possible. On the other hand, it'd be really nice if he could use his mysterious occult powers to infiltrate Jack Tedesci's mind and radically alter his views about pay-and-display car parking. But he couldn't – tried, failed – so it was no good speculating. Anyway, magic would be cheating, and if there was one thing Mr Huos prided himself on, it was the fact that he'd made his own way in the world without any undue help from anyone or anything.

He glanced at his watch: a quarter past five, which meant that if he was quick he could drop his lightweight overcoat and the trousers from his charcoal-grey suit off at the dry cleaners in Clevedon Road and still be at Jack's office before Jack got there.

A familiar pain in his throat and chest: bloody heartburn again. Jack's fault. He winced and pulled a face, then put it out of his mind. Nothing seemed to work on it – milk, bicarb, ranitidine, all the stuff they sold in Boots – presumably because it was directly linked to whatever it was (not magic) that he did with the fabric of space and time. Try explaining that to a doctor. Instead, he'd learned to ignore it, or rather pretend to himself that he was ignoring it. Also his head was aching and he had pins and needles in both hands, an effect he usually only suffered after a particularly arduous session. Mildly disturbing; what exactly had he done back there? If he turned on the TV news that evening and discovered that Brighton or Reigate had been toppled into the sea, he wouldn't half feel stupid.

He handed over the carrier bag with his laundry in, put the ticket away safely in the back of his wallet and walked briskly up Clevedon Road into Asquith Terrace, where Jack had his office.

"Mr Tedesci back yet?" he asked the receptionist. No, he wasn't, but if he'd care to wait. He grinned, sat down and picked up this month's issue of *Expensive Homes*, which he hadn't had a chance to look at before.

Blue Remembered Hills always took a centre spread in *EH*, four pages of rich colour pictures of the latest development. At the moment, this was Orchard Acres, seventy-five luxury four-bedroom eco-friendly rabbit hutches huddled, like settlers' wagons encircled against hostile Indians, in a crease in the Malvern Hills on the outskirts of picturesque, unspoiled Norton St Edgar. He considered it, and was pleased with what he saw. True enough, he'd rather sleep in a tent than live in one of those ghastly, tacky boxes. Fortunately, his preferences weren't shared by the house-buying public. It'd be misleading to say that BRHD homes sold like hot cakes; rather, hot cakes sold a bit like BRHD homes, only not nearly as well.

"Sorry, sorry." Here was Jack, bustling towards him across Reception. "Had to park half a mile away, under the railway arches. It's time they did something about parking in this town. It's killing business. Come on up and we'll get started."

It turned out to be a long session. Although Mr Huos was perfectly happy with the deal they'd outlined over the phone three days ago, Jack Tedesci was one of those annoying people who won't take yes for an answer. Accordingly they'd danced a few pointless dances, fallen out over nothing at all, made up and eventually ended up precisely where they'd started. An excellent result, Jack called it, several times. And it was, too. Mr Huos had got everything he wanted; Jack was happy; Jack's people were happy; the bank was practically incoherent with joy, and now all that was left was ordering the little people to draw up the paperwork.

"Magic," Jack summarised, and if he noticed Mr Huos wincing, he didn't comment. "I reckon this calls for a drink. What'd you say?"

Mr Huos smiled. "No," he said. "Thanks," he added, "but I really must be making tracks." Jack's face had drooped slightly, and Mr Huos was afraid he might have hurt his feelings, so he ransacked his mind for something to say that would make him feel better. "I'll say this for you, Jack, you drive a hard bargain."

He'd got that right. Jack beamed. "That's what it's all about," he replied happily. "Give no quarter, expect none, that's always been my motto." Mr Huos tuned out for a minute or so, while Jack rehearsed his repertoire of hunter-gatherer-based business clichés – eat what you kill, hungry dogs run faster, so on and so forth – then, when the performance seemed to be over, he smiled again and stood up to leave. No, really, there was no need for Jack to drive him anywhere. Really.

It was dark outside, and raining. He glanced at his watch. If he looked sharp about it, he might just be in time to pick up his laundry before they shut. He'd paid extra for the express service, in the fond hope that he'd be able to wrap things up with Jack before the shops shut. Fortunately, the dry cleaners in Clevedon Road stayed open late, which was the main reason he went there.

As he walked quickly through the fat, wet rain, he played back the negotiations in his mind, just in case he'd missed something. Everything seemed to be in order, however, and he let his mind stray a little, back to the business with the parking space, the after-effects of which were still bothering him. The numbness in his hands and fingers hadn't lasted more than half an hour, but the headache and a few other cramps and pains were still with him; likewise the heartburn. Maybe, he thought, it's cumulative: the more of this stuff I do, the worse it'll get. That would be a pity. It couldn't help but cramp his style; on the other hand, it'd be a perfect excuse for taking early retirement. Quitting the game, selling up – he'd made enough money, God knows – digging in somewhere pleasant and taking it easy. Tentatively he sniffed at the thought, like a dog smelling paint, and found it repulsive. It was, he noted, a purely intuitive revulsion (*Me, take it easy? You've got to be kidding!*) and he recorded it in the back of his mind as valuable additional data relating to the great mystery of his life. Apparently he was a single-minded workaholic. Fancy that. He wasn't quite sure if that was a good thing to be. Purposeful, driven; that's how Jack would describe it, bless him. Or you could say he was a sad, joyless individual who really ought to think hard about getting a life.

Getting a life. Ha! Good one.

If only they knew, he thought, at the same time renewing his deadly vow that they never would, not if he had anything to do with it. What mattered, after all, wasn't where he'd come from but where he was going (actually, that sounded a bit too much like something Jack would say), and if his origins were obscure and shrouded in mystery, surely that made his subsequent achievements all the more admirable. Even so, it was disconcerting sometimes to look in the mirror and say to himself, *I don't think I should talk to me. I don't know where I've been.*

By now it was tipping it down, and he could feel crawly rain seeping into his collar. He shoved open the door of the dry cleaners and dived in.

There was a nice middle-aged lady sitting behind the counter. That was fine. But...

"Excuse me," he said. "This isn't the cleaners, is it?"

The nice lady looked at him. "Alas, no," she said.

"Ah, right. Wrong shop. Sorry."

He backed out again, cursed himself for the embarrassment and looked down the street. A mobile-phone shop. A video library. The newsagent's he'd just come out of. No dry cleaners.

A ghastly thought struck him, and his hand shot into his jacket pocket. Nothing there but a handkerchief and a tape measure.

He knew it was pointless, but he dashed back into the newsagents. "Sorry to bother you," he said, "but are you sure you're not a dry cleaners?"

The lady nodded sadly.

"You're quite certain about that?"

"Alas, yes."

"Ah. Fine." He bowed his head. "Thanks anyway," he added, and went back out into the rain.

# CHAPTER THREE

Stupid, really stupid, to get so uptight about a ridiculous office darts match. What could be simpler, after all, than to pretend she had a headache and back out? Somehow, she couldn't quite bring herself to do it, so she attacked her work instead, to take her mind off it.

That's one of the few things work is good for. The drudgery, the pointlessness, the total lack of significance of most of the stuff the average office worker does during the day, acts as a powerful analgesic to the troubled mind. Maybe it's because the petty annoyances of the office routine drive out the bigger, slower-moving worries of real life, in more or less the same way as little furry rat-like mammals inherited the Earth from the dinosaurs.

Ten o'clock came and went; no word from Don about the dress, and she assumed he was still wallowing in bed. She opened a file: Plot 16 Pretty Crescent; some awkward sod of a solicitor had sent in a whole page of supplementary enquiries, and she'd been putting off doing them. She reached for a pencil and attacked the rotten lousy job, which turned out to be quite simple and straightforward after all, and then she got a phone call from the solicitor in Evesham who'd liked her voice, thanking her for sending him the whatever-it-was.

"No trouble," she replied briskly. "That's what I'm here for."

Which was, she reflected later, a terrible thing to say about yourself, even if it was true. She went to the kitchen, made herself a coffee, and took it into the library while she looked up section 144(c)(i) of the Domestic Premises Act 2001.

They called it a library, which was a bit like calling croquet on the vicarage lawn a fight to the death. All an outsider would have seen there was a slightly enlarged section of corridor with a couple of chairs parked in it and a line of bookshelves on one wall. There were books on the shelves, true enough, but they had the melancholy, something-out-of-Chekhov look of books that never get opened, because lawyers these days don't muck around with crushed-tree sandwiches; they get their information online, from comprehensive hourly-updated cyberdatabases, fast as ICBMs and just as prone to causing mayhem when they crash.

Today happened to be one of the days (on average, there were 320 of them in a year) when WebLaw was down, or playing up, or simply not in the mood, and she needed the reference. She had to stand on a chair to get the book she needed, and while she was getting it a spider ran across the back of her hand. Progress.

Section 144(c)(i) could hide, but it couldn't run; eventually she got it cornered in a footnote in an appendix, copied it out in longhand and returned the book to its eyrie. Then she put the chair back neatly where she'd got it from, picked up her coffee cup—

Which was empty.

She stood staring into it for quite some time. Nothing to see except a little dark brown sludge. That's impossible, she thought, I was here the whole time, and I *know* I didn't drink it, because I was busy the whole time; I had my hands full. She examined the floor, just in case she'd spilt it without realising, but there was no telltale stain on the pale industrial Wilton. As a last resort she held the cup up to the light, looking for tiny pinholes in the bottom.

This can't be happening, she thought.

She felt an icy calm seep through her; a natural defence mechanism, she supposed, to keep her from freaking out and screaming the place down. So what, she told herself; so there's some sort of conspiracy around here to stop me drinking coffee. Big deal. I'll show them.

She went back to the kitchen and made herself a nice strong cup of tea. She didn't like tea much, but that was hardly the point. She took it back to her room, put it down on her desk and did the business with Section 144(c)(i). That took about six minutes. Now then, she told herself. Drink your tea before it gets cold.

She took a wary sip. It was coffee.

In the time it takes a barrister to earn a pound, she'd jumped up out of her chair and hurled the cup away from her, while her other hand rubbed savagely at her lips. This time, it had gone too far. It was getting creepy, and she'd had enough. Her first instinct was to get out of there, leave the building and not come back. Only the thought of how she'd explain her actions at her next job interview made her change her mind. She was a rotten liar, and if she told the truth they'd either disbelieve her and not give her the job, or believe her and assume she was crazy. Besides, she was braver than that, she told herself (and thought, *See what I mean? Rotten liar*).

It's only coffee, she decided. Hardly life-threatening. Weren't there stories about people who'd lived in haunted houses for years, and who reckoned they regarded the ghosts as somewhere between pets and old friends? She hadn't thought of it in those terms before. So, fine. My office is haunted by an unquiet spirit who likes coffee, does some of the difficult drafting for me, sometimes answers the phone when I'm out – not a hundred percent about passing on the messages, but nobody's perfect. What exactly is so bad about that?

A slow tide of coffee was gradually dripping down the oppo-site wall. She wiped it off with a couple of tissues, and binned the bits of broken cup. It wasn't so much what the ghost did; it was knowing she didn't dare tell anybody about it – that and the extremely unpleasant hours she'd spent believing she was losing her mind, but that was all poisonous effluent under the bridge now, and she was prepared to think no more about it, provided— Provided what? That it didn't get any worse? Yes, she decided, I'll settle for that. The best thing would be to rise above it, fail to take official notice, like a government not recognising a nasty foreign regime. She wasn't sure that'd be possible, but she could see no reasonable alternative to giving it a try.

The phone rang; she sat down and answered it, but it wasn't Don, just some woman. It turned out that she and her husband had bought a house on the development before last, and she wanted to know some trivial detail about boundaries. Of course it wasn't BRHD's place to advise her on that, now that the pur-chase was completed. As it happened, though, she still had the file in her cabinet, and the woman seemed perfectly nice and polite. She got the file out and looked through it.

"Before my time, actually," she said. "My predecessor han-dled your purchase. But it's all here in the file. Hold on, let's see. Yes, you're responsible for the east-facing fence, and your neighbour owns the other side. I can send you a copy of the plan if you like."

That would be ever so kind of her. No problem, it was her pleasure.

"It's such a nice house," the woman was saying. "We're so pleased with it. Such a good neighbourhood, and of course, the views are wonderful. We love sitting out on the patio in the evening looking out over the woods, with the hills in the back-ground."

She made it sound as though Polly had designed and built the house with her own two hands, just for them, which was rather nice, and all the better for being unexpected. "Thank you," she said awkwardly. "I'm glad you're settling in so well."

"Best thing we ever did, dear, moving here. We always wanted to retire to the country, but prices are so terrible, especially these days. I honestly don't know how you do it for the money."

A few more pleasantries of that sort, and the woman rang off. A satisfied customer, apparently. For some reason, Polly felt better because of that. Being a lawyer, therefore bred to cynicism the way collies are raised to chase sheep, she'd taken it for granted that the houses they built and sold were nasty, over-priced little boxes and their customers were gullible fools. Maybe not; in which case, maybe her job and therefore her life weren't as pointless and malign as she'd always assumed. She gathered up the papers and started putting them back in the file.

Hold on a moment. There was something written on the inside cover; written in such teeny-tiny handwriting that she could barely read it. Luckily she had a magnifying glass in her desk drawer, for checking out details on deed plans and the like. She retrieved it and bent her head low over the folder.

*There is something very odd going on in this office,* she read. *Well, more like lots of little very odd things. It's enough to make me think I'm going mad. Maybe I am, I don't know.*

Oh, she thought.

*If it goes on much longer, I'll have to tell someone. I can't cope with bottling it all up inside me like this. I think I'll explode. The trouble is that it all sounds so silly. But it's not silly, it's something big and dangerous, I'm sure of it. I think something bad must've happened to whoever had this job before I did. I suppose I ought to go to the police, but they'd just laugh or have me locked up. I can't go on like this. If only I didn't need this stupid job so badly. NB remember to book car in for MOT, dishwasher being delivered Friday am, collect cushion covers, 3lb calabrese, 6 onions, mince for shepherds pie, soap powder, kitchen towels, aspirins*

That was all. She read it twice, then slumped back in her chair. I could have done without that, she thought; it really doesn't help matters. All this fuss over a few cups of stupid instant coffee. And anyway, if her weird handwriting was anything to go by, a pound to a penny whoever it was that wrote that really was off her head. Which I'm not, she reminded herself firmly.

At which point the phone rang again. Don.

"Just thought I'd let you know, I haven't forgotten."

"What?"

"About your dress. I'm just off to ask about it now."

"Forget about that," she said impatiently. "Listen."

When she'd finished, he said, "Do you still want me to go and ask about your dress?"

"Bugger the stupid dress." On balance, probably a No. "What do you make of that, then?"

"I'm not sure," he said slowly. "I've got to say, it sounds a bit iffy to me."

"Me too."

"But then," he added, "so would you, if I didn't know you well enough."

"Thank you so very fucking much."

"You asked. And look, about this tea business. Are you quite sure you didn't just think about making tea and then go ahead and make coffee instead?"

"No, of course not."

"It's the sort of thing I do sometimes."

"If that's meant to reassure me," she said icily, "it doesn't. The reverse, in fact."

He knew that particular mood, and he couldn't really blame her. There did seem to be something odd going on at her office, and in her shoes he'd most likely be stressing out about it too. Even so, the important thing right now was to calm her down, before she worked herself up into a state and did something permanent. "Tell you what," he said. "Why don't you have a sudden migraine and go home? Get out of there for the rest of the day, think about it calmly and rationally—"

"I can't," she snapped. "I've got this ridiculous bloody darts match tonight."

"Screw the darts match," he said. "It's not like you actually want to go. Besides," he added slyly, "you can't go, you haven't got anything to wear. Talking of which," he continued, "do you want me to go and check out the dry cleaners or not? I will if you insist, but there's other stuff I could be doing."

"What? Oh, yes, do it. One less thing for me to worry about. And if you do manage to get my dress back, jump on a bus and bring it here straight away. All right?"

Which he took to mean that she wasn't going to take his advice and go home. Ah well. He rang off, put on his trousers, shoes and a jacket, and made for the front door. At the last moment, he remembered the fancy pencil sharpener, which he had to give back, assuming he managed to find someone to give it back to. If not, of course, he could keep it. Lucky him.

Subconsciously, in spite of what Polly had told him, he must have been expecting to find that the dry cleaners was exactly where it had been yesterday. It wasn't. The convenience store, the video library, the mobile-phone shop, but no dry cleaners. That stopped him in his tracks, and he stood quite still for a moment, staring. Then he went into the convenience store. The nice lady told him no, there was no dry cleaners there; she believed there was one in Albion Street, that's straight down the road, first left, second right, then second left, keep going till you see a (he tuned out). She and her husband had been running their store for seven years, ever since they moved down from Leicester. He bought a Mars bar and a packet of drawing-pins, thanked her and left.

He crossed the road and stood exactly opposite the store, looking closely at the invisible line dividing it from the video library. Invisible being the relevant word; no sign of a crack, join, seam, emergency filling or rendering. His guess was that the same landlord owned all the shops in the group, because the upper storeys were one continuous spread of homogenous brickwork, all painted the same colour, as far as he could judge all at the same time. The roof tiles matched and were equally discoloured. With his phone he took a couple of pictures; next, he walked up the street to the corner and then back again, past the shops, to the next road, counting the number of buildings. Then he went home.

Back at his flat, he logged on to Google Earth and zeroed in on Clevedon Road. The pictures he got were understandably hazy, but he saved them and got to work with a high-powered enhancement program he'd got free with a magazine. They were, of course, aerial photographs, so he couldn't see the shop frontages; but he counted the number of roofs, and found that it didn't tally, by one, with the count he'd made earlier. He double-checked. That was when he got the funny feeling in the pit of his stomach.

Next he uploaded the pictures from his phone and used another free program to rotate them through ninety degrees for a bird's-eye view. All that achieved was a series of straight lines, but it did give him the relative proportions of the frontages. He superimposed them onto the Google pictures and got a confused tangle of overlapping lines.

The Google people don't tell you when their wonderful images were taken, but he got lucky there. Outside the convenience store was a newspaper sandwich board; zooming in and enhancing, he was just able to make out the headline; the results of the Tonbridge by-election, which meant the photo was something like eighteen months old. At this point he got up, soaked a flannel in cold water, and laid it across his forehead. Didn't help.

The next two hours were extremely boring; but, thanks to the Net and a surprisingly helpful woman at the council offices, he established that, as far as local government records were concerned, there had never been a dry cleaners in Clevedon Road, and the block in question (built in 1926 by a local speculative builder called Morrison; sold by his daughter in 1969 to a property company, Yule Vasey) consisted of seventeen properties. Could she please confirm that; seventeen? Yes. Not eighteen? No. Thank you so much.

Yule Vasey had been taken over in 1974 by City and Suburban Property Portfolios, who in 1982 succumbed to the blandishments of Higson Trust, who in turn sold out to White Shark Property in 1995. White Shark was a wholly owned subsidiary of Western General Holdings, which had merged in 2002 with the Chen Hua Group. A nice lady at Western General promised to call him back, but didn't.

At this juncture he paused to gobble ibuprofen and take stock. Local government, his phone camera and his own two eyes all agreed that there were seventeen buildings on Clevedon Road between Chamberlain Street and Spenser Way, and that none of them was now or ever had been a dry cleaners. On the other hand, approximately eighteen months ago, Google's eye-in-the-sky had plainly seen an eighteenth roof; furthermore, the roof currently situated next door to the convenience store was something in the order of one and a half metres longer than the one Google had seen there when it glanced down from the bar of heaven.

Back to the search engines. He had to pay money for it, but he managed to get a download of the 1934 edition of the Ordnance Survey; the large-scale version used by lawyers and estate agents to draw up plans. Eighteen buildings. Next, he got on to the Land Registry, who were delighted to help on payment of the appropriate scale fee, but could only release information on receipt of the relevant form, a copy of which they sweetly put in the post to him. Something to look forward to. He also ordered a copy of the latest edition of the Ordnance Survey.

By then, however, he'd come to the conclusion that he had enough data. More than enough.

Clearly there were two opposing schools of thought here, the eighteens and the seventeens, and it didn't really matter which side the Land Registry and the OS people chose to adhere to. What mattered was the divergence of opinion. On his desk next to the computer he'd placed the receipt he'd been given when he picked up his trousers and overcoat, only yesterday. He looked at it for a long time, then closed his eyes and tried to think.

He knew there had been a dry cleaners there, because he'd seen it, been inside it; he had the receipt, the polythene wrapping his clothes had come back in (salvaged from the bin, a bit the worse for wear and coffee grounds, but undeniable in its physicality) and, of course, the pencil sharpener. He found that he was humming the old eighties song that includes the words;

*I would like a souvenir*
*Just to show the world was here.*

On the other hand (which by now was rapidly turning into the other tightly clenched fist) he'd been there, looked, walked and counted, and he had City Hall to back him up. There were seventeen buildings in that block, and none of them dry-cleaned clothes for money.

Shit, he thought.

He looked at his watch, then Googled a chart of time zone differentials. Unless they were hopeless insomniacs in Hong Kong, the Chen Hua people wouldn't be answering their phones for another eight hours. He sent them an e-mail, tried Western General again, got through to another nice lady who promised to call him back.

All right, he said to himself. So what am I supposed to do about it? I don't want to right wrongs, find out the truth that is out there or solve the fundamental mysteries of quantum fluctuations in the space/time multimatrix. I just want to get my sister's party dress back, so she'll stop worrying and get off my case. Presumably it's my civic duty to tell someone in authority, just in case this is the tip of some catastrophic iceberg, but even if I could figure out who I'm supposed to tell, they'd only laugh at me; and if not the authorities, then who? *You and Yours?* Esther Rantzen?

He spared a brief moment of compassion for all the honest people out there, in Oklahoma and places like that, who come home from being abducted by aliens to find Elvis is gabbling away in their microwaves again; people who've seen something and know it's true, but can't or daren't pass on the news to the rest of the species. Their biggest mistake, he'd always thought, was wanting to: the fatal urge to communicate to an outside world that simply doesn't want to know. Human ignorance, after all, invalidates nothing; the world was just as round before Columbus was born, and gravity would still have worked if Isaac Newton's father had never planted an apple tree in the garden. By the same token, he appeared to have stumbled across evidence of the existence of a phenomenon that could gobble up a building and partially erase its existence from the timelines. So what. Big deal. If he was prepared to miss out on paragraphs in science textbooks and having his portrait on a 50p stamp, he was under no obligation to share.

But that wouldn't get Polly her dress back. More to the point, turning a blind eye would mean he'd have to lie to her, and for some reason he didn't want to do that. Telling her the truth, on the other hand— She'd believe him. That was the awkward part. She'd believe him, and what effect was that likely to have on her already precarious mental state?

Maybe, he thought, I could just buy her another dress.

Nice idea, but it wouldn't work. For one thing, he knew how incredibly picky she was about stuff like that. It had to be exactly the right size, shape, colour, God only knew what else; there were all sorts of technical things he knew nothing about. And even if he was unbelievably lucky and managed to get her something she liked, that'd do him no good at all. *Why've you bought me a dress, Don,* she'd say, *when you couldn't even be bothered to remember my last three birthdays. If you've started buying me presents, things must be really, really bad—*

No; in order for that to work, it'd have to be an exact replica of the one that appeared to have fallen down the back of Infinity; and the chances of finding something like that were infinitesimally small. Stupid of him even to consider it.

He shifted in his chair, and something jabbed him in the thigh. It turned out to be the corner of the pencil sharpener, which was still in his pocket. He sighed, took it out and put it on the desk. Yesterday, in some weird kind of way, it had been a source of inspiration, but the mess he was facing now was something he couldn't just sharpen his way out of. He picked it up again; a ridiculous object, fussy and ostentatious—

It was warm.

Well, of course it was. He'd just taken it out of his pocket. He turned it over a couple of times. He could probably get a fiver for it on eBay.

*It came to me, my own, my precious.* But it wasn't his birthday, and it was silly to imagine that it had anything to do with him finishing off the jingle so painlessly. He sighed, and let it fall off the palm of his hand onto the desk, which cracked down the middle and split in two.

Oh, he thought.

He knelt down and picked it up from where it had landed on the carpet. Definitely warm. His desk was sagging in the middle where the top had split. I've had just about enough of this, he thought, and stood up to lift the computer to safety. With a soft click, the desktop came together again. Mended, good as new. Not even a mark, or a seam.

Reminded him of something. He frowned. It was one of those moments when he wished he did a lot of serious drugs, because then he could blame it all on a flashback. All right, he thought, here goes. He closed his hand round the pencil sharpener, until he could feel its corners digging into the palm of his hand. If you're so clever, he thought to himself (no, to *it*), what about a dress for my sister?

There was no movement, no twitch glimpsed out of the corner of his eye. It was just there, lying neatly folded on the desk, where the crack had been, with dry-cleaners' plastic all around it. Holding the pencil sharpener tight in his right hand, he reached out with his left and drew the dress towards him. At the point where the arms of the hanger were twisted round to form the hook there was a label; green, with a number, the day before yesterday's date, the name 'Mayer' in blue pen, and a printed address in Clevedon Road.

It was as though someone had kicked his knees out from under him. He landed arse-first in the chair rather than sat down, and his eyes didn't seem to want to focus. So that's it, he said angrily to himself. Magic.

Angry; he was *furious*. A lifetime of rational thought. A lifetime dedicated to the twin goals of reasonable, logical explanation and doing as little work as possible, and now he discovered that there was magic in the world. It was insulting. It was how Columbus would have felt if he'd sailed two days beyond the Azores and found himself falling off the edge.

He could just about reach the phone from where he was sitting. He dialled a number.

"Polly Mayer, please."

"One moment." Pause. "She's not answering her phone right now, can I take a message?"

He breathed out heavily. "Yes. Tell her Don called, I've got it here but she can damn well come over and pick it up."

"Got that. Thank you for calling."

Magic, for crying out loud. The superbloodynatural. One pencil sharpener to bring them all and in the darkness bind them. Well, he wasn't having that. What if (he cringed) his jingle, his masterpiece, his seven-note Brandenberg Concerto turned out to have been composed by magic, by the grossly overspecified graphite-nibbler still snuggling in his right hand,

and not by him at all? He wasn't sure he could handle that. Surely it would invalidate what should have been the crowning glory of his career, and that in turn would undermine everything else he'd ever done or would do in the future. How could he ever bear to work again?

*Yes*, whispered a little voice in his head, *but with magic you'd never need to work again. Ever.*

Pause. Backspace. What did you just say?

*With magic*, the little voice insinuated, *you could be rich. Effortlessly rich. Have anything you wanted, just like that. Well? How about it?*

Another pause. Then; *You did always say you were only in it for the money.*

Yes, he conceded, I do tend to say that, don't I? And if all I had to do was snap my fingers—

He snapped his fingers. Nothing happened.

Ah, he thought, a gadget moment. As in, you've brought it home from the shop, you've burrowed through the cardboard and the polystyrene and the shrinkwrap, you've plugged it in and switched it on, and it doesn't work, and the instructions are in Arabic, Cantonese and Lithuanian. He knew all about that. All the more reason, therefore, to ignore it. Pretend it hadn't happened, dump the pencil sharpener in a bin somewhere, go back to a world governed by Newton and Einstein and equations and times-tables, where everything makes sense eventually if you work away at it for long enough—

He looked at the dress. Horizontal stripes. Eew.

But it was there, on his broken-and-mended desk. Magic had put them both right; admittedly, magic had caused the problems in the first place. Maybe that was all it could do, clear up its own messes. But then he thought about the seventh note. Had that been magic, too? If so, how *dare* it. Intrusive, interfering, bossy, always having to know best, as bad as his mother (almost as bad). He could have got that note perfectly well on his own, given time, given a lot of time, maybe.

It was as though he'd won first prize in a competition he hadn't entered; something big and flash and horrendously expensive which he didn't actually want, but he'd won it, so there was an obligation...The thing about shrinkwrap was, of course, that once you've opened it, you can't take the product back to the shop for a refund, and you're bound by the terms and conditions, even if you never wanted it in the first place and you don't know how to make it work.

He snapped his fingers again. Zilch.

Not exactly a fair test, since he hadn't actually been wishing for anything at the time. He made a decision: stop sulking, concentrate, try and get this thing up and running.

He sat down at his desk and closed his eyes. His mind went blank. He sighed. What he needed to do was to run a controlled experiment. Quantifiable results, definitive success/failure parameters, and preferably something that wouldn't blow up the planet or bend the fabric of reality if he got it wrong. Science. Scientific method applied to the quantification of bloody magic. Crazy.

"I would like," he said out loud, "a ten-pound note."

He waited. Nothing happened.

Try saying the magic word. "Please?" Still nothing. No humming noises, tingling sensations, gusts of wind, flashes of blue light. He searched the desk, in case it had got lodged under something. Nothing there. He tried to remember exactly what he'd done when he conjured up Polly's dress. The trouble was, he couldn't remember doing anything. He could feel a tight knot of tension in his chest, the one he tended to think of as the reinstalling-AOL sensation. Then a thought occurred to him. He took out his wallet, opened it, and found a ten-pound note where there hadn't been one before.

Well, of course. Magic, it appeared, was logical. Ask for money, it delivers it to where money is kept. Where else?

That put a slightly different complexion on it. Ten quid, for doing nothing. He held the note up to the light, made sure the

Queen was looking in the right direction, ran a finger over it to see if the ink smudged. Ten quid. Hmm.

Another thought struck him. He logged in to his online banking program and called up his current account. Withdrawals: £10, today's date.

Disappointing; but at least it provided useful data. He'd wished for a dress for Polly, and what he'd been given was Polly's dress – not a brand new one materialised out of the ether, but her actual dress from the dry cleaners. The significance had escaped him at the time, because that precise dress was the one he'd wanted. Could it be that magic couldn't create anything? Thanks to a childhood's worth of story-book misinformation, he'd assumed that magic could pull stuff out of the air, like a Star Trek replicator. Maybe it couldn't do that; indeed, no reason to assume that it could. Maybe it could only affect stuff that already existed. He wanted a dress for Polly to go to her darts match in; he got the missing horizontally striped monstrosity. He wanted ten quid; they sent him ten quid that already existed, in his bank account.

No, he was missing the point. There were loads of ten-pound notes in the world; real, physical ones, pieces of printed paper. Only a tiny proportion of them was he entitled to treat as his own. Magic had selected one of that tiny subset to fulfil his order. Did this imply an ethical dimension? If magic could only handle things that already existed, then it followed that it could only affect *property*, stuff that belonged to somebody or other. Maybe magic couldn't bring him a dress or a banknote that belonged to somebody else, because that would in effect be stealing. Interesting hypothesis; how did it apply to the seventh note? It could be argued that it did apply, since he'd have found the note for himself sooner or later, and therefore (in a sense) it was *his* note in the eyes of transcendental metaphysical law. All magic had done was let him have it earlier than usual.

On one level, he quite liked that theory. It meant that the cheating aspect wasn't quite so bad. Also, it suggested that the scope of magic was severely limited, which suited his preferred view of the world. The broken desk, now; well, that fitted, too. Magic broke his desk, magic had fixed it. If he went to the flat next door and smashed a window, would magic fix that for him? He considered trying the experiment, but decided on balance not to.

On another level, it suggested that his new gadget wasn't nearly as good as he'd thought it was. He conceded a certain degree of disappointment. It was the free-with-this-issue radio alarm clock that stops working after twenty-four hours; worth exactly what he'd paid for it. Natural justice.

That's the thing about natural justice. It may be just, but it's seldom *fair*. Nature's approach to deciding which child should have the disputed toy is to break the toy.

(And then he thought, Just look at yourself, will you? Probably the most important discovery in human history, and you're grousing because maybe it doesn't do everything you were led to believe it could do by your recollections of *My First Book of Fairy Tales*. That's on a par with Archimedes vaulting out of the bath yelling, "Oh shit, I've spilt water all over the floor.")

Order, order. He pulled himself together and took stock. First, and arguably most important, he'd got Polly's dress back for her. Job done. Second, in the process of doing the first, he'd discovered that magic existed – well, that's interesting, dear, as his mother would say – and that (possibly because he was the current owner of a stupid brass pencil sharpener) he could do magic, sort of, a bit; he could break desks and then mend them again, he could retrieve lost garments, he could get money out of the bank without having to walk to the corner of the street and use the ATM. Useful accomplishments, all of them. Even so. Right now, if offered a choice between magic and a Black & Decker Workmate, with usefulness the main criterion, it'd have to be the Workmate. No contest.

So, what was he going to do about it?

He went into the living room, sat down in his fat, slightly

broken, comfortable chair, closed his eyes and tried to think. He chased thoughts up and down and round and round, holed them up in corners, waited for them to poke their noses out and pounced on them, until eventually he understood what the question really was.

Namely; do I want to get involved?

Find the question and seven times out of ten you realise you already know the answer. No, he thought, I don't. In fact, it's the last thing on earth I want. Even if it meant I could save the rainforests, find a practical alternative to fossil fuels and make the perfect omelette. Some gadgets come at too high a price, and I don't need that kind of aggravation; there's nothing I want badly enough. Which probably means (he realised with considerable surprise) I'm perfectly contented and happy with my life. Gosh. Fancy that.

Somebody was clouting his door; by the sound of it, with a clenched fist. That must be Polly. Everybody else rang the bell, but she maintained (and he had no reason to doubt her word) that she couldn't get it to work. Just press the button, he kept telling her. I did, she'd reply, and nothing happened.

"Well?" she said.

"Hello, come in," he replied.

She pushed past him. "Did you get it?"

"What are you doing here? It's only ten past four. You should still be—"

"I couldn't wait. Pretended I had toothache. Did you get it?"

He nodded. "Remember to talk funny when you get back, like your mouth's still frozen."

"Did you—?"

"*Yes.*" He led her into the living room and pointed. "There," he said. "Is that it?"

She was clawing at the plastic. Why can't women unwrap things in an orderly fashion? "Yes," she said. "So you found the place all right?"

Was it George Washington who couldn't tell a lie, or was he

thinking of Mr Spock? Either way, he felt sorry for him. "No bother," he said.

"They'd moved."

A statement, not a question. It'd have been rude to contradict her. "That's right," he said.

She was holding the dress up, examining it. "I thought that had to be it," she said. "After all, a shop doesn't just vanish into thin air."

She sounded happy. Well, maybe not positive-happy, but free from anxiety and stress. "I'd better be getting back to the office," she said; then, on the doorstep, very much the afterthought, "Thanks."

And then she was gone. "No problem," he said to the gap where she'd been.

# CHAPTER FOUR

He woke up, yawned, reached out blind for the alarm clock, flipped the off button and lay still for a moment, enjoying the absence of that horrible shrill buzzing noise. Another day, apparently.

Next to him, his wife snarled, grabbed a fistful of duvet and dragged it towards her, like a wolf ripping apart a carcass. Sweetest woman in the world when awake, thirty years of marriage and never a cross word; asleep, a ravening monster. Carefully, like a man carrying a flask of nitroglycerine across a minefield past a hundred sleeping lions, he swung his legs out of bed, snuggled his feet into his slippers and crossed the landing to the kitchen.

Start every day with a nice cup of tea. While the kettle boiled he cut four precise slices off the loaf, put two in the toaster, opened the cupboard and took out a jar of marmalade and a packet of muesli. Milk from the fridge, a knife for spreading butter, two bowls, two spoons. The curtains were drawn in the kitchen. He left them that way.

Tea made, stirred; toast buttered and marmaladed; muesli milk-soaked; the entire assembly on a tray. He tiptoed into the bedroom, took a deep breath, then cooed, "Morning, dear."

Snarl. Grendel's mother. He put the tea within arm's reach of where she lay, smothered in snatched duvet like a dragon on its hoard, and deposited the tray on her dressing table. Then he went back into the kitchen and ate his breakfast.

Oh well, he thought, as he finished his second slice of toast. Better get it over with.

He stood up, crossed to the window and pinched the corner of the curtain between forefinger and thumb. Some days he tweaked it back, just a little corner, and peeped through. Other days he yanked it aside, like pulling off a plaster. Today he closed his eyes and drew those curtains slowly and steadily. Variations, small ways of coping with the horror bit by bit. He opened his eyes and looked out.

She must have heard the curtain moving on its rail. "Where are we?" she called out, voice still fuzzy with sleep.

He paused before answering. "It's raining," he said. "Narrow street, old-fashioned, cobbles."

"Salford?"

"Could be." Personally, he thought probably a bit further south – Leicester, maybe, or Nottingham. He'd learned a hell of a lot about regional styles of domestic architecture over the past few years. "Nowhere we've been before," he added.

"Look on the satnav," she told him irritably, like she always did.

The satnav had been a godsend; it saved the embarrassment of wandering out into the street in your dressing gown and slippers, stopping a passer-by and asking, "Where is this?" The satnav just *knew*, as soon as you switched it on. Just like magic, she'd said, when they first got it. He didn't agree. The satnav was helpful, reliable, useful and safe. Not like magic at all.

He switched it on, then did the dishes while he waited for it to warm up. When eventually the little map appeared, he did the zoom-out thing and found that they were in Derby.

"Derby," she repeated. "My sister Annie's husband came from Derby. You remember him. Jim. Big bloke, bald head, moustache."

He didn't. She had five sisters, all of whom had married men he couldn't stand. Fortunately, the chances of Annie and Jim coming into the shop while they were there didn't seem to be all that great. Indeed, one of the few good things about his life, ever since It happened, was that he hadn't had to meet or be civil to any of her relatives. Or his own, come to that. Silver lining, he thought, and took another look out of the window.

He washed his face, shaved, combed his hair, got dressed. Eight o'clock, time to start getting ready for the working day. He was missing something.

"Eileen," he called out, "have you seen my blue cardigan?"

"It's in the wash," she called back. "Wear your fawn one."

He went downstairs, unlocked the connecting door and walked into the shop. To his left, the machines, to his right the counter, the racks where the cleaned and pressed clothes were hung up, and the door to the street. He drew back the bolts, unlocked the door and looked out. He quite liked the smell of rain on pavement, but it made the newspaper soggy. He picked it up, along with the milk, and closed the door.

So many mysteries connected with It, but the one which puzzled him most of all was how the paper boy and the milkman managed to find them. And they did. No matter where the shop pitched up, from Stornaway to Truro, every morning when he opened the front door, there were two pints of semiskimmed and the *Daily Express*, regular as clockwork. True, he felt a bit bad about the fact that they never knew where the papers or the milk came from, so they hadn't paid for either commodity ever since It started. On the other hand, the more ruthless side of his nature argued, if we've got to put up with It, we're entitled to a few perks. Milk and a paper's the least they can do, whoever they may be.

It. He had no other way of describing what had happened, what had been happening, to his wife and himself for the past . . . he couldn't actually remember any more – a very long time, at any rate. Once upon a time they'd run a nice little dry-cleaning business in a pleasant part of west London. One morning they'd woken up to find that they'd moved – to Norwich, as it happened. The shop had uprooted itself, travelled halfway across the country while he and his wife slept, and snuggled itself into a small row of shops in the southern suburbs of the city.

That had been a bad day. Phone calls: they'd tried ringing the police, the fire brigade, the city and county councils, the BBC, the seismology departments of the major universities, but either the lines were engaged or they were asked to hold, and, twenty minutes of Vivaldi or Beatles-arranged-for-string-quartet later, a click and a buzz... Meanwhile, people had been hammering on the door, with their coats and trousers and pure-wool skirts. Explain to them, they wouldn't listen, didn't seem to hear; it was as though the words that reached their ears were completely different – ordinary, to do with the business of laundering clothes. Leaving the shop proved impossible; they'd get as far as the door and another customer would come bustling in with another rush job – Do you think you could possibly have it done by five thirty? I'm going to my best friend's hen night – and by the time they'd got rid of her, another one was there in the doorway. At 6 p.m. they closed the door and shot the bolts, then collapsed in the tiny downstairs kitchen.

"Put the kettle on," she'd said.

And that was that, the last time they'd even tried to discuss It, except tangentially, in passing. No need. By then both of them understood. Whatever It was, It was bigger and stronger and cleverer than they were. Trying to outrun or outsmart It could only end in tears. The sensible thing (the only course of action open to them) was to burrow their heads as comfortably as possible into the nice warm sand and wait for It to stop. With any luck, they didn't say to each other, tomorrow morning...

Which came, alarm-ushered and rainswept, and there they still were, in Norwich, with no explanations and a shopful of cleaning, pressing, mending and ironing to get done. And they thought (no need for words when you've been married as long as they had), Well, we might as well get on with it. It's what we do all day, caring for other people's clothes. The only thing that's changed is the view out of the windows, and there's precious little time for window-gazing when you're in business for yourself. People, real people, as far as they could tell, were relying on them, and they paid in real money. Business as usual – just like the war, in fact.

Working furiously, they got everything done, handed back and paid for by six; after which they were too tired to do anything more strenuous than cook a couple of ready meals out of the freezer and go to bed. Next morning, they found themselves in Portsmouth.

And so it went on. The rules, it turned out, were fairly simple. Never more than forty-eight hours in one place. The freezer restocked itself at some point during the night – such a saving on the grocery bills; ditto the water, the gas and the electric, which they got for free; ditto the consumable supplies they needed for the business. Once the takings in the till (including cheques) went over a thousand pounds, it all vanished, apart from a generous float. Once a month they got a bank statement, addressed to them at wherever they happened to be that day. It was mounting up very nicely indeed, partly because they never spent any of it, because they never had time to nip out to the bank and withdraw anything. As and when It stopped, there'd be enough there for a very comfortable retirement (Portugal, Florida even); meanwhile, they worked hard all day, as they'd always done, and tried not to think about anything longer term or further away than they could help. It meant they'd completely lost touch with their families and their old friends (when they thought about it, they were pleasantly stunned by how little they missed them); on the other hand, each of them was prepared to swear blind that the other hadn't aged a day since It started. They had their work, and they had each other. No weekends, apparently – go to bed on Friday night, wake up on Monday morning – but they never felt more than comfortably tired, and neither of them had had as much as a cold or a sore throat since they first landed in Norwich. His view (he'd never asked his wife for her opinion) was that whoever was doing It was pretty damn smart: he gave them just enough perks to make them turn a blind eye to the rest of it – the weird stuff, the endless work, the unvarying routine. In all the time It had been going on, they'd never once tried to escape, or made any serious effort to find out what was going on, or even to tell anybody about It. Could be worse, they both felt, and it's bound to stop of its own accord sooner or later. Just let It run its course.

The longer It went on, in fact, the less they wanted it to stop. The world outside had changed since they were first isolated from it. If the *Daily Express* was to be believed (as far as they were concerned, it was), the outside world was a horrible scary place, where you were lucky if you got through the day without being blown up by terrorists or stabbed by youths or poisoned by your food or laid low by some appalling new disease. They'd had a car back in west London, but they wouldn't be able to afford to run it now, and weren't gas and electric a terrible price? They really didn't know how people managed. Safe inside the world of It, life was better in so many little ways. For example, they were still getting 1987's television. The programme listings in the paper didn't sound nearly as good: all these makeover shows and talent shows and reality shows, when what they enjoyed was a nice comedy, or a serial. Also, both of them had secretly always fancied travelling – not abroad, just seeing a bit more of this country – but neither of them could abide the fuss and bother of holidays. Thanks to It, they'd been to every settlement in the United Kingdom bigger than a village, and all without having to leave the comfort of their home.

Even so.

But he didn't think about that. Mostly, when he thought outside his box at all, he wondered what happened to the stuff that wasn't collected before they moved on. It stayed on the rack for a day, and then it wasn't there any more. He hoped very much that it somehow found its way back to its owners, and didn't get too badly creased in the process. They got paid for it, at any rate.

He'd begun to wonder when they watched a thing on TV about the legend of the Flying Dutchman, which he'd wanted to see under the impression that it'd be about steam trains. Not so, apparently. The Flying Dutchman was some poor sod of a sea captain who was cursed by the Devil on account of some trivial infringement of the rules, and who spent all eternity wandering the seven seas in an old ship. It had made him think. Had he done something wrong? Short-changed a customer; lost someone's favourite blouse; shrunk someone's trousers? As far as he knew his conscience was clear, but you never know, do you? There were days when he worried a lot about that, until he remembered the perks. If he was being punished for something, would It pay all his bills and arrange for the milk and the papers? On balance, he thought not. So that was all right.

And that was all, really (apart from that other business): an unconventional life that didn't really suit but not without its benefits. You just had to shrug your shoulders, play the hand you'd been dealt, keep your head down and your nose clean and get on with it, and never under any circumstances whatsoever use the downstairs toilet between ten fifteen and a quarter to twelve. There were, as he often remarked to his wife, a heck of a lot of people worse off than they were. Look at all those earthquakes in the Middle East or wherever, and the wars, and global whatsit and the council tax.

He opened the paper at random and scanned it for a story he could relate to. Not so easy this morning, since he couldn't get *Celebrity Big Brother* on their telly, he'd never done the lottery and he'd stopped following football years ago. Property prices, he smiled at those. In the staying-put world house prices were through the roof one moment and down the toilet the next.

Another thing they didn't have to worry about. According to their bank statement, It had paid off their mortgage, and the business loan too. The bit in the paper said that people who couldn't afford to buy a conventional house were turning to mobile homes as a more affordable option. Well, quite.

In the business section there was a profile of some bloke called Huos who ran a development company, Blue Remembered Hills. There was a photo, and it rang a bell. *I know that face,* he thought. He had a remarkable memory for faces – not a particularly relevant asset, the way things were these days – and he was positive he'd seen that man before.

"Him?" She peered at the picture over the top of her glasses. Another of It's more welcome side effects; she didn't need glasses to read any more, though she couldn't get out of the habit of putting them on. "Oh yes, I remember him. Wasn't he—"

The shop bell rang. A nervous, harassed-looking man with a shirt. There were, they noticed, lipstick marks on the collar. "My wife's back from her mother's tonight," he explained, "and I don't know how to use the washing machine."

They promised it'd be ready by lunchtime, and the man looked ever so relieved. On his way out he bumped into a woman with red wine stains on a cashmere coat, who in turn was replaced by a man who needed his suit for a funeral, and so it went on. Busy, needed, providing a service; neither of them had a chance to draw breath before the ten-thirty lull.

There was always a lull at ten thirty: twenty minutes, just long enough to put the kettle on, drink a cup of tea and munch a ginger nut from the self-refilling jar in the kitchen, before the inevitable customer came in at ten to eleven. At ten forty-five both of them remembered that they'd been discussing something just before the first customer of the day arrived, but neither of them could recall what it was.

As they passed the toilet, on their way back from the kitchen to the shop, they heard a few notes of plainsong, a clank, a muffled scream, the distinctive *tzing* of a sword being drawn from a scabbard. "At it again," she muttered, and he nodded. Then the shop bell rang.

Later, around three in the afternoon, he remembered what they'd been talking about earlier: that man in the paper, what was his name? But a lot of customers came in between three and six, and drove the whole thing clean out of his mind.

The pub was called the Slug & Lettuce, and things went downhill from there. The Blue Remembered Hills team consisted of: Alan Stevens (captain); Terry Lopez from Sales, a tall, fat, pink young man who bumped into tables; Gordon Smith from Accounts, short, bald, with his own set of molybdenum carbide Pro-Flite match darts; Joe Vetterli from Planning, who talked for hours to anybody who'd stay still long enough, but nobody could ever remember anything he said; and Polly Mayer from Legal, standing on the edge of the group wishing she was somewhere else. The Thames Water team turned up wearing matching darts shirts with their logo on the fronts and their names on the backs in sequins. They were all called Paul. One of them wore glasses.

She'd been a bit apprehensive beforehand about being the only female. Needn't have worried about that. Far more daunting was being the only human being. She allowed herself to be furnished with a half of lager (she loathed beer in any form) and tried to think herself a cloaking device.

Alan Stevens (captain) was slaughtered in the opening game, still vainly popping away at double top by the time his opponent hit double bull first dart to win. Since Mr Stevens was their star player, that more or less set the tone for the evening. The Pauls were very good-natured and sportsmanlike about it all, mooing encouragingly whenever a BRHD player actually managed to hit the board, murmuring condolingly every time a dart ended up sticking in the wall or a tabletop. One of them, presumably the designated first-aider, was on the scene immediately when

Terry Lopez's ricochet hit the Australian barman on the ear. Mr Vetterli, given free rein to network, was broadcasting on all channels, and one of the Pauls actually appeared to be listening. Time passed in that unique blur you only get with quintessential boredom, and then it was her turn to play.

Her opponent was the Paul with glasses. He speared double sixteen with deadly precision and started pounding the twenty like an artillery barrage. At this point Team BRHD was down four–nil with just her game left to play; after which, as far as she could judge, she was free to feign a headache and go home. The sensible thing, therefore, would be to lose as quickly and efficiently as possible. The last thing she wanted to do was incur the lasting hatred of her teammates by winning.

She was using the pub darts (blunt, tatty, mix-and-match flights), and as she stepped up to the line she called to mind just how long it had actually been since she'd played this stupid game, and how rarely she'd won at it. Dad always beat her, of course, and Don had spent most of his university years in the union bar studying biochemistry and ballistics. It was all, she couldn't help thinking, a bit like Life.

At which thought a hitherto unsuspected caged lion began to growl softly inside her head. Of course it didn't matter, and of course she was expected to lose, and of course it'd be easier and less trouble to herself and others if she didn't even bother to try. Instead, she felt a cold fury seeping through her veins. Suddenly, all her enemies were subsumed into the dartboard, and the dart in her hand was a spear. If she listened very carefully, she wondered, would she be able to hear double eighteen scream when she transfixed it? She could just fancy that.

It didn't. Instead there was a split second of pure silence, followed by bemused but sincere expressions of delight from the Pauls, which only made her bloodlust stronger. I'll give them something to cheer about, she thought grimly, and drove the remaining two darts barrel-deep into treble twenty.

There then followed the sort of performance which, recalled

in leisurely tranquillity, makes your colon pucker with embarrassment. Mercifully it didn't last long, and then Paul-with-glasses was burbling well-done-thanks-for-the-game, and Mr Smith with the molybdenum carbide darts was giving her a scowl that would have stripped chrome plating, and Mr Vetterli had stopped trying to network and was staring at her as though she'd just grown a tail, and Terry Lopez was back from the bar with a tray of glasses, asking, "Well, who won that one?" and not getting a reply, and she asked herself, *What the hell did you want to go and do that for?* At which point the caged lion inside her head made a sort of mewing noise and tried to hide behind her subconscious. She muttered something even she didn't catch, fled to the ladies' and stayed there for five minutes, until the dripping of a tap drove her out again.

By the time she got back, Team BRHD and the Pauls had oil-and-watered into two separate knots of listless not-talking standers. She couldn't face her lot, so she walked up to the Pauls and smiled.

Cracking game, they said; where did she learn to play like that? So she embarked on the authorised biography – brought up in a pub, used to practise with her brother after school before the bar opened, leading on to general observations about growing up on licensed premises. She'd been through it often enough to be able to recite it without thinking, and it went down well with the Pauls, who asked all the usual questions, laughed at the purportedly funny bits, world without end, amen. She was, in fact, making quite a hit with Thames Water's finest, which was the professed purpose of the exercise, while Captain Stevens and his platoon stood sullenly by and scowled at the back of her head. Just goes to show. If there's one thing the British can never forgive, it's winning.

She rounded off the pub soliloquy with the usual peroration and looked for a lull in the conversation through which she could make her escape. Instead, Paul-with-glasses said, "I've got an aunt in Norton St Edgar."

Where? Oh, yes, right. "Great," she said feebly.

Paul-with-glasses had that distinctive soft-Lancashire accent that always made her think of *Gardeners' Question Time.* "She lives just down the street from your houses. She says they're very nice."

"Thank you," she said.

He accepted her thanks with a graceful dip of the head. "Apparently, everybody in the village was really worried when your company put in for planning," he went on. "Thought it'd spoil the neighbourhood, all that sort of stuff. But no, she reckons they're tucked in so unobtrusively you wouldn't know they're there."

"Glad to hear it," she said. And then a little bell rang in the secret depths of her mind where the cowardly lion had been a short while earlier, and she asked, "Which lot are we talking about?"

Puzzled face. "Excuse me?"

"Well," she said, "we've built a lot of developments round Norton St Edgar. In fact, by now the place is probably about the size of Liverpool. Which estate was your aunt talking about?"

He looked at her. "There's just the one," he said.

"Sorry?"

"Just the one lot of houses your people built," he said. "About a dozen of them, down the bottom of the village, between the church and the pub. Very tasteful, my aunt says they are, all faced with the local stone and blended in nicely."

For five seconds or thereabouts her mouth wasn't working. Then she said, "Norton St Edgar, Worcestershire?"

"Yes, that's right. Twelve minutes from Malvern on the main road. We stopped off there year before last on our way back from the Lake District."

Not long after that she played the headache card and escaped into the cool night rain. It was no more than a gentle plant-mister drizzle, the kind that you hardly register until you're soaked to the skin. She wouldn't have noticed if a big cedarwood boat loaded down with pairs of animals had gone drifting past her, swept along on a tide of floodwater.

Only one development in Norton St Edgar, tucked in unobtrusively between the pub and the church. You wouldn't know it was there. She tried to remember how many brand new houses in Norton St Edgar she personally had conveyed to their new owners. Definitely more than fifty, maybe as many as fifty-five. She'd only been there a relatively short time; before that, her predecessor (*There is something very odd going on in this office*, she'd written in teeny-tiny letters so small nobody would notice them) must have dealt with scores, hundreds of transactions, all of them in or around Norton St Edgar. The company employed six full-time conveyancers apart from herself; that must mean *thousands* of houses.

Hang on, she thought, I've seen a map. Ordnance Survey, definitive as the Pope. Norton St Edgar fitted onto just one sheet. It was *tiny*.

She went home, took off her dress and stuffed it in the laundry basket and went to bed. For an hour she lay in the dark staring at the ceiling, until the soothing whale song of the central heating system lulled her to sleep. Then she had a dream.

In her dream she was back in the office. On her desk was a stack of files, sales of houses in Norton St Edgar. Beside the stack was an unsolicited cup of coffee, which some kind, anonymous person had made for her. She opened a file and looked at it to see what needed doing. Ah yes, she remembered this one. Plot 16 Pretty Crescent – some awkward sod of a solicitor had sent in a whole page of supplementary enquiries, and she'd been putting off doing them. She reached for a pencil, then realised that the work had already been done for her.

Just a moment, she thought.

She opened her desk diary. Today's date. Pencilled in at the bottom of the page, *Darts match*. She stared at the scrawl, her handwriting, for a moment or so, then turned the page, picked up a red pen and wrote *HELP* in big capital letters. Then the alarm went, and she woke up.

B&J Removals turned off the motorway at Junction 15, followed the A road to Malvern, turned on the satnav and pottered along quiet lanes until the snooty bitch told them they'd arrived at their destination. Maybe she knew them too well; she'd brought them to a pub.

Since it was still only a quarter to nine in the morning, satnav's kindness was misplaced. The pub stood at the end of a quaint, tourist-board-approved village street. Opposite, flaked paintwork on a board identified the church as St Edgar's.

"Bloody thing," said B. "We got a map?"

In the passenger seat J shook his head. "Fourteen Attractive Close, Norton St Edgar," he said. "That's all it says here."

B craned his neck and looked round. The street they were in, like Clint Eastwood in his signature role, had no name. "We'd better find someone to ask," he said.

Easier said than done. The street was deserted. B and J walked a few yards, stopped, turned round, walked back the other way. They were beginning to wonder if something was wrong.

"You sure this is the place?" J said.

His scepticism was perfectly reasonable in the circumstances. There was one street, comprising a dozen thatched, half-timbered cottages, the pub and the church. Beyond that was a drive with a hand-painted board saying *Home Farm*. Beyond that, mere bucolic wilderness.

"Must be the wrong village," B said firmly. They walked on a few yards further, until they came to a road sign, NORTON ST EDGAR, and below that, in smaller letters, *"Please drive carefully."*

"That's odd," J said.

"Maybe there's two villages with the same name," B suggested. "You get that sometimes."

So they went back to the van and dug the road atlas out from under the empty sandwich cartons in the passenger-side footwell. Just the one Norton St Edgar.

"We need to find someone to ask," J said.

At that precise moment a middle-aged woman in a scarf came out of one of the cottages, with a dog on a lead. B and J looked at each other. Now, their body language said, we're going to get somewhere.

B wasn't good with the public, so it was J who asked the question, at which the woman frowned. "Never heard of it."

J repeated the address. The woman looked blank. "There's just the one street," she said. "This one. It's called The Street. Sorry."

The dog was pulling at its lead, anxious to be off. She let it drag her away, leaving B and J standing still and decidedly thoughtful.

B looked at his watch. "It's gone nine," he said. "Phone the estate agents."

J went back to the van, got the piece of paper and prodded buttons on his phone. "Where?" said the voice he was eventually connected with.

J was getting tired of saying it. "Fourteen Attractive Close, Norton St Edgar."

Pause. "What close?"

"Attractive."

"Please hold."

J had sharp ears. He could hear muttering in the background, then the voice came back. "Sorry," it said, "that's not one of ours. You're sure you've got the right office?"

"Yes," J said, keeping his temper. "It's here on the top of the letter."

"Please hold."

This time they played music at him. Probably not a good sign.

"Well?" B asked.

"I'm holding."

"You sure you rang the right place?"

"Don't you start."

Long wait; J feared for his battery. Then the voice came back. "Sorry," it said, "there's nothing like that on our books. What was the developer's name again?"

"Blue Remembered Hills Developments."

"Blue what?"

No such company on their books. No record of any properties in Norton St Edgar. She *was* the manager. *Click.*

They were both very quiet for a while. Then B said, "All right, ring the customer."

J shrugged, found the number and rang it. No reply. Well, there wouldn't be, not on the landline. Try the mobile.

"Hello," J said, "this is Jim, B & J Removals. Listen, we're at the address, but there doesn't seem to be any—"

"Who is this?" said the woman at the other end of the line.

"B & J Removals," J said, rather desperately. "We're moving your stuff for you."

"Stuff?"

"All your furniture and stuff. From your house. We were over your place last night—"

"No, you weren't."

"Yes, we *were*." There was panic in his voice. "We came over and loaded up, so we could get up here early. You specifically asked—"

"But we're not moving."

"We've got all your stuff in our van."

"No, you haven't. It's here. I'm looking at it."

"Listen—"

*Click.*

J looked at B. "Did you . . ."

B nodded. He had that empty look.

"We went over there," J said, "last night."

"That's right," B said. "And loaded up. There was that big old sideboard."

"That's it," J replied eagerly. "And that crummy wardrobe that wouldn't go through the door. And that bloody tropical fish tank with all the wires out the back."

A thin filament of hope stretched between them, tense and brittle. They went back to the van, unlocked the padlock on the up-and-over door and slid it up. They looked inside.

The van was empty.

# CHAPTER FIVE

Ever since Don was a small child, he'd had this recurring nightmare. It was Christmas. The pub was shut for the day and the whole family was gathered round the tree. Mum and Dad were handing out presents, some for Polly and some for him. Polly's presents all had little labels on – from Mum and Dad, from Aunt Jane with love, the usual – and when she opened them they were all in their proper as-seen-on-TV packaging, with the maker's name prominently displayed on the carton. But his presents had no labels, and as soon as he ripped them out of their glossy wrapping he could tell there was something wrong with them. No packaging. No plastic blister packs, nothing to say that batteries weren't included. They were old-fashioned, crude. They looked (he could feel tears of disappointment and anger burning in the corners of his eyes) *home-made*, or if not actually that, then not made in a proper factory, by machines.

"Well, of course not," said his mother. "They're made by Santa's elves."

"At the North Pole," added his father.

"Don't be stupid," he snapped peevishly. "There's no elves.

The North Pole's nothing but snow and ice, I saw it on David Attenborough. Santa's not *real.*"

Mum and Dad looked at each other nervously. Then Dad said, "Well, actually..."

Something in his tone of voice, perhaps. Or maybe it was loads of tiny snippets of evidence, rejected over the years by his conscious mind but gradually building up in his subconscious till they reached an unsustainable level. Anyhow, he *knew.* Everybody – his sister, the other kids at school, even the teachers – had been deliberately lying to him all these years. There genuinely was a Father Christmas. Santa Claus *existed.*

At that point in his dream he'd burst into hysterical sobs and wake up, falling sharply and reassuringly into a world where E equalled $MC^2$, and where to every action there was an equal and opposite reaction. Even though he knew at that moment that it had all been a ghastly nightmare, even so the relief, the glorious realisation that it wasn't true, always filled him with joyous gratitude, together with a renewed determination not to have rich food and black coffee after nine o'clock at night.

Today he woke up, opened his eyes and stared at the silent alarm clock beside his bed. Eight a.m. He blinked at it – he believed in the existence of eight a.m., but only in the sense that he believed in Alpha Centauri: it was out there somewhere, but he'd never live to go there – and remembered.

"Oh God," he moaned.

Yesterday, here in this very flat, his *home,* magic had happened. He had done magic. A lifetime of rational scepticism had gone gurgling down the toilet. He could almost hear sleigh bells.

Imagine the feelings of a dead atheist as he gazes into the smirking face of St Peter. He cringed. It was all so bitterly unfair. Out there in the world, he knew, there were millions of poor credulous, benighted fools who'd give anything for the knowledge that was burning him up like refluxed acid. And what next? If there was magic, where was the line to be drawn? Aliens? The Loch Ness monster? How about the Tooth Fairy? They couldn't actually force him to believe, could they?

No need. He'd seen for himself. Existence, as he'd known it, was over. All he could do was pick himself up and start again. He'd start, he decided, by putting on his underpants.

He opened the drawer. An arm, sleeved in white samite, reached out and handed them to him.

He jumped – a crane fly doing a Basil Fawlty impression – and his back hit the wall. He stared. The hand (slender, pale, feminine) was perfectly still, with his pants – ironed, he couldn't help noticing, and neatly folded – draped over its palm like a posh waiter's white cloth. But *his* pants, nonetheless. Present from his mother, birthday before last.

Mum, he thought, there's a strange lady in my underwear drawer. He thought about that. Well, for one thing, a very brave strange lady, and presumably not afflicted by claustrophobia. He cleared his throat nervously and mumbled, "Hello?"

(Then he thought, No, not possible. What's the cubic capacity of a pants drawer, even when empty? Say a metre by half a metre by twenty centimetres. In his weakened state the mental arithmetic was too much for him, but it was not a lot. Not enough for a whole human body, not even if cut up and squashed in. But then, he added quickly, it'd be dead, in which case it couldn't pass me my pants. Not, oh *God*, without magic.)

No reply. One of those strong, silent disjointed magic arms? No, that one was obvious. Of course it couldn't answer him – unless, of course, the head, larynx and lungs were in his sock drawer. That was a possibility he didn't feel up to investigating straight away. That said, he needed his pants.

How frail is our grip on our lives, how easy it is for a determined supernatural terrorist to hold us hostage. Deprive a man of his underwear and you've got him pinned down. Even if he's brave enough or scared enough to run out into the street in his pyjamas, he won't get far, and he knows it. Don had no illusions about his mental fortitude. Faced with a choice between embarrassment and arrest on the one hand, and the other hand (magic, clad in white samite, holding his boxers), there was only one way he could go. Very slowly, like a nervous city dweller in a red shirt approaching a bull, he edged forward, snatched the pants off the hand's extended palm and shot back up against the wall, breathing hard.

"Thanks," he heard himself mutter.

The hand snaked back inside the drawer, which slid quietly shut, just as the sock drawer crawled open. Another hand, also in white samite but this time fringed with a tasteful lace cuff, rose out of it like a snake, holding a pair of socks. Maybe it took pity on him: it lobbed the socks with an easy underarm throw. He fumbled the catch, retrieved the socks and fled to the bathroom, bolting the door behind him.

*You do realise,* said a voice in his head, as he perched on the edge of the bath and hyperventilated, *that it's trying to be helpful. Saving you trouble. It's somehow sensed that you're an idle git, too lazy to get dressed in the morning unless you absolutely have to, so it's helping out. Like, sort of, Jeeves.*

Yes, Don countered, that's fine. On balance, though, a some-assembly-required Jeeves that jumps out at me from inside the furniture isn't really an improvement in my quality of life. Nice thought, but no thanks.

*Don't tell me that,* replied the voice. *Tell it.*

Well, he could see the logic in that approach, he supposed. He put on the pants and socks, wrapped himself comprehensively in his towelling robe and went back into the bedroom.

The sock drawer had closed again, but he didn't feel inclined to get any closer to it than he had to. Instead, he said, in a loud, clear voice, "Excuse me."

No reply, naturally. See above.

Yes, but just because it couldn't talk back didn't mean it couldn't hear, or at least understand. "Excuse me," he repeated, "but if it's all the same to you I'd really rather get my own clothes, thanks ever so much. OK?" Pause. "If you can hear me, open a drawer or something."

Nothing moved. That's a bit rude, he thought. Or maybe it can't hear me after all.

Maybe, but his situation now was, if anything, even worse than it had been. Whereas before he'd been in his pyjamas, now he was standing there wearing nothing but pants and socks. Escape simply wasn't an option. He inched towards the wardrobe, watching the line where the doors met like a hawk. He was no further than two feet away from it when the doors swung open, and a hand, a *third* one, held out a hanger. His saved-for-best jeans and his light blue shirt.

Oh, he thought.

To be fair, though, he'd taken and put on the underwear the other two hands had offered him and nothing bad had happened. Maybe he was looking at this the wrong way. Admittedly, he didn't think that shirt and those jeans went at all well together, but he was perfectly prepared to admit that fashion sense wasn't one of his greatest assets. Not his strong suit, ha ha. Oh *God*.

I will not crack up, he commanded himself. I am the captain of my soul, and if they want to break me, they won't do it by handing me my own clothes in my own bloody flat. On the contrary. I will be strong. I will take these clothes, put them on, check I look all right in the mirror, then leave the flat, run like buggery to the nearest travel agent and book myself on the first available flight to Sumatra.

My *best* jeans, he thought. My best shirt, now I come to think of it – best in the sense of least tatty, anyhow. Sod it, the samite female is trying to tidy me up. Like my mother. Or a wife. The thought made him shudder. If he left the flat now, when he came back would it be all neat and tidy, his stuff put away where he'd never be able to find it again, his comfortable scruffy clothes bundled up in a black bin bag and spirited away? Jesus, he thought.

Going to Sumatra wasn't the answer, he knew. It was *magic*, for crying out loud; it couldn't be cheated of its prey by mere geography. It could follow him or bring him back. There was, he knew, only one course of action open to him.

He took the hanger, went into the bathroom again and got dressed. On his way back to the bedroom, the doors opened for him. "Don't do that," he pleaded. They shut behind him too.

Logic: if Samite Girl didn't have ears to hear him with, it followed that she didn't have eyes to watch him get dressed with. Indeed. But in the presence of magic, logic is a chocolate frying pan and a Zimbabwean government stock. He slithered into his dressing gown, turned his back on the chest of drawers and, hopping energetically on each leg in turn, put on his trousers. He had to doff the dressing gown to get inside his shirt, but he didn't mind that so much. He slid his keys off the bedside table and stuffed them into his trouser pocket. A hand reared up from under the bed, holding his shoes. The laces had been undone and they'd been polished till they shone – a pity, that, since they were trainers. He sat on the bed and dragged them on. Something touched the back of his head like a wasp, but noiseless and tugging gently. His hair was being combed.

(He thought, I *wish* I used an electric razor.) "I'm growing a beard," he said loudly, then counted to ten under his breath. Nothing happened. He breathed a sigh of heartfelt relief, just as a white-sleeved hand shot out through the bathroom door and stuck his toothbrush in his mouth.

He held perfectly still while the hand brushed his teeth. It seemed to be the sensible thing to do. He thought, I really need to go to the loo, but maybe I'd better not. To be fair to it, the hand proved to be quite competent with a toothbrush. Toilet paper, however, was another matter entirely.

He waited. When he'd said he was growing a beard, the hands had refrained from flying at his throat with a razor. That was reason to believe, surely, that they were able to hear and understand him after all (also that they could be lied to, come to that). Their earlier failure to obey or acknowledge...He thought about that, and the phrase *Nanny knows best* popped neatly into his mind like merchandise from a vending machine. Well, he thought, we'll see about that. Until such time as I can figure out how to make it stop, go away, leave me alone, I'm going to have to come to terms with it, sure. But I'm not going to smarten myself up; I'm not going to write my thank-you letters and I'm sure as hell not going to eat up my nice greens.

"You got that?" he said aloud.

No reply. Something told him, however, that they'd heard him just fine. There was that very faint but unmistakable tension quivering in the air, the sort he knew only too well from his childhood, the sort he'd been so very keen to get away from. This way to the battle of wills, it said to him, and he felt his muscles clench. He was the sort of man who'd rather bite off his own toe than get involved in scenes and melodrama, and ever since he'd escaped from the family nest he'd done his best to design his life to be scene-proof and melodrama-free. All that, he had a nasty feeling, was about to change. Oh well, he thought. Back to the trenches.

He looked round the room, letting his eye rest in turn on all the dark and hidden places that had produced hands at him since he woke up. He cleared his throat as though about to address a hostile board meeting.

"Maybe," he said, "we should sort out a few ground rules."

God, but he felt stupid, talking to the furniture. Quite probably they were counting on that. He hardened his heart and his skin and went on, "Rule one. No doing stuff for my own good. OK?"

Nothing stirred. But that was all right. He'd tuned into the appropriate wavelength now. He *knew* the room was listening. Almost, in the disposition of the furniture, the interplay of light and shadow, he thought he could make out an expression – a grim expression, corners of a metaphorical mouth turned down, eyes cold and hard, and was that the faint clicking of a virtual tongue? Never mind. He hated this sort of thing, but he was rather good at it. "Next," he said. "I know you can hear me, so it's only good manners if you answer me when I talk to you. Well?"

Reluctance. The room was ...

"Rule three," he said briskly. "No sulking."

Had the curtains moved? He wasn't sure, but he didn't think so. It was just the shifting of the balance between light and shade as the sun went behind a cloud that gave the impression that the room was scowling at him.

"Sorry," he said. "I didn't quite catch that."

And then the room spoke to him. It was the creaking of floor-boards, the groan of drawers not sitting perfectly square on their runners, the squeak of the hinge of a door overloaded by the weight of coats hung behind it, the flatulence of plumbing and central heating, the whimper of a chair as you stand up and the compressed foam-rubber cushion reflates, the whistle of curtains on their tracks, the click of switches, the hum of a CPU fan. Blended together, a symphony of sounds so familiar they're never heard, they said, "Yes."

It was a moment or so before he realised what he'd heard, or that he'd heard anything at all. You know how sometimes you pick something up on the beach, a slightly different shape among the pebbles, and you can't immediately tell if it's just another small, rounded stone or a human artefact, smoothed and sanded and ground down by the infinite patience of the sea until it's virtually unrecognisable. To be on the safe side, he said, "Sorry?"

The room said, "Yes."

Briefly he found himself thinking, It was bad enough when I was talking to the room, this must be very bad indeed. But that sort of thing wasn't likely to help. So, baby's first word. Talking of which, all the experts stress the value of starting as you mean to go on.

"Yes, what?"

Maybe it was the room thinking, very slowly, or maybe it was the pause while the unwilling speaker grits his teeth and forces himself to say the magic word.

"Yes, *sir*."

He wasn't sure if he'd been expecting that or not. Anyway, it'd do. "That's better," he said. "Now, the rules. Do we have an agreement?"

"Yes, *sir*."

"Excellent. Any questions?"

Pause. "No, *sir*."

One step at a time, he told himself. We've established a dialogue, which is a major step and exactly what Captain Picard would have done. We can deal with attitude tomorrow, maybe. "So," he said, "how does all this stuff work, exactly? Do I get a specified number of wishes, or is it more open-ended?"

The room seemed to shudder, as though at some ghastly lapse of protocol, and he decided he wasn't going to get an answer to that one. Pity. He took a deep breath and reformulated the question. "Um, is there a manual or a user's guide or anything like that? Only—"

A book lifted an inch off the bookshelf and flew at him across the room. He had to bat it away with his hand or it'd have smacked him in the face. It fell, pages spreadeagled, on the floor, and he picked it up quickly before it could have another go at him.

Not a book he'd seen before. It was thick enough, something in the order of a thousand pages at a guess, and handsomely bound in red leather with loads of gold leaf. Unfortunately, it wasn't in English. Damned, in fact, if he knew what it was in. Instead of words made up out of letters there were pictograms – squat, chunky, rather menacing symbols that reminded him of old-fashioned arcade game Space Invaders. Ah, he thought. Like that, is it?

"Excuse me," he said. "Is there a translation?"

"No, *sir*. Sorry, *sir*."

At that he could feel his attitude starting to shift. It came, he later rationalised to himself, from the contrariness of his own nature. Magic, it appeared, was only doing what he himself would have done in its position: messing him about to make him go away, because it didn't like him. That put a new complexion on the whole business.

It was just like, he realised, the coffee frother, one of those little plastic battery-operated whisk things which had come free with something or other. Don was take-it-or-leave-it-alone when it came to cappuccino and foamy hot chocolate and the like, and being able to concoct such things in his own kitchen was way down in the southern hemisphere of his list of priorities, only just ahead of voting in local elections and dusting. But when he'd tried it, the coffee frother didn't work. Press button, no dice, nothing; so he'd taken the batteries out and put them back in again, making sure they were the right way round, and it still didn't work; so he'd opened the casing up and checked for visibly loose connections, and there weren't any; which left him with no alternative but to call the supplier of the something or other the coffee frother had come free with, who referred him to a distributor, who put him on to an importer, who turned out to have gone bankrupt three weeks earlier, but whose liquidators suggested he take the matter up with the manufacturer. By the time the trail finally went cold, he was on oh-it's-you-again terms with four different officials at the trade delegation at the Chinese embassy, and the first thing he'd done after finally admitting defeat was go out and buy a proper coffee frother, one that actually went *whizz* when you pressed the button.

That, he'd long since acknowledged, was simply the way he was, and it was too late to do anything much about it now. Anybody could sell him anything, if only they knew about that aspect of his personality. Just tell him, "You can't have it," and immediately he couldn't live without one.

First things first, however. "Magic," he said. "Did you give me the last note of my jingle, or was it all my own work?"

"Yes, *sir.*"

He sighed. He was a patient man, but some coffee frothers come at too high a price. He was wondering whether he could be bothered to rephrase the question when his train of thought was derailed by a furious hammering at his door.

It was his upstairs neighbour, the amateur guitarist, and he was obviously upset about something. "You," he snapped. "What the hell are you *doing* in there?"

Good question. "Me? Nothing."

"Balls," replied the guitarist. "You're up to something all right. It's making the walls shake. There's plaster coming down off my ceiling."

Don smiled pleasantly. "Is that right?"

"Yes," the guitarist replied, and Don thought of the evenings he'd spent with cotton wool stuck in his ears to protect him from the sound of his favourite tunes being murdered. Also, now he came to think of it, when the guitarist wasn't being a guitarist, he was something to do with insurance. "You think it's funny, do you?"

Oh go away, Don thought. And he did.

Don couldn't be sure whether the guitarist had just vanished, or whether, a split second before he disappeared, there'd been a sort of blurry shimmer and a very faint crackling noise. Not that it really mattered; the net effect was the same. One moment there'd been a stroppy loss adjuster standing in his doorway, the next moment there wasn't.

Ah, Don thought. This is quite bad.

He found himself looking at the patch of carpet the guitarist had been standing on. No scorch marks, which was something. Next he glanced up and down the hall: mercifully, no witnesses. Everything seemed to be happening very, very slowly, with the sound turned right down, but he was confident that was just plain ordinary natural shock, bewilderment and terror.

He thought, I just killed someone. Did I just kill someone?

But I can't have done, he reasoned, because if I'd killed someone, there'd be a body, and there isn't one, that's the whole *point*. He checked the carpet again, just to make sure. No blood. No shrivelled scraps of hair or skin. Well, he thought, if there's nothing to show, at least they can't prove anything.

Wash your mind out with soap and water. A fellow human being has just been vanished – by magic, by me – and the important thing is to get him back, as quickly as possible. That had to be possible, surely? Well, of course.

He thought. He thought *hard*. Nothing happened.

This was where the instruction manual would have been so useful. Another quick glance up and down the hall. Then he said, "Magic? Are you there?"

"Yes, *sir*."

"I think maybe we can forget about the *sir* business," he said. "I didn't mean to offend you or anything. All right?"

"Yes, *master*."

He closed his eyes, then opened them again. "The man who was here just now," he said, "what happened to him."

"*Master* sent him away."

"Quite," Don said. "Now, can you bring him back again, please?"

"No, *master*."

Like when you're hanging off a strap in a Tube train, and

some clumsy idiot elbows you in the pit of the stomach. "No?"

"Alas, *master*, it cannot be done."

So that was that, then. Murder. Just one stupid little passing thought, and he'd killed a man. He hadn't meant to, not really. Trouble is, I didn't realise it was loaded is a pretty poor excuse at the best of times. "Is he ... dead?"

"No, *master*."

"Will you please stop calling me that."

"Yes, *boss*."

He knew he was getting angry but he couldn't help it. "You will address me," he said, "without any form of title. Got that?"

(Which meant, of course, that it had won, but that hardly mattered any more.) "Yes," rumbled the walls and the floor and the ceiling. Smug rumbling is a rare skill, but Magic seemed to have a flair for it. Now, back to the matter in hand.

He realised he was still standing in the doorway, where anybody passing could see him. He went inside and shut the door.

"Magic," he said, trying to sound pleasant, "if he's gone away but he's not dead, where is he?"

No answer. It was, however, a silence he recognised – from way back, from school, when the teacher asks you a question to which you ought to know the answer if you've done the homework, but you haven't, so you don't.

"Do you know where he's gone?" he asked.

"No." This time it was a very subdued rumble, barely a quiver.

"You sent him somewhere, but you don't know where."

The awkward silence that, in the same context as the example above, means yes. At the back of Don's mind a tiny silver bell tinkled. He asked it to hold the line.

"But he's still alive somewhere," he said. "You're sure of that."

A faint architectural shudder gave him the impression that Magic wasn't a 100-per-cent proud of itself. A certain degree of embarrassment, maybe even a suggestion of guilt and remorse. And quite right, too.

"Is he all right, do you think? I mean, has he got food and water? You don't know," he pre-empted. "Fair enough, let's move on. Is there any way of finding out where he's got to? Anybody you could ask, perhaps?"

The silence that means no, and another fragment of the puzzle dropped into place. Not, unfortunately, the important problem, namely the fate of his upstairs neighbour; the lesser mystery, about the nature of magic. He rather thought he might have a line on that.

"Magic," he said, "come out here where I can see you."

No apparent movement. He was about to repeat the command when a familiar voice called out, "I'm in here," from the bedroom.

Progress of a sort. "Hang on, I'm coming," he replied. In the bedroom. "Where—"

"Under the bed."

Does not compute. There wasn't anything under the bed apart from dust.

Dust, and his suitcase. And in his suitcase various items from his earlier life, things he couldn't bring himself to bin but which he didn't want to have anywhere where he could see them and be reminded of what they represented. His teddy bear, for example. His Blue Peter badge. Stuff like that.

He knelt down, pulled out the suitcase and opened the lid. "In here, right?"

"Yes." He should have guessed. The voice was coming from his old photo album, the tatty one with racing cars on the front cover. The voice had been familiar because once, long ago, it had been his own.

If his theory was correct (and he had a nasty feeling it was) he ought to be able to figure out where to open the album. He turned the pages, stopping every now and again to wince and shrivel at the images of his past self, until he found what he was looking for.

It was, needless to say, his mother's favourite picture of him, the one she'd had framed on her mantelpiece. He'd always hated it. In it he was seven years old, wearing a bobble hat his gran had knitted, sitting on a bench in the park feeding ducks on a pond. He remembered the day it had been taken. It was the day he'd stopped believing in magic.

A small, simple thing, it had happened about an hour after the picture was taken. He'd got it into his head that there were fairies living in the clump of nettles at the bottom of the pub garden. According to well-established precedent, if you gave the fairies saucers of bread and milk for a period of fourteen days, they were obliged to grant your dearest wish (a games console with joystick and GoreFest II loaded as standard). That day had been the fifteenth day, and he'd trotted down the garden path with his saucer of milky pap and a review of the console from his computer magazine, just to make sure the fairies had ordered the right model. But there weren't any fairies after all. He trampled about in the nettles getting stung, trying to flush them out, but all he found was a dead blackbird and next door's cat, predictably irritable about being disturbed. No fairies, no magic. From that moment on, his world had changed for ever.

Or so he'd thought at the time. Apparently not. He concentrated on the horrible photo, and after a moment the boy in the stupid bobble hat turned and looked at him.

"Hello," said the boy, wretchedly.

"Hello," he replied.

"You got it worked out then."

"Yes."

"Took you long enough."

He ignored that. It was, after all, fair comment. He should have guessed as soon as the room started calling him *sir* in that particular tone of voice. It was of course his own speciality. He'd refined it over an extended period of time to aggravate his parents, teachers at school, anybody who insisted on being shown respect. The same perfectly attuned ear that made him able to write the world's best jingles had led to the creation of the most irritating sarky-bolshy-snotty voice the human race had ever known. It was brilliant in its way, unique and unmistakable. He should have recognised it instantly the first time he heard it.

"It's me," he said. "Isn't it?"

The boy in the picture shrugged. "Who else would it be?" he said, and Don could see his point. "I mean, what did you think it was? Spells and stuff?"

Put like that, his preconceptions did seem a bit silly. "Is that all it is, though? Just believing?"

The boy pulled a scornful face. "No, of course not," he replied. "Else, everybody could do it."

"So what is it then? The pencil sharpener?"

The boy grinned unpleasantly at him, and he understood for the first time what a particularly loathsome child he must have been. "It's not really a pencil sharpener," he said; "that's just what you turned it into."

"Ah."

"Could be anything," the child went on. "When Mr Huos had it, it was a ring."

That sounded a bit more like it. More canonically correct. "So why a pencil sharpener?"

Shrug. "Don't ask me. Wasn't my idea. I think having it as a pencil sharpener's really stupid."

Time, Don decided, to move on, rather than get bogged down in minutiae. "So how did I get it?"

Another shrug. "Don't know," the child replied. "Happened before I was awake. You should know, you were there. Don't you remember?"

A whole new world of respect for his parents. The patience of saints, evidently. "So," he said briskly, "I come into possession of this thing, whatever the hell it is, and it starts from there. That's when you—"

"Woke up, yeah." The child really didn't look happy about it.

He thought back. "The first thing you did was break my desk."

"Sorry." Mechanical, resentful, typical child's apology.

"That's quite all right," said Don. "So then you fixed the desk."

"That's right."

"And then you got Polly's dress from wherever..." He paused, frowned. "Exactly where did you get it from?"

"Not allowed to tell."

Sigh. "All right, that's fine. Then I asked you for a ten-pound note."

"Mphm."

"Which you took," he went on, "from my bank account."

"That's right."

He nodded. "Because," he said, "you didn't know where you were supposed to get it from, and you were afraid of getting in trouble if you took it from someone else."

The child scowled at him. "You can't go taking other people's money," it said. "That's wrong. It's stealing."

"Quite," said Don. "We couldn't have that, could we? Whereas sending my upstairs neighbour somewhere and not being able to get him back, that's perfectly all right."

The child looked up. "Is it?" it said hopefully.

"No," Don replied. "It bloody well is not all right. What in God's name were you thinking of?"

Nasty look from under the hat. "You were the one doing the thinking," it pointed out. "*Go away*, you thought."

"Yes, but I didn't mean it—"

"How'm I supposed to know that?"

He knew the answer to that one. "Because you're me."

"Uh-huh." Shake of head, patronising smirk. "I *was* you. Or you were me. Whatever. Anyway, what that means is, you don't think like me any more." Short pause. "So it's not my fault, it's yours. Right?"

Well, to be fair, yes. "Tell you what," he said. "Instead of getting bogged down in whose fault it was, why don't we concentrate on figuring out how to get him back? Well? How does that sound?"

In a sense it was cheating, because he knew how the child's mind worked. Subconsciously, no matter how strenuous or justified its denials, it believed that it had to be to blame for the bad stuff happening, simply because it always had been to blame for everything. Appearing to let it off the hook, therefore, was a sure way to win its heart and mind. "Yeah, all right," the child replied. "So, how do we do that then?"

"I don't know, do I?" He stopped. Just then he'd sounded like, well, a grown-up. "Sorry," he said. "Didn't mean to snap at you like that. Only I'd assumed you'd know."

Shake of head.

"All right," Don said, trying to sound unflustered and unconcerned, "let's try another approach, shall we? What did you do to make him go away?"

"Magic."

"Yes, all right, but what *kind* of—"

"I don't know." The child looked away, angry with itself. "I don't know how it works; I just think of stuff and it happens. But thinking about bringing him back won't work."

"How d'you know that?"

"Tried it."

Naturally. The scientific approach even then. "Try it again."

"Why? It won't work."

*Because I say so.* But he couldn't bring himself to say that, not to himself, so instead he tried, "Please?"

"All right." The boy in the bobble hat screwed up his slightly faded eyes, pulled a rather vague face (low resolution, cheap and grainy special-offer film, Dad's crappy old camera) and held it for about seven seconds. "Didn't work. Told you."

"Thanks for trying, anyway," he remembered to say because nobody ever had, and he'd hated that; instead they said, *You can't have done it right; do it again.* "You got any ideas?"

A different kind of thoughtful look. "We could try looking it up in the book."

Yes, but I can't read those— Hang on. "You can read that stuff?"

Disdainful stare. "Course I can. I'm not stupid."

A few dribbles of relief started to seep through at the seams of his mind. "Excellent. Let's do that then."

Two-dimensional erstwhile Don turned full face and frowned at him. "How?"

Ah. The boy was in the photograph. The book was out here, in the room. "How about if I held it up for you to see? Would that work?"

"Suppose it might."

Just as helpful as he remembered himself being. "Where do I start? Which page?"

Shrug.

And then he thought, magic. Open it anywhere, and it'll be the right page. "Here," he said, cutting the pages like a deck of cards and holding the book parallel to the album (he didn't half feel silly doing it, but that, apparently, was what his life had devolved into). "What does it say?"

"Mm. Mmmm mm mmmm m."

"What? Oh, sorry."

He lifted the book away. The child glowered at him, then said, "That was a spell for getting rid of warts."

"Oh."

"You got the wrong page."

"Evidently."

He could feel the will to carry on ebbing away. It was all a bit too intense for him, a bit too energetic. What he wouldn't give for a nice lie-down.

"Do you want me to translate it for you?"

It was a friendly gesture, practically a unilateral declaration of peace. As it was, he only just managed to keep himself from saying something unkind and brusque. "You can do that?"

"Course I can."

"But you said—"

"Said there wasn't a translation. You didn't ask if I could make one for you."

He smiled. It was the only thing he could think of to do. "So I didn't," he said. "Silly me. Can you start with the index?"

The boy in the photograph nodded, then, "What's an index?"

"The bit at the back. Lots of names, with page numbers next to them."

"Oh that. Hang on. Right, all done."

Don flipped through the pages, all still covered with those vaguely malevolent-looking hieroglyphs, until he got to the end. Nothing there he could understand, just—

"Hold *on*, will you? Don't be in such a rush all the time."

The pictograms seemed to smudge, like watercolour when a raindrop falls on it. They blurred, ran, reformed themselves into pixels, into letters.

Magic, he thought. You know, it's not right; it shouldn't work. It ought to take twenty years and a supercomputer to decipher this lot. "Thanks," he said, as he realised he had no idea what to look for.

"Try *bringing people back*," suggested the child.

He was about to explain patiently that indexes didn't work like that when he caught sight of one of the entries, under B.

*Bringing people back.* See under; *Back, bringing people*

A blank moment. Then he said, "I see. The book's not real; it's just..." He scrabbled in his head for what he actually wanted to say. "It's just an externalisation of what's in your mind."

The child gave him a classic well-if-you're-going-to-use-long-words look and said, "You going to read what it says, or what?"

Page 743. Of course, all the page numbers were still pictograms. He pointed this out, and got looked at for his trouble, but it did get him proper Arabic numerals at the foot of each page.

"Got it. When you're ready."

Page 743 did the blurring and refocusing bit, and he was looking at a page of normal English text, with a bold subheading about a third of the way down: **Bringing People Back.** Under which, the single word: *Can't.*

# CHAPTER SIX

L ack of sleep more than anything else finally made his mind up for him. Mr Huos had always slept soundly, nine hours a night for as long as he could remember, from 9 p.m. to 6 a.m.; out like a light, a selection from his extensive repertoire of strange and disturbing recurring dreams, then instantly wide awake without the need of an alarm. Insomnia was a new one on him, and he really didn't like it, not even for one night. So, he decided, *Yes, I suppose I'll have to.*

At nine sharp he made a call. At nine thirty-five Reception buzzed him to let him know Mr Gogerty was here to see him.

Mr Huos closed his eyes. "Show him in."

He'd only ever spoken to Stan Gogerty on the phone, so all his assumptions were based on the voice. He'd been expecting a short man, probably fat, quite possibly bald and with thick glasses. He was, therefore, mildly disconcerted when Reception ushered in seven feet of lean muscle. He'd been right about bald, but only because Mr Gogerty shaved his head.

"Stan," he said, "thanks for coming round so quickly."

"No bother." Mr Gogerty folded his tremendous limbs and sat down. "What's the problem?"

For a moment Mr Huos felt sure he wouldn't be able to

go through with it after all. To his surprise, he found he was stronger than that. Or just plain desperate. "I need you to find something for me."

Mr Gogerty nodded. "That's what I do," he said. "What am I looking for?"

Mr Huos smiled. "I don't know."

"All right. What sort of thing?"

Mr Huos shrugged. "That's it," he said. "I don't *know*. It could be anything. Thimble, twelve-millimetre wing nut, bottle top, belt buckle, doorknob. There's a fair chance it's either brass or gold, but I can't guarantee that. I've got no idea how it might react to somebody else, you see." He paused, then said, "You think I've gone mad, don't you?"

Not the slightest flicker of emotion on Mr Gogerty's face. "Not necessarily," he said. "Besides, several of my best clients are mad. Absolutely barking. But if they want something found and they can afford to pay..."

Mr Huos got up and crossed to the window. Fantastic view from up here; you could see for miles. Ironic, really. "Stan," he said, "I'm going to tell you something I've never told anybody before. Discretion."

"Of course."

"Fine." His neck was itching. He loosened his tie, undid his top button, ran a finger round inside his collar. "Not quite sure where to start, to be honest with you. All right, let's try this. How long have we known each other?"

Mr Gogerty thought for a moment. "Five years, isn't it?"

"Something like that." Mr Huos turned away from the window, caught sight of the Ordnance Survey map on his desk and winced. "I call you Stan, but you don't know my first name. Well, do you?"

"No."

Mr Huos nodded. "Neither do I," he said. "In fact, I've got no reason to suppose I've even got one. You've no idea what a nuisance— I mean, take signatures. I do a sort of doctor's squiggle. I've been told that some of my business rivals hired the world's leading handwriting expert to study my signature, try and find out from it what makes me tick. I haven't got a clue what conclusion he came to, but it's bound to be way off beam. I do the squiggle because I haven't got any bloody initials. Simple as that."

Mr Gogerty was frowning – ever so slightly, but that was enough. "You mean you've forgotten..."

"Maybe." Mr Huos shrugged. "Maybe there wasn't ever anything to forget. Do you know the first thing I can remember, my earliest memory? No, of course you don't, stupid question." He sighed, took a deep breath. "My earliest memory is looking at myself in a full-length mirror in the lobby of a two-star hotel in Tshkinvall – that's a city in Georgia, in the foothills of the Caucasus Mountains. I was wearing a rather dusty light grey suit with a pale blue shirt and a blue and green striped tie, plain brown shoes and odd socks. I had one hundred thousand US dollars in large-denomination notes stuffed in my trouser pockets, a galvanised steel earring in each ear, a small brass ring in my shirt pocket and *Huos* written on the back of my left hand in blue felt-tip marker. That was ten years ago."

Mr Gogerty's face hadn't moved, except for his eyes. They were quite round. "Oh," he said.

Mr Huos nodded. "I went to the Reception desk – I knew I was in a hotel and what a hotel was – and I had the presence of mind to ask for my key. The clerk gave me one and said the abbot had called while I was out. Luckily, there was a number for me to call. I could understand the desk clerk perfectly. I can understand any language in the world, by the way; I don't even hear any difference. Chinese, Polish, Congolese, Tamil, to me it's just someone talking. I could understand the numbers on the bit of paper the clerk gave me – what I mean is, I knew what the figure seven stood for and so forth – but writing was just squiggles. It took me a year to learn to read."

Mr Huos paused for a while, as though he'd just carried a heavy weight up a long flight of stairs.

"Anyway," he continued, "I went up to the room. No luggage, nothing at all that belonged to me. I called the number, asked to speak to the abbot. Nice man," he added, "very sympathetic. Apparently, he ran a very old, very small monastery way up in the mountains – Russian Orthodox. Always had a soft spot for them because of that. They'd found me on a mountaintop, way up high. Twenty kilometres from the nearest road. You could only get there on foot, you couldn't even get a helicopter in there. But the soles of my shoes were hardly scuffed at all."

At that, Mr Gogerty lifted his head a whole inch.

"The abbot said I was out cold," Mr Huos went on. "Not ill or anything, which was odd, because if I'd been there more than an hour I ought to have been suffering from exposure, hypothermia, something of the sort. Just fast asleep. The monks carried me down off the mountain. Really good, kind thing to do; must've been a hell of a job. I've been back there since, of course, many times. Anyway, when I woke up, they said, all I did for an hour was crouch in a corner making animal noises."

"Animal noises," Mr Gogerty repeated.

"Quite. Woof, grunt, bark, snuffle, that sort of thing. The monks reckoned I was possessed by devils. Can't say I blame them, really. Anyhow, after about an hour of that I went back to sleep, and when they checked up on me a bit later, I was sitting up in bed asking for acorns. They sent for a doctor, but there wasn't anyone who could come out to them, so they took me down into town in their donkey cart. I can't remember any of that. I guess they'd found the money in my pockets, so they booked me into the hotel. Told the clerk I was American. And that," Mr Huos said, with a sigh that seemed to start in his socks and pick up momentum along the way, "is all I remember. The finest Harley Street specialists reckon I'm somewhere between forty and sixty years old, can't be more specific than that; perfect health, except some of my internal organs are in very unusual places – they work just fine, though, so what the hell – and I've never had more than a cold since. I came to this country after I made my first million – dollars, of course, not pounds. Since then, I haven't looked back. You can read all about it in the financial papers."

He stopped, and Mr Gogerty looked at him in silence for about ten seconds. Then he said, "Acorns?"

"So they told me. I'm sure they were telling the truth. Monks don't lie, in my experience. I offered to build them a new monastery, the year before last, but they wouldn't have it. They like the old one, they said. Wouldn't take any money, but they finally accepted a golf cart. Only sort of vehicle that can handle the terrain," he explained.

Mr Gogerty nodded. "So presumably you're Russian," he said.

"No idea. I don't *feel* Russian. Don't feel anything. I've got a Russian passport, of course. Cost me a thousand dollars, and it's full of spelling mistakes. I keep it for sentimental reasons." Mr Huos grinned. "I should think this is where you say that was the weirdest story you ever heard."

"No, actually," Mr Gogerty replied. "Far from it, in fact." He rubbed his chin with his fingertips, then asked, "The earrings, you still got them?"

"Of course. I've had a team of forensic scientists working on them for the past two years, cost me half a million dollars. Result: they're galvanised steel earrings. Why?"

"No inscription? Letters, numbers..."

"Completely plain."

Mr Gogerty made a doesn't-matter gesture with his hands. "And the other ring."

"Probably a curtain ring, but they didn't want to commit themselves."

"Worn?"

Mr Huos frowned. "Sorry?"

"Was it worn down at all? Like it had been rubbed hard against something."

Mr Huos was impressed. "Slightly," he said. "On one side. What made you ask that?"

"Just a hunch," Mr Gogerty said dismissively. "And brass, you said."

"Yes."

"And that's what you've lost." Mr Gogerty steepled his fingers.

"Yes. How did you—"

Mr Gogerty raised a hand for silence. Very polite, the way a bishop would have done it. "But you said it could be anything."

Mr Huos sighed. "This is where it starts to get profoundly screwy," he said. "It changes."

"Changes."

"Turns into things, yes." Mr Huos paused. "You don't seem..."

A slow, thoughtful smile crept over Mr Gogerty's face, changing it almost out of recognition. "When I said I worked for a lot of mad people," he said, "I didn't mean to imply I don't believe them. Except when I know they're lying, of course. It turns into things."

"Yes." Mr Huos nodded vigorously. "In fact, I only know it's really the brass ring because I've always kept it in a little box – you know, a jewellery box, with a catch you press to open it. I know it couldn't have got out of there, and nothing else could've got in. But when I open it, well, pot luck, you might say. No idea what I'm going to find in there. As long as it's brass or gold and it fits in the box, it can be any damn thing."

Mr Gogerty looked down at his hands. "Sooner or later," he said, "one of us is going to have to use the M-word."

"I'd rather we didn't."

"As you wish. We both know, though. It's that stuff, isn't it?"

Mr Huos said nothing, and nodded.

"Good," Mr Gogerty said, "that's that out of the way. Tell me, do you like apples?"

"Love 'em."

"This business of not having a first name." Mr Gogerty's eyebrows twitched together. "I can see what a pain that must be. So, why didn't you simply give yourself one? Make one up?"

It was as though Mr Huos couldn't grasp the concept. "I couldn't do that," he said.

"Because?"

Frown. "It wouldn't be right. I mean, it's not my place."

"To give yourself a name? Surely you've got every right."

Maybe it had never occurred to Mr Huos before to see it in that light. "I don't think so," he said. "I wouldn't feel comfortable. Like I was lying all the time. Pretending to be someone I'm not."

Mr Gogerty frowned, but all he said was, "Interesting." It was one of his key words, and he practised saying it in front of the mirror every night before going to bed. He knew thirty-six different inflections for the word interesting. On his lips, it was practically a language in itself. On this occasion, however, it didn't seem to have its usual sedative effect.

"Well?" Mr Huos barked.

"Like I said, interesting." (Number twenty-four: *in*-teresting.) "Now then, where do you last remember seeing it?"

Mr Huos smiled, a rather grim, sinister-circus-clown sort of effort. "It was in its box, in the right outside pocket of my light-weight navy-blue overcoat."

Mr Gogerty's left eyebrow twitched. "That's quite precise."

"I remember it distinctly."

"Excellent. Any idea when?"

Mr Huos nodded. "About a quarter to five, day before yesterday. Before you ask, Asquith Street."

"That's just off Clevedon Road, isn't it?"

"That's right. I remember it clearly because I made a mental note not to forget to take it out of my pocket before I took the coat in to be cleaned."

"But you forgot."

Mr Huos looked puzzled for a moment. "That's right," he

said. "Bloody odd, actually. All the years I've had the thing, I've developed a sort of sixth sense about it. No matter where I am or what I'm doing, I always know, at the back of my mind, exactly where it is. Sort of like a mum and her toddler, I suppose you could say."

"Well, you would," Mr Gogerty said, "since it's clearly very important to you. I'm like that with my car keys."

Mr Huos shook his head. "No, you're not," he said. "No offence, but there's no comparison. You may be careful with stuff. I spend a huge proportion of my life making sure I know where that box is. It's no exaggeration to say it's an obsession."

"But not this time," Mr Gogerty prompted him.

"That's the weird thing," Mr Huos replied with a sigh. "I left the bloody thing in my coat pocket. I simply can't account for it."

"All right." Mr Gogerty shrugged gracefully. "Be that as it may," he said, "I can't see there's much of a problem. If it was in your pocket when you took the coat in, then presumably it's still there. In the coat, at the cleaners."

Mr Huos' creepy smile burst out again. "Quite possibly," he said. "But that's fuck all help to me."

"Why?"

"The cleaners. Gone."

"Ah." For a fraction of a second, Mr Huos flattered himself that he might finally have fazed Stan Gogerty. No way of proving it, of course. "Gone as in . . ."

"Not there any more. And that's not all. I asked, and the woman in the shop where it used to be reckoned there never had been a cleaners there. Well?"

In the depths of Mr Gogerty's Hovis-brown eyes a tiny spurt of light flickered. Then the ARP warden of self-control made him put it out, and he nodded. "And wherever it's gone, it's taken your coat with it."

"I couldn't give a stuff about the coat."

"Well, of course not." Perish the thought, added the line

of Mr Gogerty's jaw. "You don't happen to remember the name..."

Mr Huos took a little green ticket from his shirt pocket and handed it over. Mr Gogerty reached for it, checked himself, took a pair of dentists' forceps from inside his jacket and used them to lower the ticket carefully into a little clear plastic bag, which he then sealed before putting it away. "Thanks," he said. "That could be very important. But you didn't answer my question. The name over the door ..."

"I don't know," Mr Huos said feebly. "Never occurred to me to look. I've only ever thought of it as the dry cleaners in Clevedon Road. Just human nature."

Mr Gogerty smiled primly. "That's assuming you're human," he said. "I can't afford to make presumptions like—"

"Not human?" Mr Huos' eyes were large, perfect circles. "What in hell's that supposed to mean?"

As soon as Mr Huos raised his voice, it was as though some kind of shutter had come down over Mr Gogerty's face. That one-way glass they use for identity parades, maybe. "No offence," he said, "but given what you've just told me about yourself, it's not something I can take for granted."

Mr Huos was grappling with the implications of that like a one-armed man assembling a flat-pack wardrobe. "So you're saying there's people out there who look human, but really..."

Mr Gogerty nodded, an I'm-glad-you-asked-me-that-question look. "You'd be surprised," he said.

Mr Huos, serious expression: "No, I wouldn't."

Mr Gogerty, total lack of expression: "Yes, you would. But let's not get sidetracked. You're right, it is odd, you forgetting like that. Interesting." He produced a little spiral-bound notebook. It had yellow roses on the cover. "Nothing else unusual, out of the ordinary?"

"Nothing that springs to mind."

Mr Gogerty found that interesting too, but he knew better than to say so. "Well," he said, "you've given me plenty to go on."

"I have?"

"Oh yes. Several promising leads." He paused, clearly considering something. "Mind if I ask you a personal question?"

"Fire away."

Mr Gogerty took a moment to choose his words. "Would you call yourself a tidy person? Fastidious in matters of cleanliness, that sort of thing."

"I guess so," Mr Huos replied. Then he added, "Very much so, actually. In fact, that's probably the main reason my wife left me."

"Really?"

Mr Huos pulled a sad face. "She had a problem with me washing up the pots and pans before we'd actually eaten the meal," he said. "And colour-coding her wardrobe."

"Excuse me?"

Shrug. "I'd go through her clothes putting them in colour order. All the blues, then the greens, then the yellows…"

"Ah," Mr Gogerty said.

"In rainbow order," Mr Huos went on. "You know, the order in which they appear in the spectrum."

"And she didn't like that."

Another shrug. "Made perfect sense to me," Mr Huos said. "After all, that's the order colours are supposed to be in, in nature."

Mr Gogerty looked at him for a moment, then wrote something in his notebook. "Married long?"

"Six weeks."

"Anyway." Mr Gogerty stood up. "As soon as I've got anything, I'll let you know."

"Thanks." Mr Huos was looking past him, at the wall. "If you can hurry it along, I'd be very grateful."

"It's my top priority," Mr Gogerty said.

Out in the street, Mr Gogerty found a substantial-looking lamp post and leaned against it while he pulled himself together. He'd had to put in an enormous amount of effort to keep his professional cool during the interview. Now his legs felt weak and his brain was seething like a saucepan of pasta, full of strange shapes moving at random.

Fifteen years in the trade, and he'd never heard the like; never from a client, not from his college tutors, not even after closing time at the 666 Club, when the old-timers like Ricky Wurmtoter and Kurt Lundqvist used to huddle in the darkened back room over a bottle of triple-distilled kvass and tell the stories they never told anywhere else. But they were all dead now, or gone to strange, dark places even he didn't like to think about, and there was no one left he could ask, not about something like this.

Mr Huos liked apples...

Prising himself off the lamp post, he straightened his back, fished out his mobile and fired off a terse text message to the Regius professor of Ancient Greek at Oxford, who owed him a favour. Circumstantial evidence, even if his memory was correct. But there was so much of it. Acorns. Signs of wear on one side only of a plain brass ring. Galvanised steel, no numbers, but Schliemann and Chang, in their 1976 paper for the Nairobi conference, had postulated that data would inevitably be lost in the metempsychotic flux inversion. If he was right, if he was right...

He put his phone carefully back in his pocket. I am not an academic, he reminded himself; I'm a practitioner, which means I carry out the instructions of my clients. His mission was to find a misplaced object, nothing more. It was an inviolable rule of the profession: no conducting pure research into the customers without their express permission (which in this case might be forthcoming, but then again it might not; he could always ask, he supposed, but a refusal would probably bring with it a cancellation of his retainer, and Mr Huos paid so very, very well).

A taxi went by, its yellow light off but no passenger inside. Mr Gogerty frowned. The taxi slowed to a halt and reversed, annoying a great many road users in the process, until its passenger door was level with Mr Gogerty's outstretched hand. By the time it got there, its FOR HIRE light was glowing.

"Where to?" the driver asked in a mildly bewildered voice.

Mr Gogerty gave him the address and the taxi moved off. For the first five minutes of the ride Mr Gogerty sat perfectly still and quiet. Then he took his phone out again, and used it to access the Net (the other Net, the one that was old when Merlin was resitting S-level geomancy). He called up the text of Schliemann and Chang, read it twice, then switched off.

Yes, he said to himself, but this case is different. I don't think I'll be able to do the job I'm being paid for unless I find out at least a few basic facts about Mr Huos' interesting past, and if that means a bit of pure research along the way, then so be it. And if I don't, I'll have to call him up and say I'm sorry but I haven't got a clue how to proceed – no clues, no leads; it could be anywhere. True, strictly speaking he ought to explain all that to the client before he went poking about in the obscurities of his backstory; but he knew Mr Huos pretty well by now. A busy man. Wouldn't want to be bothered with details every five minutes.

Oddly enough, the traffic lights were green all the way, so it wasn't long before Mr Gogerty reached his destination. As he barged through the revolving door and crossed the marble-tiled lobby to the security desk, he thought, One little paper can't do anybody any harm. After all, only the trade'll ever read it, and we're broad-minded, God knows.

(Yes, he added, as the guard checked his security pass, but our corporate morality doesn't really bear inspection and we tend to have about as many scruples as a bomb. Also, we're quite fond of money, and blackmail can be a lucrative sideline.)

The fifth floor of the building (it has no number, but the postmen seem to be able to find it all right) houses the Paul Carpenter Memorial Library. Founded by his enemies to commemorate the centenary of one of the trade's most eminent practitioners (founded before he was born, as it happened; that was a story that cropped up in exam questions nearly every year), the Carpenter Library's collection encompassed every aspect of the profession, both applied and theoretical. It was Mr Gogerty's spiritual home, the place he'd dreamed of seeing ever since he'd first heard of it, as a boy growing up in the back-streets of Port of Spain. Now he came here most days, used it as an office, a resource, a washroom and cafeteria, occasionally as a hotel room, but the thrill that went with pushing open the great bronze-faced cedar doors and walking into the main reading room was still as electric as ever. It was where Mr Gogerty sincerely hoped he'd go when he died, assuming he'd been very, very good.

He knew exactly where to look for what he needed. Most of the Carpenter's books were still paper, usually with leather or vellum bindings (for insulation); attempts to store them on microfiche or digitally tended to result in an explosion and a shower of sparks visible from planetary orbit. Van Spee and Viswanath's *Manual of Transdimensional Displacement* (the 1831 edition, with the addenda and the charming period illustrations) was still the standard work, and one of Mr Gogerty's favourite reads. There was only one copy in existence, in this reality at least, and here he was taking it down from the shelf, blowing off the dust as though breathing into his lover's ear, opening it at the index...

*If you have enjoyed this book*...No, gone too far. He turned back a few pages and ran his finger down the nearside column until he came to *Tshkinvall (Georgia)*. He found the entry, which was short and to the point. Then he closed the book and laid it down carefully on the desk in front of him.

It was possible, then. The thought both elated and chilled him. Dragunov's experiments in 1803 had achieved a really quite similar result, albeit in reverse. But there had to be a *cause* – rephrase that, shorn of teleological implications. There had to have been an originating event, whether deliberate or

accidental. Figure that out. He shook his head. That'd be like
trying to find the end of a circle. If you had the cause, sorry,
the event, you could trace the consequences, as Dragunov had
done. Piece of cake, A-level stuff, and in any case, outside of
a classroom why would you ever want to? But the other way
round...

He tried to find an appropriate visual image. All right, what
about a bottle? A great big bottle with a narrow neck and
mouth. Fine. Pouring water out of the bottle. Easy. Pouring the
water back in again, blindfolded, particularly if you don't happen to have a funnel...

Nice, but in the end unhelpful. Far more to it than that.
Dragunov himself had tried it in 1804, and they flooded the re-
sulting crater and used it for yacht races.

Frustrating. He leaned back in his chair, eyes closed, drawing on the library like a battery. What did that mean, in
practical terms, as far as finding Mr Huos' missing ring was
concerned? Well, it meant he had no starting point, because he
couldn't ascertain where the ring had come from in the first
place, and without that he could only make an educated guess
as to what it actually did. No matter. If he couldn't solve the
puzzle by starting at the beginning, the next logical place to try
was at the end; which, in this case –

(The really disturbing thing, of course, was that no matter
what they do to it, the chemicals they pump in, the filtration
systems they instal, the water of Dragunov's lake resolutely
stays *white*...)

– meant the site of a vanished dry cleaners in, where was
it again, Clevedon Road, where, if he was lucky, he might be
able to pick up traces of coherent sub-atomic resonances which
might just possibly allow him to extrapolate where the dry
cleaners was now.

Or he could look in the Yellow Pages.

The thought made him grin. Stranger things had happened,
and Schliemann and Chang had speculated, in a footnote

deleted from all printed copies of their work except the Dutch book club edition, about what happened to all the data that got wiped in transfer. Information, they'd argued, can't simply disappear, just as matter can't just cease to exist. Instead, it turns into something else or goes somewhere, just as burned wood becomes smoke and carbon. Admittedly, they went on to hypothesise that all the data lost when your hard drive crashes eventually drifts back, like volcanic ash, in the form of spam e-mails, and that was presumably the point at which their editors (with the exception of the Dutch) had lost patience and started scrabbling for the blue pencil. Maybe, though, there was a nugget of truth poking out of the drivel. At any rate, it couldn't hurt to look. Besides, he admitted to himself, it'd be an excuse for a trip to the Stack.

Like most of the profession's libraries, the Carpenter had solved its storage problems by expanding into the useful, though rather disreputable, dimension known to the trade as Van Spee Space (named after the megalomaniac genius who'd first encountered it). Neither parallel nor tangential, Van Spee Space bears roughly the same relation to the Einsteinian continuum as the personal injury lawyers who advertise on daytime TV bear to the mainstream legal profession. It's there, lots of people use it and nothing can be done about it right now, not for want of trying, but it's best not to harp on about it when talking to respectable scientists, for fear of causing offence. Properly engineered and installed, with all the appropriate safeguards in place, a Van Spee enclave allows a property owner to double, triple, quadruple his floor space regardless of location, with no disturbance or inconvenience to adjoining properties. The enclave can be accessed by a conventional door, and (since the existence of Van Spee Space isn't recognised under British law) it's not subject to council tax, planning law, building regulations, listed buildings approval or environmental legislation. You can have a thousand-acre country estate in your one-room flat, complete with skyscraper blocks, a rave venue, an artillery firing range and a nuclear power station, and nobody can stop you or charge you a penny. The downside, of course, is cost. There are only three registered Van Spee installers in the industrialised West, and their charges reflect the complexity of the work, the difficulty and danger of handling the lethally unstable materials involved, the years of training and hands-on experience and, of course, their limitless greed. All in all, it'd be cheaper to buy a large island and pay the inhabitants handsomely to relocate. The trustees of the Carpenter were able to afford a Van Spee enclave because Zauberwerke AG generously provided the materials and labour at cost.

They used the space to store books, at least one copy of every book ever written for or about the profession. Note the word ever; in Van Spee space, the concept of flexitime takes root and blossoms like an orchid in a hothouse. Sections 9 to 999,999,999 are where they store the books that haven't been written yet. It goes without saying that nobody's allowed anywhere near them, at least until realtime catches up with them, but, as the trustees put it, it's nice to know they're there. The telephone directories are in Section 4, next to Gardening.

It can take several hours to get at the Yellow Pages in Section 4, depending on whether there's a crane available. As it happened, Mr Gogerty had once done a substantial favour for one of the crane drivers, so the usual rules didn't apply to him.

"Thanks, George," he shouted, as the crane's massive hydraulic arm gently lowered the book into its reinforced steel cradle, disconnected its bearing chains and slid back along the gleaming rails into its siding. "I can manage from here."

Turning those thin, flimsy yellow pages calls for specialised equipment, since each leaf measures ten metres by six, and the book is almost as thick as it's wide. Mr Gogerty clambered into the cab, settled himself in the seat, turned the power on and started manipulating levers. The letters of the alphabet were helpfully stencilled onto the gate of the main selector panel. He slid the lever up into D for dry cleaners, and waited as the huge machine purred smoothly into action.

"D selected" appeared on the LCD panel in front of him. "Input search criteria."

He typed in "Clevedon Road, 1900–2009" and hit the red starter button. A motorised winch started to wind, ratchets clattered. The process always made him think of raising a draw-bridge, with the added complication that the bridge was only 0.04 millimetres thick. He reached in his pocket, found his palmtop and occupied himself usefully for the next twenty min-utes going over his recent invoices.

A bell sounded to tell him the search was complete. He looked up. A laser pointer was picking out a spot on the page raised sail-like in front of him. He climbed out of the cab and into the cherry-picker box mounted on a telescopic arm, which would lift him up close enough to read his selected entry. He closed the safety bar behind him and carefully guided the joy-stick. The box lifted off the ground and up into the air. Just as well he didn't suffer from vertigo.

Two minutes to get there. He stopped the box and put the brake on, then leaned forward until his nose was almost touch-ing the point on the page where the red laser spot glowed like a bullet wound. He took out his pocket magnifier and read,

"SpeediKleen Dry Cleaners, 77 Clevedon Road."

And that was it: no postcode, no date and (significant omis-sion in context) no phone number. Still, at least he had a name. SpeediKleen. He guided the box back to ground level, hopped back into the cab and engaged the cross-reference drive.

There were 1,825 entries for SpeediKleen in the dry cleaning section. He hit the copy button, which sent a camera drone buzzing away to photograph the relevant entries. "Time esti-mate, 6 hours." He glanced at his watch and decided he'd go away and come back.

Progress. Well, maybe. "Cheers, George," he called out. "I've left the keys in, OK?" A grunt by way of reply, which was more than he usually got; George must be in a good mood today. He left the annexe and walked slowly back along the corridor to the main library. As always, he was sure he felt a slight tremor as he crossed from Van Spee into realspace, though that wasn't supposed to happen, then across the Great Hall, left then right and into the coffee shop.

"A latte, an apple Danish and a fast forward, please," he said to the sad-looking man behind the counter, who murmured, "Coming right up," and disappeared through the beaded curtain into the back room. He came back about two minutes later with the coffee and the Danish, and a small white plastic alarm clock.

"Six hours, please," Mr Gogerty said.

The sad man nodded and turned a dial on the back of the clock, then put it on a tray with the rest of Mr Gogerty's order. "Cash?" he asked. "Or on the tab?"

"The tab, thanks, Mike."

"You're welcome."

Mr Gogerty found a table in the corner, put down the tray, looked round – nobody else in the coffee shop, good – and sat down. Fast forwards weren't really his style – a waste, he couldn't help thinking, and human life is so very short. But right now his impatience was getting the better of his will to live sequentially, and besides Mr Huos paid him by the hour. First, though, he drank the coffee and ate half the Danish. Only then did he tap the bright red button on the top of the clock, whose arms immediately started to move. Mr Gogerty checked his watch: 11:35 a.m.

Nobody really knows why they sell the fast forwards in the coffee shop. The likeliest theory is that it's a quiet, peaceful place with a pleasant, low-stress atmosphere, where your body can slump motionless for six hours or so while your consciousness skips the tedium and suspense of waiting around. Further, or alternatively, it's perfectly normal to see someone huddle for ages over one cup of coffee in a coffee shop. Cynics maintain that the chief librarian doesn't like having fast forwarders in the reading room, because he reckons they make the place look untidy.

At 5:35 p.m., Mr Gogerty sat bolt upright, opened his eyes, blinked twice and reached for the other half of his Danish. Fast forwarding always left him hungry and with a sour taste in his mouth, like falling asleep on a train. He took his time making his way down to the Stack, where a fat Manila envelope was sitting waiting for him at the enquiries desk, with an invoice laid on top of it like a bride's nightgown on her pillow. He paid by card – his Banco De Los Muertos Neutronium card, the highest credit limit in the multiverse, just about covered it – signed the invoice and retired to the Club Room.

He liked the Club Room, though not for the reason that made it so hugely popular – it's the duly accredited Victorian embassy and, just as the French embassy is legally French territory, in the eyes of the law it's firmly situated in 1897 (linked to the rest of the building by a Van Spee conduit), which makes it the only public lounge area in London where you can smoke. Mr Gogerty liked the deep leather armchairs and the oak panelling. He ordered a whisky and soda, paid for it with one of the genuine Victorian shillings he always kept by him for that express purpose, opened his envelope and hooked out a massive wad of printout.

He was less than a third of the way through when the bell rang, warning him that the club would be closing in five minutes. He scrabbled in his pocket, found his packet of Slow-Me-Downs and took enough for three hours. The last thing he needed was a break in his concentration.

The special merit of the Carpenter copy of the Yellow Pages is that it lists businesses whether they ask it to or not: every commercial enterprise conducted in the United Kingdom since 1880, listed with addresses, phone numbers where applicable, names of proprietors and dates. SpeediKleen, it seemed, had been pretty well everywhere over the past ten years, from

Liskeard to Wick, but it had never stayed in the same place for more than forty-eight hours. It had to be the same business, because the proprietors were the same, George and Eileen Williams. Sure enough, they'd been in business at 77 Clevedon Road on the relevant date; after that, they'd gone to Derby. The most recent entry – today, in fact – was 108 Commercial Road, Bexhill.

He glanced at his watch, then took out his mobile. No reply. Closed for the night and, come morning, they could be anywhere. Still, the Yellow Pages would find them, and if he got here bright and early, he'd have a whole day to track them down. He allowed himself a gentle smirk as he crammed the printouts back in the envelope, just as his last Slow-Me-Down wore off and he slid painlessly back into real time. Two minutes till the bar closed. He ordered another whisky and soda and knocked it back in one, then left the library, summoned a taxi and went home.

That night, the Paul Carpenter Memorial Library burned to the ground.

# CHAPTER SEVEN

The daily commute is a joyful thing. In our secular society it's taken the place of morning prayers: a time to meditate, reflect, get one's head together, to consider the challenges and opportunities of the day ahead and decide how best to engage with them for the greater good of oneself and others.

Or something like that. In the bus scrum someone grazed his heel down the side of Polly's ankle, laddering her tights and de-laminating her skin – but he muttered, "Sorry," so that was all right. The Tube escalator had broken down, so she got some healthy exercise. One handle of her shoulder bag gave way, spilling her possessions onto the pavement like a Medici fling-ing gold to the masses in the piazza. All good fun.

She was two minutes late at the office, something which, she felt sure, hadn't escaped the notice of Reception, who didn't like her very much. The phone was ringing when she reached her desk. She flopped into her chair, grabbed the receiver and snapped, "Yes?"

"Huos here. Can you spare me a minute?"

The boss. Wonderful. She made a sort of gabbling noise. Mr Huos thanked her and rang off before she had a chance to ask whether he was coming to visit her or whether she should make a pilgrimage to the Presence. She closed her eyes. At least, she thought, she didn't have a hangover.

Three minutes later there was a knock at her door. She squeaked, and there was Mr Huos. She had no idea whether she was supposed to stand up, like at school, or stay sitting. She compromised by leaning forward, lifting her bum three inches off the seat and sitting down again.

"Sorry to bother you," Mr Huos said. "Are you doing Satisfactory Crescent?"

She nodded, like an old-fashioned car mirror ornament.

Mr Huos appeared to hesitate, almost as though he was feeling guilty about something. "Look," he said, "if you get any screwy-sounding calls about it this morning, just take no notice, all right?"

Words were suddenly scarcer than refined palladium. She made a sort of grunting noise.

"Same with Attractive Close," Mr Huos added. "It could be that some people might ring in, and what they say may not seem to make very much sense. Just don't worry about it, OK? It's no big deal, all be sorted out soon. Just tell them..." Mr Huos' face assumed a being-strangled look, like an actor who's forgotten his lines. "Just say we know all about it and it's under control and we'll get right back to them asap. Got that?"

She nodded.

"Great. Any questions?"

He'd asked it automatically, she knew, and she had no idea what prompted her, but—

"Mr Huos?"

"Mm?"

"Who chooses the names for the streets?"

Mr Huos looked at her. "Sorry?"

"The street names." She'd started, so she had to finish. "In Norton St Edgar. Who makes them up?"

It was as if she'd just asked a middle-aged woman how old she was. "I do."

"Ah. Thanks."

"That's all right." Automated response. There's no personality in here right now to take your call, but if you'd like to leave a message . . . "So, remember, any odd-sounding calls, everything's fine and we'll ring them."

"Got that."

"Splendid." He paused. "How was the darts match?"

"Sorry?"

"Last night. Against Southern Electricity or something like that. Who won?"

"They did."

"Ah." Mr Huos frowned, a bit like God, on hearing that someone in the Garden had been scrumping apples. "Never mind. Better luck next time." On which note he departed, leaving a hole in the air you could have fitted an elephant into.

It was at that point that Polly once again gave serious thought to getting another job. Boredom she could cope with. Weirdness she could just about handle. But the two together, indissolubly mixed like metals in an alloy, might well prove too much for her. Weighed in the balance against the fact that this was the only job she'd been able to get, it fell short by some way. But it was there. Definitely.

The phone rang. Messrs Hopkins and Allen, in Malvern, re 88 Attractive Close. The file was already on her desk. She reached for it, tucked the phone under her ear and stretched for a pen.

"Number 88 Attractive Close," said a man's voice.

"That's right, yes." She'd found the place in the file. "Let's see, we were looking at exchange of contracts by the end of this week."

"It's gone."

Ah, she thought. "Gone?"

"That's right," the man's voice said. "Apparently, my clients went over there yesterday afternoon after work to measure up for curtains, and it's not there any more."

Well, she thought. "How do you mean, not—"

"It's not bloody *there*. It's vanished. The whole bloody estate, disappeared."

Just as well we haven't exchanged contracts yet. "Disappeared how? A big hole in the ground, or—"

"Green fields, apparently." The voice at the other end of the line sounded thin, as if a great weight had landed on it and squashed it flat. "Which doesn't make sense, because they were there three days ago and there was a housing estate, built by your client. And before you say it, no, they weren't lost, no, they hadn't taken a wrong turning."

At that precise moment she happened to glance down at her desk diary, which lay open in front of her. Today's date; someone had written *HELP* in big red letters.

Christ, she thought. "It's perfectly all right," she heard herself say. "There's been a little tiny glitch, bit of a nuisance but we're right on top of it. We'll have it all sorted in a jiffy and we're still looking at exchange by close of business Friday. Is that still all right with you?"

The voice that answered her reminded her of the creak of an iceberg about to calve – the unspeakable inner tension, the first crack. "Of course it's not bloody all right. Look, the house has *gone*." Pause. "I've been out there myself and had a look. It's just grass and cows and stuff, as far as the eye can—"

Later, she was quite proud of herself for her reply. "Mr...I'm sorry, I didn't catch your name."

"Hopkins. Ed Hopkins."

"Mr Hopkins," she said, "houses don't just vanish. There is a perfectly rational explanation." Um. "The fact is, we had a bit of a misunderstanding with the planning office and, to cut a long story short, they insisted we didn't have planning

and we had to put it all back exactly how it was. So we did."
Deep breath. "But we went back to them on appeal and now
we've definitely got planning. I've got a copy of it right here on
the desk in front of me, so we can go ahead and rebuild the
houses, and that should all be done by – what's the time now,
nine fifteen – it should all be done by lunchtime, but give it
till this time tomorrow just to be on the safe side, all right? If
the houses aren't back again by then, give me a ring and I'll
see it gets top priority. Or, better still, as soon as we get the
word from our contractors, I'll ring you and you can pass on
the good news to your clients. All right?"

(*HELP* In big red letters. She tried very hard not to look at
it.)

"I suppose so," Mr Hopkins mumbled. "Look, I've got your
word on that, OK?"

"Of course."

"Only my clients are really upset. They've already sold their
old house, you see, and—"

"You have my word, Mr Hopkins, as a fellow professional.
You do trust me, don't you?"

Her heart bled for him as he muttered, "Yes, all right," and
rang off. She recognised the special quality of his voice, a fellow
human being suddenly confronted with weirdness so extreme
that it couldn't be questioned or resisted; all you could do was
hang on and hope it would stop, before it reached the point
where pretending it wasn't happening was no longer possible.

Someone had written *HELP* in her diary, in red ink, in great
big capital letters. It wasn't, she hastened to point out to herself, her handwriting. It wasn't any handwriting she recognised,
come to that. The list of potential suspects was, of course, endless; anybody in the building could have sneaked into her office
while her back was turned and written *HELP* in her diary (in
red ink, in whopping great big letters, just like she'd done in
her dream) and there were all sorts of reasons why someone

should do such a thing, just as there were plausible explanations for how work got done on her files without her knowing about it, or what happened to all those cups of coffee. There were even tenable hypotheses to explain how a housing estate in rural Worcestershire could suddenly vanish; she'd been able to think of one just like *that*, on the spur of the moment, with no advance warning whatsoever. Maybe the dream was just a suppressed memory, and it had been her own hand that had guided the red pen (there was no red pen on her desk, in the drawer, in her bag, fallen down behind the radiator, anywhere in the damn room), and for some reason, presumably connected with some traumatic event which she was also suppressing, she'd chosen to forget all about it. Maybe, while she was talking to Mr Hopkins on the phone, a subconscious memory of the dream had prompted her to write *HELP* in her diary without realising she was doing it (with a red pen that had subsequently vanished, like all the houses in Attractive Close; and the other one is positively festooned with bells, pull it and you could do a passable Quasimodo impression). Maybe her enemy, whoever he or she was, the one who did her work for her and drank her coffee, had written in her diary and then hypnotised her so she'd have a dream in which—

The phone rang. A Mr Hughes, from Deane Adams in Worcester. Was she aware that Satisfactory Crescent, Norton St Edgar, was missing? Yes, Mr Hughes, we do know that, thanks all the same, and is there anything else I can help you with? No? Bye, then.

But then, as the darkness seemed to be closing in all around her, a tiny spark of light flickered in her mind. Her dress. Her dress which she'd taken to a dry cleaners that had subsequently vanished-off-the-face et-bloody-cetera; but it hadn't, had it, because Don, her hero brother, had gone after it, found it and restored it to her. And he couldn't have done that, could he, if the dry cleaners really had melted away into the air as though it had never been. No way. Instead, there had been some sort of misunderstanding or cock-up, probably something quite simple and straightforward once you knew all the facts. Don had unravelled the mystery, gone somewhere and got her dress, and everything was just fine. So, if that weirdness, which at the time had seemed insuperably baffling, had resolved itself and submitted to the healing forces of normality, then why not all the others: her dream, the diary, the vanishing houses? And besides, Mr Huos knew about the houses thing too, which meant it couldn't just be her diseased imagination. It was all right. Everything was OK. Silly old her, for getting in such a state.

*Clever old Don*, whispered the voice in her head she'd never liked very much, for finding your dress so quickly and easily. Now, how did he do it? I wonder. And wouldn't it be a good idea to ring him up right now and ask?

Her fingertips were no more than a centimetre from the handset when the phone rang. She rocked back in her chair and snatched her hand away, then picked it up.

"Your brother for you," Reception said, frostbiting her ear.

Ah, she thought. "Don, I was just about to call you."

"Listen."

She knew that voice, though its exact significance was rather hard to pin down. Sometimes it could mean *you/me/both of us in serious trouble*. Other times he'd used it to tell her that he'd been to see the new *Star Wars* film and actually it wasn't that great, or that Tim Henman (this to a woman who had trouble telling tennis apart from baseball) had just been knocked out of Wimbledon; and then she'd tell him, "Don, I couldn't give a stuff," and there'd be genuine bewilderment in his voice when he replied, "Why not?" Don was funny that way. He actually cared about separatist tendencies in the Anglican communion or who'd won the general election in Portugal.

"What?" she said.

"Look, are you very busy right now?"

"Yes."

He also had the knack of not hearing answers to questions. "Can you come over here? Right now. I need—"

"Don, don't be bloody stupid, I'm at work. I can't just—"

"What? Oh, right, of course you are. In that case, I'll come to you. Don't go anywhere; I'll be right over."

"*Don.*"

*Click, buzz.* She scowled at the phone, as though a vaguely banana-shaped plastic moulding was somehow to blame for everything, then slapped it back in its cradle. Sometimes she wondered if he really understood about work – real work, as opposed to sitting round in a dressing gown making up little tunes. Then it occurred to her that she'd been on the point of phoning him, and why? Because, every time Destiny put a spider in her bath of Life, it was Don who had to leave what he was doing and come sprinting over to hook it out. Whether it was a blocked sink or a broken heart, no hesitation, no recrimination, no squash-your-own-bloody-spiders-I'm-busy. Query, she reflected, whether a man could be so selflessly useful if he had to live in the real world and do normal stuff like everybody else.

She did a bit of work, just to pass the time away, and then he was there in the waiting room, pretending to be a surveyor so as not to embarrass her – but how many surveyors call on important clients dressed in a colander pullover, jeans and sandals?

"Well?" she said.

He turned and looked at her, and she knew at once that it wasn't Tim Henman or the failure of the Iowa sorghum harvest. "Polly," he said, "I think I'm in trouble."

Payback time. "Oh?"

"Yes." He nodded gravely, looked across the room, then said, "I think I may have killed someone."

Dead silence, for as long as it takes to change a light bulb. "Let's go through into the interview room," she said.

Not the big interview room, of course. She wasn't nearly grand enough to use that without booking it a week in advance and clearing it with Mr Stevens and the office manager. Nor the middling interview room, because the door was shut and she could hear voices. That left the Confessional, a cramped box where you could just about sit down with a client or a professional colleague without rubbing noses or brushing lips.

"Sorry about this," she said, as she breathed in to slide past the table to her chair. "It's a bit cosy, but—"

"That's quite all right," Don snapped. "Good practice for when I get locked up for the rest of my fucking life. Did you happen to hear what I said just now? I think I may have murdered somebody." He stopped, breathed out then deeply in. "I was wondering if I could trouble you for a bit of free legal advice."

"Of course." She wriggled her back into the strange angle of the chair and tried to remember back to law school. "The police," she said. "Have you made a statement? Signed anything?"

"I haven't called the police," he said.

"Witnesses? I mean, did anybody see?"

He shook his head. "Nobody. Well," he added, "maybe an earlier incarnation of me, though I'm not entirely sure about that. Look, shouldn't I start at the beginning and tell you the whole thing?"

"Oh, right." She nodded. "Carry on."

He frowned. "You know," he said, "I'm not sure I can. On account of I'm really not at all sure whether I believe any of it myself. I mean, I *do*, because of the table and your dress and the ten pounds and the dry cleaners not being there but showing up on Google." He looked up at her. "I'm talking drivel," he said, "and you're not staring at me or asking if I'm feeling all right. That's a bit worrying, actually."

She nodded gravely. "Listen," she said, and told him about

Attractive Close and *HELP* in big red letters in her diary. "All right? Fine. Your turn."

He nodded slowly. "What was it Arkwright used to say? It's been a funny old day. Of course," he added, "it could be that there's insanity running in our family and we're both going mad, but on balance I think that's probably too much to hope for. Anyway, here goes."

She listened in dead silence, without interrupting once. That should have been a momentous occasion, something to be commemorated with a special issue of stamps and United Nations Polly-Didn't-Interrupt Day. As it was, Don hardly noticed. A perfectly good miracle wasted.

Then she said, "You're kidding."

Don breathed out heavily through his nose. "Actually, no," he said. "So, where do I stand legally? Did I just murder an innocent stranger, or what?"

"Magic," she said. She was looking at him with a curious blend of awe and revulsion, like someone watching John Prescott juggling. "You can do magic."

"Apparently. Look—"

"That's amazing," she said. "You just looked at him and—"

"Yes." That was Polly all right. For her, tact was the past participle of the verb to tack. "Will you please answer the bloody question? Is it murder or isn't it?"

She frowned. "Well, they can't prove anything," she said. "And that's all that matters. If they can't prove it . . ."

Don made a sort of muffled exploding noise. "Fine," he said. "Thank you so much. I should've known better than to ask, really." He tried to stand up, banged his knee on the underside of the table and sat down again.

"You don't seem pleased," she said.

"What?"

"You can do *magic*." She looked like she was watching for an expected reaction; apparently it didn't come. "Magic is real, it actually exists, and you can do it. You ought to be—"

"Are you out of your mind?" He didn't want to get angry, but it seemed he wasn't to be allowed the choice. "My whole world view's just been blown to bits and I've killed someone. If there's anything in that to be cheerful about, maybe you could write it out for me on a bit of paper so I can study it carefully when I've—"

"Why don't you just throw it away?"

He stopped in mid-flow. Indeed. Why not? He'd intended to give the pencil-sharpener thing back to the people in the dry cleaners, but apparently that wasn't possible. So why not just bin it, or throw it in a pond somewhere?

"I can't," he replied. "I've got to try and get that poor bastard back, remember. If I sent him away with magic, it stands to reason I'll need it to get him back."

She was giving him one of her head-on-one-side looks, the ones that meant, *Nice try, only I happen to know you're lying.* "But otherwise," she said, "if it wasn't for that, you'd get rid of it. Well?"

"Yes, of course."

"Well?"

"Maybe," he said. "I don't know, do I?"

"You don't mean that."

"Look." He hadn't meant to shout. He never shouted. "That's beside the point, isn't it? The fact of the matter is I'm stuck with this appalling problem and I want to know just how much trouble I'm in. Anything else—"

There was something about the way she was looking at him that he didn't like. It was almost an accusation. She was good at those, always had been. But this just wasn't the time. He needed her to be on his side. It wasn't much to ask. After all, he'd got her stupid dress back for her.

"By the way," he said, "how was the match?"

"What?"

"The darts match. Who won?"

"They did."

"Ah well. Better luck next—"

"Don, you're a complete bastard, do you know that?"

(Oh God, he thought, what've I done now?)

"You come bursting in here and you tell me magic's for real and you can do it, and all the stuff that's been happening to me's – well, I still can't explain it, but maybe it could make sense, if only we *knew*. And you stand there drivelling about bloody darts. The whole world's changed for ever, and you aren't even *interested*."

"It's not a toy," he retorted. "It's not natural and it's dangerous and I want it to go away, but first I've got to try and save that poor bugger I vanished into thin air. After that –" he shook his head "– if we manage to get out of this in one piece, I'm going to forget all about it, and you're never ever going to mention it again, understood? Not one word. All right?"

But she frowned at him. "Don, that's stupid," she said. "It's like using a winning lottery ticket to start a bonfire with. It's—" She stopped and looked at him. "It's bad, isn't it?"

He nodded. "I think so, yes. And I don't think it's just me, either. I mean, I don't think it's a coincidence that you've had all this weird stuff happening to you at the same time as – well, that stuff. You know what?" He shook his head. "I think we're two hobbits caught up in someone's billion-dollar movie, and any minute now a huge army of horrible goblins is going to come charging over the hill straight at us. Which means," he added briskly, "it'd probably be sensible if we started running now, rather than waiting for the cameras and the lights. Only we don't know which way to run."

She looked at him. "How'd it be if we asked someone?" she said.

He blinked. "Who did you have in mind?"

"How about Mr Huos?" she said.

"Your boss? Why?"

"Something he said," she replied. "Or at least, the way he said it – when he came in my room and said there'd be a load of crazy phone calls but not to worry. It's like . . ." She thought for a moment. "It's like he knew what was going on. He knew there'd be people ringing in talking about vanishing houses and stuff like that, so doesn't it stand to reason he knows about the – well, magic and all that? I don't know, maybe he's the cause of it all. I mean, it's his firm; he must know what's going on."

"You think he's been drinking your coffee?"

She thought about that too. "No, why should he? He *owns* the bloody coffee. And I don't think he wrote in my diary, either. I think I did that. Only—"

"All right," Don said quickly. "Let's not go there quite yet. About what you said." He sighed. "I don't like it. We've got no idea what all this is about. We can't go trusting someone just because he might be able to explain it to us. I mean, explaining's what the villain does in a Bond movie when he's about to blow up the world."

Polly had a sudden mental image of Mr Huos with a fluffy white cat on his lap, but it didn't look right at all. Not a cat person, in her opinion. "He seems all right to me. OK, I've only met him twice, but—"

"If he's mixed up with this magic stuff, I don't imagine he's very nice," Don said harshly. "Do you think he makes people disappear too? Well, come on. If he disappears houses, then why not?"

Oh, she thought. "You reckon he . . . But why'd he do that?" she countered. "He built the houses; why'd he want to get rid of them? Quite apart from everything else, he'd lose millions of pounds. It doesn't make sense."

"Yes, but we don't *know*." He shrugged. "I guess that's what's bugging me the most, not knowing. I'm not used to it." He stood up (carefully this time, sliding himself out from under the table like a letter from an envelope). "All my life – well, you know me. Technology. Gadgets. When I was five years old, I was the only one who could get the timer on the video to work. And it was because I did what nobody else was prepared to do. I read the manual." He closed his eyes for a moment and breathed in deeply. "I didn't try and do it by light of nature, intuition or divine revelation. I read the book and followed the instructions and, guess what? I made it work." He covered his face with his hands, then ran his fingers through his hair. "You can't imagine the feeling of power something like that gives you. Control. The ability to make things work when nobody else can. And all because there was always a book or a Read Me or a leaflet or a photocopied sheet. That was the basis of my entire world. It made sense. I can say, 'Use of unauthorised components will void the manufacturer's warranty,' in sixteen languages." He turned to face the wall. "And now there's this new gadget, quite possibly a gadget of infinite power for good or evil that could change the life of everybody on the planet for ever, and *there's no fucking handbook*." He paused, breathed in deeply. "Well, actually, there is. But it's written in a language nobody can understand. Actually, that's not strictly true. There's a photograph of me when I'm six that can understand it, but he's me when I'm six, so he's no bloody help at all. And finally, when I persuade me to look it up and read me what it says, what do I get? I can send people away, but I can't bring them back. *God*, that's frustrating."

She gave him a moment, then asked, "Are you feeling better now?"

"No."

"Oh."

He turned away from the wall and looked at her. "But I've made my mind up," he said. "First, I'm going to get that bloody guitar player back."

"But the book says—"

"Screw the book," Don snapped viciously. "I'm through with the fucking book. You know what? The rest of you were right all along. We don't need the book; it's useless. We'll figure it out for ourselves. And then," he added, "as soon as we've put things right, that bloody pencil sharpener's going somewhere it can't do anybody any harm, ever again."

He was falling.

He was falling upwards, which was a novelty. He was being acted upon by a perversely different kind of gravity, one that shot you up instead of down. Not weightlessness, where you just drift, and if you throw up it follows you slowly round the room like a spaniel. It was your actual falling – the headlong out-of-control tumbling, the rush of the slipstream, the inexorable drag, thirty-two feet per second per second incremental velocity – just up, that was all.

He had a feeling it wasn't going to end well. Falling down rarely results in a pleasing outcome, and from what he'd gathered so far, there was no reason to assume that falling up would be much better. Maybe he'd burn up in the atmosphere rather than splat on the ground, but it hardly mattered. Any moment now, he was going to...

Once upon a time he was seventeen, just got his first motorbike – precisioneered alloy frame, carbon fibre super-aerodynamic fairing and a teeny little engine that sounded like a bumblebee on heat. Going flat out down a quiet suburban street, needle jammed right up to thirty-six miles per hour, and some poo-for-brains woman in a Fiesta had come out of a side turning without looking. *Wham*, straight into the side of her, and he'd taken off, the human cannonball, flying through the air without benefit of aircraft. As it turned out he landed in a newly dug flower bed and came out of it without a scratch, but while he was flying, Death looming over him, scythe, eye sockets, the full English, all he'd been able to think was, Oh well. That was it. No panic. No loosening of the bladder, no excruciating muscle cramps, no screams. Total absence of his life flashing before his eyes. Oh well, and then *thud* into the bedding plants.

It was the same now, except that the first time he'd been airborne for maybe a second and a half, and now he'd been falling for *ages*. Ironic; he'd always fancied having a go at skydiving – free-falling with his arms and legs outstretched, watching the flat earth spinning like old-fashioned vinyl on a turntable. But all he could see was...

Light. A big shiny cloudy doughnut of light, into which he was falling upwards. As the air slapped his face and scoured his eyeballs dry, he thought, This isn't right. This is *silly*.

Particularly so in context. The last thing he could remember before falling was putting down his guitar, stomping down the stairs and giving that little turd in the flat below a piece of his mind about the...

Odd. Maybe there was a piece missing, because it was hard to join up the dots of cause and effect. Anti-gravity sucking furiously on his toes, he cast his mind further back in search of some kind of explanation. An average day at the office, answering calls, doing paperwork. Meeting friends in the pub later, but enough time in hand before he had to leave for half an hour trying to straighten out the tricky chords in "Stairway to Heaven." And that was all, really. Nothing there that should have led him to anti-tumble, the wrong way up nature's most inviolable one-way street, to a messy and premature death.

The injustice of it surged inside him like heartburn. It was wrong. It wasn't on. He had a good mind to send someone a really nasty e-mail about it, except he never would, because any moment now he'd be blotted out like a bug on a windscreen. Bitch.

Oh well, he thought.

And landed.

*Really* soft landing. Two months ago he and a bunch of friends had flown out to the Greek islands, and coming in to land the aircraft had gone hoppity-skippety-jump down the runway, but now, one moment he was all movement in every plane, the next he was standing perfectly still, on one leg, on straw.

Oh, he thought. Not dead. Jolly good.

On straw, though. He looked down at his feet, then up, sideways. Then down again. His feet.

Not his feet, though. Where his feet should have been, due south of his body at the end of his legs, all he could see was a pair of claws. Scaly, avian, three toes ending in bloody great spikes. Also, not quite as important as the feet/claws issue but probably significant, it wasn't straw, it was long yellow tubes the length and thickness of scaffold poles. Looked like straw, hence the initial confusion, but wasn't. Too big, even for GM.

He considered that analytically. By rights, he oughtn't to be able to stand upright on a stack of bloody great big yellow poles, not with human feet encased in stylish designer trainers. It'd be a different matter entirely if you had claws (say). Also, the building he was in: great big wooden structure, size and scale of a major railway terminus but built from planks. It was almost as if...

I'm in a chicken shed, he thought. And I'm a chicken.

One of those flashes of insight, the sort you're far better off without, but they do have the nasty habit of being right. But, hang on, I'm not a fucking chicken. I know precisely what I am. I'm a thirty-year-old loss adjuster working for Amalgamated General Mutual, and on each foot I have five toes. Five, not three. Five. Five.

A shadow passed over him and he knew he wasn't alone. He was about to turn his head but realised he didn't need to; his field of vision had expanded enormously (almost as though he had eyes on the sides of his head, rather than in front athwart his nose), and he could plainly see the huge, enormous, massive *chicken* who'd just hopped in through the square opening in the far wall.

Quite possibly the biggest bipedal life form he'd ever encountered: a feathered mountain, its apex a luxuriously crested head with two mad, staring round eyes and a beak like a bale spike, the whole monstrous thing supported by two scaly grey legs culminating in two triple-toed claws, with another gut-scrambling spike sticking out of the back of each ankle at ninety degrees.

Not a lady chicken, he guessed. A gentleman chicken.

He didn't know all that much about poultry, but he did remember hearing about the holiday some of his friends had been on in Thailand or somewhere out that way, where cock fighting was still a thriving spectator sport. Essentially, you put two gentlemen chickens together in a closed space, and immediately they went for each other with razor beak and pitiless spur, not stopping until at least one of them was a bloody mess of broken bone and feather. Pure instinct, apparently. If two cock birds meet, alternative dispute resolution isn't an option.

"You looking at me?" growled the cock.

This time, it was worth noting, he didn't think, Oh well. This time he ran through the entire repertoire of conventional terror symptoms, from trembling and heart-pounding to loosened bowels and clogged windpipe. The prospect of hitting a solid surface at high speed had been depressing, but he hadn't really felt frightened. Clearly, when death was to be accompanied by extreme violence, a different set of instincts cut in: adrenalin (he hoped) and also the fear-based products. Scared; he was petrified. A coward. Chicken. A poultroon.

"Me?" he heard himself cluck. "Gosh, no."

"I said, you looking at me?" the cock growled softly (and the collar of feathers round his neck started to rise).

"No, I'm not. Really."

"You calling me a liar?"

"Absolutely not," he clucked back, unable to take his eyes off the ankle spurs. "What I should've said was, yes, I was looking at you and I realise how very wrong of me that was and I apologise and it absolutely won't happen again, I promise faithfully, only please don't..."

One hubcap-sized perfectly round eye was scanning him, reiterating the male chicken's prime directive. There was going to be a fight any second – well, you wouldn't call it a fight, more of an execution – and pretty soon he'd be dead, so really there wasn't much point in idly speculating how he'd got there, or why he'd apparently Sam Becketted into a chicken. A waste of what little precious time he had left.

"Excuse me," he said.

The cock, who'd been edging forward, tense as a coiled spring, stopped. "You talking to me?"

He nodded. "Sorry to bother you," he said, "but I was wondering. You wouldn't happen to have any idea how I got here, would you?"

"You what?"

"Only," he continued quickly, "it's all a bit odd and, I don't know, I just feel it'd be such a shame if I died not knowing the truth, so I thought, it can't do any harm if I just ask, on the off chance."

The cock was motionless, as though its feet were glued down. Clearly something new and disturbing was happening inside its tiny little brain, something so far beyond the scope of its inherent programming that it had no idea how to cope. "You what?" it repeated.

"I only just arrived, you see," he said. "A moment ago I was somewhere else – actually, more to the point, I was some*thing* else. A human. And then I was falling, only up rather than down, and then I was here and you showed up, and there's got to be some sort of rational explanation, and since you're from around here – at least I assume you are – I figured that maybe you could tell me before you peck me to death. If it's no bother, I mean."

The cock stared at him for a long time. "You what?" it said.

Like that, is it? Scheherazade with feathers. Well, he was game, no pun intended. "For a start," he went on, "am I actually a chicken, or am I a human being who thinks he's a chicken, or is there a third possibility I haven't even considered yet? Maybe this is all a dream, though it doesn't feel like one, because for one thing if this was a dream I'd be arriving late for a project tactics meeting and I wouldn't have any clothes on, though now I come to think of it, I haven't got any clothes on, just feathers. How about you? Are you real, or just dreaming that you're real when in fact you're a figment of my imagination?"

"Urrk," replied the cock. Then its head went sharply down, and it pecked up a grain of corn the size of a goose egg. As far as it was concerned, he apparently no longer existed. Too difficult, evidently.

"Excuse me," he said, and sidled past–out through the hole in the wall, mind the step, and suddenly he was under a broad blue sky, bathed in glorious sunshine and surrounded by a bevy of lady chickens. Hens.

Cor, he thought.

And then, *what* did I just think?

A hen looked up from pecking in the dust and peered at him dubiously. He looked back; he couldn't help it.

(A *chicken*, for God's sake. You've got to stop this immediately, or...)

"Hi," he heard himself say.

He always said "Hi" under such circumstances. "Hello" never worked for him; it tended to come out like meeting the panel at a job interview, or a politician kissing babies, or Leslie Phillips. He'd flirted briefly with "Hiya" and "Hi there," but there wasn't an atom of romance in either of them. "Hi," on the other hand, was a skill he'd gradually mastered (like wood-turning, or playing the violin), and he flattered himself that he wasn't bad at it.

"You're not from round here," said the hen.

As a feed line it was unexceptional. It left him a lot of work to do, but it had possibilities. "That's right," he said, "I'm from out of town."

He stopped. It was hard to be certain, because the words had come out simultaneously, but he could've sworn that instead of "town" he'd said "coop." But that was impossible. So he tried it again. Town, he said.

"Coop."

"What?"

"Sorry. I mean, yes."

The hen twitched her head, a routine preprogrammed quick-look-round to make sure no foxes had crept up on her in the five seconds since she last looked. "Does Boris know you're here?"

That didn't just not make sense, it made the opposite of sense, anti-sense. Then intuition kicked in and told him Boris must be the cock. "Oh yes," he said, and caught himself adding, "I sorted him out all right."

The fixed stare in the hen's lentil eye seemed to soften just a little. "You did, did you?"

"Let's say we both know where we stand."

The hen's neck darted down, and she gobbled up a stray lay-ers' pellet. "You don't look like you've been fighting."

He tried to grin, but you can't, with a beak. "Oh, it didn't come to that," he replied. "I don't believe in pointless violence."

"Pointless." The hen did the twitch again, and he realised he'd just done the same thing, without realising. "You mean, like blunt."

"Sorry?" And then he got it: *pointless*, in a world of beaks, claws and spurs, hadn't been the best choice of words. "I mean, unnecessary violence."

"Oh."

It was one of those points of balance you get in chat-ups, a moment when, following an advance, things could go either way. "I mean," he went on quickly, "sometimes you've got to get in there with the beak and do the business, sure. But I tend to think there's rather more to being a cock than that."

"Really? What?"

Time, his years of experience told him, to change the subject. Unfortunately, 99 per cent of his extensive repertoire of gear shifts couldn't possibly apply here. "That's a really great set of feathers you're..." he began, then stopped. The hen was sitting down, snuggling herself into the dust, arranging her wings tidily. She was about to lay an egg.

"Sorry," he said, looking away quickly. "I'll, um, leave you to it."

"Oh."

Disappointment, which was good, but it also had the subtext *Don't bother coming back* woven into it, like gold filigree in a luxury fabric. "Or I might hang around here for a moment," he mumbled. "If that's OK with you."

"Do what you like."

The hen was wriggling about. He prided himself that he wasn't excessively squeamish, but he shared the male's natural diffidence at witnessing the process of parturition. Laying eggs, he thought. Eew.

(And then a tiny echo of a former existence, already so far away that light from it would take a year to reach him, asked him what the bloody hell he thought he was playing at, and did he realise he'd just been chatting up a *chicken*, and there was a word for people like him and it wasn't very nice. He considered that, and part of him could see what the echo was getting at, the point it was trying to make, but he wasn't convinced. Nah, he thought. When in Rome. Go for it.)

"So," he said. "Been here long?"

"All my life," the hen replied. "Where are you from?"

He tried to say Walton-on-Thames, but he couldn't get his beak around it. No palate, no lips to form the component sounds. "Far away," he substituted.

"Don't know your breed."

Clearly, political correctness hadn't filtered this far down the evolutionary chain. "I'm a pedigree," he said, trying to sound offhand about it. "Rare breed, actually."

"Oh." Grudgingly impressed. Good. Then she made an extraordinary noise, and he flinched. It was a noise that only a true chicken or Hugh Fearnley-Whittingstall could find remotely attractive. It was definitely too gynaecological for his taste, and he started to edge away.

"Where are you going?" said the hen.

He thought quickly. On the ground at his feet was a grain of corn. He dipped his head, snatched it up and swallowed. Actually, not bad. Tasted a bit like chicken.

"So," he said. "Is this your, um, first time?"

"First today, you mean?"

Oh God, he thought. Also, strange how one aspect of the same basic process can be so enthralling, while another is so very yuck. "Good heavens, is that the time? I really ought to be..."

The hen made a noise he knew he'd never forget, then she shook herself, stood up and walked away. In the dust, hull down like a Tiger tank in the desert, he could see a light brown egg.

"Um," he said, "will it be all right like that?"

The question had slipped out before he had a chance to vet it for embarrassment potential. "What?"

"The egg," he said (the word stuck in his throat and came

out as a sort of clucked hiccough). "It's OK, is it, just like sort of leaving it there?"

The look she gave him made him wish he was coated in breadcrumbs. "Course it's all right," she said. "They'll be along any minute."

He really shouldn't have, but he did. "They?"

"You *know*." Twitch, peck, look of utter bemusement and scorn. "Them."

Well, he'd blown it with her already, and besides, after the whole egg thing he wasn't really in the mood. "I'm not sure we've got Them where I come from," he said.

"Course you have," she said. "Everybody's got Them. If there wasn't any Them, there'd be no us."

He wondered why he wasn't sweating. Maybe chickens don't. "Maybe we're talking at cross purposes here. When you say Them—"

"*Them*," she insisted, and he could tell he was starting to get right up her beak. "You know. Them as feeds us and fills the water and puts down straw and made the Wire to keep the foxes away. Them up There."

She arched her neck, as though looking up at something very tall; in proportion, adjusting for altered perspectives, about human-head height.

"Oh," he said. "Them."

Her relief was obvious. "That's it," she said. "They'll be along very soon now, to top up the water and pick up the eggs. So that's all right."

All right, he admitted it. She'd shocked him. He wanted to say, But that's your *egg*, your offspring, flesh of your flesh, and some tall bastard's going to come along any second now and steal it and beat it into an omelette or scramble it. Your crazy, mixed-up kid. He didn't say any of that, but he did manage, "And that's – I mean, you're OK with that."

Hens can shrug. In fact, they do it rather well. "Course I

am," she said. "I mean, it's what's best for them, isn't it? And it's so kind and good of Them, after all."

"Is it?" he croaked.

"Course. I mean," she went on, "what's going to become of them if they stay here? Dead end, basically. Just pecking around in the dirt. Instead, thanks to Them, they get a really good start in life. Boarding school, then university, then a really good job – doctors, lawyers, dentists, accountants. They're not going to get anything like that if they stay here and I hatch 'em, are they?"

He cringed, from wattles to claws. "So that's what They do, is it? Send them away to—"

"Well, course." Her eye could be really beady when she wanted it to. "What else would They be doing it for?"

"And you know that, for a fact? I mean..."

Twitch. "Stands to reason, doesn't it? I mean, why else'd They take the eggs? The way you're going on," she added corrosively, "anybody'd think you thought They were up to no good."

"Well..."

"Which'd be daft," the hen went on firmly. "Like, if They mean us any harm, why do They go to all that trouble feeding and looking after us? No, everybody knows They're good and kind and nice, and They take the eggs and hatch them out for us and give them a really good education so they can make something of themselves. Course," she added, more to herself than him, "it'd be nice if just once they'd ring or text or send us a letter, even, just to say hello, let us know how they're getting on. Still, if it was me, I guess I'd want to forget about this place as quick as I could. If I'd had the chance to go to uni, I'd've been off like a shot, no messing. And I don't suppose I'd have been in any rush to keep in touch with home, either. Can't really blame them, can you?"

Silently he cursed his exceptionally keen memory, thanks to

which he could just about remember the boiled egg he'd had for breakfast that morning. *It could've been somebody*, he thought. It could've been a contender, only some vicious bastard smashed its head in and stuck toast in it. "That's right," he whimpered. "It's a world of opportunity out there. Well worth crossing the road for."

"What road?"

He screwed up his face, trying to concentrate. It was so far away, a very faint signal, almost out of range. "It's a sort of saying," he said. "Well, a joke. Why did the chicken cross the road? It's..." He shook his head. "Forget it," he said.

The hen was looking at him. "What's a joke?"

Good question. He couldn't quite remember. And could he really have eaten an egg that morning? Were his protein and calcium levels really that deficient? "I don't know," he confessed. "I think it's a—" He shook his head, then twitched it from side to side. No foxes. "I don't know. Can't be important."

"You want to stay away from roads," the hen said. "There's great big fast things on roads that can squash you flat. Best to stay in the coop, where it's safe. That's what They built it for."

Well, of course. And They (he stooped, pecked up a grain of corn) knew best; you had to believe that, or nothing made sense. All that stuff, the echoes in his mind; maybe he'd pecked a bad nettle or something.

The hen had wandered off. He stood on one leg for a moment, preening his wing feathers. He was beginning to see things straight now. For some bizarre reason for a moment there he'd got it into his head that once he'd been one of Them. Crazy. But it was all right now, he was better again. He knew exactly who and what he was. He was—

"Excuse me."

Another hen was standing next to him. Quick check (no foxes), and he looked at her. Wattles rather pale, no sheen to her feathers, hardly worth mating with but nevertheless...

"No," the hen said, "not now. Listen. I need to talk to you."

There was something different about this hen. Odd. Didn't move right. He glared at her suspiciously. "Why?"

"Just now." Ten seconds, and she hadn't once checked for foxes. "You said something. About a road."

"What road?"

She was looking at him. "You said, 'Why did the chicken cross the road?'"

He scuffed at the ground with his claws. "Wasn't feeling right. Don't know why I said that. Forget it."

"'Why did the chicken cross the road?'" the hen repeated. "That's what you said. I heard you."

"All *right*," he snapped. "Don't go on about it. I wasn't feeling well, but I'm better now. All just a figment of my—"

"To get," the hen said, "to the other side."

Click. "What did you just..."

"It's a joke," the hen said. "A very old joke. A human joke."

"What's a..."

The hen came a little closer and lowered her voice. "You know what a joke is," she said. "You know, because you're..."

Instinctively, he knew he didn't want to hear. He threw his head back and crowed until he thought his lungs would burst. But the hen just stood there.

"All right," she said, "try this. Which came first, the chicken or the..."

He turned to run, as though all the foxes in the world were crowding in on him. Then he stopped. "Egg," he said. "The chicken or the egg."

Slowly the hen nodded. "And the answer is?"

The word came from deep inside him somewhere, a place he didn't know existed. "Neither," he said.

"What did come first?"

"Transdimensional phase shift relocation," he replied, and the words squeezed out of him like (say) a square egg. "Setting

up a differential feedback loop which in turn triggers a fundamental temporal paradox sequence, giving rise to what we
subjectively term reality."

"Thank you," the hen said gravely. "Now, how do you feel?"

He considered his answer. "Bloody strange," he said. "You
know what, for a moment there, I could have sworn I was a
ch—"

"Don't," the hen hissed, "look down. Or sideways. Just keep
looking at me, all right?"

He nodded.

"Good. Now then, what can you see?"

He looked, and saw a smartly dressed middle-aged woman
in heavy square-rimmed glasses. And feathers, but somehow
he knew they weren't really real, as though she was wearing a
transparent disguise. "Who are you?" he said.

"My name's Mary," she replied. "Mary Byron."

"Kevin Briggs," he replied automatically. "Pleased to meet
you."

# CHAPTER EIGHT

"Eileen," he called out, "where're my slippers?"

No reply. She was still in the toilet. He scowled and put on his brown shoes instead, even though they hurt his feet if he wore them for more than an hour. Then he went through to see to the customer.

A blouse, dry clean only, gravy stains down the front. A wool coat. Ready by half five, he told her. She looked pleased.

That was the sad irony. They offered a really quick, reliable service, as good as you'd find anywhere; by rights, they should've built up an impressive reputation by now, except they were never anywhere long enough. All that hard work for nothing. Sometimes he wondered why they bothered, except that if they didn't turn the stuff around inside twenty-four hours, there was all the fuss of getting it back to the customer.

George glanced at his watch. Business had been steady but not brisk. He hung the blouse on a hanger on the rail and made a note in the book.

"Eileen?" he called again.

No reply. Ten past ten. How long had she been in there, anyway? She knew better than to be in the downstairs loo at ten fifteen. She'd be out of there in plenty of time – except, he couldn't help thinking, she was still in there with only five minutes to go. What if she'd fallen asleep or something?

Hardly likely. The bell rang: a man with a grey Marks suit, looked like it had been slept in, a few other mishaps that didn't want thinking about too closely. Not for him to pass judgement on the customers, of course. In his view a dry cleaner is like a priest. He knows everything there is to know about human frailty. His job is to get rid of the stains.

Hang up the suit, write it in the book. Suddenly he remembered the time.

"Eileen?"

He looked at his watch, and a cold panic spread upwards from his solar plexus, following his veins until it flooded every part of him. He yelled her name again, then roared it. She must've heard him, so why hadn't she replied? Oh God, he thought, she's in there.

Neither of them had the faintest idea what took place in their downstairs toilet between ten fifteen and a quarter to twelve every day. They had more sense than to look. The strange noises, though nearly always the same, were so bizarre and so diverse that they offered no intelligible clue. They'd never discussed it. Best not to think about it. After all, whatever it was had always stayed in there – it wasn't really any trouble. By 11:46 everything was back to normal, more or less. A little water spilt on the floor, a new toilet roll in the holder and a faint smell of almonds, not at all unpleasant. They could live with it, not that they had any real choice.

But today, as far as he could tell, it was 10:14 and Eileen was still in there, which meant he had to do something. He broke away from the counter, dashed into the back, arrived at the door and stopped dead.

I'm not going in there, he thought.

Yes, but he had to. His wife was in there. She'd fallen asleep, or had a heart attack or a stroke, and it was due to begin in a matter of seconds. He had to...

His hand on the handle. He twisted it. The door was locked.

It was as though he and It had a deal: you respect my space and I'll respect yours. It was a bit like sharing a house with a polite, well-behaved werewolf. Just as long as you're out of the way at certain times, there's absolutely no reason why it can't be made to work indefinitely. But once you cross the line...

Very gently, he tapped at the door. "Eileen?" he whispered.

Then he heard a clanking noise, which meant it had begun. He closed his eyes.

For a long time, maybe five seconds, he stood there completely still. It was as though the universe had asked him a question, and there were two answers, each one completely contradicting the other, both – he knew it intuitively – entirely true. The answers were—

You've got to do something.

I'm not going in there. Not for *anything*.

George had never thought of himself as a coward. He'd always assumed, on the incredibly rare occasions when it occurred to him to consider the matter, that if it came right down to it (house on fire, kiddie drowning in a pond, stuff like that) he'd probably do the right thing, because he'd have no choice. And, most likely, if the test had been one of fire or water, he'd have found the necessary courage. But it wasn't fire or water in there, or if either fire or water were involved, he knew they'd be the least of his worries. Instead, what was in there was It. If that was cowardice, he was as yellow as a canary. End of story.

Yes, he thought, but it's *Eileen* in there. And if something happens to her, and she never comes out again...Well, he thought, it's going to be very lonely, stuck in this place for ever, without anyone to talk to. Besides, there was the business to think of.

He clenched his fist and banged it against the door. *Ouch.* "Eileen?"

No reply, just the sound of steel being drawn across stone and a snatch of plainsong. Suddenly he felt a spurt of anger – irrational, unexpected, in the circumstances exactly what he needed. Who the hell did they think they were, anyhow, taking over someone else's downstairs bog for an hour and a half every day without so much as a thank you, playing with chains and knives and *singing*, and no consideration for other people? Well, he thought, it was about time he put a stop to it.

He wrenched the handle again. Stuck solid.

When he'd been a kid and had gone regularly to the cinema, they used to make the sort of film where strong, admirable men regularly broke down doors. Generally they shoulder-charged them; there was something a bit low or not-quite-nice about kicking them in. He considered the door. It was pretty solid, none of your two sheets of hardboard nailed to a deal frame when they built this house. Maybe if he got a bit of wire, he could fiddle about and try and work the latch.

No time for that. In the films they took a bit of a run-up, then straight at it, and the next thing you saw was the hero bursting into the previously inaccessible room (his good side always facing the camera). It was one of those things where you've seen it done a thousand times but never really picked up the details of technique you actually need in order to be able to do it yourself.

Oh well, he thought, it's hardly rocket science. He paced off five yards, broke into a gentle trot, walloped into the door and bounced off, howling with pain.

Clearly, more to it than that. Rubbing his shoulder (his arm had gone numb), he retreated to the start of his run-up and tried to analyse the problem sensibly.

Kicking it was a non-starter; he established that very quickly. Just as well, in fact, that he was wearing his brown shoes and not his slippers, or he'd have a broken toe to contend with as well as everything else. So, what else did the heroes in movies do? Well, if they were policemen, they shot off the lock, but he wasn't a policeman and he didn't have a gun, so that was out of the window straight away. What else? In Robin Hood films he'd known them to batter down doors with benches. That, however, was strictly a two-man job. Slowly it dawned on him that, after a lifetime of subconsciously believing in the movies, he'd reached a sort of anti-road-to-Damascus moment, and his faith was gone for ever.

In which case, he'd have to get by with just plain common sense and basic engineering. He thought, All right, what would a professional do? A burglar, say.

Easy. Burglars had jemmies; they carried them, presumably, in their bags marked SWAG. Needless to say, he didn't have a jemmy; he wasn't even sure he'd recognise one if he saw one, let alone know how to use it. But the principle was quite simple, and he did have a long stout screwdriver and a hammer.

As he closed the lid of his toolbox, he checked his watch again. Twenty-one minutes past ten. She'd been in there for six minutes already, with It. Furious with himself, he charged back to the door, located the screwdriver blade as close as he could get to the point where the latch entered the mortice, and started bashing with the hammer.

Turned out to be a piece of cake. Once the blade was in, he leaned his hip against the screwdriver handle and the door just popped open.

Eileen was sitting on the toilet, unharmed as far as he could tell, an unopened magazine in her lap. She didn't look round as he came crashing through the door, and when he called out her name, she answered, "Sh." He opened his mouth defiantly, but then he followed her line of sight and his tongue froze, leaving him standing perfectly still and deathly quiet, like a statue. Stiller, even, than a statue. As still as one of those whitened-faced mimes who stand around pretending to be statues, and you can't get much stiller or quieter than that.

Where the back wall should have been, there was landscape, loads of it, rolling downland undulating away as far as the eye could see. More or less centre, about where the toilet-roll holder used to be, he saw an old, fallen-down sort of a building, yellow stone with a grey slate roof and a distinctly churchy sort of air to it, though it was a bit small and didn't have a spire or anything like that. Bigger than a shed, smaller than a house, very old-fashioned and quaint, the most remarkable thing about it was that nobody had converted it into a tea shop.

"Eileen," he heard himself whisper, "what's happened to our wall?"

"Sh," and he could see her point. Standing in front of the building's massive nail-studded oak door was a knight in armour, shiny but black, which covered him from head to toe. George wasn't one to jump to conclusions, but he was fairly sure the knight wasn't a stray customer who'd taken a wrong turning, even though his clothes were most definitely dry clean only.

"What's he..." he hissed, but Eileen glowered at him and he subsided, just in time to see another knight striding round the corner of the building.

The newcomer was fully armoured too, but his steelware was mirror-bright and gleaming, and he was leading a Persil-white horse by the bridle. If this was anything at all like the movies (and George had just seen how fallible they could be), Mr Sparkles here had to be the hero. The horse alone practically guaranteed it. None of which explained what either of them thought he was doing trespassing in someone else's un-naturally distended bog.

With a shrill grating noise (So that's what that is, he thought) the black knight drew his sword and waggled it – supposed to be threatening, presumably, but George thought, He could put his eye out with that thing if he's not careful. The white knight, however, responded at once by drawing his own sword, and a moment later they were bashing at each other like panel beaters. It can't have been something either of them had said, because not a word had been spoken, but it was fairly obvious they didn't like each other. On the other hand, thanks to all the sheet metal, neither of them seemed the slightest bit affected by the clobbering he was getting. It all reminded George a bit of *Jeux Sans Frontières*, except that they were using swords instead of water-filled balloons.

Then, for no obvious reason, the black knight suddenly keeled over and landed on his back, *flump*, making the floor shake and the toothbrushes rattle in their mug. Without knowing the rules it was hard to know precisely what had been achieved, but the white knight stepped back and sheathed his sword in a let-that-be-a-lesson-to-you manner, so presumably he'd won. Quick glance at watch. All that had only taken five minutes, which meant an hour and twenty minutes still to go.

"Here," Eileen muttered, "d'you think he's all right? The one lying down. Maybe we should call an ambulance."

His turn. "Sh."

"Yes, but if anything happens to him, what'll it do to our insurance?"

Valid point, made irrelevant by the disappearance into thin air of the black knight. The white knight either hadn't noticed or thought nothing of it. He was standing in front of the door, belting it with his clenched fist. Three massive thuds and the door was opened by a monk in a hoody, sorry, cowl, who beckoned to the knight in slow motion, whereupon...

They were inside the building, which was a bit disconcerting. The walls were pale grey stone, the roof was high and vaulted, and directly ahead was a church altar. (Last time he'd been this close to one of them, he'd been saying, "I do," while Eileen's mum's eyes had been blistering the back of his neck. The parallel comforted him rather. That had seemed strange and disconcerting at the time, but it hadn't turned out too badly.)

It's all just It, he told himself. It doesn't matter, as long as we can get away from It, which we can do at any time, just by running to the toilet door. With that reassurance firmly in mind, he admitted to himself that he wouldn't mind finding out what was going to happen next.

The monk led the knight to the altar and pointed at it, then bowed low and backed away. George took his eye off him for a moment, and then the monk wasn't there any more. That didn't seem to matter. The knight went down on one knee, as if proposing. Somewhere offstage, a choir started singing monksong. The knight clasped his hands together in prayer. Eileen suddenly gasped, as if in pain.

"What?" he whispered.

"Pins and needles," she replied, and rubbed her leg.

Gradually, so slowly it was almost imperceptible, the altar began to glow. The unseen choir hit a high note and held it. The glow was now too bright to look at comfortably (Bloody hell, he thought, Steven Spielberg in our downstairs toilet) and he looked away. Then the plainsong stopped, and he looked up.

The altar had stopped glowing. The knight, who'd turned away to avoid the glare, started to get up, then froze, then dropped down on both knees with a creak of straining rivets. George felt a stiff breeze on his face, in his hair. A cloud of dust was slowly rising from the altar, swirling, forming a double helix. Definitely Spielberg, he thought, and then the helices collapsed, and there on the altar, sitting next to each other, were a chicken and an egg.

He stared at them, and then movement from the knight caught his eye. The knight had jumped up as if starting a race, then he stopped, paralysed, then he raised his right hand, balled his fist and crashed it with terrible force against his armoured thigh and yelled, not with pain but desperate frustration and despair. The vaulted roof caught his yell and played tennis with it, backwards and forwards from wall to wall, and that set the choir off again, chanting their slow measured harmonies. The knight lunged at the altar, whereupon the chicken and the egg both vanished. The knight stopped dead in his tracks; they reappeared, and he took another step; they vanished, and he juddered to a halt. The knight sank to his knees again, moaning softly, and this time George could just make out the words.

"Which came first?" the knight whimpered. "Which came *first?*"

Then the whole toilet shook, as a great voice that seemed to draw its power from the very stones boomed out in perfectly modulated quadrophonic sound, "You are not worthy. Go, and never return." The knight bowed his head, stood for a long time as if unable or unwilling to move, then turned on his heel and walked slowly out of the chapel.

Outside again. No sign of the white knight, but the black knight was back on duty in front of the chapel door. ("Oh, he's all right, then," Eileen muttered. "I was a bit concerned.") The white knight appeared round the corner of the chapel, leading his horse.

That was it. "Come on," he hissed, grabbing Eileen by the wrist. "Let's get out of here."

"But I want—"

"Come on," he repeated, and towed her after him towards the door – the real one, which he'd forced open with a screwdriver less than fifteen minutes ago, but there didn't seem to be any sign of his onslaught now. There wasn't a mark on it, and it was firmly shut. He reached for the handle and wrenched at it. It came off in his hand.

Behind them, the two knights were at it again, crash-bangwallop, like a car smash or a breaker's yard. George stood quite still, looking at the plain brass doorknob in his hand, with two screws still in their holes in the mounting plate, and a shadow fell across him, and he turned to find he was looking into the gentle grey eyes of the monk, who shook his head sadly, and said, "You can't leave. I'm sorry."

He was about to shout, quite probably something nasty, but Eileen beat him to it. She looked at the monk, and asked quietly, "So which did come first?"

The monk shook his head again, and the folds of his cowl flapped like an elephant's ears. "I'm sorry," he repeated.

For some reason that made George very angry. "Look, you," he growled. "My wife just asked you a civil question."

The monk sighed softly. "That information is not available. Also, you're standing on my foot."

"What? Oh, sorry." He stepped back quickly, and the monk smiled.

"Thank you," he said. "We apologise for any inconvenience. If you have further queries, say *stop*. If you would like to return to the chapel, say *stop*. If you would like to leave the room and return to your normal environment—"

"Stop."

"That function is not available at this time," the monk said smoothly. "Please try later. If you have further queries—"

Under normal circumstances George wasn't a violent man; in fact the last time he'd hit someone, it had been about a disputed conkers match and Harold Macmillan had been prime minister. He clenched his right fist and swung it at the monk's face, which turned to mist and faded away.

"You shouldn't have done that," Eileen said.

"You're not helping."

In the background, bloody plainsong again. "I want to go back in," Eileen said. "I want to find out what happens."

That made him shudder. Got to get out of there; the question was how? Breaking down the door, been there, done that; on this side, however, the door opened *inwards*. Come on, he thought, this isn't the first time in the history of the world someone's got stuck in a toilet. He considered the handle, but the bit of square-section bar the handle fits over had vanished from the door, so just putting the handle assembly back on wasn't going to solve anything.

"Come on." Eileen was tugging at his sleeve. "I want to know which came first."

"Don't be stupid; it's just a kids' riddle," he said (and as he said it, he knew he was lying). "There's no answer, that's the whole point." Maybe there was something in the chapel he could use instead of the square bar – a bit of wood, a window stay, or what about the point of the knight's sword? All he had to do was make the turny thing in the lock turn ninety degrees and they could be out of there, safe, gone. Oh, if only he still had his Boy Scout penknife.

"Idiot," he said aloud, and dropped to his hands and knees. It had to be there somewhere. True, things vanished into thin air around here, but not, he was prepared to bet, stuff that had been brought in from outside. There were rules, there had to be. Say what you like about It, there had always been rules, and they'd always been complied with.

He felt something under his foot, stooped down and found what he'd been looking for: the screwdriver he'd used to jemmy the door. It was a wonderful moment, like finding yourself in a foreign city and hearing an English voice. He straightened up, stuck the blade of the screwdriver into the hole in the lock where the square-section bar should have been, and turned.

The door opened.

He grabbed it and pulled it wide open. Beyond the threshold, one small step, was the worn carpet of his downstairs back corridor, every frayed edge and tea stain as precious to him as life itself. The plainsong had stopped. Round about now the great voice was presumably telling the white knight to go away, which meant that any moment now the whole process would start again. He turned round to collect Eileen and saw to his horror that she'd got up from the toilet seat and was trotting determinedly towards the chapel door. *Bloody woman*, he breathed softly to himself. As quickly as he could, he jammed the screwdriver wedge-fashion under the bottom edge of the door, then sprang after her and grabbed her arm.

"Let go," she snapped. "I want to see."

"Not now," he barked at her (thirty years and never a cross word). "Come on. I've got the door open. Please. It's not safe."

She was looking at him like he was simple or something. "Don't talk daft," she said, as to a small, timid child. "There's nothing to be afraid of. It's just a..." She frowned, trying to find the right word. "It isn't really real," she said. "It's more like a recording or something. They can't hurt us, because they're not really here."

He could see where she was coming from, but there was a lethal flaw in her reasoning; he knew it was there, but he couldn't think clearly enough to pinpoint what it was. Briefly he considered knocking her out and carrying her through the door over his shoulder, but then he thought about his back and, being a realist, decided against it. But if the caveman approach wasn't viable, what was he supposed to do?

"Eileen," he said, "I'm ordering you to..."

She wasn't listening. The black knight had reappeared outside the chapel door, and she was heading straight at him.

"Eileen."

Then, far away but quite distinct, he heard the *ting* of the shop bell. She heard it too, and for a moment she stood quite still, like a comet exactly halfway between two black holes. Then she turned round, smart as a soldier on parade, and hurried past him, through the door and into the corridor. He closed his eyes, let go of a breath he'd been holding for rather longer than was good for him, and started after her, only to be intercepted by the monk, who was smiling pleasantly and hold-ing a long-bladed screwdriver.

"That's the deal, is it?" he said to the monk. "She can go, but I've got to stay."

The monk shook his head. "Nothing like that," he said.

"Good. Then get out of my way."

The monk stepped aside. "Your screwdriver," he said.

"Thanks."

"You're welcome."

Just having the screwdriver back in his hand made him feel noticeably more secure. "All right," he said. "What do you want?"

The monk shrugged. "The time is drawing near," he said, "and you have been found worthy. Have a nice day."

"Worthy of what?" he demanded, but he got no answer. Instead, the monk pushed him out through the door and slammed it shut.

The alarm clock trilled, waking Mary Byron out of a most peculiar dream, in which she'd been a chicken, of all things. As she opened her eyes, it remained so vivid that she had to shake her head to get rid of it.

Shower, dress, breakfast (toast and black coffee), then half an hour being chewed up by the Northern Line, then work. She sat down at her desk and opened her diary to see what treats lay in store for her.

*HELP.* In big red letters.

She frowned. The bizarre poultry-haunted dream hadn't been the only disturbing thing lately; far from it. For one thing, she had a nasty suspicion she had an admirer, or something equivalently creepy. It had started small – cups of coffee left for her on her desk when she came back from meetings or trips to the loo, difficult bits of work done for her in her absence. The latter narrowed down the list of likely suspects to the other solicitors in the office, and the thought of any of them fancying her made her skin crawl. Without proof, however, she couldn't very well start firing out accusations or go to Mr Huos with a formal harassment complaint, and so far her attempts at amateur sleuthing had got her nowhere. When her unseen helper had sorted out the Attractive Avenue file, for example, all the possible suspects had had watertight alibis, vouched for by secretaries, office juniors, Reception and similarly unimpeachable witnesses, and she had been forced to admit that she had nothing to go on. That didn't help. The thought that her secret stalker was rational enough and cunning enough to cover his tracks so well was hardly encouraging. It was so bad she'd even contemplated chucking the job in, though not for long, given the depressed state of the conveyancing sector. Now, apparently, whoever it was had gone a little bit further off the rails and had started writing pleading messages in her diary. It had to stop, she decided.

As always, the day's incoming mail was in a wire tray on the left-hand side of her desk. She leafed through it, a preliminary reconnaissance only, triage rather than OR. Nothing much. None of the outstanding items she was waiting for to wrap up ongoing cases. She opened her drawer and groped for the box of paper clips; found it; found it empty.

She sighed. That was another annoying thing – not nearly as bad as the stalker, but over time it was wearing her down. Of course it was part of office life: the constant trivial pilfering of stationery from colleagues' desks when the store cupboard was bare or one simply couldn't be bothered to walk up three flights of stairs for a pencil sharpener or a refill of staples. But it was getting so you couldn't leave anything for five minutes and be sure it'd be there when you got back, and when she thought of all the time she was having to waste, traipsing back and forth to the storeroom because some thoughtless individual had robbed her of basic supplies—

The phone rang. It was only Martin.

"What do you want?" she snapped, rather more harshly than she'd intended.

"Sorry," her brother replied. "Bad day?"

"What do you want?" she repeated.

"It's a bit awkward. You see—"

She clicked her tongue. Words weren't needed when he used that tone of voice. "You're after money again," she said.

"You make it sound so—" He stopped, and started again. "It's only fifty quid," he said, "to tide me over until—"

"For crying out loud, Martin."

"I'll pay you back on Thursday, I promise you. Only I still haven't got paid for the Hanwell gig, and I'd been sort of counting on that for the rent."

She sighed. "You know what," she said. "I'm getting a bit fed up with being a patron of the arts. It was all right for the Medici and the Esterhazys, they had the money. Besides, they got something to show for it. You, on the other hand—"

"Yes, all right. I know. I'm wasting my life and why don't I get a proper job. Actually, I think I'm on the brink of getting into something really good. I'm meeting this bloke next week, and . . ."

"Martin."

"Good," he said firmly, "as in lots of money. Composing. Well, writing jingles, actually. You know, for commercials and radio stations. It's crazy what they'll pay for just seven notes, provided they're the right ones."

"Martin," she said grimly, "if I agree to lend you fifty pounds, will you promise me you'll spend a fiver of it on a dictionary, so you can look up *proper* and *job*, because I don't think you quite grasp—"

"Forget it, then," Martin said crisply. "Sorry I bothered you. I quite understand. Have a nice day."

"Martin—"

*Click, buzz.* She scowled furiously at the receiver, then slammed it back on its cradle. It was so bitterly unfair, she thought, how Martin had the knack of zooming past her and up into the snowcapped peaks of the moral high ground, when by any relevant criteria he was a sponger, a wastrel and an inefficient use of increasingly scarce resources. It wasn't as though she begrudged him the money. He'd be welcome to it, if only he had the grace to cringe and grovel for it occasionally.

Her eye fell on the diary, still open in front of her, still broadcasting a big red *HELP*. The silly thing was, she had a vague memory, a memory of a dream, a dream in which she'd been asleep and dreaming, and in her dream there'd been someone else sitting at her desk, writing in her diary, and maybe the pen she'd used had had a red cap.

Coincidence, or déjà vu. There was a scientific explanation for that; she'd heard something on the radio. There was always a scientific explanation. Unfortunately, she'd given up on science as soon as she'd had the option, a decision she'd regretted ever since. Instead, she'd set her heart on being a lawyer, in a smart suit, sitting at a desk, in control, like the captain of a starship. One of the bitterest things about her life was that she'd always achieved her ambitions to the full.

She'd give it half an hour, she decided, and then she'd call Martin back and tell him he could have his rotten fifty quid. It wouldn't be enough to regain as much as a moral foothill, but at least they'd be on speaking terms again. Besides, she thought, if he's really got a chance to go into the jingles business, there was a possibility she might be reunited with her money one of these days, in the coming by-and-by. Like he'd said, it was crazy what some people would pay for a jingle, or so she'd heard.

She opened the next file on her heap and reset her mind to work mode. A lot to do today. A great many important things requiring her undivided concentration. These standard-form requisitions on title, for example.

Like a small boat adrift on a turbulent sea, her mind floated away. A chicken, for crying out loud. As in no spring. Well, she couldn't deny that, and maybe that was all there was to it. As in *Why did the chicken cross the road?*

Someone had said that, quite recently, and in context it had seemed important. Supposedly, according to the latest research, that and the door that's a jar were the two best-known jokes in the English language. Odd that, since neither of them was particularly funny. The door thing was at least a rudimentary pun, but the chicken gag was just silly – meaningless, like a nursery rhyme. The only way she could think of in which it could carry any vestigial charge of humour was if it was shorthand, a prompt, the tip of an iceberg, serving to remind the listener of the rest of the joke (long since lost and forgotten). Otherwise, there was no possible excuse for it. In which case, who'd said it to her just lately, and why had it been so important that she remembered it?

Enough of that. She shooed all the chickens from her mind, and filled in some Land Registry forms, an exercise that left her feeling thirsty and caffeine-deficient, so she went to the kitchen and made herself a nice strong coffee, black, no sugar.

When she got back to her desk, something was different. She scowled, put her mug down on top of the filing cabinet and investigated.

Someone had closed her diary; that was all, nothing more. She opened it, found today's date and put it down in its usual place. Nothing else appeared to have been touched, which was something. Even so, she was furious. Someone had come in, the moment her back was turned (Did that imply that her movements were being watched?) and had read her diary, presumably to try and get advance notice of any trips out of the office, personal appointments, whatever. That was a new level of creepiness, and she wasn't prepared to put up with it. Not making a fuss was all very well, but there were limits, which in her view had just been exceeded. She picked up her phone and rang through to Pauline, Mr Huos' PA.

"Can I see him for a couple of minutes?" she asked. "It's important."

Getting past Pauline was usually on a par with sneaking backstage at a Springsteen gig. Today, however, Pauline chirped back, "Will today at eleven be all right?" Mary glanced at the clock on her wall. It was 10:45.

"Um, sure," she replied, slightly stunned. "If that's OK with him. I don't want to—"

"You did say it was important."

And yes, dammit, it was. "Eleven sharp, then," she said, and put the phone down. Then the shakes set in. Evidence, for crying out loud. She didn't have any. Well there was the coffee, but she could hardly go charging into Mr Huos' actual office with an empty mug in her hand and expect to be taken seriously. The work done for her; thin, perilously thin. The diary, she thought, that at least is a physical object I can put in front of him. There it was; *HELP* in big red letters.

And big green letters.

She stared at it for a moment. *HELP*. A fairly useless message because it's so vague, a bit like *Look out* suddenly yelled in your ear by your front-seat passenger. Also, the handwriting was different, though, given the degree of cunning displayed so far by her tormentor, there wasn't anything surprising in that. Well, she thought, that's evidence. Nobody could look at that and deny that she had a case to put before an industrial tribunal, if she chose to go down that route. Not that she had any reason to believe that Mr Huos wouldn't be as shocked and appalled as she was.

Another glance at the clock. Might as well make a move; it was a long way to Mr Huos' office, even when the lifts were running OK. Tucking the diary under her arm, she walked briskly up the corridor, past the printer room and the small interview room and the closed file store, left at Denny Brock's room, along more corridor, then sharp right and directly into the lift, which was waiting for her with its door conveniently open. She pressed the button for the seventh floor, and the door closed with a soft *whoosh*.

The lift went straight up, from three to seven. The door opened. Mr Huos was in his office, expecting her. He was very kind and sympathetic, and assured her he'd look into it straight away. He went as far as to write something down on the back of a blue folder; even so, Polly got the distinct feeling that his mind was elsewhere.

Polly took the lift back to the third floor. Preoccupied with her recent encounter, she didn't look down, which was probably just as well. If she had, she couldn't have helped noticing the stray wisps of straw, the four light-brown feathers and the still-warm egg.

Mr Gogerty stared at the smoking ruins and wept.

Twelve fire engines were battling the fire, which was still roaring away in outlying parts of the building. They weren't having much luck. Water didn't seem to have much effect, especially on the bright green flames welling up out of what looked like a perfectly ordinary toilet bowl on the second floor. Depending on the water pressure and the angle from which the jets were directed, the flames either rose higher, doubled their heat output or played selections from *Phantom of the Opera* (the original cast recording). Fire-suppressant foam turned the fire purple, with a faint green pinstripe, and worried-looking men in bulky orange suits were muttering to each other about blowing the remains of the building up with dynamite.

It was just as well Mr Gogerty overheard them. He slid

through the crowd, ducked under the incident tape, reassured the policeman with a serious nod and joined the discussion.

"Gogerty," he said, "head of operations, MP3. Whatever you do, don't use explosives. Not," he added with a wild grin, "unless you really want to annoy the Ordnance Survey."

An orange suit turned to him. "The what?"

"All those maps they'll have to redraw," Mr Gogerty explained. "Look, just tell your men to turn off the taps and back off. I'll deal with it."

Which he did, by taking a small packet of white powder from his top pocket and tossing it into the heart of the fire, which immediately went out. In fact, the powder was coffee sweetener, but Mr Gogerty reckoned that if he'd just given the fire a stern look and said, "Behave," to the four overexcited salamanders who'd broken out of the aquarium and were causing all the fuss, he'd have drawn unwelcome attention to himself. Instead, he explained that the powder was the latest oxygen-extraction reagent, a sample he'd liberated on a recent visit to NASA.

"What started it?" he asked.

They had no idea, though they weren't ruling out arson at this stage. Why not? Because they hadn't been able to get close enough to rule out *anything*, from an electrical fault to a fly-past by massed dragons. "Fair enough," he replied. "Well, I won't keep you. Make sure there's a report on my desk by 0900 tomorrow."

On his way back through the cordon he scooped up the salamanders, who were drooping about on the pavement looking lost and sad, and stowed them safely in his 100-per-cent-fireproof jacket pocket, on the principle that things were bad enough without four emotionally disturbed invisible fire spirits wandering about the capital. Their names, they told him, were Pinky, Perky, Boris and Patch. He promised to find them a new home as soon as he could, and they curled up and went to sleep.

He took a taxi to Blue Remembered Hills and asked to see Mr Huos. He found him sitting at his desk holding a brown chicken feather in one hand and an egg in the other, looking distinctly worried.

"Things are getting bad," Mr Huos said.

Mr Gogerty registered polite concern. "Business, you mean?" he asked. "Or the other thing?"

Mr Huos put the egg carefully in his empty coffee cup. "Both," he replied. "I'm having to lay off staff. And that's not as easy as you might think, either. In fact, I'm not sure how much longer I'll be able to. Anyway, how about you? Progress?"

Mr Gogerty frowned. "Developments," he amended. "The thing is about investigations in my field," he went on, "it's all a game of snakes and ladders." With real snakes, he didn't add, sometimes hundred-headed, and as for the ladders, even he didn't want to know. "You make what looks like a breakthrough and then suddenly you hit a brick wall. But then, if you can get past that, you'll probably find there's been another breakthrough. I won't bother you with the details."

"Oh."

"Suffice to say," Mr Gogerty went on, "as far as I'm concerned, this case has just got personal. Something very important to me...Well, anyway." He sat up a little straighter and steepled his fingers in front of him. "I wanted to ask you. Have you told anybody else about what we were talking about yesterday?"

Mr Huos grinned. "Are you serious?"

"That's a no."

"Too bloody right. When I was telling you about it, it all sounded so crazy it made me wonder if I was off my head. If some of the people I do business with ever found out—"

"Quite," Mr Gogerty said. "I just wanted to make sure there hadn't been a security breach at this end."

"Rest assured," Mr Huos said grimly. "So, now what?"

"I still have a very promising lead," Mr Gogerty replied, "which I'm just about to follow up. I'll let you know as soon as I've got anything."

Mr Huos nodded. "So, no sneak preview?"

"No."

"Tiny little hint? Cryptic clue?"

"No."

"Oh." Mr Huos pulled a face, then shrugged. "For fear of compromising security, I suppose."

"Partly," Mr Gogerty said, rising to leave. "Also, you'd probably think I'm crazy."

The Carpenter library wasn't the only place that had the definitive edition of the Yellow Pages. There was one other copy. Sort of. Mr Gogerty took a taxi to Marylebone station, a train to High Wycombe and a minicab to a small private airfield about six miles out of the town, where he was well enough known to be able to hire a helicopter at ten minutes' notice.

The pilot assigned to him was a short square man with bright blue eyes and no neck. "Where to?" he asked.

Mr Gogerty handed him a piece of paper with a map reference. The pilot nodded. "You want to land, or..."

"No."

"Just buzz round a couple of times, that sort of thing."

"I'll tell you what to do when we get there."

It was a fast, modern helicopter (bless Mr Huos and his unlimited unqueried expenses) and the flight only took an hour, during which time Mr Gogerty sat quietly in the passenger seat doing sums on a calculator with three side-by-side screens. When the pilot said, "We're here; now what?" he looked across at the instrument panel.

"Which of these is the altitude?" he said.

"That one."

Mr Gogerty looked at the readout, then down at his calculator. "Up another seventy-six metres," he said.

"Seventy-*six*." The pilot grinned. "You're sure you don't mean seventy-six point three nine five?"

"That's all right," Mr Gogerty said. "I've got long legs."

When the altitude readout was as close as he felt he was going to get, Mr Gogerty checked his calculator again. "Hold this altitude," he said, "and move three metres starboard."

The pilot shrugged. "Tricky," he said.

Mr Gogerty gave him a look he remembered for many years to come. "Give it your best shot," he said.

The pilot swung round in a shallow loop and tried again. "There," he said. "Close enough for you?"

"I hope so," Mr Gogerty said. "Right, just wait here. I won't be very long."

Before the pilot could stop him, Mr Gogerty had unbuckled his safety harness, opened his door and stepped out of the helicopter. For a split second his left foot groped cloud, then it came to rest on something invisible but solid, and Mr Gogerty shifted his weight onto it, as with his right hand he appeared to knock three times on a faint wisp of water vapour.

A door opened. The pilot tried to peer past him to see what was beyond it, but couldn't. Then the door closed. A moment later the pilot, who hadn't been paying proper attention to the controls, flew straight through the exact spot where it had been. Just as well, really, that there was nothing there.

"Stan." The old man who'd opened the door grinned broadly and clapped Mr Gogerty on the shoulder. "Wonderful to see you. It's been such a long time."

Mr Gogerty looked down at the mangy carpet under his feet, then across at the dingy nicotine-streaked woodchip on the walls. "Everything here seems pretty much the same," he said. "I thought you were going to redecorate."

"I did." The old man sounded hurt. "Don't you like it?"

On the mantelpiece at the far end of the room Mr Gogerty noticed a faded chrysanthemum in a jam jar. Last time, as he

172 • Tom Holt

recalled, it had been a faded rose. "Love what you've done with the place," he said.

"Well, don't just stand there," the old man said. "Come in, sit down, let me get you something. Coffee, tea." Two grubby-looking cups materialised on a dusty table. A plate of digestive biscuits landed on the edge of the table, wobbled and fell on the floor. "You're looking really well, Stan, really well. And doing all right for yourself, so everybody's saying."

Mr Gogerty perched on a rickety chair, which swayed under him. "Not so bad," he replied. "Ever since—"

"And your mother," the old man went on. "How's she doing?"

"Oh, fine."

"And your aunt Priscilla?"

"Fine, fine."

"And your cousin Mary?"

"Fine."

"And your second cousin Darryl? He's at medical school, isn't he?"

"That's right," Mr Gogerty said grimly. "And he's fine."

"That's grand," the old man said, picking the biscuits off the floor and dusting them on his cuff. "You be sure to give my regards to your mother. She must be very proud of you."

Mr Gogerty shuffled a little on his pinnacle of seat. "I'll do that," he said. "What I wanted—"

"You heard about the Carpenter Library?" The old man's crinkled face became terribly grave. "Wasn't that a dreadful thing?"

"I was there this morning," Mr Gogerty said. "That's one of the reasons—"

"Burned to the ground," the old man went on, shaking his head sadly (and the light from the bare bulb danced on the shiny apex of his bald head). "All those wonderful books, all gone. Irreplaceable, most of them. Makes you wonder who'd do such a thing."

"Yes," Mr Gogerty said, so firmly that the old man looked

up, as though he'd just remembered Mr Gogerty was there. "Like I was saying," he continued, "that's one of the reasons I'm here."

The old man nodded. "Not just a social call, then."

"No."

"Drink your tea, it's getting cold." The old man folded his hands in his lap and sighed. "Just think of it," he said, "the Carpenter Library, gone for ever. I used to spend hours in there when I was studying for my exams."

Which would have been sixty years ago at least, and the Carpenter had only been built for fifteen, but it was that sort of library. "Me too," Mr Gogerty said. "I'll miss the place, that's for sure. But—"

"You'll be wanting to use upstairs, then."

The old man was looking straight at him, and Mr Gogerty had forgotten how bright his eyes could be, when he wanted them to. He nodded. "The Yellow Pages," he said. "That's all right, isn't it?"

He said it lightly, as though the request was a mere formality, which it wasn't. In theory, access to the Spielmann Webb Archive, of which the bright-eyed old man was the guardian and curator, was restricted to the most eminent leaders of the profession, and even they had to submit a written request for permission to the General Ethical Council. Just turning up and asking to see the archive could result in being shown the door (bearing in mind where the door was, no laughing matter). On the other hand, the curator had been to school with Mr Gogerty's mother.

"Well," the old man said, "I don't know."

Mr Gogerty crushed his pride down into his boots. "Please, Uncle Theo."

A long sigh. "I guess so," the old man said. "Just mind you don't go telling anybody or you'll get me in trouble. And drink your tea."

Ten minutes later, Mr Gogerty stepped out of the door in the cloud into the waiting helicopter, shut the door, waved good-bye to the shiny head floating in apparently thin air and told the pilot to take him home.

The pilot looked at him. "You just—"

Mr Gogerty nodded. "Yes," he said. "And yes, you could tell someone. But who'd believe you?"

He spent the entire flight home staring at the turned-up page of his notebook, on which was written an address. From time to time he glanced at his watch and asked the pilot if he could go a bit faster.

"You're in a hurry," the pilot said eventually.

"That's right," Mr Gogerty replied. "Got to get to the dry cleaners before it shuts."

# CHAPTER NINE

"We can't do this," Polly said, while Don wrecked a perfectly valid MasterCard. "It's against the law. It's burglary."

Don straightened up and looked at his card. "There I'd venture to disagree with you," he said. "The reason we can't do this is because it's difficult. The legal aspect, well, obviously that's where you'd tend to focus, it being your chosen field of endeavour and all." He sighed. "Here, lend me your credit card, would you? I'm getting the hang of this, but..."

"Certainly not." She looked nervously up and down the corridor. "Suppose somebody comes," she said. "We'll be in all sorts of trouble."

"We're already in all sorts of trouble," Don replied grimly, putting his murdered MasterCard back in his wallet. "Murder and mucking about with the dark arts, for starters." He sighed again. "It looks so easy in films," he said. "You just ease the corner of the card into the latch, and then *click* and you're in."

"Try using magic," Polly said.

He gave her a filthy look. "I'll pretend you meant that sarcastically," he said. "Oh come on. It's just a crappy Chinese Yale rip-off; it shouldn't be a problem. If underprivileged kids from dead-end estates with no GCSEs can do it, it can't be difficult, surely. Here, give me a nail file, that might do it."

"I haven't got a nail file."

He scowled at her. "Don't be silly," he said. "You're a girl, of course you've got a nail file. Otherwise, what would you spend all day sitting at your desk filing your nails with?"

"Have you tried turning the handle?"

He made a vulgar noise. "I suppose I could try drilling the lock off," he said. "Only that'd make a hell of a racket, and—"

"No," she said. "Think. He hears you crashing about, right, so—"

"I wasn't crashing about," Don retorted. "I wasn't doing anything."

"So," she went on calmly, "he decides to nip downstairs and ask you to stop. In which case..." She reached past him and took hold of the door handle. "Since he's only planning on being out for a minute or so, wouldn't he just put the door on the latch, rather than locking it?"

She twisted the handle and the door swung open. "There," she said.

"Oh."

"We're in," Polly said, "and since we haven't forced our way in, strictly speaking it's not burglary, just civil trespass. Well, come on."

Don hadn't really known what to expect. The plan had seemed obvious back at Polly's office: go round to the vanished guitar player's flat and look for clues, anything that might give them a starting point for figuring out how to get him back. Later, while he was delaminating credit cards on the lock, it had occurred to him that he was working on movie logic, rather than the stuff that applied in the real world. In a film you'd go round to the victim's flat and there the next big clue would be, sitting waiting for you, on a bed of wild rice with saffron and rocket garnish. In reality there was absolutely no reason to suppose that there'd be anything useful here, or, even if there was, that they'd stumble across it and recognise it for what it was in the course of a hurried and cursory search.

"You know what," Polly was saying. "It's almost as bad as your place."

He resented that. The vanished guitar player's flat was a mess, a tip, a pig heap. There were unwashed-up plates and empty beer cans on practically every flat surface, discarded clothes on the floor, bits of half-dismantled electronic appliances just left lying with their guts hanging out in skeins, a TV set left negligently on standby (thereby directly contributing to the deaths of countless baby polar bears in the rapidly defrosting Arctic) and an expensive electric guitar apparently dropped on the floor and left for dead. Also, he could have pointed out, the walls were a different colour.

"Clues," he said. "Find clues."

"Such as?"

"I don't know, do I?" He looked round desperately. "It could be anything."

"Such as?"

He pleaded with the universe for inspiration. "An address book," he said. "Look for an address book."

There didn't seem to be one. Socks, yes. Underwear of all kinds, enough to fill a museum or, more appropriately, a silage clamp. No little black book, however.

"People don't use address books any more," Polly pointed out. "He'd have all that stuff on his phone or his computer. Besides, what were you planning on doing? Phoning his mother?"

"That's an idea," Don replied, picking up an empty milk carton with finger and thumb and dropping it on top of the crammed-full waste-paper basket. "We'll have a look on his computer; there might be something there."

Polly pulled a face. "You can do that," she said. "I'm going to look in the bedroom."

He waited till she was out of the room. Then he sat down on a chair, pulled a single hair from the top of his head and spat on it. For a second or two nothing happened. Then the hair started to grow, longer and thicker, until it was a brown tube about the size of a washing-up liquid bottle. He dropped it, and it fell on the floor, rolled a little way, sprouted arms, legs and a head, and sat up.

"Greetings," it said.

"Keep your voice down," Don hissed urgently. "Listen, my sister's in the next room. If she knew I was using magic, I'd never hear the last of it."

The hair nodded its curiously vague-featured head. "Understood," it whispered. "How may I be of service?"

Don looked at it with a certain degree of awe. "It works, then."

The hair smiled at him; at least a mouth appeared in the curved plane of its face, and its edges twitched upwards. "Of course," it said.

"It was in a book," Don said, "when I was a kid, and I always thought, Hey, that'd be so cool." He frowned. "Anyway, you're here now. Search the flat."

"At once," the hair replied. "Search it for what, exactly?"

"Clues."

"Consider it done. Clues to what?"

(At which point he thought, Magic's really just another kind of technology, really. You think it's the answer, but instead it's only another lot of bloody stupid questions.) "Clues to what happened to the man who used to live here," he whispered, as patiently as he could.

"Please define 'clue.' "

Something you haven't got. "Forget it," he sighed. "Um. Stand by."

The hair creature froze, neither stirring nor breathing. Don picked it up and put it on the table, hoping that when Polly came back, she'd assume it was an ornament. It looked just sufficiently naff to pass for one.

"Nothing in there apart from vintage laundry," Polly said, shutting the bedroom door behind her. "Why don't men ever wash anything until it actually starts to ferment? Oh hell," she added, staring at the front door, which was opening.

Don just had time to step in front of the hair creature (he wasn't quite sure why it was so important; he only knew the thing mustn't be seen) as a young woman in a dark business suit walked in, caught sight of them both and stopped dead in her tracks.

She didn't scream, which was nice. Instead she frowned as though they somehow didn't make sense. Then she put down her briefcase and said, "Who the devil are you?"

"We're friends of…" Don suddenly remembered he didn't know his victim's name. "The man who lives here," he added. "We, um, let ourselves in."

"Like hell you are," the woman said briskly. "Don't move. I'm calling the police."

It was her tone of voice more than anything – the scorn, the distaste, rather than fear or panic. At the back of his mind Don thought, I could send her away, just like I did with the guitar player. After all, she's such a snotty bitch, who'd miss her? And the terrible thing was, he'd actually drawn in the breath and tensed the mental muscle before he realised what he was about to do. He cancelled the operation just in time, but the effort made him choke and grab at his throat, so much so that the woman looked at him sharply and said, "Are you all right?"

"I'm fine," he gasped. "Caught my breath the wrong way, that's all."

The woman frowned. "Stay there," she said. "I'll get you a glass of water."

She headed for what was presumably the kitchen, at which point Polly hissed, "Come on. Let's get out of here. Quickly."

But he shook his head. "Clue," was all he managed to get out, because he started coughing.

"Don't be stupid, she's going to call the police."

Valid point, but he chose to disregard it. "It's all right," he said, one of his all-time most stupid remarks given the context, but before Polly could say anything further, the woman came back with a glass of water.

It helped. "Thanks," he muttered. "Look, I'll be honest with you. We lied. We're not actually friends of..."

"Kevin. My brother," she added. "And I know you aren't. I know all Kevin's friends."

"We're not burglars," Polly said.

"No." The woman took the empty glass and put it down. "I suppose you aren't; you're far too disorganised. So what are you doing here?"

The best lies are made with real truth. "I live in the flat downstairs," Don said. "This is my sister, by the way. I'm Don and she's Polly. We came to, um, complain about the noise."

The woman raised both eyebrows. "But he's not here," she said. "Therefore, not making any noise."

"Polly's a solicitor," Don said. "I brought her along to—"

The woman turned and looked at Polly. "You're a solicitor?"

"Well, yes."

"So am I," the woman said. "Rachel Briggs." She shot out a hand, which Polly warily shook. "What firm?"

Lawyers, Don thought. Here we are burgling her brother's flat, and she's networking. Polly, meanwhile, had got her inferiority-complex face on. "Actually," she said, "I'm more sort of in-house at the moment. I'm a conveyancer with—"

"Snap," the woman said. "I'm with BRHD, don't know if you've heard of them."

For a moment it was as though Polly had been turned off at

the mains. Movement drained out of her, and Don wondered if she was about to have some sort of fit. "BRHD," she repeated.

"Blue Remembered—"

"No, you're not," Polly said.

It was a plain statement, no attitude, no offence intended. Offence was, however, most definitely taken. "What did you just say?"

"You don't work for Blue Remembered Hills," Polly said. "I'm sorry," she added with just a hint of vitality, enough to make you decide that, on the balance of probabilities, she was most likely still alive. "But you just don't."

The woman opened her mouth, but nothing came out. Polly shook her head. "I know," she said. "I'm with BRHD. I'm sure I'd have noticed you by now if you worked there."

There had been a time, many years ago, when Don had had a girlfriend who liked long country walks. Fortunately for both parties it hardly lasted any time at all and no permanent damage was done, but there'd been one occasion when they'd been trudging through a huge dismal sort of forest thing, and Don had put his foot down on what looked like perfectly sensible, ordinary ground and it had turned out to be mud, about three feet deep, and his leg had vanished into it up to the knee, so he'd staggered a bit, and then his other leg went in even deeper, and there he was, suddenly, comprehensively and quite gratuitously stuck, with not the faintest idea of what to do next. "Excuse me," he said. "What did you just—"

They ignored him, of course. "That's *silly*," the woman said eventually. "Listen, my office is on the third floor, two down from the lift. Next door to me—"

"Duncan Sharp," Polly said quietly, "and next to him, the gents' toilet. And there's a green filing cabinet in the corner of the room, and the runner of the middle drawer's bent, so you have to sort of shunt it to get it to shut. Only it's not your office, it's mine."

The two women were staring at each other, so they didn't notice Don flinch when something tapped him on the shoulder.

"Not now," he hissed. "I'm busy."

"Very sorry," the hair whispered back. "I just wondered if I could be of any assistance."

"Shh."

"Of course."

"The carpet's green," Polly said eventually. "Or it was once. Now it's a sort of pale toothpaste colour, and it's all scuffed up round the doorway because the door drags a bit on its hinges. Also, there's a damp patch a bit like Wales on the wall just above the window."

"What were you doing in my office?"

"I work there," Polly said wretchedly. "Sorry, but it's true. Isn't it, Don? You've been in there."

The woman sniffed savagely. "Don't be bloody stupid," she said. "That's my office; I work there. I've been there eighteen months. Ask anybody in the building."

Polly detected a potential straw and grasped at it. "What times do you work? I mean, they've never told me there's a night shift, but—"

"Nine to five-thirty," the woman snapped back. "Look, I don't know who either of you are, why you've been stalking me or what you think you're doing in my brother's flat, but it's starting to creep me out, and I think it's time I called the—"

Three seconds of dead silence. Then Polly asked, in a terrified voice, "Don, what did you just do to her?"

"Nothing," Don replied. "Honestly. She just stopped dead. I'm as surprised as you are." He leaned forward a little and peered at her. "She's not breathing," he said. "That's bad, isn't it? Maybe we should—"

Now Polly was like it too. In fact the similarity was so strong, he felt a strange urge to stand them side by side and fill the intervening space with books. He turned round slowly and scowled at the hair-creature, which was smiling respectfully at him.

"What've you done?" he demanded.

"Profound apologies," the hair said, "but I felt it might be helpful to pause linear development in the $t$ axis of the space/time continuum for a short while, to give you an opportunity to gather your thoughts and decide on a plan of action. I hope that wasn't too presumptuous of me."

Don felt like he was trying to do quadratic equations in his head after six pints of Guinness. "What was that about the space/time continuum?"

The hair did its funny little cartoon smile. "I stopped time," it said. "Just for a minute or two."

"You did that?"

"It's perfectly all right," the hair assured him. "Linear development in the $t$ axis won't be permanently affected. You get a little breathing space, that's all. If you're interested, there's a handy ready-to-use application you can buy – Slow-Me-Down from Zauberwerke, just seventy-nine ninety-nine for a packet of twelve. I can order you some, if you like."

"No, please don't." Don groped for a chair and sat down. "You can do that. Stop time."

"Of course."

"Oh God." He shook his head, which made him feel dizzy. "All right," he said, "since we've got a few minutes, you can start by telling me what's going on."

"Certainly." The hair thing cleared its throat. "You and your sister Polly are in the flat above your own. The young lady over there is the sister of the man who lives here. It would appear that she works for the same company as your sister, though paradoxically neither of them is aware of the fact. The young lady, whose name incidentally is Briggs, seems to have formed the impression that you and your sister are lying to her – which, to be fair, is not entirely without foundation. Will that be all, or can I help you with something else?"

Two more pints and an ouzo chaser; now do it all again in base six. "You call that explaining?"

"Yes."

"But I know all that."

"Yes."

Don sighed. "In other words, you don't know, do you? You're as much in the dark as I am."

"With respect." The hair gave him a reproachful look. "Please bear in mind that I am no more than a hair from your head, into which you have temporarily channelled the supernatural abilities you're currently drawing from the T317G transponder unit. I can do magic, but I can't work miracles."

"Oh. Can't you?"

"No."

He thought about it for a moment. "You can do stuff I can't, but you only know what I know."

The hair beamed at him. "Correct. And very well put, if I may say so."

"Fine." He didn't feel quite so drunk. Instead, he felt hungover, which was worse. "All right," he said. "Granted you don't *know*, but would you care to speculate? Hazard a guess, maybe?"

The hair formed a chin for itself and rubbed it. "If you ask me," it said, "something isn't quite right around here."

Don waited in case there was more, but there wasn't. "Thanks ever so much," he said. "I guess I won't be needing you any more. Can you . . ."

The hair thing shrank, smaller and shorter, and vanished. Without counting Don couldn't be sure, but he had an idea he now had an extra hair on the top of his head.

"Police," the Briggs woman said. Normal service had evidently been resumed. Pity.

"Don't do that," Don said quickly. "Look, you'll have to forgive my sister. Sometimes she gets these fixations on people."

"Shut up, Don. And you, whoever you are, you go ahead and call who you like. Come to think of it, I've got Alan Stevens' number on my mobile." She paused and glared at the Briggs female. "You know Alan. Short bloke with a neck like a turkey."

"I should think so," she replied icily. "He's my boyfriend."

The rest of the suggestion (Get Alan over here. He'll vouch for me and tell you you're an imposter or you don't exist.) suddenly lost its appeal, so she didn't make it. Ms Briggs, meanwhile, was feeling about in her handbag, presumably for her phone. There was just one last thing she could think of to try, so she said, "Did you write *HELP* in my diary?"

She had the phone in her hand, but she wasn't pressing buttons. "What did you just say?"

"Someone wrote *HELP* in my diary," Polly said. "In big red letters."

"Green."

"I beg your pardon?"

"Not big red letters. Green letters." Ms Briggs was frowning, not anger this time, but concern. "Was that you?"

Polly shook her head. "I promise you, it wasn't," she said. "All right, how about this? Do you make cups of coffee for yourself, and then, if you leave the room and come back, someone's been and drunk them?"

Ms Briggs' face suddenly went very pale. "No," she said.

"Oh."

"No," she repeated. "But quite often, if I leave the room, when I come back there's a coffee on my desk, and I know I didn't make it."

Polly found she could scarcely breathe. "Milk and one sugar?"

Ms Briggs nodded. "Bit too much milk for my taste, actually." Her frown deepened, and it looked like she'd forgotten about the phone completely. "Listen," she said. "Sometimes I open a file to do a job, and—"

"You find someone's already done it for you," Polly said in a rush. "Or you get a call from a purchaser's solicitor about a letter—"

"I know I haven't written yet. Oh God," Ms Briggs said solemnly. "This is so creepy."

"Excuse me," Don said.

They both shushed him precisely simultaneously; in context, creepier still. At least it had the effect of shutting them both up long enough for him to say, "Ms Briggs. Rachel. Your brother plays the guitar, right?"

She nodded.

"Just a hobby?"

"Yes," she replied, "he's terrible at it. That's why he works in insurance." She hesitated then added, "But when he was a kid, he really wanted to be a musician. Why?"

"Musician," Don replied. "As in playing in a band, that sort of thing?"

She nodded. "Actually," she added, "he really fancied writing songs, but Dad insisted— What's that got to do with anything?"

"I write songs," Don said quietly. "Or at least right now I'm doing more sort of jingles. But writing songs is what I've always wanted to do. Ever since I was small."

Little wheels were going round behind Ms Briggs' eyes. Eventually they stopped, and – "Where's Kevin?" she asked. "He should be here."

Silence, brittle as an icicle. Then, "Yes," Don said. "Yes, he should."

"Something's going on, isn't it?" There was a distinct change in Ms Briggs' voice. Anger was turning into fear, the way sugar ferments into alcohol. Probably not good. "It's all right," Polly said, and realised as soon as the words had passed the gate of her teeth that if any statement could make matters worse, that was it. She added, "Honestly," but for some reason that didn't help. Ms Briggs had remembered that she was holding her phone. Indeed, she was covering both of them with it, as if it was a gun.

"You're weird, both of you," she said. "I'm calling the police."

Later, Don was rather proud of what he said next, or at least the way he said it. Calmly, reasonably. Not tripping over his words. "Really," he said. "And what are you going to tell them?"

Like a fish hook in her lip, the point had caught her for a moment. "That my brother's missing, and you two freaks—"

"He's out," Polly said. "That's not quite the same as missing, is it? I mean," she went on, "you don't say, 'I'm just going missing to the shops. I'll be back in ten minutes.' Just because he's not here right now doesn't mean anything bad's happened."

Gradually it dawned on Ms Briggs that her phone wasn't loaded. She lowered it. "What about you?" she barked at Polly. "You've been spying on me at work. That's harassment."

Polly sighed. "Please," she said, "will you just listen to me for a moment? I haven't been spying on you, or stalking you, or anything like that. I really do work for BRHD. And clearly you do too. Look, can't you see there's something really strange happening, and we're both caught up in it? So really we should be on the same side, not snarling at each other. Together, we might be able to figure it out."

Ah, Don thought, the United Nations approach. And if only it worked, what a wonderful world this would be. As it was, he could see that Ms Briggs had a severe case of weirdness poisoning, and any moment now she was going to do something all of them would end up regretting. In which case there was really only one thing he could do.

"Hey," Ms Briggs snapped. "What are you—"

But by then Don had yanked out one of his hairs and spat on it, and it was starting to grow.

"Won't take a jiffy," he said cheerfully, and it didn't. When the hair was the size of a small French stick, with dear little arms and legs and the funniest little bobble for a head, he said, "Freeze time," and the hair just looked at him.

At which point it occurred to him that it probably wasn't the same hair as last time. In fact, the odds were several hundred thousand to one. A frantic rummage through his memory produced a phrase. "Slow-Me-Down," he added quickly.

"Oh, right," the hair said, and time froze.

"That's a tenner you owe me," said the hair.

Under other circumstances Don would have pointed out that twelve into seventy-nine ninety-nine wasn't ten, even allowing for VAT and carriage, but just then he was in no mood to quibble. "Fine," he said. "And thanks. Now, how do we get out of here?"

The hair looked at him, then at the two motionless women. "I'd run for it if I was you," the hair said.

"What about Polly? I can't just leave her here."

The hair grew shoulders and shrugged them. "If you say so," it said. "Don't see the problem myself, but you're the doctor." It thought for a moment, then said, "You'll just have to carry her."

"Oh." Not the reply he'd been expecting. "You couldn't..."

"No."

The hair seemed pretty definite about that, so there didn't seem to be much point trying to negotiate. "Fine," he said sadly, and considered the best way to do it.

Several false starts. At the moment of freezing Polly had just taken a step back. One arm was by her side, the other was sticking out at an inconvenient angle. You couldn't call her fat exactly, not if you didn't want shouting and tears and angst for a fortnight. Big bones. Anyway, when he tried just grabbing hold and lifting, he got little coloured lights in front of his eyes and had to stop for a moment to catch his breath. In the end he managed to tip her sideways until she sort of fell across his shoulder, then straightened his legs and staggered towards the door, which was shut. He didn't dare loosen his hold on whatever it was he was holding on to (he really didn't want to know), so he looked round for the hair, which was examining itself in a mirror, and said, "Excuse me."

"What?"

"You couldn't just get the door for me?"

"What? Oh, right."

On the stairs he almost collided with the middle-aged lady who lived on the top floor. She stared.

"Afternoon," he said brightly. "Sorry, can I just squeeze past?"

The woman shuffled sideways, and as he crept by her, his shoulder in agony, she said, "What—"

He sighed. "I've told her a thousand times," he said. "I told her, if you do that, one of these days you'll stick like it. But would she listen? Oh sorry, was that your foot?"

He hurried past, straight down to street level, propped Polly up against the front door and said, "All right, you can unfreeze."

Whereupon Polly squeaked and fell over him, and he felt a tiny tingle in his scalp, which he hoped meant the hair had gone back where it belonged. Polly stood up, looked at him and said, "What the hell just happened?"

He sighed. "We escaped," he replied. "Which is good. On the other hand, that Briggs woman now knows who I am and where I live, so I can't go back there any more, and it looks like this whole mess just got weirder. Come on," he added, grabbing her sleeve. "Let's get away from here before she comes looking for us."

They caught a bus at the end of the road. The top deck was

empty, so they were able to hold an extended council of war without the risk of being overheard. "That was magic, wasn't it?" Polly said. "You did magic to get us out of there."

Little Miss Tact. "Not necessarily," he said. "Look, forget about it, will you? And tell me what that stuff about Blue Remembered Hills was all about."

She frowned, not at him but past him. "Actually," she said, "I've got a theory about that. Trouble is, it's so utterly bizarre I don't even want to admit I'm capable of thinking of it. If it's true..." She shuddered. "Don, let's pretend none of this is happening. It'd be so much better."

"If only," he replied sadly. "But I can't. I disappeared that miserable cow's brother, remember? Let's hear your theory. It can't be screwier than the one I've got."

"Well." She took a deep breath. "Suppose you're an employer," she said, looking past him out of the window. "Your biggest overhead is the wage bill, right? Say you employ five people at forty-five thousand a year, plus pension and National Insurance contributions and all the trimmings. So that's around a quarter of a million quid. Lot of money, yes?"

Don nodded. "So?"

"So," Polly said, "all that expense comes about because these people are working for you..." She screwed up her face with the effort of getting her head around what she wanted to say. "In parallel" was the best she could come up with. "Five people in five offices drawing five wage packets. But what if you could have those five people working for you *simultaneously?* For example," she said quickly, as though the words tasted really bad and she wanted to get rid of them as soon as possible, "suppose you had your offices on the site of an interdimensional rift, where alternative realities somehow intersect. Suppose you had five different *versions* of the same employee, in five different dimensions, all sitting at the same desk in the same chair at the same time, but each one of them doing different work?"

Don's eyebrows shot up. "It'd be the same as having five employees, but—"

"You'd only be paying them one wage," Polly said, "one lot of NI stamps, one lot of pension contributions. Fifty K a year wage bill instead of a quarter-million." Suddenly she grinned. "Job sharing," she said, "taken to its logical conclusion."

"That's..." Don paused. "Actually, that's pretty neat," he said. "Or it would be, if only it wasn't impossible. Which it is, thank God."

"Not with magic."

For some reason that really annoyed him. "Just shut up about bloody magic, will you? Forget about it, it's just – well, technology. Pretty useless technology at that. It doesn't work the way you think it does."

"How do you know that?" she objected, sounding somewhat miffed. "Just because you can't get it to work. You were the same about broadband when it first came in."

"It's nothing like—"

"You couldn't get it to run," Polly reminisced pitilessly, "therefore it was fundamentally flawed. It couldn't ever be made to work, and in six months' time everybody'd have forgotten about it and moved on to something else. And all the time you were plugging the yellow lead into the wrong socket."

"Anyway," Don said firmly, "so that's your theory." He pulled a deep-in-thought face, but it was hardly convincing, and Polly wasn't convinced.

"Admit it," she said. "You're scared stiff, aren't you?"

There was a world of relief in his single quick nod of the head. "Petrified," he replied. "Not so much fear of getting killed or horribly mutilated, though those are experiences I could definitely do without. It's more..." He paused, concentrating fiercely on the search for the right words. "It's like I'm Columbus and I've reached the edge of the world and my ship's just about to sail over it and drop off, and I'm saying to myself,

This can't be right, I know the world is bloody round so why is this happening to me? And also," he added painfully, "I killed that aggravating woman's brother."

"You don't know that. He could be—"

"And I came within a whisker of killing her too," he went on, riding over her reassurance like a tank crossing a fence. "Could've done it so easily, just because she was in the way and getting so far up my nose she was practically coming out of my ear. I had to stop myself." He closed his eyes for a moment. "You know what? It took a real effort. It made me realise something about myself. There's times when the only thing stopping me from doing bad stuff is being afraid of getting caught or found out. But suppose there was no risk of that. It bothers me a lot."

"Glad to hear it," Polly said crisply. "Look at me and tell me the truth. Did you use magic to get us out of there?"

He nodded. "Also, I tried to use it to look for clues. Did me a fat lot of good, though."

"So you really can—" She stopped. "But you don't want to. Fair enough." The bus had stopped, and she looked out of the window. Snarled up in traffic. With magic you could do something about that. You could make the bus sprout wings, could you? Her intuition told her that you probably couldn't, or if you did, they'd just flap up and down and the bus would stay resolutely earth-bound. Magic could get you out of traffic, but only if you vanished all the other road users. Of course, there were people who'd do that, and presumably that was why magic wasn't used, and why it was kept a secret. "So," she said, "what about my theory?"

"I don't know," he replied. "I guess it fits the facts as we know them, but it's pretty hard to swallow. I mean, think about it for a moment. If you could access other dimensions and do all that stuff, would you really need to piddle about saving on wages? Surely you'd have better things to do."

She looked down at her feet. "I suppose so," she said. "Or you could ask, since we can put men on the moon and do micro-surgery and build amazing computers and manipulate DNA and I don't know what else, surely it's ridiculous to imagine we'd still be fighting wars and allowing millions of people to starve to death and poisoning the atmosphere; surely we'd have more sense, if we were that clever? But I don't suppose it works quite like that. Suppose magic's just better technology. What do people do with wonderful technology? They patent it, so they can keep it all to themselves, and then they figure out how to use it to make money. Maybe magic can do all sorts of wonderful stuff, but it's not actually very useful commercially. Maybe it can't turn base metals into gold or mass-produce dollar bills or anything like that."

(He thought about the ten-pound note, debited from his bank account.)

"And maybe," she went on, "the only way you can get magic to *pay* is by using it to do petty, mean things, like paying five people one wage between them. That makes sense, doesn't it? Because otherwise..." She frowned, concentrating like mad. "Magic exists, right? We're pretty sure about that. But magicians don't rule the world; only a few people know about it; there's no sign that it's being used all over the place. If it could be used to make money, don't you think that's what all the industrialists and entrepreneurs and miserable, craggy-faced men from *Dragons' Den* would be doing, right, left and centre? And they wouldn't bother being discreet about it, because the government'd be right behind them, because magic'd mean massive tax revenues and probably better weapons, not to mention a listening elf in every living room. I think it's only a deadly secret because nobody's found out how to get rich with it."

"Except your boss," Don said quietly.

She shook her head. "But he builds houses," she replied. "That's not magic. I mean, he hasn't got goblins and zombies

194 • Tom Holt

laying bricks and running up and down ladders, just a lot of eastern Europeans, like everybody else. He builds houses and then he sells them to people. He's made a lot of money, but only because he builds reasonable houses and sells them for a fair price. That's not magic, it's just business."

Don nodded. "So your theory doesn't stand up then," he said. "It fails the *why bother* test. Because it's a hell of a lot of trouble to go to, just to save—"

"Two hundred thousand pounds a year," she pointed out. "That's a lot of money."

"True." He scowled at his hands, folded in his lap. "But it's not that much. How much does your company charge for a smallish bungalow, say?"

"About two hundred thousand."

"And there you have it," Don said. "In the context of all the dosh he must be scooping in, it's not actually all that much. And you're saying that for this relatively small sum, he's playing silly buggers with the laws of reality as we understand them, quite possibly putting the stability of the space/time continuum at serious risk, not to mention all the work and effort he must've put into figuring out how to do it. I don't know," he confessed wearily. "If I was a wealthy, successful property developer, I don't think I'd bother trashing Newton and Einstein for less than seven figures. I'd just squeeze a couple more little boxes into my next development and save myself the aggravation."

For some reason she found that infuriating. "Fine," she snapped. "So what are you saying? I'm making it all up, or what?"

"No, of course not." He scratched his head in a despairing sort of a way. "But like you said yourself, it was just a theory. That's the trouble," he said angrily. "Magic, for crying out loud. There's no *rules*. Or if there are, we don't know them. It's like those stories where you're playing chess with Death with your life at stake. Only," he added bitterly, "it's not chess; it's Mornington bloody Crescent. It's not fair. There ought to be someone we could ask, or a number we could ring." Suddenly he leaned forward, a wild look on his face. "Maybe there is," he said. "Maybe it's as simple as that. Phone."

"What?"

"Your phone." He grabbed it out of her hand when she offered it. "You can access the Net on this thing, right?"

"Yes. You just—"

"I know." He was stabbing buttons. "Well, it's worth a try," he said. "It's just a matter of finding the right keywords to google." He paused, caught in the headlights of indecision. "How about...?"

"Commercial thaumaturgical consultants," Polly said.

He looked at her, impressed. "All right," he said. "We'll try that."

Polly's phone was three months old, practically antique. It took a frustratingly long time, but then...

"My God," she said in a tiny voice. "There's *dozens*."

Don was staring at the miniature screen. "You know what," he said. "I think we've just stumbled across a whole bloody industry. It's like finding one of those lost cities in the jungle."

Polly took the phone from him. "By the addresses," she said, "I reckon over half of these are in America." She frowned. "Germany, Australia, Japan, India. Not many round here, by the looks of it. Hang on, I'll refine the search." She tapped in "London." "That's more like it," she said. "That just leaves five."

"Five," Don repeated in a haunted voice. "Which means there's enough work in the magic business to keep at least five people full-time employed. That's—"

"How about this one?" Polly said. "'S. Gogerty, freelance commercial thaumaturgical consultant,' followed by a double helping of alphabet soup – FBASM, FRIW, all that stuff. Looks pretty impressive, don't you think?"

Don peered over her shoulder then shrugged. "Let's have a look," he said in a bewildered voice.

A rather plain website, austere even. Name, an expanded version of the list of meaningless qualifications, contact details, areas of expertise (temporal phase shift anomaly resolution, dimensional variance management, matter/energy disparity transposition – what the hell was all that about?), a brief CV, a tariff of charges.

"Better take a look at that," Don said.

A table of figures came up on the screen. They both stared at it for a moment. Then Don gave a low whistle.

"And I thought lawyers were expensive," Polly said.

"That's an awful lot of noughts chasing one lonely integer," Don agreed. "Hardly seems fair."

Polly looked at him. "We can't afford him," she said.

Don thought for a moment. "We'll have to," he said. "I mean, just look at all this stuff. I haven't got the faintest idea what any of it means, but you can tell just by glancing at it. It's complicated. Difficult. Technical. 'High-energy metamorphic resonance modulation,' for crying out loud. I have an idea that's the sort of thing you're not recommended to try at home with a Ouija board and a set of box spanners. Even if we knew where to start, we could do serious damage blundering about trying to DIY it. Worse," he added quietly, "than I've done already. And that's saying something."

Polly conceded the point with a slight nod. "I suppose people who do this stuff all the time have insurance to cover the costs," she said. "Wish we did."

"To hell with it," Don said. "I'm going to call him."

Polly wavered, then said, "All right. But no small talk, right? Nice-weather-we've-been-having-lately looks like it'd cost me a month's salary."

Don jotted down the phone number on the back of his cuff, then logged off the Net and pecked it in.

*Ring ring*, then "You have reached Stanley Gogerty. I'm afraid I can't take your call right now –"

"Sod it," Don snarled.

"– but if you'd care to leave your name, species and number, I'll get back to you as soon as—"

"Species," Polly repeated. "I do so hope that's supposed to be a joke."

Don recorded a brief message, then rang off. "Well," he said, "you never know. He might be the answer to our prayers, he might not. Anyway, we tried. Beyond that, I really don't know what we can do next."

"Go home," Polly replied.

"That's all right for you," Don said sourly. "I can't. That Briggs woman's probably got my flat surrounded by police marksmen by now. I'll have to stay at your place for the time being."

"Oh." Brief moment in which Polly failed to refute the suggestion that this wasn't the best news she'd ever heard in her life. "Of course, yes, you're welcome. Only..."

"Only what?"

"No, that's fine," Polly said firmly. "You're my brother and we're both in this together. Just..."

"Just?"

She pulled ever such a sad little face. "*Please* can you try and remember to put the toilet seat down after you've—"

"Yes, all right."

"And try not to overfill the bath, because the water slops out over the side. And if you have to use the cooker while I'm not there—"

"It's all right," Don said. "I can go and sleep in a cardboard box in a shop doorway somewhere."

"There's no need to be like that about it. All I'm asking is—"

"I think this is our stop," Don said firmly. "Come on."

★ ★ ★

Five minutes after Mr Gogerty had left him, Uncle Theo got up from his comfy armchair, padded across the room, opened a cupboard, dug about like a dog in a rat hole and came out with a small tin, the sort that small drills, screws and Rawlplugs tend to nest in. He opened it and took out a pear-shaped red jewel, which he laid flat on the palm of his hand. He sighed.

"So what are we doing," Kevin asked, "being chickens?"

The hen, whose name apparently was Mary Byron, looked at him. "Let me guess," she said. "You're some sort of musician."

"How did you—"

"Well?"

"Yes," Kevin said. "I play the guitar. Well, it's a hobby. There was a time when I thought I could make a—"

"And you've got a sister," Ms Byron went on, "who's a lawyer."

If he hadn't been gripped by an unconquerable urge to look round for foxes, Kevin would have stared at her. "That's right," he said. "How in God's name...?"

Ms Byron clucked sternly. "The cockerel you met earlier," she said, "his real name's Charles Mynott-Harrison and he used to be the conductor of the Liverpool Philharmonic. His sister was once a partner in Broadhead and Symes, specialising in mergers and acquisitions. That's her," she added, jabbing her beak in the direction of a sad-looking hen with no tail feathers and a drooping comb, "over there. Next to her, the Plymouth Rock with the twisted beak, that's Ginny Speke, commercial leaseholds with Steinway Ross. Her brother was the drummer with Painted Roses, if you can remember them. Very big in the late eighties."

Kevin's throat was dry. "What happened?"

She pecked up a speck of grit. "This is a farmyard, Mr

Briggs," she said, "which means the rules are different from what you've been used to. If you have more than one cockerel in a farmyard, they fight." She paused to nibble behind her wing. "Charles won."

"Oh."

"In fact," she went on, "I'm rather surprised he let you go. Funny, really. By all accounts he was a very promising young conductor – built up quite a reputation with the Mahler symphonies. These days..." She shrugged. "I'd watch out for him if I were you," she said. "Of course, in a day or two you'll probably be challenging him yourself. If," she added meaningfully, "you last that long."

"Oh my God."

"There's a pattern to it, you see," Ms Byron went on. "All the hens here used to be solicitors. And all the cocks were their brothers and something to do with music. About thirty-six hours after they get here, their memories of being human are completely wiped."

"Except yours."

A very odd look came into Ms Byron's perfectly round eyes. "No," she said. "That's the funny thing. My memory went earlier than most, as a matter of fact. I'm not sure how long I've been here, but when I arrived it was winter, so it's been a while, and all that time I was convinced I was a chicken, always had been. It'd never have occurred to me that I was one of Them once. Then, quite suddenly, not long before you showed up –" she stood on one leg, using her free foot to scrabble at her tummy "– it all came back to me, wham, like it'd never been away. Very odd indeed. Doesn't seem like any of the others are remembering anything, though. I've asked them, and all they say is 'cluck.' Which is also odd," she added, "because before I could understand them perfectly. In chicken language, I mean. Excuse me," she added. "I need to go and lay an egg. I'll be back in a few minutes. Don't go away."

Kevin didn't want to be left alone, but he really didn't want to be present at the birth, so he edged away into the corner of the run and pretended to be very interested in a small pile of rat droppings (which wasn't very hard, actually, and he was surprised he'd never taken an intelligent interest in rat droppings before, because they were really quite fascinating. No, he ordered himself, stop that, right now) until he became aware of a shadow falling across him.

"You looking at me?" said a horribly familiar voice.

Knowing it was really the former conductor of the Liverpool Philharmonic should have taken all the terror and mortal dread out of it, but it didn't. Instead, he remembered Ms Byron saying *if you have more than one cockerel in a farmyard, they fight.* He told himself, To hell with it. I'm a goddamn chartered actuary, I can take a sissy conductor with one wing tied behind my back. The shadow moved a little, blotting out the light. Oh no, I couldn't, he thought.

"I asked you a question," said the voice. "You looking at me or what?"

Exactly how long, he wondered, does it take to lay an egg? Perhaps Ms Byron would come back and save him. Perhaps not. She hadn't stuck her neck out to save the drummer of the Painted Roses, so presumably either she didn't care or there was nothing she could do.

"What you looking at?" said the cockerel, and his voice was a cracked record, a recorded message. "You looking at me?"

Kevin turned round slowly. The erstwhile Mahler-botherer was very big and his spurs were very long and sharp. "Now I am," Kevin said, and if his voice was a bit high and squeaky, it could have been higher and squeakier. "Big deal. I'm so impressed."

"What did you just say?"

Oh well, Kevin thought. It really couldn't matter less, but since he had the choice, he'd prefer the last thing he heard to be his own voice, saying something cutting and sardonic. "I said," he replied, barely high and only very slightly squeaky, "that you take the second movement of Mahler's Third way too fast. It's a piece of classical music, not a drag race. Also, you clearly can't tell a bassoon from a rocket-propelled grenade, because you make the third movement sound like the Paris rush hour. As for the violin solo in the first—"

The cockerel was taut with fury. "Take that back," he said.

"I will not," Kevin said. "And you may notice I'm speaking very loudly and very slowly, because you're clearly as deaf as a post, otherwise you couldn't have failed to notice what a bog you made of the opening of 'Das Lied Von Der Erde.' The plain fact is, you couldn't conduct a bus."

The cockerel quivered. "You can't say that to me," he said. "That's totally unfair. The *New York Times* compared me to Karajan."

Kevin smiled. "They must've meant Hank Karajan," he said. "Minor country and western star, had a voice like a pig in a blender. Or maybe they were thinking of Howling Bill Klemperer. Mind you, if I were Hank or Howling Bill I'd sue over that. At least they were *professionals*."

Big chickens don't cry. Neither do small ones. No tear ducts. But the cockerel's eyes were red and puffy, and was that a tiny teardrop soaking into its cheek feathers? Hang on, Kevin thought.

"You," he snapped. "Tell me your name."

"You know perfectly well," the cockerel replied, and his words constituted a genuine, authentic snivel.

"Tell me anyway. Come on," Kevin barked. "What's your bloody name?"

"Charles Mynott-Harrison," the cockerel snuffled. "And I think you're perfectly horrible, and I can't begin to imagine why you're picking on me like this, I haven't done anything to—"

He stopped in mid-whine. A light had come on behind those

202 • Tom Holt

empty button eyes. He started to look round for foxes, then stopped.

"Go on," said Kevin gently.

"I'm Charles Mynott-Harrison," the cockerel said, his voice heavy with wonder. "Oh my God, what am I doing here? What's happened to me? What are all these horrid *feathers*?"

Kevin tried to smile. The beak wouldn't let him, of course, but at least he could remember how a smile worked. "That," he said, "is a very good question. Allow me to introduce myself, by the way. I'm Kevin Briggs." He held out his hand, realised it was a wing, and tucked it away again. "You have no idea," he said, "how pleased I am to meet you. And I take it back about the slow movement."

"Really?"

"Trust me," Kevin said. He could see Ms Byron approaching, just as a frantic clucking from the direction of the hen house turned into a wail of horror and disgust, from which Kevin deduced that a lady solicitor had just laid an egg.

# CHAPTER TEN

M r Gogerty glanced at his watch.

There are any number of mail order catalogues where you can buy fancy watches: titanium-cased, extra-shockproof, special-forces-approved, with all manner of wonderful functions that only James Bond could ever find a use for. Mr Gogerty's watch didn't come from one of them. It was built by Feinwerkhaus of Suhl, back in the days when people really knew how to make stuff. It was small, plain to the point of austerity, with a blue steel case, white face, thin spring-steel blue hands – and three dials. That was the whole point. Mr Gogerty's watch (one of only nine ever made by the greatest watchmaker the world has ever seen) told the time in the present, the past and the future.

The middle dial told him it was a quarter past five, and he breathed a sigh of relief. The satnav built into his phone (Beckmesser & Schmidt of Augsburg, a hundred years before Marconi was born, but that's another story) told him he was where he needed to be: 47 New Road, Sidmouth, Devon, standing in front of SpeediKleen Dry Cleaners, est. 1975. The last bit made him smile, a special trade-only grin that about a dozen people in the whole world would have understood properly.

Right, he said to himself. Here goes.

He pushed the door, and a little bell rang as he walked into what looked like every ma-and-pa dry cleaners he'd ever been in, from Reykjavik to Tierra del Fuego. There was a counter, well used rather than shabby; a rack behind it, half-filled with carefully lynched garments in their blue polythene shrouds; a till. If this was, as he suspected, the fulcrum of multiple intersecting realities, there wasn't exactly a lot to see. Mr Gogerty, however, knew better than to rely on appearances.

A man, late middle age, short, thinning grey hair, thick-lensed glasses, a beige cardigan with carefully patched elbows, carpet slippers; but Mr Gogerty, who treated chimeras and manticores as though they were badly trained Yorkshire terriers, took a step back as he approached. The man was positively saturated, marinaded in chronomorphic resonances, enough to trigger a Brigadoon syndrome big enough to dislocate San Francisco. He tried to pull himself together, but his voice shook a little as he said, "Mr Williams?"

The man hadn't been expecting that, almost as if nobody had called him by his name for a very long time. "That's me," he said.

"My name's Gogerty. Is there somewhere we can talk?"

Mr Williams frowned. "How do you mean?"

"Privately. Where we won't be disturbed."

Confusion, apprehension. Mr Williams tensed up like a clenched fist. "You from the council?"

"Yes," Mr Gogerty replied.

"Oh."

"I need to ask you some questions," Mr Gogerty said. "About the shop. You understand, I'm sure."

Mr Williams nodded as though he had lead bricks taped to the back of his head. Something he'd been dreading for a long time was about to happen. "You'd better come through into the back," he said. "Just a tick." He edged past Mr Gogerty and turned the sign in the window to CLOSED. "We in trouble, then?"

Deep breath, because he was about to do something rather mean and cruel, though clearly it had to be done. "I'm sure we can sort something out," he said. "But you're going to have to be completely honest with me. Do you understand?"

Mr Williams nodded. "I'd better call Eileen," he said. "I suppose you'll be wanting to talk to her as well."

"Not necessarily," Mr Gogerty said. "It may be possible to keep her out of this, if you really try hard and cooperate."

A flicker of hope behind those burning-glass lenses, and for the first time Mr Gogerty was grateful for the unique accident he'd suffered a few years back, as a result of which he no longer showed up in mirrors. Looking himself in the face wouldn't have been a comfortable experience. "You think so?"

"No promises," Mr Gogerty replied. "But like I just said, it really all depends on you."

The back room was comfortable, the way a pair of shoes is comfortable a month or so before it's only fit for the bin. Constant use had bent, strained, creased and warped everything in it into the shape of a routine that hadn't changed in a very long time. Mr Gogerty lowered himself into a tired-but-faithful-looking chair and took out a notebook and a pen.

"First things first," he said. "Full name and date of birth."

George Edward Williams, born in war and brought up in bombed-out streets, spoke slowly, calm as a steer waiting in a stall in a slaughterhouse. He told Mr Gogerty how he'd used his redundancy from the tyre factory to start up the business, how it had been everything he'd ever wanted until the day came when everything changed. He described it all, looking down at his feet or his hands, from the first terrible morning right down to the visions he'd seen in his downstairs toilet earlier that day. When he'd finished, he looked up and said, "That's all there is to it, really. We didn't mean anybody any harm," and Mr Gogerty, who'd seen it all and learned the hard way never, ever to get personally involved, silently vowed to put things right for Mr Williams and his wife, or die trying.

"I see," he said. "Now, I'd like you to look at this photograph and tell me if you recognise this man."

Mr Williams peered at the picture of Mr Huos then nodded firmly. "Oh, I know him," he said. "He was in the paper the other day."

"But have you ever seen him in the flesh, so to speak?"

"Oh yes. He was in here, not so long back. We were in London. He came in with a coat. Nice quality, decent bit of material. Nice bloke. Polite."

Mr Gogerty's throat was the Nullarbor in high summer. "Can you remember," he said, "if there was anything in the pockets?"

Blank look, then suspicion began to seep in. Mr Williams might be placid by nature – had to be, to have stayed sane all those years – but he clearly wasn't stupid. "Don't think so," he said. "Why? What's that got to do with anything?"

"It's very important," Mr Gogerty said, and managed to stop himself adding, "trust me," because anyone as smart as Mr Williams would instinctively know that anybody who says 'trust me' is likely to be about as trustworthy as a petrol station watch. "Are you sure you can't remember? You seem to have a remarkably good memory."

Mr Williams frowned. "Yes," he said. "Matter of fact, I do. Which is a bit funny," he went on, "because before, well, It –" he paused and a very slight shudder passed through him "– I had a very bad memory. Eileen used to make jokes about it. Memory like a tea bag, she used to say. But not nowadays," he said. "I can remember stuff now like it was yesterday."

Of course he could, Mr Gogerty didn't explain, because to all intents and purposes every day since the initial temporal excursion *was* yesterday. "So," he pressed on, "if there had been something in this man's coat pockets, you'd remember."

"Might do." Very suspicious. Any moment now, he'll ask for ID. Which wouldn't be a problem, of course. Mr Gogerty carried identity cards for all major intelligence and law enforcement agencies, and 90 percent of them were quite genuine. "But anyhow," he went on, "if there had been, we'd have given it back to him. We're very particular about that."

Mr Gogerty nodded. "Of course," he said. "I expect you've got a system for when that happens."

"Oh yes." Mr Williams leaned back a little in his chair, knowing he was on safe ground. "Anything that's left in a pocket, we put it in a plastic bag with the job number on it, in a box under the counter next to the ticket tray. Then, when a customer comes in to collect, we always check the box before we hand the garment back, just to see if there's a bag with that number on it."

"That's a good system," Mr Gogerty said.

"Never had any complaints," Mr Williams replied. "Well," he added sadly, "we never get any complaints about anything, cos we're always gone the next day. But we're very careful about customers' things. Got to be. Position of trust, you see."

"Quite," Mr Gogerty said. "But just supposing – and I'm not implying anything, this is just for argument's sake – just supposing there had been something in that coat pocket and for some reason you didn't give it back, then there's a good chance it'd still be in your box, right?"

Mr Williams didn't like that question at all. "Well, I suppose it might be, yes. But like I just told you, we're extra-specially careful about stuff like that. And ninety-nine times out of a hundred, we'd remember anyway, without needing to look."

Suddenly Mr Gogerty's throat was very tight. Forming the next words he spoke made the tendons in his neck rub against each other, like cables. "Maybe we should just go through your box to make sure," he said.

He'd blown it. Mr Williams' forehead crinkled up, like paper in a fire. "You did say you're from the council," he said.

"That's right. Trading standards. And planning." Mr Gogerty pulled out his card wallet (Zauberwerke AG of Hallstadt; only four made, and then they had to blow up the whole valley, just to seal the rift), flicked through and found what he was looking for. East Devon District Council and a photograph of him looking as though he'd just been taken down off the gallows. "I'm afraid I'm going to have to insist, Mr Williams," he said. "This is a very serious business. Naturally, I don't want to have to involve the police, but..."

The P-word. Does it every time. Here was a man who'd just watched two knights beating each other up with swords over and over again in his toilet and could still function normally, but threaten him with the police and he fell apart. The British, Mr Gogerty thought, God bless them.

"Maybe you could ask your wife if she can spare me a moment," he said.

"No, that's all right." Mr Williams' eyes closed, just for a moment. "Come on through."

It was just a box. Once it had held two dozen packets of Walkers crisps. Mr Williams put it down on the counter, then started looking in the book for the ticket number. Someone was banging on the shop door, some poor fool whose laundry was hanging on the rail, presumably. Mr Williams looked up, but Mr Gogerty shook his head.

"Here you go," Mr Williams said. "Ticket number 776598. It'll be on the plastic bag, if it's there."

The search didn't take long. There were only five bags in the box, and none of them had that number on it. Not that Mr Gogerty needed to look. If it had been there, he'd have felt it through his fingertips like gripping a wet electric fence.

"That's fine," he said wearily. "Sorry to have bothered you."

Not there, he thought (and took a small black disc, a little smaller than a pound coin, out of his shirt pocket, slipped it into the palm of his hand and clenched his fingers round it). Which meant that either his entire hypothesis was wrong or else it had left Mr Huos' coat pocket and somehow found its way—

"Can you tell me," he said, looking away, "anything about the other customers who left stuff to be cleaned, the day that

Mr . . . that the man whose picture I showed you came in? Just basic information," he added, throwaway voice, no big deal. "Just names and addresses, that sort of thing."

Mr Williams looked shocked and scared. "I don't know," he muttered. "I mean, it was a long time ago."

"No, it wasn't," Mr Gogerty said pleasantly. "Also, I'm sure you make a note of that sort of thing. It seems to me you've got a really impressive routine going here, very orderly and methodical. I imagine you write down all the names and addresses so you can be sure people get their things back – if they don't come in to collect, for example, before you move on. A conscientious man like you, I'm sure you take a lot of trouble over just that kind of detail." He smiled, all teeth and predator DNA. "You don't strike me as the computerised type, so it'd either be a book or index cards. Well?"

Like watching a very small giant trying to carry the weight of a very large planet on his shoulders, you could see him gradually buckle and give way. "Book," Mr Williams said. "There, on the counter, the blue one. You'll have to excuse my handwriting."

"No problem," Mr Gogerty said. He was already standing over the book, reaching for it. "Let's see," he said. "Date order. Well, we know the date. Here we are." He ran his finger down the list. Ten customers, not a particularly busy day. Mr Huos had been the fifth. While he was at it, he pressed the locator device he'd palmed earlier on to the underside of the counter. "I'll just take a picture of this page," he said, slipping his phone out of his inside pocket. "There, all done. Thank you very much; you've been extremely helpful."

Mr Williams frowned at him. "That's it?"

"For now," Mr Gogerty said. "I may need to talk to you again."

"How'll you find me? I haven't got a clue where we'll fetch up next."

Another of those smiles. "Oh, that won't be a problem." Nor

would it be, with the handy 5D transponder unit clinging to the underside of the counter like a Borg limpet.

"Is there..." Mr Williams tried to look him in the eye but couldn't quite manage it. "Is there anything anybody can do? To stop it, I mean?"

Mr Gogerty shivered, but not so anybody'd notice. "No promises," he said, "but there may be. If I can, I will. I give you my word."

"Thanks."

"Don't thank me yet," Mr Gogerty said. "We're not out of the woods, not by a long chalk. Still, there are various approaches we can try."

Mr Williams swallowed hard, almost like someone choking back tears. "I feel better just for knowing someone else knows about it," he said. "It's been difficult, keeping it to ourselves all this time."

Difficult. What a word to choose. The kind of pressure required to crush everything he must have been through into 'difficult' would be enough to turn a red giant into a black hole.

Mr Williams went with him to the door, unlocked it, even opened it for him. "I'll be in touch," Mr Gogerty said, as he stood with one foot on carpet, the other on pavement.

"Will you?"

"Oh yes."

"You couldn't..." Big spaniel eyes. "You know, give us a clue where we're going next."

"Sorry," Mr Gogerty replied. "Rules, you know."

"Ah, right. Hope you don't mind me asking."

What an appalling existence, Mr Gogerty thought, as he walked away. Like what would happen if the Tardis' navigation system got replaced by the computer that runs baggage handling at Heathrow. The theory that was gradually building in his mind would explain most of it, fitted 90 percent of the established facts. If it proved to be correct, it was all Mr Huos' fault. Maybe he could nudge Mr Huos into a nice, neighbourly ex gratia compensation payment, when it was all over. When. If.

Before anything fuzzy and heart-warming could happen, however, he had to do the job he was being paid for, and his best and only lead was the wodge of digital information stored in his phone: the customers who'd brought clothes in to be cleaned on the same day Mr Huos took in his coat. Plain, ordinary investigation, simple legwork, *Rockford Files* stuff.

He found a low wall to sit on, took out his phone and called up the picture he'd taken of the page in Mr Williams' book. He concentrated on the first name on the list.

The first name was Kevin Briggs.

She understood protocol the way a fish understands water. All good lawyers do; it's the element that gave them birth and nourishes them, from which they came and to which they will ultimately return. This morning, however, she was hopping mad. So, instead of knocking and waiting for Alan's reedy "Come" to filter through the woodwork, she clubbed the door with the heel of her hand, twisted the handle as if killing poultry and burst in.

Alan was on the phone. She scowled at him. He flinched as though she'd just hit him but carried on with his call. Angrily she dropped into a chair and started picking at the frayed upholstery.

He wasn't the most sensitive man on the planet, but he had the good sense to wind his call up quickly and put the phone down. "Rachel," he said.

She raked him with a glare. "Where were you last night?" she said.

The sort of question no fiancé likes to have staring him in the face first thing in the morning. Luckily his conscience was clear. "I had a late meeting at Burridge's," he replied. "Why?"

"I rang you at eleven."

"I didn't get home till gone midnight."

212 · Tom Holt

"Your mobile was off."

"Like I said, I was in a meeting."

She took a deep breath and let it go, and with it went a certain proportion of her rage. "The most extraordinary thing happened last evening," she said. "That's why I was trying to get hold of you."

"You should've left—" He didn't bother to complete the recommendation. Rachel didn't leave messages. He had an idea she saw it as a sign of weakness. "What happened?"

Her frown deepened. "I met this madwoman," she said. "Total nutter. And Kevin's disappeared."

Item, one silver lining, Alan didn't say. If his future brother-in-law really had vanished off the face of the earth, it'd be a sweet, beautiful thing and a cause for lasting joy. Highly unlikely of course. "Oh?" he said.

"I found the madwoman in Kevin's flat."

Figures, Alan thought. Any woman would have to be mad to go there, or at least utterly desperate. "New girlfriend?"

She shook her head so fiercely it was a miracle she didn't centrifuge her brain. "She claimed she works here," she said.

You don't have to be mad to work here, Alan was tempted to argue. Wisely he didn't. "She doesn't, I take it."

"Of course she doesn't. Listen," she added, and told the story. Being a lawyer, she knew how to pick out the salient facts and arrange them in due order. When she'd finished, she had his undivided attention.

"That's mad," he said.

"The disturbing thing is," Rachel went on, "how much she knew about me. Obviously she's been in my office – more than once, quite likely."

"One of the cleaners?"

"Doubt it. I know all the cleaners by sight. I'm usually here when they come round, after all."

Rachel was a great one for working late. Until she'd joined the company, Alan had held the coveted Last Man Sitting award for voluntary unpaid overtime. These days, he wasn't in the running. "You're sure you didn't recognise her?"

"Of course I didn't. Don't be ridiculous." She picked a pencil off his desk, broke it in two and dropped it in the bin provided. "You haven't seen anybody hanging round the place lately, have you?"

He shook his head. "She could've been here for a meeting," he suggested. "There's people in here all the time."

"Not roaming around the place sneaking into people's rooms," she snapped. "And anyway, why would anybody want to do something like that? It's not like I'm a movie star or a TV presenter or anything. It's weird."

Alan racked his brains for some useful contribution he could make. "Have you noticed if anything's gone missing?" he asked. "Not anything big necessarily. That's what stalkers do, I gather. They just like to take things. Underwear, mostly, but—"

"Shut up, Alan; you're not helping," Rachel said with a shiver. "And I'm not in the habit of keeping my knickers in my desk drawer, thank you so much." She frowned thoughtfully. "Actually," she said, "stuff *has* been disappearing lately, but it's the sort of stuff you don't think twice about. You know – staples and envelopes, rubber bands, that sort of thing."

"That's just being in an office," Alan pointed out.

"Maybe. Also," she added, "someone keeps making me cups of coffee."

"Ah." That sounded a bit more like it. "It didn't taste funny, did it?"

She shook her head. "I assumed it was Pauline," she replied.

"Pauline never makes me coffee."

"Well, no," Rachel replied. "She's there to answer the phone and do photocopying, not run a buffet service. I just thought ..." She shrugged. "I don't know," she said. "Maybe we ought to involve the police."

The look on Alan's face told her what he thought of that idea. What is it about men and not making a fuss till it's too late? Too late, she thought, and the implications weren't very nice. "Well, we've got to tell *someone*," she said firmly. "After all, if there's a weirdo wandering about the office, we can't just ignore it and hope it stops. Something'll have to be done about it."

Alan nodded slowly. "You're quite right," he said. "Who do you suggest we go to?"

She gave him a stern look. "Well," she said, "I've just gone to you, because you're my head of department. Far be it from me..."

"All right," he said wearily. "I guess I'll have to talk to Mr Huos about it."

There was more than a hint of fear in his voice. Pathetic, she thought. Chicken. "Also," she said, "I want you to come with me this evening when I go round to the flat directly under Kevin's. I want to see if that man I told you about really lives there."

Oh what fun. "I don't think that's such a good idea," Alan said quickly. "I mean, what if...?"

"Fine. I'll call the police then."

She'd trapped him neatly, caught him between his terror of physical confrontation and his morbid dread of getting mixed up in trouble-with-the-police. She was interested, from a purely psychological and sociological point of view, to see which dilemma-horn he'd ultimately choose to impale himself on.

"Tonight's a bad time for me," he said. "I've got this contract I really need to get finished."

She was almost proud of him; it was a valiant attempt. "I'll ring the police then."

"No."

(And for a moment she remembered what she'd once seen in him, before they got engaged and love duly atrophied. It takes character to be able to decide instinctively which of two very scary things you're most afraid of.)

"Then you'll come with me."

"Yes, all right."

She beamed at him, partly to reward obedience, partly from satisfaction that she'd already trained him so well. "Excellent," she said. "I'll meet you downstairs at half past six. And afterwards," she conceded sweetly, "you can buy me dinner."

On her way back to her office she reflected on the life choice she'd made when she induced him to propose, and decided that it was still valid. True, Alan did look a bit like he'd been shrunk in the wash and inexpertly dried over a radiator. On the other hand, he did what he was told. Five years of marriage and she'd have him chasing after sticks and fetching the daily paper in his mouth.

Back to her office, where she quickly churned through some routine trivia and had a refreshingly bracing run-in with a solicitor from Derby who phoned up to upbraid her for not sending him a copy of some inspection certificate or other. The stupid man swore blind he'd spoken to her only the day before yesterday and she'd promised faithfully the certificate would be in the DX that night.

"I don't think so," she'd replied sweetly. "In fact, I'm quite sure of it. What time did you call?"

"Just after eleven," the Derby man replied. "Got a note of it here, as a matter of fact. *Phoned BRHD 11:05 re cert; promised in post asap.* So..."

"Not possible," she cooed back at him. "You see, I'm looking at my diary for the day before yesterday, and it's reminding me that I was in a meeting from ten to 11:45. So, I don't know who you were talking to, but it most certainly wasn't me."

"Look, does it matter?" The Derby man sounded thoroughly rattled, which was how it should be. "I need that certificate as soon as possible, or I won't be able to complete on schedule."

"No problem," she trilled back at him. "I'll make sure it's in tonight's DX." Slight pause then, "Anything else I can help you with, or was that all?"

When the stupid man had rung off, with a muffled snorting

noise that she felt entirely justified in taking as an admission of defeat, she reached across her desk for her diary and flicked forward a page or two, just to remind herself what she'd be doing over the next few days. She was about to close the book when an entry caught her eye and made her frown. It was only *Lutterworth 10:30*, and she knew Mr Lutterworth was an accountant from Splice Watershed – vaguely, she remembered making the appointment – but the entry wasn't in her handwriting, nor was it a hand she recognised.

Someone had been writing in her diary. Another point for Alan to raise with Mr Huos. Better look and see if there had been any further violations. Sure enough, she found another one, for next Monday: *9:30 Stevens assessment.*

Her eyebrows shot up like oil prices. Stevens. Yes, nominally she had an appointment to see Alan to discuss the quality of her work over the past three months. It was a regular fixture; in fact, it had been in the course of the assessment before last that she'd finally choked a proposal of marriage out of him. But she'd have written *Alan*, and she'd have left out the demeaning *assessment*, and that most definitely wasn't her writing.

Nor, she realised, was it the same hand that had written *Lutterworth 10:30* on the previous page. *Two* people scribbling in her diary, one of them demonstrably creepy. She scowled horribly and went through the diary page by page, first the future, then the past. When she'd finished, she pushed the diary off the desk onto the floor as if it was crawling with spiders and instinctively wiped her hands on her sleeves.

Not just two entries in two different hands; there were *dozens* of them. Well, five at least. Furthermore (and this was the truly spooky bit) there were entries for appointments and meetings which she could clearly remember having made and written in herself, but which appeared on the diary page in handwriting most decidedly not her own, while of her own entries (she could practically see herself writing them down) there was no sign, not even Tipp-Ex splodges or the marks of rubbed-out pencil. Finally, to add insult to gross weirdness with intent to cause alarm and despondency, in the useful-phone-numbers section at the back of the diary, each of the interloping hands had written, in a different colour ink, the extraordinary line, *Which came first, the   or the   ?*

Mr Huos woke from a dream of acorn sandwiches and turnip sorbet to find he'd fallen asleep at his desk. He shook himself, rubbed his shoulder against the edge of the desk and reached for the phone.

"Mandy."

"Yes, Mr Huos?"

"Has Mr Gogerty called yet?"

"No, Mr Huos."

"Any messages at all?"

"Lots," Mandy replied succinctly. "Shall I bring them in?"

He sighed. "Might as well."

"Lots" was no exaggeration. Restored to life, the Post-It notes alone would have been enough for a medium-sized Scots pine. Then there were the printed-out e-mails and the internal memos. Everybody in the world, it seemed, wanted to talk to him.

Actually, not talk to. Shout at. One example at random: the site manager in charge of the new Far From the Madding Crowd development (a hundred and ninety luxury bungalows on the northern edge of Norton St Edgar) had turned up for work at nine sharp to find that the site wasn't there any more. Hares lolloped and roe deer grazed on unsullied pasture where yesterday he'd had a dozen JCBs gouging out footings, and there was no sign at all that he and his men had ever been there. An explanation, please, and were they to forget it or start all over again? Meanwhile, the building inspector who'd come out to sign off on the Paradise Regained development was a bit put out because there weren't any buildings for him to inspect – rather a surprise, since he'd been there a month earlier and they were just putting the roofs on. Had Mr Huos ordered the demolition of the properties in question, and if so was he aware that planning consent was required before any such demolition could take place? Those, and a dozen or so more like them, were bad enough. What made Mr Huos wince, however, was the sheaf of memos from the legal department – eleven of them, all asking the same question about the same property.

Oh hell, he thought.

He picked up the phone. "Get Gogerty on his mobile," he barked. "Now."

His own stupid fault, he was perfectly willing to concede, for trying to be clever. One scam at a time, his inner voice had yelled at him, but no, he hadn't been able to resist the lure of the extra refinement, the tweak too far. Now everything was unravelling on him simultaneously, and he shuddered to think where it would end, unless something could be done about it. Unfortunately, right now the only person in the world who could sort it out for him was Gogerty, who when last spoken to had burbled to him about promising leads and intriguing potential lines of enquiry – translated into English, diddly squat. He couldn't in all conscience criticise Gogerty on that score. The job he'd been set was, after all, monstrously difficult, quite likely impossible: looking for a phase-shifting needle in a polydimensional haystack, blindfold and wearing wicketkeepers' gloves. The more he thought about it, in fact, the more depressing it became. What if Gogerty failed, and the whole horrible contrivance came apart at the seams? That was the trouble with using technology (for want of a better word) when you had no idea how it actually worked. Absolutely fine when it's running smoothly, but as soon as the little red lights go on and the burning smell gets too rank to ignore, you're in the hands of repair men and technicians, and if they don't know how to fix it . . .

*Brrr.* "Mr Gogerty for you."

"Put him on."

Mr Gogerty sounded hassled, which was as unpromising as

it was uncharacteristic. "Nothing so far," he reported. "I'm following up an angle that might lead somewhere, but it'll take time."

"That's a bit awkward," Mr Huos said. "The fact is, I'm under a certain amount of pressure right now. I really do need this business sorted out as soon as possible." He realised how that must have sounded, and added, "I know you're doing your best. Do you need any more resources? Money?"

"No," Mr Gogerty said. "It's nothing like that. It's just that I can't be in two places at once."

Been there, Mr Huos thought, done that. As for the other way round, that was what had caused all this mess to begin with. "Ah well," he said, "I thought I'd ask, just in case. I'm holding you up. I'll let you get on. Call me as soon as you've got anything at all."

No hope there then. That really only left him one possible course of action, and it was something he'd wanted desperately not to have to do. He sent for Alan Stevens.

"It's like this," he explained. "I need to lay off staff in your department. It's the economic climate. Just not enough work to justify current staffing levels."

Mr Stevens stared at him. Respectfully, of course, a bit like a senior courtier staring at George III on one of his bad days. "Oh," he said. "I was sort of under the impression we were rushed off our feet."

"Not really," Mr Huos said. "Probably it just feels like it from where you're sitting. The view from my desk is that we need to slim down our operation a bit. In fact," he went on, "I'm closing the whole department. From now on, we'll be outsourcing our legal work. That," he added quickly, "doesn't include you, of course." The agonised look on Mr Stevens' face thinned a bit, but he still looked very sad indeed, like a spaniel whose bone has just been stolen by an Alsatian. "I'll need you to, um –" (If he was outsourcing everything, what could he possibly need Mr Stevens for?) "– to coordinate the legal side of the business and, um, supervise things. If that's all right with you, of course."

Mr Stevens nodded so rapidly his head was a blur. "Of course," he said, and any worries Mr Huos may have had about Mr Stevens resigning in solidarity evaporated like water in a furnace. "I'm sure I'll be up to the extra responsibility."

You had to admire a man like that, someone with the cool and the vision to turn a narrow escape from the dustbin into promotion. The sort of man you'd want at your side, if only so you could make sure he didn't sneak up behind you with an ice pick. "We'll discuss a new package to cover your, um, career restructuring." A pay rise, in other words. Well, why not? For some reason thirty pieces of silver was the sum that sprang immediately to mind. "Well," he went on with an effort, "I'd better let you get on. You've got a fairly miserable day ahead of you."

"Have I?"

Mr Huos didn't answer, whereupon it occurred to Mr Stevens that telling the legal department it had just got the sack was to be part of his extra responsibilities. He took it better than Mr Huos had expected, in that he didn't audibly whimper. Instead, he stood frozen stiff for about ten seconds, then turned slowly and wordlessly and left the room.

Mr Huos slopped back into his chair, like cheese melting into toast. Nasty business and he felt truly rotten about it, but at least that was one small part of the mess dealt with, for now. The greater part was out of his hands. Only Mr Gogerty could save him now.

Pam and Trevor McPherson liked living in Norton St Edgar. It was their sort of place. As they stood on their drive at the top of the hill on a Sunday morning, they could look down on an apparently endless vista of salmon-pink bungalow roofs and neatly cut lawns, on an army of neighbours walking dogs, weeding borders and washing cars. If only, they sometimes thought, the whole world could be like Norton. It was the perfect place to retire to, an island of calm, order, homogeneity and sanity in a universe of wild men and madmen. The only thing it lacked, Mr McPherson had been known to say, was a moat and a drawbridge.

Today, however, they had to leave Norton, just for a little while, to drive into Malvern and stock up at Tesco. Under the warm mid-morning sun they got into the car, waved cheerfully at their neighbours, who waved cheerfully back, and set off down Attractive Drive towards what passed for a main road. At the T-junction they turned left, past the massive oak tree, past the track that led to Priory Farm, and found themselves back at the top of the hill, outside their house.

Trevor McPherson frowned, checked his mirror, indicated and pulled over. His wife looked at him.

"Didn't we just..."

He shrugged. "Can't have," he replied, and drove on.

Down Attractive Drive (Mrs Clayton was pruning her roses; Mr Burgoyne was painting his windowsills), at the junction turn left, past the beautiful old oak tree in which Charles II was supposed to have hidden when escaping from the Roundheads, though he'd have had a job, since it was only two hundred years old, past the track that led to Priory Farm, over a slight rise, back in front of their house.

His wife scowled at him. "What are you doing?" she asked.

"I'm not doing anything," he barked. "We just—"

"I thought we did."

He shook his head. "We can't have."

He drove on. Down Attractive Drive (Mrs Clayton too wrapped up in her roses to look up; Mr Burgoyne frowning slightly as he watched them go past), at the end of the road turn left, past the tree, past the farm drive, over the little bump...

"This is daft," Mr McPherson said.

His wife was getting edgy, he could tell. "I don't like this," she said. "Let's go back in the house."

The same thought had crossed his mind, but, since she'd suggested it, honour dictated that he couldn't. "Don't be silly," he said. "We're going shopping, all right?"

He drove on. Down Attractive Drive (Mrs Clayton, straightening up, secateurs in hand, waved cheerily, but they didn't wave back), at the junction turn left, past the tree, past the farm, over the bump and, "Stop the car," said Mrs McPherson, "I want to get out."

"Shut up," Mr McPherson reasoned with her. "All right," he said grimly and drove on, down Attractive Drive, at the junction turn *right* –

"I thought we were going to Tesco," said Mrs McPherson.

– through the village, past the church, past the pub, past the site where they were building the new houses, round the sharpish left-hand bend, and there they were again, opposite their front door.

"That does it," Mrs McPherson said, reaching for the door handle. "I'm getting out."

"Stay where you are," Mr McPherson commanded, as she slammed the door behind her and marched up to the front door. Well, fine. "Stupid woman," he muttered under his breath, and let the clutch in.

This time, he performed a flawless three-point turn and drove up the hill instead of down, over the little bump, out onto the narrow single-track road that meandered its way between tall hedges to the neighbouring village of Bawton. For the first minute his heart was in his mouth, but the road carried on being the road, the familiar landmarks (gateways, overhanging trees, a derelict barn) were all where they were supposed to be, and he gradually allowed himself to unclench a little. He was actually pleased when he met a tractor coming the other way and, having crammed himself into the hedge to let it crawl by, he wound down his window and hailed the driver.

"Excuse me," he shouted. "Have you noticed anything odd?"

The driver looked at him as if to say, Yes, you. "Odd?"

Obviously not. "Sorry," Mr McPherson said. "Forget about it."

He drove on, past the long, wide right-hand curve with the lay-by, past the stack of silage bales, past the track to Priory Farm, past the oak tree Charles II couldn't possibly have hidden in.

He stopped. On his right, the mouth of Attractive Drive. He swore loudly and drove on; through the village, past the pub, church, new development, round the bend, over the little bump, back to his own front bloody door.

He stopped, put on the handbrake, let go of the steering wheel and began to shake all over. He was still quivering when his wife banged on the window. He wound it down.

"Well?" she said. He shook his head.

He'd never seen her look like that before. "I tried ringing the council," she said, "but the phone's out of order."

"Try your mobile."

"No signal."

Forty years in the road haulage business, twelve of them as regional manager, Mr McPherson reckoned he was pretty well bombproof, and with good reason. Spilled loads on the M6 hadn't phased him, nor snowdrifts, Operation Stack, fuel excise duty, not even the French. He knew better than most the risks of setting tyre to tarmac. Just as mariners gathered together in dockside bars whisper strange tales about the mysteries of the deep, hauliers have their own Flying Dutchmen, Marie Celestes, sea serpents, islands that turn out to be giant turtles. They know that geography isn't such a set of absolute constants as they'd have you believe. He'd heard about the demon motorway junction in Pembrokeshire that swallows up those unwise enough to take it, leaving no trace; of the phantom Lutterworth bypass that only appears for six hours every five years and leads to a place that nobody who's been there will ever talk about; of the M25 tailback in '92 that became so dense it achieved critical mass and collapsed into a black hole. He'd raised more than one glass to honour a driver who'd set off into the vast uncertainty of the highway and never been seen or heard of again. There were worse things out there than feedback loops, and he'd met men who'd faced them down and lived to tell the tale.

"Sod it," he said. "I'm going to get to the bottom of this. I may be some time."

"Trevor, don't be so bloody stupid," his wife said, but by then he'd turned the ignition key and put the car in gear. The last she saw of him was his brake lights, as he slowed to a halt at the T-junction. Then he was gone.

Mrs McPherson went back into the house, made herself a cup of tea and turned the TV on for her afternoon soap. All she got was a black-and-white snowstorm. She tried channel-hopping, but they were all the same. She had another go at ringing the council, but the line was still dead.

She went next door and rang the bell. When her neighbour came out, she said, "My telly's on the blink. Mind if I watch with you?"

A shake of the head. "Mine too. I was just about to come round to your house."

"Can I use your phone?"

"It's not working."

They looked at each other, and each of them saw no panic, only resigned, irritable acceptance. Intuitively, both of them knew that whatever this strange inconvenience might be, the root cause must lie with some man somewhere, trying to fix something he didn't understand rather than send for a proper engineer and pay the call-out fee. Hence, no cause for concern, since sooner or later the man's wife would make him see sense, the proper authorities would be sent for, and normal service would eventually be resumed.

Then an ugly thought occurred to Mrs McPherson, and she asked, "Where's Dave?"

"He went into town to get some plywood," her neighbour

replied. "He's been ever such a long time. Still, once he goes in one of those DIY places, he loses all track of time."

Mrs McPherson replied that Trevor was just as bad, but her heart wasn't in it. If asked, she reckoned she could advance a pretty good theory about why Dave was so long at the fair. The point was, though, that she hadn't been asked, and it'd serve no useful purpose to scare her neighbour out of her wits when, for all she knew, council workmen were at that precise moment swinging into action and sorting it all out; whereupon the roads would be open again, the TV and the phones would start working, and she'd be able to ring the council offices and have a good moan about why it had taken them so long. Until then the only sensible course of action was to keep quiet and spirit-of-the-Blitz it out.

She went home and did some vacuuming. About half an hour later the electricity went off.

That, she felt, was taking things just a bit too far. Unfortunately, there was absolutely nothing she could do about any of it – not unless she fancied trying to walk into Malvern, assuming she could get out of Norton, which she felt fairly sure was impossible.

She read a book until it was too dark to make out the words, then sat quietly in front of her silent TV and her stone-cold-dead gas fire.

Just gone nine, Trevor came home. He was limping and his back was bent. He'd run out of petrol, he explained, and he'd had to leave the car at the top of Burridge Lane, which was incidentally about as far as it was possible to get before It sent you back home again. He'd tried everywhere, he went on, every road or lane out of Norton, and it was the same story all over. Eventually, when the petrol gave out, he'd tried walking up the footpath that wound its way through the woods to Bawton. He'd trudged on for well over an hour, and he'd been on the point of letting himself hope when he'd climbed over a stile to find himself back in Attractive Drive, two doors down from home.

"This is no good," his wife told him. "We've got to tell some-one."

He no longer had enough energy to be irritated. "They'll find out soon enough," he said, dragging off his shoes and collapsing into a chair. "I expect the electric being off's going to get their attention."

"But somebody's got to do something."

He looked at her. "Such as?"

"Oh, you're just useless," she said, storming off and colliding with the rocking chair, and, although he felt she was maybe being a bit harsh, he wasn't inclined to disagree. He'd come to the end of his resources when the petrol tank ran dry. All his life he'd been a man of action, and now he was faced with the depressing fact that there was nothing he could do. His wife, by contrast, was a – what was the word? A catalyst. She suggested, urged, mithered, complained until someone else, the properly constituted authorities, took action. But with no phones, no roads by which postmen could come to collect letters, no means of communication whatsoever, she was as ineffectual as he was. They couldn't even have a nice cup of tea, with no electric. Still, he thought, it wasn't as though it was going to last very long. By now the outside world must have noticed. Rescue was on its way, and any minute now the lights would go on, the phones would ring, the roads would reopen and all would be well.

For now, however, he was sitting in the pitch dark, and it bothered him. Without visual stimuli to distract him, he found it hard to keep his mind from coming up with increasingly bizarre and disturbing theories about what was going on: alien invasions, nuclear catastrophies so violent they'd buggered up the laws of physics, stuff so weird and wonderful he'd never take any of it seriously for one second in the light but which spawned and grew alarmingly in the darkness. Bugger that, he thought. It had been a cloudless blue-sky day, so the moon and stars would be out; hardly a substitute for a hundred-watt bulb, but surely better than no light at all.

He got up and felt his way slowly and carefully to the back door. Outside, the night was still and warm. An owl hooted sleepily in the distance. The air was sweet and rich with the heavy scent of lavender and night-scented stocks. But it was dark.

He craned his neck to look up at the sky. Clouds, he said to himself. Please let it be just clouds.

No stars. No moon.

# CHAPTER ELEVEN

"Where is he?" roared Jack Tedesci, as he surged through the front office like a tidal wave and broke against Reception. "I'll kill him."

The receptionist smiled at him. As luck would have it, Mrs Hacksmith had just started a two-week holiday, and the temp who was filling in for her was young and beautiful, and Jack Tedesci noticed things like that, the way a spy satellite notices troop movements. His anger and sense of purpose both dissipated a little. "Is your boss in?" he said.

Still the smile. "Sorry, I'm new here. This is my first day. Who were you wanting?"

"Mr Huos."

"I'll see if he's available for you."

Four minutes went by, during which Mr Tedesci learned some really quite interesting stuff about Wayne and Colleen from a nine-month-old copy of *Hello!*. He was holding the magazine sideways and grinning when Mr Huos came out and apologised for keeping him waiting.

"No bother," Mr Tedesci replied, absent-mindedly folding the magazine lengthwise and stuffing it into his coat pocket. "Good of you to see me at such short notice."

"Come on through," Mr Huos said, and ushered him into the lift. "So, Jack, how's things?"

The use of his first name may not have quite woken the sleeping tiger of Mr Tedesci's wrath, but it nudged the tip of its tail. Why was it, he wondered, after all the deals they'd done together, that Mr Huos called him Jack, but he didn't even know what Huos' first name was. A bit stand-offish, he'd often thought, a wee tad superior; like at school, where the teachers can call you any damn thing they like, but you've got to call them sir. He'd toyed with hailing Mr Huos as Huey or Huzza, but decided that would be going too far, so he'd shelved the matter and let it fester as a class-three minor grudge.

"Not so good," he replied. "You know that land you sold me?"

"Mm?"

"It's gone."

Whatever the reply he'd been expecting, it hadn't been "Oh," or at least not "Oh" in that tone of voice. "I'm sorry to hear that, Jack," Mr Huos went on. "I can see why you're probably a bit concerned."

A bit concerned. Like describing the Vietnam War as "a bit of a scrap." "You don't sound all that surprised," he said.

"I'm not." The lift stopped. Mr Huos made an after-you herding gesture. "Truth is, you're not the first person I've heard that from today, not by a long chalk."

Mr Tedesci walked a few steps, then stopped dead, like a mule. "Are we talking about the same thing? When I said it's gone—"

Sigh. "I should think so, yes. Let's see, you went out there to take a look at it, and you couldn't find it."

"If you're suggesting I can't read a map . . ."

Mr Huos didn't seem to have heard him. "Nothing to see, I don't suppose. No great big gaping hole or anything like that. Just, well, not there any more. Like all the surrounding fields had sort of healed up around where it used to be. Well?"

"Pretty much," Mr Tedesci said feebly. "Look, what the hell's going on? You're making it sound like it's *normal* or something."

Mr Huos just looked tired. "Naturally, you'll get your money back," he said. "And it'd only be fair if I covered all your out-of-pocket expenses: surveyors, architects, planning consultants and so on. If you'll get your people to mail me a breakdown..."

"Listen." Mr Tedesci realised he'd grabbed Mr Huos' arm. It was like stone. He quickly let go. "Listen," he repeated. "Screw the money."

"That's very generous of you, Jack."

"Tell me," Mr Tedesci shouted in his face, "what's going on."

Mr Huos shifted his head a degree or so and looked straight at him; at which moment, if he'd been offered the choice, Mr Tedesci would cheerfully have torn up the contract, forfeited the money and undertaken never to mention the deal ever again, just as long as Mr Huos stopped looking at him like that. "And why not?" he sighed. "You know what: I might just do that. I've never told anybody, you see, not even Stan Gogerty. Sorry, you don't know him. Just forget you heard the name. But what the hell." Suddenly he was alive again, alert, almost crackling with energy. "In here," he said, pushing a door open. Not an office, Mr Tedesci noticed. More a sort of—

"That's a toilet," he pointed out.

"Fine. I'll stand, you can have the seat." Mr Huos sort of nudged him, only a little gentle pressure, but so expertly applied that Mr Tedesci had no choice. He lost his footing, stumbled a yard or so, backed into something solid, flumped down onto it and found he was sitting on a closed toilet lid. "Are you sitting comfortably?" Mr Huos asked cheerfully as he closed and bolted the door. "Then I'll begin."

★ ★ ★

It was bad enough facing a crowd of thirty women, all staring at him expectantly and impatiently. It certainly didn't help that, although they were definitely human, he could also see them as chickens. But what was really screwing him up was the knowledge that all of them were lawyers.

He cleared his throat. "Ladies," he said. All thirty of them glowered at him. That was the moment when he realised that if he'd been born a fox, he'd have starved to death years ago. "Um," he said, and then his voice stopped working, a failure so abrupt and total it was hard to believe Microsoft didn't have anything to do with it. He looked back to see if his fellow male was going to help him out, but that didn't seem likely. Charles Mynott-Harrison, former conductor of the Liverpool Philharmonic, slayer of rival cockerels and currently the coop's designated alpha male, was hiding behind him, shaking like a leaf.

Fortunately, that was when Ms Byron took charge, stepping in front of him and gently edging him out of the way. "Listen, everyone," she said. "Will everybody who's really a human please raise their wing. Hand. All right," she went on, as a forest of wings lifted into the air, waited to be counted and then, from sheer force of habit, flapped. "Looks like that's all of us. All right," she continued. "Wings up, anyone who's *not* a lawyer."

Not a feather stirred, and Ms Byron nodded. "Now then," she said, "wings up, anybody who hasn't got a brother who's a musician of some sort."

Chickens have no eyebrows, so Kevin couldn't do a bewildered frown. *All* of them?

"Something very screwy," Ms Byron said, slowly and clearly, like a good teacher, "has been going on, but it looks like it may be getting better, though I can't say that for sure.

"Fine," Ms Byron said, and her voice was quieter, as though she was trying to deal with a whole lot of implications all at once. "The question is, what are we going to do?"

If she'd been expecting suggestions, she was out of luck. Kevin waited to see what she'd say next.

"All right," Ms Byron went on, and now she sounded like what she was, the duly-elected-leader-by-default. "So, here's how I see it. Here we are, thirty-seven human beings who've somehow or other been turned into chickens. I don't know—" She raised her voice to quell the incipient low hum of clucking. "I don't know how it happened – none of us knows that. I don't know why it's happened to us, or why we're all women lawyers with brothers who play musical instruments. To be perfectly honest with you, I really couldn't give a damn, as long as there's some way we can make it stop and get back to normal." She paused. Dead silence. She had their undivided attention. "I suggest," she said, "we get help."

It didn't go down terribly well, but they were still listening. "And how, you may well ask," she went on, "do we go about doing that? Good question. Obviously we can't talk to humans, even if we could find a human to talk to. Anybody remember seeing one lately? No? Me neither. We can't talk, we can't phone, but –" she paused for effect "– we can *text*. Or send an e-mail. Agreed?"

Thirty-odd pairs of round eyes were watching her intently, but nobody clucked.

"Which means," she went on, "we need to get to a phone or a computer. Which in turn means we need to get out of this coop. If we can do that—"

A large brown Speckled Sussex in the front row interrupted her. "Just who do you propose we contact?" she said. "The police? The army? The RSPCA? Who the hell is going to believe—"

"We'll cross that bridge when we come to it," Ms Byron replied, so firmly that the Speckled Sussex took a step back and stood on one leg. "Whatever we're going to do, we can't do it stuck in here. Put it another way: nobody could admire Gandhi more than I do, but I really don't think passive resistance and non-violent protest is going to cut it for us, not in these circumstances. We've got to get out of here, get into the nearest house and find something we can type into. Now, has anybody got any ideas about how we can do that?"

Thirty-seven chickens looked around. They saw a framework of twelve solid three-inch-thick seven-foot-high posts, to which had been nailed an impenetrable barrier of wire netting, the whole area covered on top with a tarpaulin, to comply with anti-bird flu regulations. There was one door, a wooden frame covered in inch mesh, securely tied top and bottom with baler twine. It was Alcatraz, and they were the bird women.

Depression and despair, multiplied by thirty-six. But Ms Byron's head was still held high, and her perfectly round eyes were still bright as she scuffed at the dusty floor with her triple-toed claw-ended feet.

"Only one thing for it," she said. "We dig a tunnel."

Back at his office, Mr Gogerty washed, shaved, changed his underwear and shirt and brushed his teeth. A cup of tea would be nice. He looked in the Tupperware box next to the kettle, but all the tea bags were gone. There was, however, half a pot of cold tea left over from the day before yesterday, so he put the spout between his lips and glugged four times. Fine. Now he'd go and visit Kevin Briggs.

First, however, he checked his messages, just in case. Sandersons; could he ring Mr Ibrahim at his earliest convenience about the Eye of Odin case? He frowned and made a note on the pad. The Massachusetts Institute of Thaumaturgy wanted to consult him about a potential product liability suit; could he call asap? He sighed. MIT was just the sort of client he was anxious to attract, but right now he couldn't spare the time. Schlager & Chang; any progress with the missing ten years from the seventeenth century? He was quite glad he'd missed that call. Someone by the name of Don Mayer wanting to consult him about some really weird stuff which he couldn't explain on the phone; please could he ring back on this number (he wrote it down out of force of habit) or else he could reach him at this address—

Mr Gogerty stopped dead, frozen in the act of knotting his tie. Then he rewound and played back the last bit of the message. Except for one number, the address was the same as the one he'd written in his notebook when he'd looked up Kevin Briggs.

Hooray for serendipity. He sat down and pecked in the number with the butt of his pencil. Three rings before rather high, slightly nerdish man's voice helloed.

"Stanley Gogerty," he said, "returning your call."

"What? Oh, right, yes, hello. Thanks for calling back. Um."

Ah, Mr Gogerty thought, the public. Not an entity he ever chose to do business with. Not that he had anything against them as such, but whenever they were involved in a case, they tended to complicate it. For one thing, they didn't think properly. Professional people think in straight lines, the shortest distance between the two relevant points. At their best and brightest, the public think in a series of wide concentric loops, their thought processes in slow, lazy orbit around the matter in hand.

"You wanted to consult me about a problem," Mr Gogerty prompted.

"Yes."

Mr Gogerty closed his eyes and counted to ten. After a lifetime of dealing with the public, he'd learned to count to ten very, very quickly. "What did you want to talk to me about?"

Arguably, of course, it wasn't entirely their fault. They've been trained practically since birth to live in awe of the professional classes, so naturally they get a bit tongue-tied. Understandable but annoying. "Well, it's complicated," the voice said. "I'm not sure where to begin, really. And I'd rather not discuss it over the phone. Can we come and see you or something?"

Mr Gogerty noticed the change from singular to plural.

"Better still," he said. "It so happens I've got a call to make in your neck of the woods, so I'll drop in and see you." He glanced at his watch, automatically correlating the triplicate reading. "Would, say, half past ten be convenient?"

"Um."

There's a particular tone of voice, immediately recognisable, that's only ever used by an Englishman who thinks someone's about to try and sell him something. Mr Gogerty frowned. He didn't want to scare this Mayer character off by sounding too enthusiastic, but the prospect of a possible new lead was flooding him with nervous energy. "Well?" he snapped. "Sorry to rush you, but I'm on a schedule."

Mr Mayer was discussing something with an offstage female voice. He heard it hiss, "Oh for crying out loud, Don," and that seemed to resolve the issue. "Yes, that's fine," said Mr Mayer. "Half ten, my place. See you there."

If asked, Mr Gogerty would deny he was an intuitive sort of guy. Conclusions firmly based on solid evidence refined by logical analysis; that was how he liked to conduct his business. Hunches were for amateurs and charlatans. It was a bit galling, therefore, to have to admit to himself that he had a hunch – not just any hunch, a megahunch, a hunch the size of the Sydney Opera House – about this Mayer person. Defiantly, as he finished knotting his tie and doing up his shoelaces, he tried to rationalise it. The synchronicity, for one thing. He wished he'd had the presence of mind to ask Mr Mayer how he'd heard about him. Something else as well: a certain desperation in his manner, a hint of honest-to-goodness panic – understandable in a member of the public coming up against some manifestation of the world of the profession for the first time, but maybe there was a bit more to it than that. Also, he remembered, Mr Mayer hadn't asked him what his charges were. A significant omission, but one that could mean many things.

Well, no point speculating without data. He shut the office door and locked it, sprinted briskly down the stairs into the street and hailed a passing taxi. It drove straight past him without stopping.

He frowned. That wasn't supposed to happen. Among his many accomplishments, Mr Gogerty had a firm grasp of the Words of Command. He could raise storms and quell them, subdue lions, elephants and small, yapping dogs, bring about partial eclipses of the sun, summon lifts, attract the attention of barmen and waiters and, up till that precise moment, hail taxis. Basic stuff. Asking him to do it was like asking Gordon Ramsay to boil an egg.

No more taxis to be seen anywhere. He glanced at his watch. Wouldn't do to be late. He started to walk, heading east, and caught the Tube at Livingstone Square. A train came along straight away, and he had the carriage to himself.

Coincidence, he thought, as the train rattled deep into the earth. Coincidence is a technical term for a pattern of events you're too stupid to identify. He called up a street map on his phone screen and zoomed in on the immediate vicinity of Clevedon Road. There was, he felt certain, something basic and obvious that he'd been missing right from the start. Furthermore, it was a wood-for-trees sort of thing, the kind of thing he might overlook but which would be obvious to an untrained civilian. He hated those. Frowning, he turned the map upside down, and then rotated it to the left through ninety degrees.

The train stopped, the way they do. At first he barely noticed, then he told himself to be patient, then he looked at his watch. Only one dial.

Bad. He ordered himself to stay calm and looked slowly round the empty carriage. Nothing to see, no sinister shapes lurking in shadows. Everything was as normal and mundane as it could possibly be. But his hands were sweating, his heart was going like a lawnmower engine and his watch had only one dial, instead of the three it had been made with.

It was then that he remembered that the Livingstone Square Tube station wouldn't be built until 2016.

★ ★ ★

Well, thought Mr Williams, peering through the shop window. Never been here before.

Not that he minded. It had been a very long time since he'd seen anything other than pavement, tarmac, the frontages of other shops. Today, the view from the window was of a beautiful green meadow, with a backdrop of mist-wreathed hills. He unlocked the front door and stepped outside to find himself standing on the verge of a single-track lane. Stone me, he thought, the countryside.

"Eileen," he called out. "Come and look at this."

She'd be pleased. She used to like the countryside, back in the days before It. That was all so long ago now that he wasn't sure there was still any countryside left; the rate they were building houses nowadays, he wouldn't be at all surprised if they'd used it all up. Apparently not. From where he was standing, he couldn't see a single man-made structure, unless you counted gates and hedges. Not, he couldn't help thinking, an ideal spot for a dry cleaners, but since they'd only be there for a day, it didn't matter terribly much. Maybe – the idea burst in his mind like a firework – they could shut the shop and go for a walk; take a picnic lunch even, make a day of it. Could this possibly be Its way of granting them a well-deserved, much-needed holiday?

"Where's this, then?" Eileen said.

"Dunno." He turned and smiled at her. "Nice, though, isn't it?"

"It's the middle of nowhere."

"Yes." Suddenly his heart was full of joy and certainty. "Eileen, love, how about taking the day off?"

She stared at him. "What, you mean not open the shop?"

"That's right."

"We can't."

"Why not?"

"We *can't*." She'd lowered her voice as if she was afraid It might hear her. "We've got to open the shop. Otherwise..."

He smiled. "But there're no customers," he said gently. "Like you said, it's the middle of nowhere." Now it was his turn to whisper. "Know what I think? I reckon It wants us to have the day off. Otherwise, why bring us here, where there's no people?"

"You don't know that," she said. "There could be a town or something nearby."

"Where?" He pointed through the open door. "Just think, Eileen," he said. "We could go for a stroll, just the two of us. Fresh air. When was the last time we walked more than ten yards without coming up against a wall?"

She shrank back a step. "I don't like it," she said. "It doesn't feel right. Shut the door, for crying out loud; it's giving me the creeps."

"That's just because it's been so long," he replied gently. "Think about it. When was the last time we went out that door and shut it behind us?"

She shook her head. "I don't know."

"And you know why?" Light was spreading inside his head, and he wanted to laugh out loud. "Because every time we even think about leaving the shop, some bugger comes in with a load of dirty clothes that want cleaning, so we never get time." He stood perfectly still and quiet, as though waiting. "See?" he said happily. "No customers."

"That's because you still got the CLOSED sign up."

She had a point. He reached back and twisted the sign round. "There," he said. "Now we're open for business, official." He waited again, ten seconds. "Well?"

She looked up at him, and mixed in with the fear in her eyes there was hope. "You're right," she said. "Normally, we'd have had a customer in by now."

"We could take a picnic."

He'd chosen the right line of argument. Her eyes softened

and widened, and she whispered, "I've got that cold chicken."

"Fantastic."

"And a bit of cheese and some salad. Oh, could we? It'd be..."

Yes, he thought, it would. "Come on," he said. "Before anyone comes along."

It didn't take her long to pack the picnic basket. She didn't even stop to do her hair or put on a face. Ten minutes later they locked the shop door behind them and set off down the lane, not looking back. In the distance sheep were bleating, birds were singing, and those were the only sounds: no subliminal rumble of traffic, no dull pulse of someone else's music vibrating through the walls, no background hum of the machines, no gabbling voices of customers. The sun was bright and gently warm – real light, not electric; they'd forgotten how different real light was – and a faint breeze stirred the leaves in the hedge, just enough to cool them. They walked for ten minutes, following the lazy curves of the lane, and then Eileen said, "Did I remember to turn off the gas?"

"Probably," he replied.

"Maybe we should go back and—"

"No."

She didn't argue. In fact, she hardly said a word. She was too busy looking about her, as if she'd never seen anything like this before. They stopped in a gateway and took in the view. Below them, a great meadow rolled gently down to a beech-shaded river, then swept back up to a distant skyline. There were cows, black and white against the green, and a red tractor crept along the top of the ridge, slow as a beetle.

She looked at him. "How long?"

"No need to rush," he replied.

The lane started to climb, a gradient so slight they hardly noticed it. They passed a small wood, beyond which the hedge gave way to post-and-rail fencing, so they could see even further. A rabbit darted out in front of them, paused for a moment to stare, then bolted into the long grass at the side of the lane.

"This is really nice," he said.

"Yes," she replied.

A bend in the lane brought them to a cluster of buildings: a farmhouse, presumably, with a yard and outbuildings. They peered over a low wall and saw a big fat pig sprawled comfortably in the doorway of its sty. It reminded them both of Eileen's cousin Norman, but neither of them said anything.

"He looks happy," Eileen said.

"It's a she," he pointed out.

"So it is."

Neither of them mentioned the fact that it was the first life form they'd been that close to in years whose washing they hadn't had to do. It didn't need saying. They were out of the shop and they were together and the sun was shining. Compared with those three enormous facts, anything else was so small and trivial it didn't merit attention, except as a component of the most beautiful day either of them could remember.

"It's so *normal*," she said at last. "That's why it's so special."

At which point an engine revved wildly in one of the buildings. They turned to look, and saw an elderly Ford Cortina, draped in cobwebs and plastered with mud and straw, burst through the side of a long wooden shed, scattering splinters of plank and weatherboard like confetti. It raced across the yard, swerved to avoid a parked tractor, scrunched its offside wing against a wall, backed up, hit the corner of a barn and stalled.

It appeared to be being driven by chickens.

"He's late," Don said nervously.

It had taken all his courage to go back to the flat. He'd been sure they'd get there to find the police waiting for them, or the army, or the SAS, or sinister men in grey suits or white coats, or, worse still, Ms Briggs.

"She'll be at work," Polly had pointed out.

"She might not be. She could've taken the day off. After all, it's her brother. If I'd gone missing, you'd take the day off."

"Possibly. It'd depend on how busy we were."

How sweet, he thought. "Anyhow, he's late," he said, peering through the sitting-room window, which commanded a superlative view of the dustbins in the yard below. "I don't think he's going to show."

"He's five minutes late," Polly pointed out. "Maybe he's been held up in traffic. Look," she added, as he started pacing again, "this has got to stop, right? This is your home; you live here. Sooner or later you've got to get a grip and..."

Move back in, she didn't say. It hadn't been easy, having her brother as a house guest. On balance, she'd have preferred rats.

"That's easy for you to say," he retorted. "You're not the one who murdered his next-door neighbour."

"Don't start that again."

"Why not? Strikes me it's the leading issue of the day." The phone rang, and he jumped a foot in the air. "You get that," he hissed. "Pretend it's a wrong number."

She gave him a very sour look and picked up the phone. "Hello? Sorry, he's not here right now. Can I— Oh yes, right. Yes, got that. Thanks then. Bye."

She put the phone down and turned to face him. He'd gone ever such a funny colour: pale pink with natural-yoghurt highlights. "Well?" he hissed.

"They can deliver your new fridge on Wednesday," she said. "For pity's sake, Don, don't be such a *baby*."

"Well, I wasn't to—"

"I'm going to get something to drink."

She went into the kitchen, leaving him sunk boneless in his chair. Magic, he thought. If it's so much hassle, why the hell would anybody want it in the first place? She was right about one thing, though. He couldn't go on like this for much longer – scared of the phone, driven out of his own flat, forced to live with his sister (never again, he vowed; he'd rather buy an old van and sleep in that). Maybe it was time he pulled himself together and just said no.

Polly came back into the room. "Your fridge is on the blink," she said. "The little light's not coming on, and everything inside is rapidly turning into compost."

One second, then they stared at each other.

"Just as well," Don said quietly, "they're delivering a new one on Wednesday."

Her eyes widened. "You mean you haven't..."

"Last time I looked, that one was working just fine. So no, I haven't ordered a new one."

"Oh." She backed up against the sofa and sat down. "That's—"

"And before you say it," he said angrily, "yes, I'm sure I didn't buy a new fridge, yes, I'm absolutely bloody positive the old one was working a couple of days ago." He froze, then lifted his head and stared at her. "What's the date today?"

"It's the..." She frowned. "I don't know; I've lost track. Hang on, I'll look on my phone."

"No, don't," he said quickly. "I don't think I want to know after all. Was there any beer in the fridge?"

"What? No."

"Pity." The last time he'd opened it, he'd put six cans in there. Time wasn't just messing him about, it was helping itself to his beer. That, he felt, was going too far. "We need that Gogerty bloke," he said heavily. "Someone's got to sort out this mess. I can't do it; you can't do it. There must be something—"

He realised what he was doing. In books, old-fashioned ones, people in a state of heightened emotion tear out their hair. He'd never known anybody do it for real, except, apparently, him. He looked at the wisps of hair he was clutching between finger and thumb. Well, he thought. Pity for it to go to waste.

"Don," Polly said, "what are you..."

He spat on the hairs and dropped them, and they grew.

When they were the size of rolling pins, they sprouted heads, arms and legs. Polly made a horrified squealing noise, but he shushed her. "Magic," he explained.

The hairs, there were seven of them, stopped wriggling on the floor, stood up, formed a line and bowed to him. "At your service," they chorused.

Embarrassing or what? Nevertheless, he gave them what he hoped was an encouraging nod. "Go and find Stanley Gogerty and bring him here," he said. "Assuming he wants to come," he added quickly, but by then it was too late. The hairs had already shot up into the air, where they hovered for a split second before zooming, rocket-like, through the window, which opened itself at the very last moment to let them through.

Polly was giving him a look that would probably have etched steel. "You said..."

"Changed my mind. Look, I've had it up to here with the weird stuff. I just want it to stop. This Gogerty bloke..." He sighed. "If he can't help us, maybe he can tell us who can. If that doesn't work, I don't know what I can do. That's it, basically. That's me finished." He sat down and slumped forward, elbows on knees, a picture of despair. Not a Rubens or a Titian or a Degas or even a Picasso of despair; other works by this artist you might enjoy include *Gypsy Dancer* and *Lady of Spain*, and can be bought off the railings in the Bayswater Road.

"Pack it in, Don," Polly said crisply. "Why didn't you tell me you've been doing magic?"

"I haven't," Don growled back. "Only the hair trick. I got us away from that horrible Briggs woman with it. Otherwise, it's been useless."

"But you can do it."

"No. Well, maybe. I don't know. Don't want to know, either."

"But Don—"

"For crying out loud," he yelled at the floor. "This isn't some handy labour-saving gadget. It killed that stupid idiot upstairs.

We can't use it, Polly. It'd be like trying to use a nuclear bomb to shift stubborn stains."

"You just did."

Polly had a real gift for that sort of thing: being right in teeny-weeny matters of detail, while being utterly wrong about the big stuff. "Yes," he said.

"You sent *magical creatures* to *abduct* a perfect stranger and *drag* him here."

"Well, he shouldn't be late for appointments," Don replied. "If I ran my business like that, I'd be—"

"You're never on time for anything. You told me yourself."

Once, when he was young, on a visit to the aquarium he'd stood in front of the piranha tank and wondered what it'd be like to be nibbled to death by hundreds of tiny jaws. Since then he'd had many lively debates with his sister, and reckoned he could guess just fine. "All right," he said. "You suggest something. Got any bright ideas?"

Polly was quiet for about a second. "Yes," she said. "Where's that thing?"

Amazingly, he was able, through long experience, to translate. "You mean the pencil sharpener?"

"Yes. Fetch it here. I want to see it."

Another man might have asked why. Another man might have put his foot in the apparently calm and placid waters, only to have it stripped to the bone in a millisecond. "All right," he said. "Hang on, I'll get it."

He'd hidden it, after much internal debate, in the carrier bag in which he stockpiled his used underwear until such time as supplies ran out and laundry became inevitable. Nobody, he reasoned, not even the most determined thief, would go in there after it. He reappeared with the bag, took the pencil sharpener out, wiped it on the tail of his shirt and put it down in the exact centre of the living-room table.

"That's it?"

"Yes."

"You're sure?"

"Of course not," he snapped. "It's just an inference I draw from the fact that my life started going down the toilet the moment I first set eyes on the bloody thing. It'd probably be better if you didn't..."

She already had, and was turning it over in her hand. "Oh look," she said. "There's writing on it."

"Which I'm hoping this Gogerty bloke will be able to read. I can't. You can't."

"Yes, I can."

Freewheeling too fast downhill on his bicycle and suddenly finding the brakes didn't work, the same sudden feeling of Oh. "You can?"

"Mm. It says—"

"But you *can't*," Don insisted. "It's magic writing. Probably you've got to chuck it in a fire or something, to make the letters show through."

"It's Russian," Polly said calmly. "I did Russian GCSE, remember? It says..."

"Well?"

She put the pencil sharpener back on the table. "I don't know," she said. "I only got a D. But that's all right," she went on brightly. "I've still got my dictionary. I can look it up."

"*Russian?*"

She nodded. "Cyrillic alphabet. What did you think it was?"

He pretended he hadn't heard that. "No reason why they shouldn't have magic in Russia if we've got it over here," he said grudgingly. "You sure you can't make out what it says?"

"Hang on, I'll have another look. It's something something and then I think it's just initials. Oh."

"What?"

"Really I'm just guessing, but..."

"*What?*"

"Made in the USSR," she said, and dumped the pencil sharpener unceremoniously on the table. "Oh well."

Don sighed. "Never mind," he said. "At least we know *something* about it, even if that something is no bloody use at all." He frowned. "If it's Soviet era, maybe it's some kind of spy stuff. You know, KGB department of dirty tricks."

She shrugged. "Maybe. So what?"

"At least then it'd be proper technology," he said, a bit more cheerfully, "as opposed to the sodding supernatural. Maybe it's an experimental hi-tech device that went wrong. During the Cold War both sides were researching some pretty wacky stuff."

She looked at him in mild disbelief. "I see," she said. "So if it's a dimension-bending, reality-skewing *gadget*, it's all right, just as long as it's not magic. Don, you're strange."

"Think about it," he urged. "If it's technology, then somewhere there's some laws of physics it's got to obey. In which case, maybe we could figure it out. At least it wouldn't be *cheating.*"

"It really makes a difference to you, doesn't it?"

A sad look spread across his face like melted ice cream. "Just kidding myself," he said. "Even if it's man-made rather than superbloodynatural, it can still vanish people and turn hairs into flying robots. We're still screwed, unless this Gogerty bloke can sort it all out."

Digging the tunnel hadn't been nearly as hard as he'd imagined it would be. Chicken feet are designed to shift earth. Chicken feet motivated by human minds got the job done in no time flat.

Ms Byron organised them into teams: 10 per cent of the workforce (three chickens) worked the face, scrabbling dirt and stones backwards, to be cleared out of the tunnel by the rest of the flock, stationed in a continuous relay the length of a chicken leg apart. It was a bit like playing football in a narrow corridor, with only reverse passing allowed. Kevin quite enjoyed it; it reminded him of kicking up drifts of dry leaves when he was a kid.

Once they'd broken through and emerged warily into the vast, uncertain, fox-infested wilderness beyond the wire, it took all Ms Byron's moral authority to keep them from scuttling back down the hole again, or wandering off in search of worms and protein-rich earwigs. She did it, though. Standing on one leg while scratching at dottles of mud in her belly plumage with the other, she was practically Churchillian as she urged them not to waver in their quest. A phone, she reminded them, all they needed was a phone, or a PC, or a fax machine, and before they knew it they'd be human again, and in a position to go back to their desks and their loved ones. If she believed that, nobody else did, but it sounded very fine when she said it.

She split them up into seven search parties and dispatched them to investigate the outbuildings. Kevin felt very proud when she chose him to be in her team, and it was pretty well inevitable that they should be the ones to make the discovery. It wasn't what they were supposed to be looking for, of course. It was a mouldy old car. There's one in every shed in every farmyard in the country.

"It's exactly what we need," Ms Byron said firmly. "All we've got to do is get it started and drive to the nearest town."

It's a clear sign that you're a born leader when nobody agrees with you but nobody disagrees with you either, at least not out loud. Getting inside the car was no big deal, since the driver's-side window had been helpfully left wound down. Keys in the lock were, of course, too much to hope for.

"We don't need keys," Ms Byron said scornfully. "Get the bonnet open and hot-wire it."

The bonnet opener, tucked down under the dashboard, was one small plastic lever for a man, but a giant immovable girder for chickenkind. They tried flying up and hanging on it with their beaks. They tried forming a poultry pyramid by standing on each others' heads and leaning on it. One particularly resourceful Buff Orpington flew out of the car window and came back with a yard of baler twine clenched in her beak. They tied one end to the lever (a small miracle in itself), looped it round the gear lever as a capstan and hauled on the other end till the lever snapped off, leaving a half-inch stub. Only then did a small, nervous Maran bantam point out that there was a whole mess of wires hanging down where the dashboard had come loose, and maybe they could trace them back and figure out which two connected to the ignition. Once they'd done that, it was a simple matter of pecking off the insulation and holding two ends of bare copper twist together. Incredibly, the battery wasn't flat. With a roar that sent two nervous Warrens into a premature moult, the engine started.

"Right," Ms Byron said. "You four, perch on the steering wheel. You two, stand by to shift the gear lever into first. You two, see what you can do with the rest of the gear lever. I'll do the accelerator myself."

By the time they hit the side of the shed they must have been doing at least fifteen. The plank wall didn't stand a chance. After that, things got a bit out of claw for a while, but (as Ms Byron maintained later) they were just getting the hang of it when they hit the stupid barn and stalled the engine.

"Look," Kevin said. "Humans."

Man or chicken, he was used to people not listening to him. Fair enough; he never had anything important to say. This time, though, he couldn't help feeling, was different. He raised his voice quite a lot and said, "Excuse me."

Ms Byron was pecking angrily at the tangle of wires drooping out of the dashboard. "What do you mean, you can't remember which ones go to the battery?" she clucked. "Here, get out of the way. Let me do it. Honestly, you're hopeless. One little thing goes wrong and you're all fussing around like a lot of headless—"

"Excuse me," Kevin repeated. Nobody paid him any attention. A bulky Leghorn cross had got her claw on one wire and another in her beak, just as a Plymouth Rock connected two other bits of wire together. For a split second the Leghorn was hanging in mid-air with no visible means of support, and when it finally landed, its plumage was fluffed wildly out like a feather duster.

Kevin looked back. The humans were still there, but they could wander off at any moment. Nothing for it. He stuck his chest out, threw his head back and crowed for all he was worth.

It got him noticed, at any rate. The hens all stopped what they were doing and stared, while Ms Byron gave him a filthy look and said, "What are you making that ridiculous noise for?"

"Humans," he replied, as soon as he'd got his breath back. "Over there."

To her credit, Ms Byron didn't need to be told twice. Spreading her wings, she flew up off the dashboard, through the window and quite some way across the yard before touching down, and as soon as her claws met the concrete, she started running, with thirty hens in close pursuit. For some reason, Kevin didn't follow her. He stayed where he was and watched as Ms Byron hurtled towards the humans, yelling, "We come in peace! Take us to your leader!"

It was a valiant effort, he thought, but he had a feeling she'd forgotten something.

"Oh look," Eileen said. "Chickens."

Her husband had already seen them for himself. Though a townie to the core, he'd seen chickens before. When he was a kid, just after the war, several families in their street had kept a few hens in their back gardens, and he could remember being allowed to poke bits of wilted cabbage through the wire at them, that being what passed for excitement in austerity-era Britain. So, although he hardly regarded himself as an expert, he reckoned he knew a little bit about poultry – enough, at least, to be fairly sure they weren't supposed to charge at you making bloodcurdling squawking noises. Also, he'd seen *The*

*Birds* when it first came out, and it had made quite an impression on him.

"Come on, Eileen," he said, trying to sound calm so as not to alarm her. "Let's go, shall we?"

"Why are those chickens...?"

Indeed. Why did the chicken cross the yard? One of life's mysteries. "I said come on," he said. "Let's get out of here."

He didn't have to argue his case any further. The feathered horde was sweeping towards them like an incoming wave, and Eileen had seen Hitchcock's masterpiece too. In fact, they'd seen it together, in the back row of the one-and-nines, which was why there were large chunks of the film they were quite hazy about. But they remembered the gist of it.

"Let's run," Eileen said.

Trouble was, the chickens could run faster. Quite soon, the horrible things were flowing round their ankles, clucking and flapping their nasty wings, and they didn't seem inclined to take "Shoo" for an answer. George and Eileen couldn't bring themselves to tread on them, and if they'd had the dexterity to kick moving chickens while running they would have been playing in the Premier League instead of running a dry cleaning business. In fact, things could've turned quite nasty if Mr Williams hadn't spotted—

"Quick," he said. "In here."

The gate was tied with a strand or two of heavily frayed baler twine, but it came loose when he yanked hard at it. They darted through and slammed the gate behind them, scattering chickens like sea spray. Eileen leaned against it, while he fumbled to reconnect the bits of string into a coherent fastening.

"That's all right," he said, breathing heavily. "For a moment there..."

"George," said Eileen, "there's a pig in here."

So there was. A great big thing, pink with black spots and a ring through its nose, like a teenager. On the other hand, it wasn't a chicken. "Don't tease it," he said. "It'll leave us alone."

"I'm not teasing it," Eileen replied. "George, do something."

It wasn't quite his finest hour, but it made the shortlist. Stepping carefully round the pig and grimly not looking down at what he was walking in, he went to the other end of the high-walled concrete enclosure, opened a little gate and held it for her while she scuttled through. Not a word. The parfait gentil knight.

"Let's go home," he said.

They took a long detour to make sure they stayed well away from the other side of the yard, just in case the chickens reappeared, but they got back to the road without any further trouble. They didn't talk much on the walk back. The view didn't seem quite so charming, now they knew the sort of savage creatures likely to be roaming about in it. They had a nasty moment when they came round a bend and saw a cow's head sticking over a gate, staring at them, but they crossed over to the other side of the lane and ignored it, and nothing bad happened.

"George," said Eileen, "those chickens. They were driving that car."

"I know."

She didn't say any more, but she didn't need to. Chickens that drove old Cortinas and mobbed humans didn't belong in the normal world; they had to be another manifestation of It, which meant It didn't stop at the shop door, and they couldn't just walk away, even for a little while. Clearly there was no point complaining, making a fuss; no point ringing the local paper or *You and Yours*, or writing to their MP, even if they ever stopped still in one place long enough to have one. All they could do was knuckle down and put up with It, and hope that eventually, one day, It'd stop of Its own accord. Not much of a hope, but still...

"George."

They stood rooted to the ground. Here, in this lay-by, next to this gate, opposite that double helping of landscape, was where their ill-starred walk had started. Here was where the shop had been when they set out. Here was now where the shop wasn't.

"Oh God," George said.

The shop had moved on again, and this time it had left without them.

# CHAPTER TWELVE

"Anyway," said Mr Huos, "that's all I know about my early life. Sad, isn't it?"

Jack Tedesci nodded vaguely. He'd never thought of himself as a timid sort of guy before. If anything, he was a bit concerned about coming across as a trifle bumptious, a little on the loud and aggressive side, maybe just a mini-tad scary to people who didn't know him. It was only now, wedged into a cramped men's toilet with Mr Huos looming over him and telling him all this crazy stuff with that wild look in his eye, that Jack realised he was at heart a frightened little animal who wanted nothing more out of life than to find a nice safe hole in the ground and burrow right down into it as far as he could go.

"Very," he mumbled. "Very sad indeed."

It would have been all right if he hadn't believed what he'd been hearing. The ravings of a loon, even a big, tall loon like Mr Huos, wouldn't have disturbed him particularly, any more than if he'd been screamed at in the street by a wino. It was the content, not the manner of presentation, that was messing with Jack Tedesci's head. At first he'd assumed he was listening to an amnesia story – found unconscious on a Georgian mountainside, pockets stuffed with money, couldn't remember his own name – but as the narrative went relentlessly on, details jumped out at him and hung like bats from the inner fabric of his mind. The steel earrings, for example; the ability to understand any language immediately. The fact that his internal organs weren't where *Gray's Anatomy* reckoned they ought to be. Really, he didn't like the sound of that at all.

Mr Huos was looking at him contemplatively, either like an artist considering a work in progress or like a spider checking out its silk-wrapped larder, he wasn't quite sure which. "I expect," Mr Huos said, "all that stuff sounds pretty screwy to you."

When all else fails, honesty. "Yes," said Jack.

Mr Huos grinned like a dog. "You ain't heard nothing yet. Listen."

I told you (Mr Huos said) about the brass ring. What I didn't tell you was that it started acting funny.

No, belay that. I'm getting ahead of myself. There I was in the Caucasus, with nothing except the shirt on my back and one hundred thousand bucks in cash. Naturally, the first thing I did was invest heavily in real estate.

I was lucky right from the start. I bought this forest. I was still living in the hotel at the time, but I could see this forest from my bedroom window and I just knew I had to have it. So I went to see the owners. They were a timber consortium that was just on the point of going bust; cash in hand suited them very well, especially hard currency. We rushed though the formalities. They made themselves scarce – came over here, actually; settled down, did quite nicely for themselves, even bought a football team – and I had my forest, which was all I—

Quite. You may well ask. Really, there wasn't a logical reason I could put my finger on, then or now. I just wanted it. Actually, I had this crazy notion there might have been truffles growing in it. Anyway, a week after I'd completed the deal, one of the megabig Russian oil companies came looking for me. Apparently they'd struck oil nearby, and they desperately needed my land for a pipeline. I turned my one hundred thousand into ten million, thanked them very much and looked round for something else to put my money into.

I won't bore you with the details. Everything I touched came good. I bought swamps, deserts, deserted villages contaminated by nuclear disasters, and within hours there'd be some nutcase desperate to quintuple my money for me if only I'd sell out to them. It was all so easy – so *natural*, if you follow me, like this was what was meant to happen – I really couldn't understand why everybody else on the planet wasn't doing exactly the same thing. Anyway, at the time life seemed pretty good. Straightforward. Or so I thought.

That was when the brass ring started playing up.

I used to carry it round with me in a little box. Don't ask me why. It seemed the right thing to do. From time to time I'd take it out and look at it. Yes, I know what you're thinking, but it wasn't like that at all. I wasn't continually putting it on, and when I did I didn't vanish or anything like that. Rather, it was as though just by looking at it, I thought I might remember some stuff from my previous life. It's like when you know there's an answer to some problem that's driving you nuts and it's staring you in the face but you can't quite see it. I was absolutely sure that daft brass ring meant something, and if I studied it hard enough, the penny would eventually drop and then I'd *know*.

But it didn't work out like that, and then the ring started changing. Yes, literally changing. One day it'd be a ring, next day it'd be a nail file or a ten-millimetre carriage bolt or a pair of nail scissors or a bit off an intake valve. I only knew it was really my brass ring because it was in the box. It started to bother me, so instead of carrying it round all the time, I hired a safe deposit box in a bank in Tashkent and left it there.

Almost straight away, everything started going down the pan. I bought more swamps and deserts and nuclear disaster sites, but nobody wanted to buy them off me. Deals I'd made earlier started unravelling horribly. The tax people came after me with a vengeance. I managed to piss off some rather heavy people sort of in and around the government – they thought I was political, which I obviously wasn't, but try getting them to believe that. All in all, I was in a bit of a mess. I did a basic stock take of my assets, liabilities and life generally, and realised that I was exactly, to the kopek, back where I'd started from. I'd lost the four hundred million or so I'd made, but I still had a hundred thousand US, in cash, in my safe deposit box. That was all that was left. The nasty men had made it pretty clear they wanted me to go away somewhere, so that's what I did, taking the cash and my brass ring with me. I wandered around for a bit, then hit on the UK as a fairly nice place to be. I came here, got off the plane at Heathrow, took a taxi to Slough and bought a disused sewage farm. Why? Because the derelict warehouse and the burned-out factory site were too much money, of course.

Next day some fixers from a supermarket chain came knocking at my hotel room door and offered me five million for my sewage farm. So that was all right. I was back in business.

After that, I took a couple of weeks off and did some thinking. Didn't take me long to figure out that my luck depended on having the brass ring on my person at all times. Well, fine, I thought. It's not exactly a hardship. But that was easy enough to say. The fact was, lugging the bloody thing about the place was beginning to prey on my mind really badly. I put up with it for as long as I could, and then I just couldn't hack it any longer. I chucked the ring and the box in a pond in a field out in the middle of nowhere, turned round and kept walking. About an hour later I got struck by lightning.

I remember waking up, and I was on a hillside. I looked round, expecting to see Russian Orthodox monks zooming towards me in a golf buggy, but not this time, apparently. I was feeling like shit, though there were no bones broken or anything. I got up and walked around for a bit, till I came to this farmyard. There didn't seem to be anybody about and I was dead on my feet, so I crawled inside the first outbuilding I came to and fell asleep.

You aren't going to like the next bit, but never mind. While I was asleep, the brass ring appeared to me in a dream. It told me we couldn't go on like this; I was using it up at a rate of knots, and if I carried on like that it'd have to kill me and find someone else. I didn't like the sound of that one bit, so I asked it what it wanted me to do. Easy, it replied. Buy this farm, get planning permission, build a load of houses on it, sell them and make a nice profit. All right, I said, I'll give it a go, and then what? At which, the ring gave me a very funny look and said, no, I didn't understand. I was to go on doing that indefinitely, or at least until the ring told me to stop. And then I woke up.

You don't argue with something like that. Well, maybe you would, but you've had a rather more conventional upbringing than me. I ran back to the pond and splashed about in the mud till I found the box. Then I walked to the nearest town, discovered who owned the farm and offered him ten times what it was worth. Planning permission was a breeze, and we started building. Then things started to get weird.

Basically, it was like this. We built the houses, and we sold them, and the day after we'd sold the last one, the whole lot vanished. Gone without a trace. I remember walking up the lane to where the housing estate ought to have been, and there was nothing there: just green grass and hedgerows and birds singing and rabbits scampering about at the side of the road, and not a house or a JCB or a big pile of bricks to be seen anywhere. Meanwhile, according to the Land Registry and the council and everybody else who presumably ought to know, I still owned the land and I had full planning consent to build as many houses on it as I could contrive to squeeze in. The only thing that hadn't vanished, in fact, was the money. So, naturally, I started all over again. I built another housing estate and sold the houses, and sure enough, twenty-four hours after completion on the final sale, I was right back where I'd started. Grass, birds, rabbits, deeds, planning and a tidy sum put aside in the bank for a rainy day.

And that (Mr Huos said) is basically what I've been doing ever since. I've lost count of how many times. Must be twenty, at least. Which means I've built and sold hundreds of houses and bungalows and maisonettes and studio apartments, all on the same scrubby little bit of land, and I can't face looking at my bank statements any more because the thought of all that money makes me feel sick. But I daren't even think of stopping, because every time I do, I get this dream where the ring reminds me of what'll happen to me if I don't cooperate; and maybe it's bluffing and maybe it isn't, but I really don't want to find out which. And that's not all it's made me do. A while back it pointed out to me that I could save a bundle on my wage bill if I hired my legal staff simultaneously rather than consecutively, and I didn't dare argue; I just did as I was told. I haven't got a clue how, but I had about sixteen qualified lawyers working for me and I was only paying four lots of wages, and there's only four offices in that part of the building.

"So the land you sold me..."

Mr Huos nodded. "The same land," he said. "Sometimes, just for a change, I sell it to another developer instead of building on it myself. Makes no odds. As soon as the other guy's built and sold his development, it goes straight back to green fields and gambolling wildlife. But nobody's ever complained," Mr Huos added, and his voice was as taut as a guitar string. "That's the bit that gets to me. You know Jimmy Bouzek, Greystoke Properties? Sold him the land about nine months ago, got it back about six weeks later, and I bump into Jimmy all the time and he's never said a word about our deal. Or Frank Panizo; he bought the land off me just before Christmas, and apparently he's been going around telling everybody what a good deal he made and what a right sucker I was to let him have it so cheap. Satisfied customers, in other words. Which was why," he added sadly, "I sold it to you, because I had no reason to suppose it wouldn't be perfectly all right."

Jack Tedesci looked at him for a long time, then took a deep breath. "Let me get this straight," he said. "You've been selling the same bit of land over and over again, and all the houses vanish, and nobody *minds*?"

Mr Huos didn't reply, and Jack Tedesci, usually about as sensitive as a policeman's boot, realised it would probably be best not to press him on the issue. He was a simple man at heart, single-minded, tenacious, not without a considerable degree of basic predator's cunning, but he believed that the world was made up of straight lines, numbers, causes and effects. Now he was in the excruciatingly uncomfortable position of believing two things simultaneously: one, that Mr Huos was as crazy as three ferrets in a blender; two, that at least some of what he'd just been told was probably true. Faced with something like that, the only course of action he could envisage was to get out of there as quickly as possible, forget everything he'd heard, and get his accountants busy on finding a way of writing off the stupendous sum of money he'd just lost against tax.

"Anyway," Mr Huos was saying, "that's what's going on, more or less. For some reason everything seems to have chosen this particular moment to come unstuck. Bloody nuisance," he added with a death's-head grin. "I've just had to fire all my in-house lawyers, for one thing. Apparently, they're sort of leaking into one another, and that's more aggravation than I can handle, so I thought the simplest thing'd be to get rid of the lot of them. Hopefully all this'll blow over and I can hire them again. I wouldn't want to leave them stranded – they're a good bunch of people, by and large. More worrying is that the land seems to have vanished completely. Well," he added, "you know that already don't you? Anyhow, that's about it." He grinned again, then added, "You did ask."

260 • Tom Holt

"Yes," Jack said. "I did, didn't I?"

Mr Huos stood back and unbolted the lavatory door. "One thing," he said. "Would you mind very much keeping all this to yourself? Only..."

Jack laughed, a harsh, rasping noise, like a man just saved from drowning coughing up water. "No worries on that score," he said. "If I tried to tell anyone what you just told me..." He shook his head so hard he nearly sprained something. "Safe with me," he said firmly. "Just stay away from me, all right? I never want to see or hear from you ever again, got that?"

Mr Huos walked him back to Reception. "I'm sorry," he said, but Jack just turned his back and lunged out into the street. Mr Huos sighed and went back to his office, where he called the bank and arranged for Jack's money to be sent back to him. The least he could do, but not nearly enough.

*Come on, Stan,* he said fervently to himself. *Where are you when I need you?*

Mr Gogerty looked at his watch. It was blank. Where there used to be three dials, there was now only a flat sheet of brush-finished stainless steel. Oh, he thought.

The train didn't seem to be going particularly fast, but it was definitely moving. He looked out of the window, but all he could see was his reflection against a black background. This, he thought, and someone burned down the Carpenter Library. The only possible conclusion: enemy action.

If there's enemy action, it stands to reason there must be an enemy. Mr Gogerty slipped his mind into calm mode and considered what he knew about his presumed assailant. Not very much; but from what little he had, he might be able to build up a profile.

Competent, you had to give him that. Burning down the Carpenter couldn't have been easy. Because of the very nature of what was stored there, the building was protected by the highest level of security known to the trade. Admittedly, the biggest concern had always been spontaneous combustion rather than arson, but the defences against the one should have protected it against the other, unless the arsonist was cunning, resourceful, imaginative and very, very good indeed at doing the business. As for this other thing: creating a biosignature-specific temporal portal, just so Stanley Gogerty could be induced to board a train to seven years in the future, wasn't just impressive, it was showing off. Look how clever I am, his opponent was telling him; you don't want to mess with someone like me. It was also a remarkably humane way of getting rid of him, he couldn't help thinking. There were far worse things, and they were much cheaper and easier to use. If Mr Gogerty had been called upon to take someone out, he'd have gone for something like a consequence mine, probability well, Better Mousetrap or McKinley bomb – tried and tested, devastatingly effective, practically impossible to detect or counter and (since British law didn't recognise the existence of the profession) perfectly legal, even though the effect on the victim was either fatal or worse. Temporal phase engineering was much harder to do, substantially more expensive, considerably less reliable and totally forbidden under the trade's own ferociously enforced by-laws; it was also, to someone of Mr Gogerty's abilities, relatively easy to get out of, eventually. His enemy, therefore, was someone who wanted him out of the way for a certain length of time (no pun intended) but who meant him no lasting harm, and who probably wanted to impress on him that he wasn't playing the blind school. Burning down the Carpenter, on the other hand, implied a rather scary degree of ruthlessness. This time, his unknown enemy was telling him, nobody needs to get hurt. Next time...

Mr Gogerty was mildly impressed; he knew quite a lot about his enemy, after all. That in itself was significant. In the small, claustrophobic village of the profession, such a profile narrowed the list of suspects down considerably, and obviously his enemy knew that. It was almost as though Stan was deliberately being offered a set of clues to an identity – a signature, in fact, albeit a squiggly, illegible doctors-and-solicitors signature that either you recognised or you didn't. It's somebody I know, Mr Gogerty's intuition yelled in his inner ear, somebody I know quite well. Definitely somebody who knows me, or else how...?

He frowned. Leaving the blindingly obvious till last was a fault of his, one that he regretted. The temporal portal had been laid by somebody who could accurately predict his movements. Now that *was* scary. He'd only taken the Tube because he couldn't get a taxi. Refine search parameters. It was pretty unusual that he hadn't been able to get a taxi, since his summoning technology was extremely sophisticated. He reviewed it. Rated Grade 6, it was guaranteed to bring him a taxi in Stoke Newington at 3 a.m. within twenty-five seconds of issuing the summons. A dampening field, therefore. His enemy had neutralised the summons in order to make him take a Tube, before cutting an access portal through time so he'd walk into an Underground station that wouldn't be built for another seven years. Leaving aside the quite remarkable achievement this represented, it begged the question of how Mr Enemy had known which future Tube stop to access; the answer to which was that he'd known the direction Stanley Gogerty intended to travel in. Given the ad hoc nature of the decision, whoever it was must have exceptionally accurate, up-to-the-minute information about his plans and intentions. In other words, a tracking device. A bug.

Where there's a bug there's a bugger. At some point in the fairly recent past someone had got close enough to plant a tracking device on him, someone with a strong incentive for hindering his current mission. That really narrowed it down while, at the same time, throwing it wide open. Someone who'd come within arm's reach of him. Someone who, presumably, really didn't like Mr Huos. Someone with a Grade 9 or higher trade rating.

Um.

Meanwhile, he decided, it would probably be a good idea to stop the train and get off. He got up and walked along the carriage, looking for the red emergency-stop button. There wasn't one. That, he had to concede, made things awkward. A Tube train in motion in an underground tunnel isn't the easiest thing in the world to disembark from. He could smash a window and crawl/jump/fall out, but only if he didn't mind the high probability of being killed or horribly mangled. He tried the connecting door into the next carriage, with a view to getting to the driver's cab. It was locked, and not just with a physical mechanism. When he touched it, it was as though he'd loaded up on LSD and stuck his hand in a bacon slicer. He took a moment to recover, then tried prodding the handle very gently with a pencil, which promptly turned into a green mamba and tried to crawl up his sleeve. He dropped it quickly and retreated to the other end of the compartment. Someone had put a Grade 6 jamming protocol on the door. Laying it on with a trowel, he couldn't help thinking.

His respect for his unidentified enemy ratcheted up a notch or two. Eventually, the train would arrive somewhere (because a stable temporal stasis field, though theoretically possible, would be inconceivably expensive to produce) and he'd be able to get off and find his way back to his own proper time and place. Until then, he was forced to concede, he was stuck. Mr Enemy – it hurt him to admit it, but he had no choice – was better at this sort of thing than he was. Grade 6 jamming protocols. He shuddered and issued a mental apology to his client. Sorry, Mr Huos, but you're on your own. Stanley Gogerty is off the case. He sighed, opened his briefcase, took out the forensics report for the Mendoza Consortium inquiry and began to read.

It was fairly engrossing stuff (maybe he'd been wrong to focus exclusively on the penguins-in-June angle after all) and he'd read fifteen pages before he looked up to discover that there was someone sitting next to him. Mr Gogerty didn't do double takes or sitting high jumps. Instead, he put the report back in his briefcase and clicked the locks shut before turning his head, taking a long, steady look at the newcomer and saying, "I'm Stanley Gogerty. Who the hell are you?"

He'd gone with *who* mostly out of politeness, but *what* would have been more appropriate. It was humanoid, more or less. It had arms and legs and a perfectly spherical blob for a head, snowman eyes in an otherwise blank face. A six-foot 3D gingerbread man badly rendered in CGI.

"Hello," it replied.

The voice told him what it was. Unlike the body, the voice was packed with information. It had a slight London accent; it sounded male and early thirties, diffident, self-conscious, a bit like it needed to go to the lavatory very soon indeed. Its master's voice, Mr Gogerty concluded, which meant it was some form of trfade artefact, a golem or Henderson projection, or possibly a good old-fashioned spat-upon hair.

"How long have you been sitting there?" Mr Gogerty asked.

"Oh, about five minutes," it replied. "I didn't want to disturb you."

Probably not an assassin in that case. "Who sent you?"

It opened the slit in its face, but no words came out, and since it had no lips Mr Gogerty couldn't lip-read. It had been a trick question, in any case. Animated proxy artefacts can't do proper nouns.

"I see," Mr Gogerty said. "Well, what can I do for you?"

"You must come with me at once," it replied. "Life and death. If convenient."

Mr Gogerty smiled. "I'd like to do that," he said. "Unfortunately, I don't think that'd be possible. This train is ..."

This train was, in fact, slowing down. Mr Gogerty glanced through the window and saw VICTORIA in a red circle with a bar through it. As the train drew smoothly to a halt, he checked his watch. Three dials.

"How did you do that?" he asked.

It smiled. "I have no idea," it replied. "Follow me, please."

Out onto the platform, up the escalator, out into the street. Oddly enough, none of the hundreds of people swarming about in Victoria station seemed to notice that Mr Gogerty's companion was a featureless, asexual, biscuit-coloured nude, or that it didn't have a valid ticket. Outside, it raised its arm above its head and a taxi immediately drew up beside it – driven, Mr Gogerty noticed, by what could only be the thing's identical twin brother. His escort didn't specify an address, but the taxi drove off anyway.

Neither of the gingerbread men said a word after that, so Mr Gogerty took the opportunity to read a bit more of the Mendoza report. He didn't feel in the least apprehensive, which was good. His only regret was that his boyhood promise to his mother, not to get into a motor vehicle with strange men, was now completely and irrevocably broken. On the plus side, according to his watch he'd re-entered conventional linear time only three minutes after he'd left it. To a self-employed man who charged by the hour, that was a small mercy worth being grateful for.

The taxi stopped, and Mr Gogerty looked up and put the report away in his briefcase. He frowned. If he didn't know any better...

"Where are we?" he asked.

"Here," the thing replied, with as beautiful a smile as it's possible to produce without a conventional mouth. The taxi door swung open, and Mr Gogerty got out.

Briefly, in the time it would take a photon to travel twenty yards, Mr Gogerty considered running for it. After all, it hadn't been precisely established whether he'd been (a) rescued or (b) abducted, though he suspected it was really (c) both. It was possible – more than possible, given the vicissitudes of his trade – that he'd been brought here by an enemy, though presumably not the enemy who'd marooned him briefly on a Tube train in the future, and that if he now

266 • Tom Holt

went where he was led, he'd have cause to regret it. It didn't feel like that, however, and Mr Gogerty was quite good at sensing impending danger, a talent which explained the fact he'd lived long enough to own more than six pairs of shoes. Also, he was confoundedly curious, and if he was right about where he'd been brought to...

"Follow," said the thing. "Please," it added. So Mr Gogerty followed.

A glimpse of a street name, and then of the number on the front door, confirmed at least part of his hunch. The interesting question now was which flat in the block he'd be taken to. It also occurred to him to wonder what his enemy – his original enemy, the one who'd planted on him a tracking device which he hadn't so far been able to identify and remove – was making of all this.

The thing led him up the stairs, with the other thing, the one who'd been driving the taxi, following on behind at a discreet distance. The number on the door they stopped at answered the most pressing question in his mind, so when the door was opened (by a tall, thin, pale young man with long, shaggy hair and glasses) he knew what to say.

"Hello," he said, "you must be Donald Mayer. I'm Stanley Gogerty."

Surprisingly, the young man didn't seem to have been expecting that. "Um," he said. "I mean, I'm sorry. You're late."

Mr Gogerty considered him. To survive for any length of time in the profession, it helped to be a good – and very, very quick – judge of character. Mr Gogerty's very first impression was that Mr Mayer was a pretty gormless young man. No, not just gormless, but a black hole into which gorm falls and is utterly consumed. Why he revised that opinion a fraction of a second later he wasn't entirely sure, but once the revision had been made he was quite happy to abide by it. Gormless, yes, but inside the oyster of his gormlessness lurked a tiny seed pearl of something else, which was why, accused of lateness,

Mr Gogerty nodded gravely and said, "Sorry about that. I was held up. This—" He nodded at the thing.

"I know," Mr Mayer interrupted. "I sent them. I think," he added. "Hair?"

The two things nodded enthusiastically, then jumped into Mr Mayer's hand, shrinking as they went. By the time they landed on his palm, they were two carrot-red hairs, which Mr Mayer put back with an embarrassed look, like a man doing up his fly in public.

"I hope they didn't—"

"Not at all," Mr Gogerty replied briskly. "In fact, they rescued me from a temporal vortex, so I'm much obliged to you. Shall I come in?"

Mr Mayer looked at him as though he'd just been told he'd been chosen to lead the human race in its crusade against the Marshmallow People. "Um," he replied. "Sorry. Yes."

"After you, then."

"What? Oh, right. This way."

Mr Gogerty followed, and as he crossed the threshold he felt it, the presence of a trade artefact: something like having your skull squeezed in a bench vice while ants run riot inside your clothes. Strong. In fact... He paused to steady himself on the door frame.

There aren't any Oscars in the profession – no Emmys, no Pulitzers, Nobels or Bookers. There're the Siegfrieds, but they're really only for dragon slaying, vampire kebabbing and the like, while these days the Merlins are little more than a popularity contest, a means of recognising the fact that so-and-so's managed to complete thirty years in the trade without being killed, transfigured or imprisoned for ever in the heart of a glacier. The only meaningful accolade left is the four-yearly Shumway Award (nowadays it's the Carlstein Lager-Bank of the Dead-Kawaguchiya Integrated Circuits-Shumway Award), presented to the practitioner responsible for a truly significant advance in professional research. Past winners have included

Arne Mortensen, Li Huan-Chi, Theo van Spee, Frank Carpenter and the Shaftgrave sisters, and it's widely recognised as the only gong in the biz that money or threats can't buy. The irony is that nine times out of ten, the recipient is some otherwise run-of-the-mill individual who happened to be in the right place at the right time: Mortensen on the steps of the Smithsonian at the exact moment when Krakatoa erupted, Li history-kibbitzing in Sir Isaac Newton's garden when the apple parted from the tree and slowly floated upwards, Molly Shaftgrave inadvertently trapped inside her own suitcase at Heathrow Terminal 5 and shipped across the interdimensional void to the parallel universe where Bing Crosby was cast as the Man With No Name in *A Fistful of Dollars*. In the past Mr Gogerty had felt bitterly aggrieved at the sheer dumb luck that had brought these losers the trade's most coveted accolade, knowing full well that he'd never get that lucky. Or maybe (the waves of pressure emanating from whatever-it-was made his ears hum like an extractor fan) not.

"My sister Polly," said Mr Mayer, wobbling his hand in the general direction of some female.

It was somewhere in this room. "Pleased to meet you," said Mr Gogerty, trying not to be too obvious as his eyes flicked from table to floor to ceiling. "You wanted to see me."

"That's right," said Mr Mayer's sister Polly. "There's something really screwy going on, and we want to know how to make it stop."

It took Mr Gogerty quite an effort to remember how to smile. "Screwy is my business," he said, sitting down on the sofa and only just managing not to groan at the pounding of blood in his forehead. "Tell me all about it."

So she did, and to his credit Mr Gogerty managed to concentrate just enough to get the gist of it. A pencil sharpener.

"Excuse me," he interrupted. "A brass pencil sharpener?"

Mr Mayer nodded eagerly. "Could be brass, yes."

"In a box?"

"What? Sorry. No, there wasn't a box."

"I see. Please, carry on."

( Why not ask to see it? He wasn't sure. Maybe it was simple fear. Any closer to the source of all that energy and the fillings in his teeth would start melting. Maybe subconsciously he was prolonging the moment of triumph, quite possibly the crowning glory of his entire career. Or maybe, before he actually confronted the thing, he needed to know what had become of the box. The Lifetime Achievement Shumway would look just right on his mantelpiece, in between the alabaster Minoan vase and his uncle Desmond's clock, but boxes don't just vanish. Something, he felt it in his scar tissue, wasn't quite right.)

Something bad had happened. The upstairs neighbour gone without a trace. Mr Gogerty twitched in his chair. He'd forgotten all about the occupant of the flat above.

"That'd be Mr Kevin Briggs," he said calmly.

He'd scored a few points with that one. Both of them stared at him, and the female said, "How the hell did you know that?"

Other members of the profession reckoned a little showmanship was perfectly legitimate and good for business. Fair enough, but not when it gets in the way. "I know about Mr Briggs," he said. "He took some laundry to SpeediKleen in Clevedon Road, shortly before—" He paused. Reading his clients' faces was an important part of his business. "The name rings a bell, I take it."

"More like an international festival of campanology," the young man muttered. "That's the place where Polly took her dress, and then it—"

"Disappeared." Mr Gogerty nodded. "I know. Let me be perfectly frank with you, Mr Mayer. SpeediKleen is the main reason I'm here."

The sister – he'd suspected all along she was the brighter of the two – was looking at him. "You're searching for it," she said.

"I found it," he replied.

He'd intended to be impressive – force of professional

habit – and he'd succeeded, to the point where he was afraid he was laying himself open to charges of self-indulgence. "I think I'd better level with you both," he said. "My client – you'll excuse me if I don't tell you his name, I'm sure you understand why – is extremely anxious to trace a certain object he lost recently. He has reason to believe that it was in the pocket of an overcoat he took in to SpeediKleen in Clevedon Road. I should point out that this object is capable of doing very strange things."

"Magic," the sister said.

Mr Gogerty winced as though he was an admiral and someone at a party had asked him what kind of boat he drove. "For want of a better word," he said. "The important point is, this object is potentially very dangerous. In fact," he added, as Mr Mayer's face went the colour of ten-year-old white gloss paintwork, "there's evidence to suggest that it's already been responsible for some extremely unfortunate events, quite apart from the disappearance of your upstairs neighbour. I would therefore urge you most strongly—" (Damn it, Mr Gogerty thought, I'm starting to sound like a policeman at a press conference.) "If you can help me find it," he said, "you'd be doing me a favour, and my client, and possibly a great many other people as well."

The sister was looking at him again. "You think Don's pencil sharpener's this magic thing."

"There is that possibility, yes." (Damn it, he'd slipped back into rozzerspeak.) "If I could just . . ."

"You seem to know a lot about it. What it does."

Sharp as a bramble, that one. "Mostly guesswork," he said. "Even my client, its owner, doesn't actually know what it is or where it came from."

Ms Mayer nodded. "But you know, don't you? Or you've got a pretty good idea."

He made a vague gesture with his arms. "I've never seen this thing," he said. "I don't know what it looks like. I haven't seen a picture or anything like that. But—"

"Is that right?" Ms Mayer was after him now. He decided he didn't like her terribly much. "This client of yours hires you to find something for him, but you don't know what it looks like. But," she added with a frown, "you think it might be a pencil sharpener. Sorry if I'm being a bit slow here, but didn't your client say? I mean, to be or not to be a pencil sharpener's hardly a grey area."

"It changes shape," he said. "That's what he told me. It can be one thing one day and something else the next. He only knows it's really the same thing because it's always been kept in its box. Once it's out of the box, I imagine there's no obvious way of telling it apart from any old bit of brass junk you might find at a car boot sale. Unless, of course," he added forcefully, "you happen to be a world expert on objects of that kind. Like me."

She smiled sourly at him. "So you do know what it is."

"Yes."

"Fine." By the look of it, she didn't like him much, either. "So what is it?"

"I'm afraid I can't tell you that." Oh well, he thought, never mind. "You must understand, I have a duty to my existing client. And the object in question does belong to him, after all."

"Oh fine." A disapproving look, as though he was global warming, nuclear weapons, GM crops and the deforestation of the Amazon basin all rolled into one. "There's this incredibly dangerous shape-shifting magic thing on the loose that might hurt loads of innocent people, but your lips are sealed because your very rich client wants his toy back. I don't think that's a terribly responsible attitude, do you?"

"Polly." He'd forgotten about Mr Mayer. "Just shut up, will you?"

"Yes, but—"

"Shut up."

And it worked, remarkably. Having achieved his miracle, Mr Mayer gave him a very sad look and said, "The man I sent away. Is he dead?"

Mr Gogerty shook his head. "I don't think so," he replied. "So we can get him back?"

Mr Gogerty hesitated. He could lie and be reasonably sure of Mr Mayer's full cooperation; he could give Mr Huos back his ring today (though without the box, that box) and be sure of his most lucrative client's sincere gratitude and a cheque with noughts on it like a child blowing bubbles. He was in this business to make a living, not to right wrongs. The red cape and inside-out underwear, the blue phone box, the lobbing of enchanted bling into volcanoes; that sort of stunt he left to others, nobler men with ideals and private incomes. On the other hand, Ms Polly bloody Mayer had a point; furthermore, she'd taken her point and stuck it right up his conscience, and he didn't like that one bit. Something, he knew, was badly wrong, and if Mr Huos' ring was what he thought it was, feared it was, as long as the wretched thing was out there, it could only get worse. And furthermore, someone had burned down the Carpenter Library. Much as he'd have liked to, he couldn't overlook that.

So, "I don't know," he said. "I believe that if your pencil sharpener turns out to be the item my client is looking for, we should be able to undo what happened to Mr Briggs."

Mr Mayer looked as though he was about to burst. "We can get him back."

"We can get back something," Mr Gogerty said. "But not necessarily what you sent away."

Which quite obviously wasn't what either of them had wanted to hear. They looked at him helplessly, like would-be passengers gazing through the window of a bus pulling away just as they reached the stop. Then Mr Mayer said, "Oh."

Mr Gogerty took a deep breath. "If this thing's what I think it is," he said, "it will all depend on whether we can provide the answer to a question. If we can, all may yet be well. If not..."

"A question." Polly Mayer was back in town. "What do you mean, a question?"

"A question," Mr Gogerty repeated. "That, if my theory's correct, is what the artefact wants. If we can answer the question, there's a good chance things will sort themselves out. If not..." He shrugged. "It's not quite as clear-cut an issue as you'd like to think, Ms Mayer. If we can't answer the question, my client might as well have the item as anybody else. He's owned it for quite a while, and this is the first time it's caused any trouble, and only because it managed to get away from him. It could well be that it's as safe with him as it's possible for it to be. And yes," he added with a faint smile, "then I'd get paid my substantial fee, so at least someone'd be happy. You wouldn't begrudge me that, would you, Ms Mayer? As it happens, I've worked very hard indeed to get this far."

Ms Mayer scowled at him, then sighed. "I suppose not. But never mind about that. How do we find out what this stupid question is?"

"Oh, I know that," Mr Gogerty replied sadly. "Everyone knows the question. It's the answer that's the problem. It has been all along."

"Oh for pity's sake," Mr Mayer interrupted, jumping up and inadvertently treading on a discarded pizza tray. "If I hear one more cryptic utterance I'm going to start biting people. If you know this bloody question, tell us what it is. Then, if we don't know the answer, we'll look it up, on Google or Wikipedia. I suppose you've been so busy chasing around the place doing magic, it's never occurred to you to try something so obvious and simple."

"Actually," Mr Gogerty said mildly, "I did try it once, just to see what'd happen."

"And?"

"I got two answers," Mr Gogerty said. "But I knew them already. There are only two possible answers, you see. The difficulty lies in choosing which—"

Mr Mayer bared his teeth. It was almost certainly an empty, melodramatic gesture, but Mr Gogerty had been around long enough not to take that sort of risk. "All right," he said, "the question is this. Which came first—"

Ms Mayer groaned. "You can't be serious."

But Mr Gogerty nodded and grinned. "I'm afraid so. That's the question you need to answer. Which came first, the chicken –" he folded his arms and leaned back in his chair "– or the egg?"

# CHAPTER THIRTEEN

Dimly aware that something wasn't quite as it should be, the black knight nevertheless adjusted his grip on the handle of his shield, drew his sword, stifled a yawn and lumbered across the greensward to meet his enemy.

The white knight turned to face him, shield outstretched. There was no r in the month so it was the black knight's turn to strike first. He aimed a devastating blow at the side of his opponent's head, which the white knight deflected quite easily before countering with a backhand cut to the shoulder. The black knight took a long step back, and the slash whistled harmlessly past.

"My sister-in-law's birthday today," said the black knight. Then he parried high, checked the stroke halfway and converted it into a low cut to the knee. Unsporting, strictly speaking, but because he was the villain, he was allowed.

"Is that your sister in Argyll?" the white knight replied, moving sideways to avoid the attack and using the same motion to chop down briskly at the black knight's wrist.

"That's right," the black knight said, tilting the edge of his shield to block. "She'd have been six hundred and forty-two today." He lunged at the eye slits of the white knight's helmet, but a timely parry with the flat of the blade sent the attack off to the side. The white knight riposted with a cut to the elbow, which the black knight's armour absorbed.

"She married a Yorkshireman, didn't she?" the white knight asked.

The black knight nodded, then swung his sword in a wide, flailing arc. Ostensibly he was trying to crush the top of his opponent's helmet; what he was actually doing was giving him an opening, so he'd be able to nip smartly inside the black knight's guard, whack him hard on the collarbone and follow up with a full-strength blow to the head that would end the fight. It was a fairly recent addition to their repertoire – he'd introduced it the year before Sir Walter Raleigh brought back the first potato from the New World – but they'd both got the hang of it, more or less, and the black knight quite liked it because it meant he could lose quickly, without having to be pounded to a standstill. After all, as he'd explained to the white knight more than once over the years, just because they were both trapped for ever in endless repetitions of a bizarre and meaningless ritual, it didn't mean pain didn't hurt.

But the white knight didn't move. He just stood there, his head tilted a little to one side, like a puzzled dog. "You know what," he said. "Something's wrong."

Slowly the black knight lowered his sword. "You think so too?" he asked.

The white knight nodded, quite an achievement for a man wearing a twelve-pound helmet. "Don't ask me what it is," he said, "but something's definitely not right. It's been bothering me ever since we started this morning."

The black knight sheathed his sword. He wasn't supposed to do that. In seven centuries he'd never done it. They fought; he got knocked silly and dropped the sword, and when he came back on line again at the start of the next time around, the sword would be back in its scabbard at his side. That was probably why it took him four goes before he eventually managed it.

He waited, half expecting a bolt of lightning to fry him where he stood for breaking the rules. Nothing happened.

"It's like something's missing," the white knight said contemplatively, and the black knight thought, Yes, that's it. He's right. Something missing. A bit like walking into an empty house when you'd been sure there'd be someone at home.

They both looked around. It had been years since the black knight had actually stopped and taken any notice of his surroundings. They were still, he noticed, as dull and boring as ever.

"What do you think we should do?" the black knight said.

"Don't know," the white knight replied. "You feel it too, then."

"Definitely," the black knight confirmed quickly. "Something's been bugging me all day, but I didn't like to say anything. Thought it must just be me feeling a bit off colour or something."

"You're not feeling well?"

"No, I'm fine. Well, a bit of a headache. But I always get a bad head after you've knocked me out a couple of times."

Then the white knight did something extraordinary, something he'd never done before in all the years they'd been working together. He took his helmet off.

"I'm sorry to hear that," he said. "I didn't realise."

The white knight wasn't a bit like his colleague had expected. In fact he was a round-faced, chubby-cheeked man with small blue eyes and a big ginger moustache. "I did sort of try hinting," the black knight said. "Anyway, that's not important."

"But if I've been giving you headaches all this time..."

"Forget it." The black knight was fumbling with his own chinstrap buckle. It had been so long, he could barely remember where it was or how it worked.

"Yes, but we could change the fight a bit. How'd it be if instead of a side cut in—"

"Really," the black knight said firmly, "it's no big deal." His fingers found the loop of the strap and tugged it past the bar of the buckle. A moment later he was out of the helmet and into the light and air.

"Are you all right?" the white knight asked.

"Fine," the black knight assured him, gasping slightly. The light (it was a dull, overcast day) was blinding him, burning his eyes. "Just not used to all this space, I guess." He lifted the helmet clear of his head, lost his grip on it and dropped it. "I've been trapped in that stupid thing so long..."

"Of course," the white knight said. "I was forgetting, you don't get to take yours off, do you?" He frowned. He had a kind face. "That must be a real pain in the bum," he said.

Suddenly the black knight could feel tears welling up in the corners of his eyes, and he didn't think it was the brightness of the light. He decided to change the subject.

"So," he said. "What d'you reckon?"

The white knight shrugged. "Search me," he said. "Maybe we should ask the priest."

That sounded promising. Priests were men of God; a priest would be bound to know. "Should we?" he asked hopefully.

"Can't hurt," the white knight said. "Come on."

But the priest took one look at them walking towards him side by side when they should have been clubbing each other savagely, and ran into the chapel, slamming the door behind him. A moment later they heard bolts being rammed home.

The black knight remembered he was the bad guy. "We could break the door down," he suggested.

The white knight thought for a moment, then shook his head. "Better not," he said. "After all, it's a sort of church. Besides, he didn't look to me like he knows what's going on."

True enough; the poor man had come across as scared out of his wits. "Now what?" the black knight asked.

"I think we should keep going till we meet somebody, and ask them."

The black knight could think of several objections to that.

On the other hand, the white knight was the good guy, which presumably gave him the moral authority to decide their course of action; also, he had nothing better to suggest. "All right," he said. "Which way?"

The white knight shrugged. "Broad as it's long, I guess. This way," he added, and there was something in his voice that inspired confidence – not all that much, but some. He took a step forward, then paused and turned back. "I'm Gareth, by the way," he said.

Seven hundred years of bashing each other over the head. "I'm Mordred," the black knight replied.

The white knight held out his hand. "Pleased to meet you," he said.

Old habits die hard. It cost the black knight a special effort of will not to grab the proffered hand and twist it into an armlock. Instead, he shook it gravely. "Likewise," he said.

The next few seconds were acutely embarrassing, as was only to be expected after such a display of raw but cissy emotion. Then the white knight pulled himself together and stomped off through the long grass, and the black knight followed him.

Seven hundred years he'd worn the same armour every second he was conscious, but in all that time he'd never had occasion to walk more than a few yards. Ouch, he thought. It wasn't hard to identify the source of the discomfort. His armoured shoes (sabatons, to be pub-quiz-trivia accurate, a pair of sheet steel galoshes that looked like giant woodlice) had rubbed huge great blisters on both his heels, and every step he took was agony. He stopped to whimper, then had to break into a trot just to keep up.

"What d'you reckon that is?" the white knight said, and pointed to a curious white seat dead ahead. The black knight stopped (bliss!) and studied the thing. It wasn't like any seat, chair or throne he'd ever seen before. It had no arms, for one thing, and it was rounded in every plane. It was white, shiny like marble, with what looked like a wooden cushion. Closer inspection revealed a sort of tap, like a larger version of a beer-barrel spigot, only apparently made of brightly polished steel, sticking out of the square boxed-shaped section you were presumably meant to lean your back against.

"What's a stone chair doing in the middle of a field?" the white knight asked.

Good question. "Must be a monument of some kind. Symbolic," the black knight explained. "Maybe it's a war memorial or something."

The white knight approached it warily. "You'd think there'd be writing on it," he said. "Otherwise, how's anybody supposed to know what it's commemorating?" He extended one steel-plated finger and gently pressed down on the spigot. It moved under his hand, and from somewhere came a great sound of rushing water.

"Must be magic," the white knight said, as if repeating an article of faith. Magic explained anything, just as any bizarre or inexplicable action can be made sense of by saying it's for tax reasons. "A siege perilous, something like that. I bet if you sit in it and close your eyes, you can see all the kingdoms of the earth."

"Could be," the black knight replied diplomatically. "Or it could be a trap. Could be if you sit in it, it grabs hold of you and won't let you go."

"If you prod the shiny bar thing, you can hear the sea."

"I'd leave well alone if I were you," the black knight said. He wasn't entirely happy about his new best friend's attitude. The sort of man who, confronted in a mysterious landscape with an alien lever, presses it to see what it does isn't the kind of leader who inspires confidence.

"You're quite right," the white knight said wistfully. "Come on, then, if you're coming."

They hadn't gone more than a few steps when a patch of thin air dead ahead of them suddenly turned into a door. The white knight stopped dead in his tracks.

"It's a door," he said.

"Maybe," the black knight said warily. "Funny place for a door to be, though. For a start, there's no wall."

"Magic," the white knight said, and he was right: there could be no possible alternative explanation. But confirmed outbreaks of magic made the black knight want to run a mile, even in badly fitting sabatons, whereas the white knight made it sound like a good thing. On balance, the black knight decided, his new friend had been less trouble when he'd been bashing him on the head.

"So what do you reckon?" the white knight said. He nudged it with his foot and it swung open an inch or so. "Do we go through it or what?"

Typical good-guy mentality. Still, it was pretty well certain that the idiot was going to go through it whether the black knight approved or not, and if one of them went through, solidarity demanded that the other must follow. He groaned to himself and said, "Why not?"

So they went through, and found themselves in a corridor or cloister. Everything about it made the black knight's flesh creep. For one thing, the walls appeared to be covered with paper; what the hell was that supposed to mean? Did passing through the door mean they'd wound up inside a book? From what he'd gathered from stories he'd heard, that was exactly the sort of thing you could expect if you started messing around with magic. And as for the floor...

"Hellfire," he groaned. "This place has got woollen grass."

But the white knight shook his head. "I know about this stuff," he said. "It's called carpet. Cousin of mine brought some back from the crusades. Fiendishly expensive stuff, by all accounts. My cousin said it cost him twelve gold nobles a yard. We must be in a royal palace."

"Lucky us," the black knight muttered. It wasn't too late to turn round and go back, but he knew that if he suggested it, the white knight would only say, "You go back if you want," or words to that effect, and then he'd have to carry on to the bitter end or be shamed eternally. "After you," he said stiffly, and the white knight tore his attention away from the floor and stomped on down the corridor, until they reached another door.

"Look, there's a glass panel," the white knight said in an awed voice. "Definitely a palace."

The black knight took a deep breath. "Did you ever hear the story," he said, "of the wandering knight caught out in a terrible storm who came across a castle in the middle of nowhere, and when he knocked there was no answer, so he went in, and it turned out it wasn't a castle after all, it was the lair of the troll king, and suddenly a whole load of trolls jumped out at him from nowhere and ate him?"

"No," said the white knight. "Why?"

"Nothing," the black knight replied gloomily. "Go on, then."

So the white knight pushed the door open and lumbered through it, and the room they found on the other side was so weird and strange and unlike anything either of them had heard of that they quickened their pace and kept going, until they came to yet another door, which opened onto a lane, and green grass, and fresh air. They stumbled through it and dropped on their knees on the grass, shaking.

"That," said the white knight, "was all a bit much."

The black knight slowly hauled himself upright and looked around. "You know what," he said. "I think I know where we are."

"Really?"

Nod. "I reckon that's the abbey's twelve-acre pasture," he said, pointing. "Except there ought to be a wood over to the left and there isn't one."

Pause. Then the white knight said tactfully, "We've been away for a while."

Oh God, the black knight thought, so we have. Seven hundred years. For a moment the weight of the implications crushed him, like a ploughman's boot crushing a snail. On the other hand, he was alive, he'd escaped from the terrible endlessly repeated battle, he'd got through the troll king's palace in one piece. Always look on the bright side, his mother used to say. "Come on," he said cheerfully, and started to walk up the lane.

"Where are we going?" the white knight asked.

"You're not from round here, then." He realised how little he knew about the man he'd been fighting all these years.

"Me? Lord, no. I'm from Kent originally. So where is this?"

"Worcestershire," the black knight replied, "I think. My home territory, I grew up just over that big hill over there, look. If I'm right, we're just outside Norton St Edgar."

"Oh. Is it nice?"

The black knight shrugged. "It's home," he said.

They walked on for a while, and for some reason the blisters on the black knight's heels didn't hurt nearly as much as they had earlier, or perhaps he didn't notice or didn't care. Home, he thought, *home*! But home is a location in time as well as space.

They rounded a corner, and—

"I was right," the black knight said. "There's St Edgar's church, dead ahead. And..." He laughed. "Looks like they've turned Old Blind Wat's cottage into a pub."

"A pub," the white knight repeated thoughtfully. "Um, have you got any money on you?"

"I don't need money around here," the black knight replied. "My family owns this whole—" He stopped and thought about it. "No," he said. "No money. Sorry."

"Maybe we could try barter," the white knight said. "Nice sword or helmet, look good hanging over the bar."

The black knight tried the door. "It's shut," he said grimly.

"What do you mean, shut?" the white knight demanded angrily. "It's not Lent."

"Well," the black knight said, "it's locked and there doesn't seem to be anybody about."

"We could try breaking the door down."

No more Mr Good Guy, apparently. Talking of which...

But it had been so long, so very long, that he couldn't remember how it had started, how he'd come to meet the white knight in the first place, to fight with him, to start the endless, pitiless cycle they'd both been trapped in. Why was I the bad guy? he tried to remember. What did I do? Was it just because, when I bought my armour, the only colour they had in my size was black? He considered what little he knew about himself. He didn't feel evil, but presumably they all say that, the sackers of cities, burners of monasteries, oppressors of peasants – not that he could remember ever having done any of that stuff. And even if he had been bad seven hundred years ago, surely that was all long since gone and obsolete. Everything that had made up his world had presumably passed away and been forgotten. It occurred to him that an hour or so with some coarse-grade sandpaper and wire wool would be all it would take to make him the white knight, and then...

"Ah well," the white knight said sadly, as he tried to peer through a gap in the curtains. "Better be getting back, I suppose."

For a considerable time the black knight was so stunned he couldn't speak. "You what?"

"Getting back," the white knight said. "To the abbey. Before they notice we aren't there."

The black knight shook his head so violently he almost twisted a gorget rivet. "Not likely," he said. "I'm not going back, not ever."

"You can't be serious." The white knight sounded horrified.

"Too right I'm serious," the black knight said. "Nothing on earth could possibly make me go back in there and carry on with that ridiculous bloody farce. No, thanks all the same, this is where I make a fresh start." He paused. You can't spend seven hundred years with someone and not feel anything, even if that person's spent all that time hammering on your skull with a sixpound broadsword. "If you want to go back, that's up to you. I'm staying."

"But you can't."

Not an attempt at persuasion; a statement of fact. At the back of the black knight's memory something nasty stirred, prompted by the total conviction in the white knight's voice. It was true: he couldn't stay here, just like he couldn't flap his arms and fly like a bird. "Why not?" he asked feebly.

"You know perfectly well."

"Remind me."

The white knight's expression was a subtle blend of exasperation and fear. "Because we haven't got the answer yet. You know, to the question."

An answer to a question, how novel. But there was definitely something tapping inside the eggshell of his memory.

Eggshell.

He closed his eyes. He'd known defeat five times a day, every day for seven hundred years. Played 1,277,500. Won 0. Drawn 0. Lost 1,277,500. But that had just been swordfighting, and it didn't matter.

"Oh," he said. "That question."

"Which came first, the—"

"Yes," he snapped. "Thank you, I remember now. We can't leave till someone gets the right answer."

"Exactly." The white knight didn't half sound relieved. "And that hasn't happened yet, obviously."

A tiny flicker of hope. "Maybe it has," he said. "Maybe that's why it stopped and we were able to come out here. Maybe it's over."

The white knight shook his head slowly. "They'd have told us," he said. "There'd have been an official announcement. Heralds, that sort of thing." He gave the pub door a last pointless nudge with his hip. "No, there's just been some sort of glitch, that's all. When we get back, it'll be business as usual."

The black knight sagged. Of course it would, and fairly soon all this would feel like it had been a stupid dream. "Tell me something," he said. "After you've won the fight and I've been knocked out—"

"Killed," the white knight corrected him. "I kill you."

The black knight shrugged. "Whatever," he said. "Afterwards, what do you do? Before it all resets to zero, I mean."

So the white knight told him: the monk, the abbey, the glowing altar, the chicken, the egg; go now, you are not worthy. "And that's more or less it," he concluded.

"You're kidding."

The white knight shook his head. "Always the same," he said. "Never varies. I've tried doing something different ever so many times, but somehow, you know, I just can't."

Suddenly getting cracked on the head – killed even – didn't seem all that bad in comparison. "Rather you than me," the black knight said. "What's it all supposed to mean?"

Shrug. "Come on," the white knight said. "We really should be getting back."

Slowly they turned round and trudged back the way they'd come. The black knight's feet were killing him. Five times a day, he thought; I get killed five times a day. Frequent dier points and everything.

"Well," the white knight was saying, "it was fun while it lasted. It'll be something we can look back on. Until we forget about it, of course."

The black knight stopped. They'd turned the corner, and from that stretch of overgrown drystone wall you could see right across the valley. "It's gone," he said.

"What?"

"The building," the black knight said quietly. "You know, the one we live in. This is where we left it. But it's not here any more."

"Chicken," Polly said.

"Egg," said Don, almost but not quite simultaneously.

Mr Gogerty smiled and shook his head. "Guessing's not allowed," he said. "You've got to *know*. That's the rule," he added, "apparently."

Don gave him a puzzled look. "But there's only two possible answers," he replied. "Therefore, one of them's got to be right. So..."

Mr Gogerty stretched his impossibly long legs. "You remember in maths exams," he said. "The answer doesn't count unless you show how you got there."

"Oh." Don slumped in his chair. "So we've got to prove it is what you're saying."

Mr Gogerty rubbed his chin. "I don't think it's like proving it to a jury," he said. "As long as you know, that'd be all right. But you don't, do you?"

Don frowned. "Well, no. But it's one of those impossible things – paradoxes. The whole point of it is there isn't a right answer."

"Neither," Polly said sharply. "That's got to be it. The answer, I mean. Neither came first."

Mr Gogerty smiled at them as though they were children. "I'm not laughing at you," he said. "In fact, I spent three years trying to prove it myself. I argued that the egg represents the future, just as the chicken represents the egg, with the moment of egg laying being the present. Since any reasonably stable material object exists in all three temporal locations – I was here five seconds ago, I'm here now, I'll still be here in five seconds' time – it's pointless to differentiate between them. I'm me in all three locations. By that argument, the chicken and the egg that came out of the chicken are essentially the same, therefore indivisible in space and time. Therefore neither came first. I put it rather better in my doctoral thesis, but that's basically what I argued."

"And?"

"I won a prize," Mr Gogerty said, with more than a hint of pride. "A consolation prize, of course. E for effort. They gave me this watch." He rolled back his cuff. "One of the proudest days of my life, except it meant I'd failed. Sorry," he went on. "'neither' is not the right answer. Nor is 'both.' " He grinned. "That didn't stop them giving Otto van Helsing the Siegfried Award in 1896 for suggesting it. But it's wrong."

"Let's get this straight," Polly said, and it was interesting to see how both men cowered ever so slightly at the briskness of her voice: Mr Gogerty, who'd battled with the Undead and faced the unthinkable horror of the existential void, and Don, who was used to her by now. "This pencil sharpener—"

"A shape-shifting trade artefact of considerable power," Mr Gogerty mumbled.

"This pencil sharpener," Polly repeated, "won't let Don's upstairs neighbour come back from wherever he's gone to unless we can tell it which came first. But according to you there're only four possible answers, and they're all wrong."

Mr Gogerty had never married, and his relationships with women had all been brief and disconcerting. "Not necessarily," he said, and was taken aback when Polly made a noise like an exploding pressure cooker and stomped across the room with her arms tightly folded. "It's the difference between guessing and—"

"Yes, all right," Polly barked. "I still don't see what all that's about, but never mind. What you're saying is that, for all practical purposes, there's no way of getting that stupid man back. Well?"

"There's a theoretical possibility."

Polly snarled at him. "If people have been trying to answer your stupid puzzle since eighteen ninety-something and they still haven't managed it, then the chances of us three doing it in the foreseeable future have got to be—"

"Your watch," Don said.

Don was a master of the art of quiet interrupting, a useful and necessary art, since nothing else could be relied on to shut his sister up when she was in full flow. Mr Gogerty nodded. "What about it?"

"It's got three..."

Mr Gogerty smiled. If he'd been noticed and taken off for training twenty years ago, Don Mayer might have had a future in the profession. "That's right," he said. "It's a special watch. It tells the time in the present, the past and the future."

Polly's explosive snigger proved Mr Gogerty's long-held belief that talent doesn't always run in families. "That's silly," she said. "What you mean is one dial's a few minutes fast and one's a bit slow. So what? I could—"

Mr Gogerty lifted his arm, wrist cocked, so she could see the dials. She glanced at it, then shook her head.

"Big deal," she said. "It's a watch with three dials."

"Let me see," Don said, leaning over her to look. "She's right," he said. "It's a watch with three dials. But they're all showing the same time."

Mr Gogerty was disappointed. Don had looked at the hands, not the dials themselves, which was why he hadn't noticed that on one dial the numbers ran anticlockwise, while on another there were no numbers at all. The point, in other words, had gone so far over his head you could have bounced a radio signal off it. Never mind.

Don was looking thoughtful. "You're sure that thing works?" he asked.

"Of course," Mr Gogerty said. "I wind it twice a day, without fail. Why do you ask?"

"Nothing," Don said. "Just curious." Quite suddenly he wanted them all to go away so he could think. "Well," he said with an effort, "thanks ever so much for coming. You've explained it all just fine."

"No, he hasn't," Polly objected. "He hasn't explained a damn thing."

"And it looks," Don ground on, "as though there's nothing we can do to get that poor man back, so I suppose I'd better forget about it and get on with my life." He hesitated, then reached down the back of the sofa cushions and pulled out the brass pencil sharpener (without box). "I think you should take this," he said. "Give it back to the bloke you're working for."

"Don," Polly said dangerously. He ignored her. It got just a little bit easier each time.

Mr Gogerty was staring at the pencil sharpener a bit like a dog watching a seagull, a bit like a seagull watching a dog, a bit like stout Cortes in the poem, a bit like the plant supervisor at Chernobyl a moment or so after one of his colleagues said, "Oops." Don was holding the thing out to him, the way a cat brings you a dead mouse, almost pointing it like a gun. Mr Huos will be so pleased, Stan told himself. Or I could save the world. Save the world, tuppence a bag. Not that anybody would thank me for it, because of course nobody would ever know; whereas Mr Huos paid good money.

"Well," Don said. "Take it."

A bit like injections, Mr Gogerty thought. As a boy he had been terrified of injections. It couldn't have been the pain; someone who got into as many fights as he had wasn't bothered about pain, and anyway it's only a little prick from a needle. But every time he had to have an injection he lay awake at night trembling for a week beforehand, and when he got to the doctor's, it took his mother, his uncle Royston and two nurses to hold him down. Try as he might, he simply couldn't hold still and let them jab him, and now, try as he might, he couldn't raise his arm, reach out with his hand and take the pencil sharpener. The thought of touching it, his skin in contact with the metal, was more than he could bear to think about.

It would be different, of course, if it was in a box.

Polly was looking at him, and Don was frowning. "You wouldn't have such a thing as a plastic bag?" he asked.

"You want me to wrap it for you?"

"If you wouldn't mind," Mr Gogerty said. "The truth is, I've got an allergy to copper alloys. They make me come out in boils."

The look on Don's face said, clear as anything, You're lying to me, but *why?* "Hold on," he said. "I'll get you a carrier."

Polly waited till her brother had left the room, then leaned forward and hissed, "If you've been playing games with us, I'll sue you for every penny you've got. Understood?"

Mr Gogerty nodded. Don had left the thing on the floor while he went to the kitchen. "I don't suppose," he said slowly, "anything odd's been happening here. Apart from what you already told me. Anything to do with time."

Polly was about to say, No, of course not. Then Don came out of the kitchen, and she remembered. "The fridge," she said.

"Fridge?"

"The man from the shop called to tell Don when his new fridge was going to be delivered. But that was before we found out the old one had just died." She looked up, just sufficiently worried to forget the lie about the allergy. "Is that the sort of thing?"

She had his undivided attention. "The old fridge," Mr Gogerty said. "Has it been taken away yet?"

Don shook his head. "No, they said they'd take it when they delivered the new one."

With the speed and grace of a leaping panther, Mr Gogerty rose to his feet. "Kitchen through there?"

"Yes. Here," Don added, "don't you want this? I've wrapped it like you asked."

Mr Gogerty snatched the bag from his hand as he brushed past on the way to the kitchen. As he went, it occurred to him that he was quite possibly going to his death, and that there were so many things he'd never done – because he'd been too busy, because he'd always assumed there'd be a tomorrow. He'd never been to Florence. He'd never seen the midnight sun in Norway or the sudden, stunning sunset of the South African veldt. He hadn't won the Shumway Award, or watched his son play football, or composed a piano concerto, or sat up all night on a high mountain to greet the dawn. He hadn't surfed in

California, or hunted wild pigs the hard way in New Zealand, or walked to the South Pole or the source of the Amazon. He hadn't played chess with the Dalai Lama. He hadn't given the Mayers a bill for this consultation.

*Oh well*, he thought, and then for some reason he added, *next time*.

"Why's he gone in the kitchen?" he heard Polly say, and Don answered, "Dunno. Maybe he wants a drink of water." Not the epitaph he'd have wanted. Come to that, he'd never wanted an epitaph of any kind. He'd planned on living for ever, or as near as made no odds.

A fridge. He opened the door, and no light came on. There was a powerful smell of decayed vegetable matter, but all the shelves were Mother-Hubbard bare.

To hell with it, he thought. Then he clambered into the fridge, which sort of grew to accommodate him, and closed the door behind him.

"That," said Ms Byron, clawing the ground with her foot, "was a shambles."

Thirty female lawyers and the greatest living interpreter of *Kindertotenlieder* all tried to look away simultaneously. It was clear they felt deeply ashamed of what had just happened: the crashed car, the failed attempt to contact the two humans. They assumed it was their fault, naturally.

Kevin Briggs didn't share that view. They'd just done what they were told. The fault – if there was one, and it hadn't all just been bad luck – lay with the commander-in-chief, not the poor bloody infantry. He shuffled his feet and fluffed up his neck feathers; a bit like trying to put on an overcoat without using your hands.

It had started to rain, a fine sprinkle of small, thin drops that lay on his feathers but didn't soak through. It was weather to match the general mood of the flock, which for some reason Kevin didn't share. True, ever since they'd dug their way out of the coop they hadn't actually achieved anything, apart from scaring a middle-aged woman out of her wits, but that (Kevin reckoned) was because their entire approach had been fundamentally unsound. Get to a phone, Ms Byron had said, or a computer or something; tell the outside world, and the world will come and rescue us. But Kevin had an unpleasant feeling that it wasn't going to be that simple, which should have been depressing but somehow wasn't. In his mind a sentence beginning *All we need to do is* was trying to take shape, and although it was still very much a work-in-progress, he was quietly confident that the rest of it would follow sooner or later. Meanwhile, there was a rather enticing-looking clump of nettles in the far corner of the yard, and he was feeling (for want of a better word) peckish.

He wandered across. Hugh Fearnley-Whittingstall, he remembered, reckoned you could turn a bunch of humble nettles into a first-class gourmet feast just by adding two pints of cream, a pound of Stilton cheese, some finely diced Parma ham, a bottle of Chablis and a few other bits and bobs. Standing on tipclaw, he reached up and nipped off a corner of nettle leaf. Not bad, he thought. Tastes a bit like—

In among the nettles, something moved.

One of the more upbeat aspects of being a chicken was amazingly heightened senses. The faintest noise, the slightest movement. He stopped, assessed his tactical position, decided he had a clear escape route if he needed one and peered a bit closer to see what had attracted his attention.

The nettle heap turned out to be masking a heap of old junk, the usual accumulation of valueless non-recyclables that you'll find in a corner of any farmyard in the northern hemisphere: various bits of discarded or clapped-out farm machinery, a rusty old bike with twisted wheels, an old fridge, some plastic sacks, a tangle of wire, the corroded wreck of a galvanised watering can. It was hardly like finding a lost city of the Incas buried in the undergrowth of the rainforest. On the other hand, it was just the sort of place where a predator might hole up and wait for a very stupid chicken to come strolling by. Suddenly Kevin lost his taste for nettles. He backed away a step or two and saw it again: something was moving about in there.

What to do? Permeating chicken DNA like the lettering in seaside rock is a disinclination to turn one's back on danger, to break eye contact with the source of a potential threat. He backed away a few steps more, then stopped. The door of the battered old fridge was swinging open. A man was getting out.

The extraction process was so fascinating that Kevin had to stay and watch, in spite of a million years of avian evolution screaming at him to get the hell out of there. First, a very long leg appeared, rather in the style of John Cleese doing a silly walk. Then an arm, snaking round the fridge door and groping for something to grab hold of. Unfortunately for the arm's owner, the only grabbing-suitable articles in the vicinity were nettles. The hand unclenched and pulled back sharply, and the human said something extremely vulgar. Then the fridge wobbled a bit, and the man sort of rolled out of it, straight into the heart of the thickest clump of nettles in the patch.

When you're two feet high, all humans look big, but this was a big human by any standards. He was tall and powerfully built, with a shaved head, wearing a blue suit and what looked like hand-made shoes, and when he knelt on the coil of rusty barbed wire he jumped up with the speed and single-mindedness of a swooping falcon. Once on his feet, he dusted himself down and looked round, a what-the-hell expression on his finely chiselled face.

I can talk to him till I'm blue in the face, Kevin thought sadly, but he won't understand a word I'm saying. Pity. He had the look of a man who knew what he was doing, a resourceful type, the sort of man who might just possibly know how to turn a flock of metamorphosed lawyers back into human beings, although (Kevin couldn't help thinking) he couldn't be all that smart if he'd managed to get himself trapped inside a derelict fridge. Not that it mattered. Without a means of communication, nothing could be done.

The man reached into his jacket and produced a phone, a smart phone presumably, since he didn't use it to make a call. Instead, he tapped buttons, scowled at the screen and looked very unhappy. A built-in satnav, perhaps, or maybe he was just checking the latest commodity prices on Wall Street.

"Look," said a voice behind him somewhere. "Look, he's got a phone."

The whole flock started shouting at once. (A phone! Look, he's got a phone! Did you see that? Isn't that a Nokia 776Z?) But the man didn't seem to notice that he'd just become the centre of attention. Just chickens clucking, he must be thinking. Accordingly, when Ms Byron yelled, "Get him!" he failed to grasp the nature of the clear and present threat, at least until it was too late.

A terrible sight to see, a man suddenly overwhelmed by poultry. Ms Byron, leading by example in the manner of Alexander and Henry V, flew straight at his face. Others went for the hands, pitching on his forearms and pecking at his wrists, while Charles the ex-conductor perched on his shoulder and sank one substantial claw in the poor bugger's ear. Sheer weight of birdflesh on his arms meant he couldn't lash out or defend himself. Ms Byron had her beak firmly clamped on his nose and was hanging from it, wildly flapping her wings. It was only a matter of time (three and a quarter seconds, in the event) before the man dropped the phone. It fell on the toe of his left shoe, bounced twice and landed within easy pecking distance of where Kevin, the only flock member not participating in the general assault, was standing.

Kevin looked at the phone. Well now, he thought, that's convenient. We deliver. It was even facing the right way. All he had to do was stoop, the way he'd been doing on and off ever since the Great Change, and use his hard pointy beak to peck the keys. Using a mobile phone is simple, piece of cake. If teenagers can do it, so can a reasonably intelligent chicken. The problem, the one and only problem, was that he hadn't got the faintest idea who to send a message to, let alone what to say.

His not to reason why, though. Kevin's duty, plainly enough, was to secure the phone and remove it to a place of safety before the human had a chance to beat off the chickens. For now they had him at their mercy, but that was mostly due to the element of surprise. It couldn't be long before he drove off his persecutors and came looking for his phone, and if he managed to recover it, the whole exercise would have been a waste of time. Kevin's responsibility, therefore. The whole team, in fact, was depending on him to do his bit.

He looked at the phone and stayed exactly where he was. An overwhelming desire not to get involved surged over him like floodwater. Something wasn't quite right about all this: that he'd been the one who first noticed the human, that the phone had fallen at his feet, right way up, switched on, all ready for him. Maybe having been a chicken for a while had kick-started his basic animal survival instinct, dormant for so long in the comfortable, complacent security of being human. He couldn't bear to think what Ms Byron would do to him if he let the phone get away – something extremely violent, he assumed, and along the lines of the French method of producing goose-liver pâté. That sort of put paid to the survival instinct theory, but it made no difference. However hard he tried, he couldn't bring himself to do what was obviously required of him.

This is hopeless, he thought, as a chicken flew backwards past his ear, thudded into the side of a building, scrambled to its feet and scuttled away squawking. The human was starting to fight back, which meant it could only be a matter of time. He'd failed. Simple as that.

"You," he heard Ms Byron scream, "get that bloody phone, quick." Too late for that now. Even if he wanted to, he wouldn't have time to shove and nudge it to a place of concealment. Two more chickens whizzed past him, hurled by a furious hand.

Suddenly, he knew what to do. He dipped his head and pecked four keys, just in time. He'd just finished setting beak to the fourth one when a giant hand descended from the sky, swatted him aside, grabbed the phone and swept it away. He picked himself up and watched the human walk away, the phone almost lost in his enormous hand. Oh well, Kevin thought, I screwed that up real good.

Then the human stopped and slowly swung round to look at him.

What he'd written was, "help."

# CHAPTER FOURTEEN

The old man sighed and looked out of his bathroom window. The view from there was always the same – blue skies, bright sunlight – just as the sitting-room window always looked out on thick white cloud. Usually he kept the curtains drawn out of consideration for passing airliners. The effect on a pilot of a glimpse of the old man brushing his teeth at thirty thousand feet could easily be catastrophic.

He pottered down the stairs into his tiny kitchen and made himself a strong cup of tea the hard way, using a kettle instead of a word and a snap of the fingers. Theoretically, the result should be the same either way, but he fancied that short-cut-made tea always came out a little bit too milky and pale. He conjured up a cinnamon biscuit, changed his mind and transformed it into a small slice of lemon drizzle cake.

Something was missing, he realised – missing, presumed wrong. He wandered back into the sitting room and immediately realised what it was. There was an empty space on the mantelpiece, and behind it a rectangle of paint slightly less faded. He pulled open a drawer and took out the framed photograph he'd hidden away when he realised young Stanley was on his way to pay him a visit. A large woman in early middle age, with a huge smile. He put it back where it belonged.

*To Theo, with all my love, from Corinna.* Innocuous enough, but probably just as well if Stanley didn't see it. A boy's mother should be above suspicion, and Stanley had remarkable powers of insight and intuition. Got them from his old man, the old man thought fondly.

He glanced at the clocks on the wall, made the necessary conversions effortlessly in his head. Above all, he wished he could be sure he was doing the right thing.

"help."

Help?

A chicken had written that, pecked it with its beak; he'd watched it do it. Of course, it could be entirely random, and if his phone had been an old-fashioned typewriter, and if it had been monkeys rather than chickens and the message had read "To be or not to be that is the..." he'd have dismissed it from his mind and thought no more of it. But a chicken; that was different. He looked round and identified the bird in question – easily done, since it had been a cockerel and all the others he could see were hens. It was standing on one leg about ten yards away, looking at him. Small, scrawny-looking, its comb pale and drooping. His mother had kept chickens for a while, so he knew a bit about them. This one was a pretty poor specimen, one for the pot rather than for breeding, and it was holding unnaturally still. Help, he thought. He cleared his throat.

"Chicken?" he said.

The bird seemed to hesitate. Then, very cautiously, it came towards him, watching him with furious concentration. "Chicken," he repeated, "can you understand me?"

No, probably not. To a bird's ear his voice would come across as a huge, shapeless roar, drawn out and booming. He cleared the screen of his phone, typed in "hello," and laid it slowly on the ground. Then he backed off four strides and waited.

It took the chicken a long time to make up its mind, but in the end it came, stood over the phone, looked down at it, pecked the casing, scratched a little dust over it, pecked its own wing feathers, then looked at the word on the screen. Mr Gogerty waited, taking long, deliberate breaths. Then the chicken pecked the keypad four times, scuttled away, stopped and turned round again.

Mr Gogerty sighed. In a way it was rather wonderful, this unique moment of cross-species diplomacy. On the other hand, unless they found a way of doing without all the preliminaries, it could take a very long time.

"help." A chicken with a limited vocabulary. He tapped in "yes, how?" put the phone down and waited.

Peck, peck, peck – much quicker this time. He peered down at the result.

"don't know."

A chicken that could do apostrophes – impressive. A thought suddenly struck him, rather as though Newton had been sitting under a coconut palm rather than an apple tree at the relevant moment. He retrieved the phone and tapped in, "are you human?"

Mercifully, the chicken had got past all that backing-away-and-acting-scared stuff. Three pecks. "yes."

Mr Gogerty's mouth had gone dry. Usually it was a joyful thing, the sudden, unexpected impact of intuition; the gleam of light, the flash of gold in the mud-filled pan of routine analysis.

This time it made him feel shaky and slightly sick.

Impossible, he thought. It wouldn't count. It'd be cheating.

On the other hand, "what happened to you?" he tapped in quickly.

The reply took a while. "no idea."

He grabbed the phone and started to type. He got as far as "who are yo," then stopped, erased all that, and wrote, "are you kevin briggs?"

He didn't need the confirmation of the reply. Quite suddenly he knew, not just how Mr Briggs had got here or where this was or why he'd been turned into a chicken. Far more than that. It's no good guessing, he'd told Don and Polly Mayer; you've got to know. And now he did. After all the fuss, it was simple really. And cheating, of course.

The chicken who was also Mr Briggs was typing again. "can you get me out of here? please?" That brought him up short. He took the phone and wrote, "what about all the others?"

"human too. well, lawyers." The chicken was looking at him with those round red eyes, a plea he somehow couldn't resist.

The answer could wait. He took the phone, hit a few keys, inadvertently struck the wrong one and started a game of Minesweeper, cleared it, got back to the message screen, and finished typing, "it's all right leave it to me." He thought, just briefly, about calling up his tariff of charges and standard new client agreement, but what the hell. If he was right about all this, Mr Huos would pay. In fact, money would never be relevant again.

"Maybe he was feeling hot," Don said.

Polly looked at him. "He'll suffocate in there," she said. "You've got to get him out."

Don stayed exactly where he was. He'd seen the way the fridge had bulged, the sheet-metal sides ballooning, until the doorway was big enough for Mr Gogerty to scramble in. And then he'd watched it deflate. It couldn't do that of course. Steel has a tensile strength and a shearing point; he could find them in a book or look them up through Google. Stretched that far, it'd stay stretched. Only it hadn't.

"He's a professional," he muttered. "I'm sure he can look after himself."

"Yes," Polly snarled, "but a professional what? He didn't actually say."

Don shrugged. "I don't know. Magician."

Polly made a noise like a bursting tyre. "Sorry," she said, "but I think we've gone way past rabbits out of hats and the seven of clubs is in your top right-hand pocket. He could be dying in there."

"I don't think so," Don said. "Surely he'd bang on the door or something."

"Open the bloody fridge, Don."

"You do it."

"No," she said. "It's not my fridge."

"You have my unqualified permission."

They stood and looked at it. A fridge is just a fridge.

"I'm guessing," Don said, "that it's some kind of interdimensional portal."

"Could be. What's an interdimensional portal?"

"I have no idea." He took one step forward, then stopped. "He took the pencil sharpener."

"So?"

Don shrugged. "He'll be all right if he's got that with him. We don't need to worry. It's none of our—"

Polly pushed past him and reached for the fridge door handle. "Don," she said, "it feels warm."

"When he comes out," Don said thoughtfully, "he can tell us if the light stays on."

"Mr Gogerty." Polly waited; no reply. "Don, he's not answering. He must be in trouble."

"Not if I'm right and it's an interdimensional portal. He could be anywhere by now. In a completely different space/time continuum, for all we know."

Polly took her hand away from the handle and stepped back. "You'd better open it," she said.

He had to ask. "Why?"

"Don," she said, "a human life is in danger."

"Yes. Mine. Didn't you hear what I just said? If that thing's what I think it is—"

"It's a fridge, Don. What are you afraid of? Frostbite?"

"If," he repeated slowly (their father used to do that when she interrupted him, and she'd always hated it), "that thing is what I think it is, I could end up anywhere. Or anywhen, come to that. I think Mr Gogerty used it to go somewhere, probably somewhere he couldn't get to by any other means. I think this fridge *leads* somewhere, maybe the place I sent Kevin Briggs to. The difference is, Gogerty's a professional and presumably knows what he's doing. If I go there, how in God's name am I ever going to get back?"

"Don," said his sister, "open the fucking fridge."

A man can argue only so long. Sooner or later, he does what he's told, if only to get some peace. But there was more to it than that. To boldly go where no man has gone before – except Mr Gogerty, of course, and maybe Kevin Briggs and perhaps some other people he didn't know about – to boldly go where not many people have gone before. To see what's out there. To *know*. Up till now he'd been fighting the stuff whose name began with M for all he was worth, because it wasn't natural, it wasn't right, because it was totally unfamiliar and so, quite reasonably, he was frightened of it. But no longer. He wasn't sure why, but suddenly his personal safety didn't seem quite so all-important, not compared with the opportunity that Life was seeing fit to rub his nose in. Well, he thought, why not? He'd just take a quick look, to satisfy his curiosity.

He reached out and took hold of the door handle. Polly had been quite wrong about it. Not hot, cold as ice.

"Don," he heard her say, "be careful."

Oh for crying out loud, he thought, and opened the door.

He opened the door and, before her very eyes, it did it again. The fridge swelled up like a bubble, like a paper bag you blow into and then burst. "Don, don't," she shouted, but it was too late. Like a man in a trance, her idiot brother took a long step forward, and went inside.

She lunged for the door, but too late; it had already shut

behind him, and the fridge was back to its normal proportions. "Don," she yelled, and yanked it open.

Inside she saw half a dozen eggs, six cans of Stella Artois, two tomatoes, a pat of butter, a few crumbs of Stilton cheese in cling film, a half-empty jar of olives and an elderly-looking cucumber.

As he walked through the door, a bell rang, like in a shop. He swung round, but the door had shut behind him: a shop door, with a glass panel, through which he could see pavement. He threw himself against it, rattling the glass, but it wouldn't budge. Then he tried turning the handle, but that didn't work either. The door wouldn't open. Oh, he thought.

He turned and looked around. He knew this place. A counter, and behind it a rack of clothes all done up in blue polythene. He grabbed at a book of tickets on the counter in front of him. On each of them was printed "SpeediKleen" over a number.

So that's what an interdimensional portal looks like, he thought. No swirly lights, slo-mo, dry ice; one moment you're in one place, the next you're somewhere else. No frills, like a low-cost airline. Nobody trying to sell you socks or filled baguettes while you're hanging around waiting for something to happen. Serious travel, in other words, for serious people – a category, he reflected, into which I don't really fit.

"Hello?" he called out. "Mr Gogerty?"

No answer. He hadn't expected one. Better than even money that they'd gone (been sent) to different locations. He moved his head a little to one side and sniffed. He could have sworn he smelled cheese: Stilton, his favourite.

"Hello?" he repeated. "Shop? Anybody there?"

Apparently not. On the shelf behind the counter he saw a large, grubby-looking red ledger, corners bruised, pages well thumbed. He opened it and turned the pages back until he found what he'd expected to find: *Miss P. Mayer, one dress, clean, mend and press.* Thought so. It was *the* dry cleaners, the one that had suddenly vanished. Magic, he remembered, had retrieved Polly's dress from here and delivered it to the flat. Worth a try. He pulled out a hair and blew on it. Nothing happened. But of course it wouldn't. Mr Gogerty had the pencil sharpener and so, presumably, was now the master of all its extraordinary powers. A bit of a waste since Mr Gogerty had no hair.

The cheese smell reminded him that it had been a long time since he'd had anything to eat. It seemed sadly trivial-minded to worry about food at a time like this. It depended on how long he was likely to be here. If the answer to that question was (for example) for ever and ever, the food issue would be far from trivial. It stood to reason that the people who ran the shop had access to food – but they weren't here, were they? – A kitchen, he thought, or a larder. Or even a control centre or bridge. Taking a deep breath, he set off to explore.

Ten minutes later he was back where he'd started. He'd found a kitchen, and in it a breadbin, and in that a couple of slightly stale brown rolls, for which he was truly thankful. No sign of a command centre, but loads of cleaning plant and machinery, together with a main bedroom, a spare bedroom, a bathroom, a living room which reminded him of Uncle Jim and Auntie Pauline's house (shudder), a cupboard-under-the stairs full of coats and scarves, and a downstairs loo. Not exactly the Tardis. If it wasn't for the fact that the front door was still firmly shut (he'd found a hammer in the cupboard under the stairs, but it hadn't had any effect on the door glass) he could almost have believed he was in a perfectly ordinary dry cleaners somewhere in the real world. Which would have been nice.

Something else that appeared to be functioning within normal parameters was his bladder, which was making a bid for his urgent attention. He'd done his best to ignore it for several minutes, but action would be required quite soon. Weeing in someone else's house without asking first offended every convention he lived by; there was something inherently wrong with the idea. It was practically criminal – breaking and urinating – but, by the same token, so was helping himself to brown rolls from the kitchen. The owners wouldn't mind, he told himself (it's much easier to convince yourself of ethically dubious propositions when your legs are tightly crossed). More to the point, they'd never know. Awkwardly but quickly he retraced his steps to the downstairs toilet, barged open the door and pulled it shut behind him, and—

"George," said Eileen. "I want to go home."

They'd been walking for hours, and their feet were sore. It had been a long time since they'd walked more than a few yards or on any surface other than slightly threadbare carpet. The sun was still shining, but a few clouds had started to drift in – long, high, flat clouds that looked as though they'd been sat on by overweight angels. Eileen didn't seem to have noticed that they'd been walking in circles all the time, and they were now back at the foot of the farm drive. Mercifully, no sign of the savage attack chickens.

"Me too," George said, and realised rather to his own surprise that he meant it. Twenty-four hours ago his dearest wish would have been to escape from the shop and never go back; never to press another shirt or stare at the same implacably unchanging walls. He'd probably have stuck to his resolution if they'd been in a town, with proper pavements and buildings and lashings of people. The countryside was different, however. It was big and empty and scary, and he wished it would go away. Think of all the nice houses you could build on a wilderness like this.

"I've had about enough of this walk."

"Can't be too far now," he replied diplomatically.

"When we get home," Eileen said, "I'm going to have a nice strong cup of tea and put my feet up."

He could try explaining, he thought, but what useful purpose would it serve? "Me too," he said. "Maybe a nice hot bath."

"Did you remember to turn the immersion on?"

"Yes," he lied, and felt guilty about it even though it couldn't possibly matter. "There'll be plenty of hot water. You can have a nice bath and wash your hair."

"I'd like that." She came to a halt and looked at him as though searching for something she'd lost. "Do you think we did something wrong?" she said.

"What?"

"All this." She made a small gesture with her hands that nevertheless adequately indicated the entire universe. "Do you think it's because we did something wrong? You know, something bad."

It was the first time either of them had said it out loud. "No," he said, with practically no hesitation. "No, we're not bad people. It's just some stuff, that's all." He frowned, trying to think of comparables. "Like a burst water main," he said, "or the plagues of Egypt in the Bible. I think somebody else somewhere may've done something bad, and we got sort of swept up in it. Or maybe it's just one of those things."

She nodded, relieved to have her analysis confirmed. "Do you think it's over now?"

Hopeful, like a small kid in a car, *Are we nearly there yet?* They should make up a new range of words for times like this, he thought, words that mean the same things but with the nasty sharp edges taken off. "Wouldn't have thought so," he replied. "But you never know."

"Here, George." She grabbed his arm. "We're back at that chicken place again."

Again he'd hoped she wouldn't notice. After all, they'd already been past it half a dozen times since the incident, but she hadn't been paying attention. Women don't take in their surroundings the way men do.

"So we are," he said.

"Come on," she muttered. "Let's go back the way we just came. If those bloody chickens are still running about loose..."

"I don't think they are. I can't see them anywhere."

"There's one, look." Her arm shot out like a harpoon into a whale, and she pointed. "There, see? Near that man."

"What man?"

"That one there, see? Tall black man with a bald head."

Of course there are times when men are so busy taking in their surroundings that they overlook the howlingly obvious. "Oh him," he said, and then the description registered. He peered more closely, wishing very much he'd thought to bring his glasses.

"George," Eileen said urgently, "let's go back."

"Just a second, love." Yes, now he'd seen him properly, as it were, there was no possibility of mistaken identity. The tall man standing by the big clump of nettles talking to a chicken was the same one who'd called to see him, the scary one who'd promised—

Hang on, he thought. He's talking to a chicken.

Well, so what? People talk to animals: cats, dogs, budgies, goldfish even. Nothing weird or sinister about that. His gran on his mother's side—

"What's he doing now?"

Good question. He looked like he was typing something into a little gadget he was holding in his hand. Now he was bending down and putting the gadget on the ground, and the chicken was stooping like it was reading what he'd written (only chickens can't read, of course), and now it was pecking at the thing like it was typing in a reply, and the man was picking it up and reading it.

"Let's go back," he said firmly. "Come on."

But Eileen didn't seem to hear him. "That man might know what's going on," she said. "You could ask him."

George's heart withered inside his chest. Men don't ask; it's the rules. Correction: men don't ask strangers. But the tall man wasn't a stranger; furthermore, he was from the council or something of the sort, which made him official, so that was all right. And maybe he did know what was going on, at that. He'd seemed pretty clued up the last time.

"Good idea," George said. "You wait here while I just—"

Bad suggestion. "Not likely," Eileen said briskly. "You're not leaving me here with all them chickens wandering about."

There's also a rule that says that women are allowed to be afraid of animals; they can make as much fuss as they like, and you're not allowed to tell them to pull themselves together or get a grip. It's one of those complicated rules, like men have to carry the suitcase at airports but opening doors is male chauvinism. "All right, then," he conceded. "You know what," he added, "I think I may have seen him before somewhere."

"Don't be silly," Eileen replied. They're allowed to say things like that too.

The man – Mr Gogerty, George remembered – was concentrating so hard on typing into his gadget that he didn't realise he had company until George did some rather theatrical coughing, at which he spun round like a ballet dancer and stared.

"Hello," George said brightly. "Mr Gogerty, isn't it?"

A split second. Mr Gogerty was clearly an intelligent, perceptive man. He saw Eileen, registered the complication, and said, "That's right. And you're Mr..." He made a pantomine of trying to remember. "Mr Williams," he said. "From the dry cleaners in Clevedon Road."

"Fancy you remembering," George said. "You must have a really good memory. Eileen, this is Mr Gogerty, who came in our shop once. Mr Gogerty, this is my wife, Eileen."

Enough with the play-acting, said Mr Gogerty's eyebrows. "Pleased to meet you," he said. "May I ask..."

"What we're doing here?" George grinned sadly. "Funnily enough, I was wondering if you could tell me."

The chicken clucked. If it had been human, it would have sounded annoyed. Eileen jumped and looked terrified, and George had a flash of inspiration. "Get back, Eileen," he said. "We'll protect you."

Eileen backed away ten yards, her eyes fixed on the chicken's beak. "Nice," muttered Mr Gogerty, clearly impressed. "All right, what are you doing here?"

"Dunno," George whispered back. "The shop came here; we thought we'd go for a walk, and when we tried to find it again, it'd gone."

Mr Gogerty looked at him sharply. "Gone."

"Gone. Vanished. We've been walking round in circles ever since." He frowned, added, "We keep going in a straight line, but we always end up here. It's like—"

"That's right," Mr Gogerty said. "It's because it's what we call a pocket universe. Infinite, like the real universe, but curved." George gave him his number-one blank look. "Sorry," Mr Gogerty said. "Thinking aloud. Oh sorry, this is Kevin Briggs."

"What?"

The chicken clucked angrily, dislodging the penny, which dropped with terrible force. "What, *that*?" George said. "That's a . . ."

"As human as you or me," Mr Gogerty said. "In fact, he came into your shop once. Actually," he added, "I rather think that's why he's here."

Imagine the multiverse (Mr Huos read) as a series of concentric spheres, a set of spherical Russian dolls packed inside each other. Each universe comprised in the multiverse is by definition infinite; each universe is curved, in accordance with basic Einsteinian metaphysics.

Mr Huos paused and scratched his head. He wasn't a great reader at the best of times, and Mr Gogerty's article in the autumn 1972 edition of *Supernature* was rather hard going. Still, he was beginning to get a glimmer of the basic idea.

Each universe is infinite; how, then, can one fit inside another? To argue thus, we contend, is to allow ourselves to be confined within the bounds of a crudely materialist mindset, to envisage the boundaries of universes to be hard, solid, like the shell of an egg. Instead of a shell, let that boundary be a balloon, capable of inflating and shrinking and yet remaining essentially the same. If a universe is truly infinite, of course it can accommodate itself inside another universe; come to that, inside a football or a peanut shell. Infinite doesn't just mean infinitely big. Infinite also encompasses infinitely small.

The egg metaphor, of course, begs the great teleological question, Which came first? But for that question to have any semblance of meaning . . .

Mr Huos groaned, reached for his sandwich, peeled off the top slice of bread, shook half a dozen aspirins from the bottle on top of the amply mustarded roast beef, replaced the bread and bit largely. Such was his remarkable constitution that he could eat aspirin like sweets and come to no harm. Such was his bizarrely different physiology that he could munch aspirins all day without any effect on his headache. Still, it did no harm to try.

He skipped a page and tried again.

Let us consider Suslowicz's fifth proposition. What, he asks, is an egg but a compilation of ingredients – water, calcium, proteins – drawn from the body of the hen, matured inside her and expelled in the act of laying. Although the egg is not the whole chicken, the egg is wholly made up from the chicken. At the instant of laying every part of it is derived from the chicken; thus, by any meaningful criteria, the egg is the chicken, or at least of the chicken, and the separateness that ensues from the act of parturition is merely a geographical irrelevance. If a man's arm is cut off, Suslowicz argues, the arm is still a component of the man's body. That the egg then proceeds to hatch into a wholly separate life form is beside the point. Even the newly hatched chick is wholly composed of its mother until it takes its first externally derived bite of food and sip of water (Suslowicz ignores the fact that the eggshell is permeable, and therefore air not supplied by the mother is absorbed by the chick from the moment of laying) . . .

Naughty Suslowicz, Mr Huos thought. In fact, he was so cross with Suslowicz he skipped the whole of the rest of the page, just to teach him a lesson.

It therefore follows that the egg inside the chicken is entirely comparable to the concentric universe inside the multiverse. An egg, containing an unborn chicken, is in itself an infinity of possibilities. Within its first sixty seconds of life the chick might stand up or sit down, turn right or left, cheep or not cheep; in its entire lifetime the chick encompasses an infinity, a universe of potential choices, of moments when the continuum bifurcates and new universes are formed, each infinite but contained within the other, like our spherical Russian dolls. The hen is, by the same token, equally infinite, but when she contains the egg she contains the future infinity that will soon be the chick. Therefore, to ask the question "Which came first?" is to ignore the . . .

Mr Huos yawned and turned back to the list of contents at the front of the journal. Someone, the editor presumably, had put it rather well: "P.376 'Suslowicz reconsidered; the argument from internality.' A nice try by Stanley Gogerty."

Indeed. A nice try but drivel nonetheless. Mr Huos closed

the journal, ate the rest of his sandwich, glanced at his watch. A quarter past five, the time when, according to his usual routine, they brought him the day's letters to check and sign. His fingers itched for the pen, the way a missing tooth sometimes aches. The office felt very big and empty with just him in it.

He'd had no choice, however. Sack the lot of them, it had been the only way. Close down the entire business, cancel all the contracts, pay them all off, every single one. He winced at the thought. A few days ago, before it all went wrong, he'd been a rich man, so rich he had no idea how much money he'd got. Now, having bought himself out of all his liabilities, he was left with about fifty thousand pounds sterling, say a hundred thousand US dollars, an evocative figure, he couldn't help thinking. A hundred thousand bucks plus the clothes he stood up in. The difference this time was that he didn't have a little brass ring, slightly worn on one side. Big difference.

He sat very still and listened. There are few places on earth as quiet as a fully soundproofed modern office suite with nobody in it and the phones all disconnected and the computers and the air conditioning switched off and nobody using the plumbing. You could have heard a pin drop, except there was nobody around to drop a pin. Mr Huos frowned. Maybe he could ring the job centre and hire someone to come in and drop pins, just to ease the silence. Better not, though; he couldn't really afford indulgences like that any more. He still had Stan Gogerty's bill to pay, and he had an idea that a hundred thousand dollars would only just cover it. No, belay that. Symmetry demanded that a hundred thousand dollars would cover it exactly, leaving him with nothing because that was how it should be. Often he'd wondered why he'd had the money bestowed upon him when he was put there in the Caucasus for the monks to find. Now he knew. It was to pay Mr Gogerty's bill, when the time came.

The implication being that the time had now come. Which it had; no question about that. Jack Tedesci had been the first of many business associates past and present baying for his blood because the slab of real estate they'd bought from him had suddenly vanished. Going on was out of the question. He reached in his pocket, got out his phone and accessed his bank account. $100,036.72. Not quite, then. He still had $36.72 of time left, then, which came as a relief. If he spent it carefully it could buy him a couple of days. Long enough, anyhow, for a cup of coffee. He went to the staff kitchen, filled the kettle and switched it on, then remembered that the electricity had been cut off.

He sighed. There were still four ginger nuts in the biscuit jar. He ate them, washing them down with water. He looked around, remembering when this room had been filled with people at all times – people making themselves drinks, drinking them, chatting, doing faces and nails, getting changed ready for a night out, storing shopping in the fridge, reading magazines when they should have been at their desks working. He'd come a long way from the Caucasus but, geographical irrelevances excluded, he was right back where he started – because infinity is curved, he supposed, and according to Stan Gogerty I'm just an egg inside an egg inside a chicken, so what would I know anyhow?

It was all the brass ring's fault – easy enough to say when it wasn't here to defend itself. He thought about that thought and decided that you can take fair-mindedness too far. It hadn't ever actually talked to him in a creepy Joan-of-Arc sort of way, but he'd been keenly aware of it in his mind, as a personality – a reminder of his origins, he liked to fool himself, but more than that. You could do this, it would urge, you could do that. And this and that had turned out to involve using the M stuff: folding the space/time continuum like those cut-out paper-dolls-holding-hands, so that he could sell the same plots of land over and over again; hiring a dozen people to sit behind one desk simultaneously, in a reality layered like filo pastry. How malleable he'd been, how easily led. You could do this and that. Eat the nice apple, said the brass serpent with its tail in its mouth; it'll do you good.

What did I know? he asked himself. I'm just a poor orphan boy from the Caucasus. A brass ring tells me to fold space/time; I do it. Rude not to. And now the brass ring had gone, left him alone to clear up the mess and put everything back where he'd got it from – moved on, presumably, to a more efficient and satisfactory carrier. He walked slowly back to the front office, where, on the Reception desk, he saw a letter. He was fairly sure it hadn't been there before, but he could have been mistaken.

"Dear sir," the letter said, "please find enclosed our invoice for powdered coffee supplied to your goodselves between the following dates." He translated from sterling into US dollars. $36.72.

All right then.

He wrote out a cheque, put it in an envelope, stamped it with his last stamp, found nesting in the back of his wallet, where he also found a five-pound note and some loose change: seventy-two pence. "Goodbye, office," he said aloud, and walked down into the street, where a taxi happened to be waiting.

"Where to?" the driver asked.

"A fiver's worth," Mr Huos replied. "Wherever that takes me, that's the place."

The driver looked at him. "Quicker to walk," he said.

Mr Huos scowled at him. "Here's five pounds," he said. "Here's the tip." He dropped the coins through the open window. "Now fucking drive."

The driver looked at him again, and there was a split second when he seemed to understand. He nodded, and Mr Huos got in and sat down.

They drove for a very long time. Westway to the M40, past Oxford and Warwick, the M42 to join the M5, leaving at the Kidderminster junction, and cross-country from there.

"Are we nearly there yet?" Mr Huos asked.

He glanced at his watch, according to which the journey had lasted three minutes. Outside the window, hedgerows and green fields blurred past, with a background of big round hills. WELCOME TO ELGAR COUNTRY, shouted a road sign. Mr Huos didn't know who Elgar was ( Wasn't that the name of the famous race horse that got stolen?) but he had the strangest feeling of familiarity, of homecoming. Which was odd, since he'd never been here before in his life.

As far as he knew. Ha!

Down little lanes with grass growing up the middle. Three and a half minutes now. The sun agreed with his watch. It showed no inclination to set, but instead shone brightly in the spaces between flat, squashed-looking clouds. A cottage or two. A church. The taxi stopped.

"We're here," the driver said.

Mr Huos nodded, and opened the door. Grass under his feet, at his side the yellow stone of the churchyard wall. "Where the hell are we?" he asked.

"Norton St Edgar," the driver replied, and drove away.

"Fine," Mr Huos shouted at the rear of the disappearing taxi. "I can walk the rest of the way from here." Marvellous. He didn't like walking at the best of times, and his shoes were too tight. He looked down and realised he'd just trodden in something bucolic.

Well, he thought, so this is Norton St Edgar. Nice place; no wonder so many people were so keen to live here. Wiping his shoe carefully on a tuft of grass, he considered the view. Pretty, he decided. Nice hills and stuff. Really, it'd be a shame to build houses all over it.

Apparently, though, that hadn't happened. The magic of the plain brass ring, which had folded the universe for him and kept it folded after he'd taken the money and moved on, had all faded now. He wondered where all the houses had gone to, and the people living in them. If he'd understood what Stan Gogerty had said in the learned journal, each house he'd built was basically an egg floating anomalously in time and space. In which case, they ought to start hatching any moment now.

That wasn't a cheerful thought, and he threw it out of his mind like a bouncer ejecting a drunk, but it came back almost immediately and brought a load of its rowdy friends along with it. Exactly what had happened to all those people? If, as he'd always assumed, the magic had been keeping them in place, and the magic had stopped working, what then? He realised he had no idea. Appalling. He felt his forehead and realised he was sweating, as well he might. *All those people—*

He felt in his pocket and found something, a coin, snuggled in a fold of his hanky. He took it out and looked at it. One penny. He laughed. Not quite yet then.

He turned his head like a battleship's gun turret and took a proper look at the landscape. Once he'd reduced it to an Ordnance Survey two-dimensional shape – contour lines and salient features – it was entirely familiar. It ought to be; he'd divided it up and parcelled it out into lots often enough. He couldn't begin to remember the names of all the streets he'd built on that shape over the years, dozens of them, maybe a hundred. He grinned like a dog. A town, practically a city, but nothing to see; nothing an archaeologist could sink a trowel into.

That reminded him. He'd seen a telly programme once about archaeology, with the little scruffy man from *Blackadder* scampering energetically in the mud. Cities, he remembered, tend to come in layers, like a Big Mac. Take a really old city; it's made up of loads of different layers, where each generation has built on top of the ruins of its predecessors. Dig a vertical shaft and you can see them, like strata in rock: dozens of streets, maybe a hundred, all piled on top of each other, all occupying the same ground but separated by time. Seen from above, from the air, just one. Seen from the side, lots. On a map, or a development plan, or the plan attached to a transfer deed, you only got the bird's-eye view. What he'd done was essentially the same thing time did, except accelerated. He frowned and scratched an itch behind his ear. He had an idea he'd hit on something, a stray fragment of the explanation, but he knew he wasn't capable of recognising it for what it was. Stan Gogerty would get it; he'd know what it meant, but of course he wasn't here.

He shook his head. One moment a load of eggs floating in space, the next a slice of layer cake. Given human beings' innate need to think in metaphors, it was remarkable they'd contrived to achieve anything at all.

All those poor people trapped in collapsed archaeological strata, like earthquake victims. In Baldrick's ruined city, as previously noted, the superimposed levels were kept apart by time. Here, it had been magic, some trick or other powered by the brass ring, which strongly implied that all the king's horses and all the king's men couldn't dig the poor buggers out again.

My fault, he thought.

Once, at an airport, waiting for a plane, he'd bought a copy of *Dr Faustus*. It had been an honest mistake (he'd thought it was the book of that film with Omar Sharif and the famous shot where he opens the cattle-truck door), and by the time he realised what he'd done, he was twenty thousand feet above the Atlantic. So he'd read it, and pretty weird it turned out to be. There was a scene at the end where the hero's waiting for the Devil to come and get him, and this had stuck in his mind, like a bit of sweetcorn skin lodged between the front teeth.

Ah Faustus! Thou hast one bare hour to live,
And then thou must be damned eternally –

One hour, one penny. He opened his hand and looked at it. The Queen was on the back, but she looked away, unwilling to meet the eye of the man responsible for hundreds of innocent people getting buried alive in metaphysical choux pastry. He considered repenting, but that had never been his style. To hell with it, he thought, and chucked the penny into the hedge. Then he waited for something to happen.

He waited and waited, and then he felt something tapping on the toe of his left shoe. He looked down, and there was a chicken, pecking at the stitching of his hand-made Lobb-of-St-James's brown brogues. Very gently, he nudged it away. "Go on, chicken," he said. "Shoo."

The chicken took no notice. Peck, peck, peck. Not that it mattered any more, but each precision-aimed beakstrike was taking about a fiver off the value of his footwear.

A lesser man would have swung his leg back and booted the chicken into Worcestershire, but Mr Huos restrained himself. Far from holding the moral high ground, he was down on the moral flood plain, cricking his neck back to see the encircling peaks. He withdrew his foot gently out of pecking range, in the process taking a step back. The chicken set to work on his right foot. He sighed and gave ground once again. The chicken advanced. He retreated. It was silly – a former master of the universe being backed into a hedge by a barnyard fowl – but he accepted it with patient resignation, as befitted a man without a penny to his name. Only when his back was to the hazel branches and the bramble tendrils were nuzzling his collar did he stop and hold his ground.

"Fine," he said. "Eat my shoes, see if I care."

The chicken took one last peck, lifted its head, twitched it the way chickens do. "I've got a message for you," it said.

Oh hell, he thought, now I'm listening to talking chickens. And then he paused and thought about it. He reflected on how he'd always been able to understand any language, just hearing the words, not realising he was being talked to in foreign until the matter emerged from context. Human languages, animal languages; he'd never been conscious of understanding birdsong and beast-grunt before, but maybe that was just because he hadn't been listening. The mind blots out the voices it can't be bothered with, the background chatter, the involuntary eavesdrops. Maybe, when he'd strolled in the park or down the street, some of those voices hadn't been strictly human.

"Chicken?" he said.

"My name," the chicken replied icily, "is Mary Byron. I have a message for you from Stanley Gogerty."

# CHAPTER FIFTEEN

Looking glasses and wardrobes, his childhood reading had prepared him for those, but fridges and toilets? Appropriate, in a way. There's something mysterious and wonderful about a mirror, and at least a big old-fashioned mahogany wardrobe has class. For the Don Mayers of this world, he thought sadly, a knackered fridge is far more suitable. And a toilet, as it were, speaks for itself.

He tried the door again but it wasn't going to budge, just like the shop door, with its hammer-proof glass. A pattern emerging, he decided. All right then. Slowly and deliberately, he turned round to face the weirdness and concluded that on balance it wasn't so bad. Green fields, blue sky, distant sheep on distant hills, a Tory's vision of England. Fine, he said to himself, bring it on.

Maybe he'd have felt differently if it wasn't for the guilt, because there was no denying, it served him right. He'd sent away his annoying upstairs neighbour, and now here he was, presumably and for all he knew in the same place as his victim: poetic justice, although the poetry element was about on a level with the stuff you find written inside greetings cards. Was that stone building away yonder a ruined abbey? Practically inevitable, he decided, in the circumstances.

Being urban to the core, he drifted towards the only building in sight. Fallen-down and dilapidated it might be, but at least it had walls and the suggestion of a roof, so if it rained (he'd been on holiday to the countryside when he was young; sooner or later, it always rains in the country) he wouldn't get wet. Besides, he was pretty sure that he hadn't ended up here entirely at random. Someone had set an agenda, and it seemed more likely that it would be taking place in the only building for miles around than out in all this green vagueness. Get it over with, he told himself, and then maybe they'll let you go home. Maybe.

The ruin was further away than it had looked from the toilet door, and it took him a while to get there. Apart from the far-away sheep (and they could just as easily have been white splodges on a painted backdrop) he was the only living thing as far as the eye could see. No birds overhead, no rabbits flolloping through the long grass, no flies, midges, wasps. For someone used to sharing his horizons with a teeming mass of life, it was distinctly uncomfortable. Artificial, he thought. The designer could do vegetation, but the budget wouldn't stretch to extras from the animal kingdom. He quickened his pace, his instincts urging him to get to the cover of the building as soon as possible. Daft, but that's atavistic tendencies for you.

Sure enough, it was a ruined abbey. There was the gatehouse, and that was where the monks slept, and that big long job must be the church. In spite of himself he grinned. To whoever was doing this to him, ruined abbeys presumably meant Gothic melodrama, but to him they would always mean August afternoons when it was too wet for the beach, followed by a picnic in the car, with steamed-up windows and tea in the top of a Thermos, Mum and Dad gently bickering and Polly in one of her sulks. There was something so reassuringly mundane and boring about derelict ecclesiastical architecture, it was almost like coming home. No; if whoever it was had wanted to do heavy menace, he should have gone for a city-centre car park at 3 a.m. This was so tame it was practically National Trust.

Something moved. He stopped dead until he was able to identify it: a horse, a fellow life form at last. Not that Don was comfortable around horses. When Polly was going through her brief mad-about-ponies phase, he'd had to go to riding stables and gymkhanas, where huge looming things with hooves and teeth had eyed him up as a potential target. This horse wasn't like them, though. It had its saddle on and bits of string attached to its face, but it was quietly swishing its tail and munching grass, no bother to anyone. Maybe they only get stroppy and mad-eyed when they're being chivvied by people's sisters. In which case, he felt their pain.

"Nice horse," he said.

The horse looked at him. He shrugged and walked on past it until he reached the church wall, where there was a door, a big grey oak door, studded with nails, slightly ajar. He felt like a character in a computer game.

Very gently, using only the tips of his index and middle fingers, he pushed the door until it swung open. I don't want to go in there, he said to himself. *Like you've got a choice*, himself pointed out. He felt rather as he'd done when he was eight or nine years old and he had to go to someone's birthday party, knowing he was only there because everybody in the class had been invited. He paused on the threshold, hearing his mother's voice saying, "You'll enjoy it when you get there," which had never turned out to be the case. Oh well, he thought, and went inside.

There were several seconds before he could see anything in the comparative darkness. It was just a church, though it turned out to have rather more roof than he'd expected. He grinned. Continuity error. It made him feel a little better, though not much.

Movement in the shadows made him tense up, until it re-solved itself into a bald man in a brown dressing gown, or rather a monk, who beckoned to him without smiling, turned his back and walked up the aisle towards the altar. For some reason he wasn't a bit scared, maybe because fear comes from the unknown, and this wasn't. The elaborate mise en scène, with its painstaking attention to detail and beautifully observed touches of realism, told him everything he needed to know. It was all too perfect, too complete. The gargoyles and misericords and the polished brass of the eagle lectern and the worn brasses let into the flagstones and the deep glow of the bottom-polished oak pews was too perfectly lit, too sharply in focus. He'd been to real ruined abbeys and they weren't like this, not nearly so convincing and realistic. The unseen director was trying too hard, and that was a great comfort.

The monk arrived at the altar steps, bowed deeply and withdrew discreetly into the shadows precisely as a ray of sunlight burst through the technicolour filter of a stained-glass window. It fell on the altar, spotlighting two crisply defined objects: a chicken and an egg.

Then a great voice, welling up all around him like background noise massively amplified, boomed out and filled all the available space. "Well?" it said.

"Trevor," said his wife, peering through a gap in the lace curtains, "there's two knights in the front garden."

Trevor McPherson frowned. "Two whats?"

"Knights," Pam replied. "You know, in armour."

Trevor, who'd just been glancing through the local free newspaper to take his mind off the recent strange goings-on, nodded. "That's all right," he said. He put the paper down, went to the front door and opened it.

Two knights in armour, just as Pam had said: one shiny as a newly polished chrome bumper, the other one black. If he hadn't known what was going on, he might have been concerned. As it was, he regarded their appearance as a positive sign. "Hello, there," he called out, and went into the garden to greet them.

The white knight turned slowly to face him and lifted his visor. He seemed confused, as well he might.

"You're in the wrong place," Trevor explained.

The knight's eyes blinked under the steel rim of his helmet. "Wrong place," he repeated.

"Yes." Trevor nodded briskly. "You want Norton St Giles. This is Norton St Edgar."

The black knight advanced, gently barging his colleague out of the way. "Did you say Norton St Giles?"

"That's right," Trevor said. "Where they're having the Medieval Fayre and tournament re-enactment. It's this weekend, isn't it?"

The white knight was staring at him as though he'd never seen a retired transport manager before, as though he'd heard about such creatures in wild fireside tales but never believed they could possibly be true. "Where is this?" he said.

"I just told you: Norton St Edgar," Trevor replied. "You want to go back to the crossroads, turn left, then after half a mile take the second right, right again at the Three Pigeons and there you are." He paused, then asked with open interest, "The road's open again now, is it?"

The black knight took a step back. "Is it?"

Trevor felt his patience starting to leak away. "Well, it must be," he said, "or how else did you get here? Came down the B4197, I expect, and turned off too early. Now, what you could've done was stay on the 4197 as far as Adderbridge, then taken the first right past the Esso station, which would've brought you out the other side of Norton St Giles, and then you could've taken the right-hand turn that brings you out just past the Spar shop. Now you're here, though, your best bet's to carry straight on through the village till you..."

He tailed off. They didn't seem to be listening. It annoyed him when he gave people directions and they couldn't be bothered to listen. The white knight was staring at his cardigan, while the black knight was looking over Trevor's shoulder at the bungalow with an expression of horrified awe on his face. Well, Trevor thought, hardly surprising. He'd heard stories. The sort of people who go in for these re-enactment things, they're little better than hippies, the lot of them. Probably stoned to the eyeballs. In which case he didn't want them in his front garden. On the other hand, he did want to know if the problems with the roads (it sounded so much better put like that) had been sorted out yet. It was hard to know what to do for the best; how to get the vital intelligence he needed without ending up with a posse of rusty Dormobiles camped on his front lawn.

Light burst inside his head, and he felt in his pocket. "Tell you what," he said, producing his car keys. "I'll show you the way. You just follow on."

The two knights looked at each other. "Show us the way," the black knight repeated. "Yes, that would be . . ." He shrugged with a loud creaking of rivets and articulated steel. "That would be helpful."

The white knight didn't look too keen on the idea, or else he was too far gone to understand what was being said to him. Trevor hoped very much that someone else would be driving. At least this way, though, he could get rid of them and find out about the roads at the same time. The knights were talking in low voices, having an argument about something; he saw the white knight nudge the black knight in his lobster-shell-plated ribs and hiss, "Go on, ask him."

"Something I can help you with?" he said.

The white knight gave his colleague a shove with his elbow, and the black knight looked at Trevor and said, "Do you know which came first?"

Oink. "Which what came . . . ?"

"The chicken," said the white knight, "or the egg."

God almighty, Trevor thought, they're really far gone. "No idea, sorry," he said sharply. "Now, if you go on back to your vehicle, you can follow me out of the village." He walked away without looking round, got into the car and turned the key in the ignition. The engine fired, and instinctively he looked in the rear-view mirror.

The knights, he observed, were running away down the street. They weren't finding it easy because of all the ironmongery, but they were putting a significant degree of effort into it, as though they'd just seen something so terrifying they couldn't bear to be within a mile of it.

Well, fine, he thought, disconcerted but glad to be rid of them. The fact remained that they'd been here, and since they didn't come from Norton St Edgar, inevitably it followed that they'd come in from outside, which must mean that the roads were open again. Open, such a good word. It reduced the weirdness to a minor inconvenience, on a par with resurfacing or a lorry shedding its load. Already his busy mind was building coral reefs of normality over the absurd anomaly he'd experienced – he *thought* he'd experienced, but he could have been wrong, must have been wrong, had definitely got hold of the wrong end of the stick, and really there'd been a perfectly rational explanation.

He drove sedately up the hill to the crossroads, turned left, past the farm, past a tall man with a shiny head and a smart suit (another stranger, therefore another hopeful sign), on a bit further, past an even taller man in an even smarter suit who was striding along apparently following a chicken, on a bit further, past a nice-looking middle-aged couple (all strangers, he noted with satisfaction), on a bit further, at which point he happened to look up at the sky and saw something that made him swerve and drive clean through a dense hazel hedge into a field of maize.

"I've got a theory about that," Don said.

He waited, but the great reverberating voice said nothing. The chicken on the altar tucked its head under its wing and pecked at its feathers. The light streaming in through the stained-glass window dimmed a little, as though someone with a remote was adjusting the contrast.

"I think," he went on, "that it must've been the chicken, only it wasn't a chicken, if you get what I'm trying to say. I think that the first egg that ever hatched out a chicken was laid by something that wasn't a chicken – very nearly a chicken, naturally, but not quite. Evolution is what I'm getting at. I mean, evolution is how amoebas eventually turned into ammonites, which eventually turned into archaeopteryxes, which eventually evolved into a bird that was bloody nearly a chicken, which mated with another bird, slightly different but also bloody nearly a chicken, and when their genes got together and mixed it up, the egg with which their union was blessed turned out to be the first chicken as we know it. I mean," he went on, "it all depends on how you define what a chicken actually is, but I expect there's a specification in a biology textbook somewhere, a genome or something like that, something you can look up and use to decide whether a particular bird is a genuine certified chicken or just an uppity pheasant." He paused. "Just basic science, really. I mean, you can't argue with science." He paused again, and observed that the chicken on the altar seemed to be frozen in a pinion-feather-straightening pose, quite motionless. "All right," he said. "Give me a clue. Am I sort of warmish or completely off the beacon?"

The building shook as the great voice said, "Yes."

"Ah."

"And no."

Don nodded. "Yes and no," he repeated. "Thank you so much. Can I go home now?"

"Only," boomed the great voice, like a bell the size of Wembley, "when you have answered the question."

He wasn't having that. The voice was very loud and when it spoke the ground shook under his feet, but he'd stood up to bigger bullies before. He'd used Windows Vista. He'd installed broadband. Incomprehensible and immensely powerful forces entirely beyond his control were all in a day's work as far as he was concerned. "I just did," he said. "I chose the egg."

There was a pause: dead silence, complete stillness. Then the voice said, "That answer is unacceptable."

"Fine. So it's got to be the chicken."

"That answer is unacceptable."

Don frowned. "You mean it's wrong."

"Yes. And no."

The chicken clucked, got up, walked across the altar and pecked at the corner of the cloth. "So it's not about evolution, then."

About fifteen seconds of quiet stillness then, "An answer based on evolution is not acceptable."

Don sighed. Rather frustrating, but at least he had an inkling of what sort of process he was involved with. Appearances, after all, are deceptive. Get past them to the true essence of the thing, and you're in business. Accordingly, if it talks like technology and it thinks like technology, there's a fair chance that that's what it is. And where you have technology, you have to have rules. Only figure those rules out, and you're in with a chance.

"All right," he said, wearily but not without hope. "I think it's the chicken, and here's why. I think that you can take a bit of chicken genetic material and stick it in a Petri dish and clone a chicken, but only a chicken can lay an egg. Quite probably, though I'm not entirely sure of my facts here, you could take DNA samples from partridges and peacocks and guinea fowl and God only knows what, and you could do stuff to them and modify them and bung them in a tank full of green goo, and eventually you'd have yourself the poultry equivalent of Dolly the sheep, but growing an egg, no, I don't think that's possible. So, *if you're starting from scratch*, the chicken's got to come first, because only a chicken can make an egg. Now, strictly speaking that'd be which *comes* first, not which *came* first, but—" He stopped, sensing some slight change in ambience. "Sorry," he said. "Am I boring you?"

The walls shook. "Continue."

"I'm barking up the wrong tree, aren't I?"

"Your answer would appear to be based on an unacceptable approach."

"I've changed my mind," Don said. "It's the egg, isn't it?"

"That answer is not acceptable."

Don smiled. He didn't care about the answer any more. He'd found out something far more important, he was sure of it. The voice, the ruined abbey, the exceptionally roomy toilet, presumably the fridge as well; he was dealing with a machine. Not a human or a superhuman, but a gadget, a piece of kit. That was the point, surely. Gadgets don't just happen. Gadgets are designed and built for a purpose, to achieve an objective. This one, he felt moderately sure, was intended to find an answer to this idiotic question, and by sheer bad luck he'd managed to get himself caught up in it, like the tie of a man bending too low over a shredder. But that was, or could be, all right. Gadgets have rules.

"Define acceptable," he said.

The voice didn't hesitate this time. "Acceptable is defined as that which is liable to be accepted by the panel of judges."

Ah. "State the criteria by which the panel of judges assesses acceptibility."

"The panel of judges will accept an answer that is in accordance with the terms and conditions of the competition, as set out in the statement of terms and conditions."

"Tell me the terms and conditions."

"One, the judges' decision is final. Two, the competition is not open to fellows, staff and employees of the Paul Carpenter Foundation, their employees, contractors or families. Three, all entries must be received no later than 1 March 1362. Four, time travel is permitted under the conditions set out in Appendix A. Five..."

There were a hundred and four terms and conditions, and by the time the great voice finally fell silent Don's head felt like the inside of a kettledrum. But that was a small price to pay. Finally, against all expectations, quite probably for the first time in his life, he understood what was going on. "Thank you," he said. "In which case, the answer is, the chicken."

A silence lasting two seconds. You could have held the world stalagmite-growing championships in those two seconds – qualifiers, opening rounds, quarter-finals, semi-finals and a best-of-three knockout tournament to decide the title.

"Correct," said the voice.

"Stan," Mr Huos said.

Mr Gogerty turned and faced his employer. "You're here."

"Apparently." Mr Huos frowned. "I'd more or less given up on you."

By Mr Huos' feet a chicken clucked. Mr Gogerty gave it a not-now look. "I've found it," he said.

For a moment Mr Huos couldn't think what to say, and when he did manage to come up with a selection of words, they weren't desperately original. "You found it?"

"Yes."

"Oh."

"Here," Mr Gogerty said, and from his pocket he took a plain brass ring, which he displayed on the palm of his hand, perfectly visible but significantly out of Mr Huos' reach. "This it, isn't it?"

It could have been any old brass ring. "Yes," Mr Huos said immediately. "That's it."

"I haven't got the box," Mr Gogerty said. "Just the ring. It was a pencil sharpener, of all things."

Shrug. "I think it was a pencil sharpener once before," Mr Huos said. "I forget, it's been so many things. Well, that's fantastic. I don't know what to say."

Mr Gogerty paused as if trying to decide something. Then

he fished a bit of paper out of his top pocket with his other hand, closed his fist tight around the ring and gave Mr Huos the paper.

"My bill," he said.

Mr Huos looked at it and smiled. It came to $100,000.02.

"I'll have to owe you the penny," he said.

"That's fine," Mr Gogerty said. "I'll take a cheque."

"Got a pen?"

Mr Gogerty had a pen. He had several, including one by Schimmel & Bracht of Salzburg, circa 1927, which could write lies that anybody reading them would automatically believe, and another one by Braun of Geneva which only wrote the truth, and a rather nice chased-silver propelling pencil by Tomacek of Prague which could solve any crossword ever set. He also had a plain blue biro, which he handed to Mr Huos, who dropped it, picked it up and used it to write a cheque.

"Thanks," Mr Gogerty said.

"Pleasure," Mr Huos replied. "Now can I have my ring back, please?"

Many years ago, playing in the dusty backstreets of Port of Spain, the young Gogerty had been haunted by a recurring daydream. In it he was standing on a rostrum (an orange box draped with a pillowcase) in front of the assembled United Nations, as the President of Earth shook his hand and presented him with a gold medal the size of a dinner plate, while overhead floated a banner inscribed STANLEY GOGERTY SAVES THE WORLD. Nothing distressingly unusual in that, except that in the dream he was always thoroughly miserable, guilty, ashamed of himself, because somehow he knew that saving the world was an indulgence, an ego trip, showing off when he should be knuckling down and earning a living.

So, dilemma time. He could give Mr Huos the brass ring and keep the cheque, or he could refuse to hand over the ring, in which case Mr Huos would be entirely within his rights to

ask for his money back. The quandary was further complicated by the fact that he had no proof, only a hunch, that
withholding the ring would save the world (From what?), but
the feeling in the pit of his stomach was so strong that he
couldn't just ignore it. Besides, what if his childhood vision
had been a premonition rather than a daydream, and the mis-
ery of the young Stanley Gogerty was a foreshadowing of
precisely the angst he was feeling right now? He thought, I
can't keep it; it's not mine. Then he remembered that someone had burned down the Carpenter Library.

"I'm sorry," he said. "I can't do that."

Mr Huos wasn't angry, just confused. "Do what?"

"I can't give this thing back to you," Mr Gogerty said, and
it was like talking while wearing a ten-ton moustache. "I have
reason to believe it's extremely dangerous."

"You don't say." Mr Huos was smiling like a sunset. "That's
what I just paid you a hundred thousand dollars for – it's dangerous. Thanks, but I'd sort of reached that conclusion myself.
So," he went on, calming himself down as much as he could,
"you're going to hang on to it for safekeeping, I suppose. Make
sure it doesn't fall into the wrong hands."

Put like that, it didn't sound so good. Maybe it was a bit
late. Maybe it was in the wrong hands already. Maybe there
weren't any right hands anywhere. "You've got another suggestion?" Mr Gogerty said cautiously.

"God, no." Mr Huos was grinning again. "The way I see it,
there's only two possibilities. Try and use it to put everything
back how it was, which I'm fairly sure can't be done, or get rid
of it. Kill it, saw it in half, throw it in the sea. I don't know.
Don't suppose that's possible either. Tell you what: have your
lot got a museum or something like that? Safe place where you
can put really dangerous stuff where it's sealed in and can't get
out? Or maybe they can disarm it or something. Anyway, it's
yours. You keep it and do what the hell you like. I have absolute trust in your judgement and discretion, and I know you'll

do the right thing. And will you stop your chicken biting my ankles?"

"That's not my chicken," Mr Gogerty said, then, very quickly, as Mr Huos swung his leg back, "It's not a chicken at all, it just looks like one."

"Can I kick it anyway?"

"No."

Mr Huos sighed and put his foot back on the ground. "How can it not be a chicken?" he said. "It looks like one; it sounds like one; if I put my boot up its arse I bet you anything you like it'll fly like one."

Mr Gogerty looked straight at him. It was like facing his reflection in a mirror when he'd done something he was particularly ashamed of. "It's not a chicken," he said, "the same way you're not human."

Stunned, dissociated from reality, like someone on morphine or having an out-of-body experience, Polly reached into the fridge and picked up the cucumber, frowned at it and dropped it on the floor. She really wasn't in the right frame of mind for cucumbers.

What the hell, she asked herself, was she going to tell her mother? Yes, Mum, he got into the fridge and shut the door, and when I opened it again he'd gone. Vanished. What? Oh, eggs, tomatoes, cheese, olives, a cucumber. Look, does it really matter? Yes, I guess it does go to show he's eating properly.

Someone was ringing the doorbell. It took her a moment to identify the sound. Reluctantly she closed the fridge, then quickly opened it again, just in case something had changed. Very silly of her, except that something had. Under the Stilton crumbs, next to the olives, was a small rosewood box. She grabbed it without thinking and went to the door.

"Oh," she said. "It's you."

Rachel Briggs, sister of Don's upstairs neighbour (the one he'd presumably disintegrated, the one who'd caught the two of them burgling his flat) pushed past her, followed by a small, balding young man with a very sad face, who muttered an apology then stopped dead and stared at her. Alan Stevens, her immediate superior at BRHD.

"Alan?" Ms Briggs, Polly decided, would have made a first-class dog trainer. "Don't just stand there gawping. We're going to search this flat from top to bottom."

"Fine," Polly murmured. "Carry on. Tell me if you find anything interesting."

In spite of the word of command uttered with total authority, Mr Stevens didn't move. He knew he was disobeying a direct order and that at some point there'd be serious repercussions, but it didn't matter. He felt as though he'd just been torn in half. On one side of him stood his fiancée, Rachel Briggs, on the other, his subordinate, Polly Mayer. He knew them both very well, obviously. But – and this was what was ripping his brain to pieces – he was somehow aware that the Alan Stevens who worked with Ms Mayer wasn't the same man who was engaged to Rachel. They were both talking to him, but he couldn't make out a word they were saying. He was a trick coin, with the head of Alan Stevens on both sides. One side existed in a world with Rachel in it, the other—

"*Star Trek*," he said.

At least that had the effect of shutting them both up instantly. He didn't explain. He didn't bother trying to tell them about the episode of *Star Trek* where the matter and antimatter universes collide, and the guest star from the antimatter universe gets loose in the matter universe, and, well, he hadn't understood it at the time, but it was all right because it was only sci-fi and a pretext for William Shatner to charge around in a torn shirt. Naturally, if he'd thought that one day it would happen to him, he'd have paid closer attention.

Rachel was in his face, yelling at him; under other circumstances, something he'd have done anything to avoid. Lazily, he extended his arm and pushed her out of the way (stupid, aggressive woman, no idea what he'd ever seen in her). It was bloody *Star Trek*, that's what it was, and here he was bang in the middle of it. Also, just to make things a little bit more interesting, he was feeling very strange: dizzy, bunged up like a bad cold, woozy like a hangover, more than a little nauseous (watch out shoes, here comes lunch) and somehow as though he wasn't altogether there. Maybe, he thought, and grinned, Scotty's beaming me out of here, in the nick of time. Good old Sco—

He vanished.

Rachel Briggs stared at the cubic metre of air that no longer encompassed her fiancé and screamed. Polly, who'd always had a secret fondness for loud noises, let her rip for two and a bit seconds, then smacked her round the face. She'd always wanted a legitimate opportunity to do that.

"It's all right," she said, rubbing her hand. "He's gone."

The contradiction in that statement wasn't lost on her. Ms Briggs' brother, her brother and now Alan Stevens: three, to her certain knowledge. Maybe "all right" was stretching it a bit. Oh yes, and Mr Gogerty. Four. Well, at least they'd none of them be lonely.

"Now do you believe me?" she said.

Ms Briggs looked at her as if she was the ground, and Ms Briggs' parachute had somehow failed to open. "What happened?"

"We think it's magic," Polly said. "Sit down and I'll make us both a coffee."

"He just—"

"I know." With a gentle hand on her shoulder she steered Ms Briggs to the sofa and folded her onto it. "So," she said, "how long have you been working at BRHD?"

Ms Briggs' eyes were a very pale blue and completely blank. "What's that got to do with anything?"

"Lots," Polly said. "Sit still while I get the coffee."

Making coffee meant being in the kitchen, where the fridge was. She tried to keep as far away from it as she could. While the kettle was boiling, she examined the rosewood box, thinking about something Mr Gogerty had said, about a box. When she felt brave enough, she opened it, but it was empty. Just an empty box, a bit like the fridge, if you didn't count Stilton crumbs and cucumbers.

She frowned. Maybe that was it. Maybe you had to count *everything*.

Ms Briggs hadn't moved while she was away. Polly pushed the coffee mug into her hands, and Ms Briggs grabbed it like a lifebelt, spilling a bit. "Now then," Polly said briskly, like a nurse. "We know that there's something going on. Don and I used the word magic because, well, it seems to be doing magic-like stuff, and we don't know what else to call it. We know it's something to do with Blue Remembered Hills. Don had a theory."

Ms Briggs looked at her helplessly. "Don's your brother?"

"Yes, that's right." Firm, reassuring nod of the head. "His idea was that there was a whole lot of us working at BRHD, and we were all sort of there simultaneously, if you get what I'm saying. We couldn't see or hear each other, but we were occupying the same space at the same time, but in a different..."

"Dimension?"

"That's right," Polly said quickly. "And I know it sounds weird, but please hear me out, all right, because I think I know where I'm going and I need someone to tell it to, just to see if it really hangs together. You're all right for time, are you? Not on your way anywhere?"

Ms Briggs shook her head, though her eyes stayed fixed on Polly.

"All right then." Polly took a moment to shepherd her thoughts. "We have no idea how long it's being going on for, but my guess is, it's been a while, and up till very recently it was working just fine. Then, a few days ago, everything started to go wrong. The darts match," she remembered. "Do you know anything about a darts match?"

Ms Briggs pulled a deep-concentration face. "Alan said something. He's..."

"Captain of the office team," Polly prompted. "That's right. You don't play darts, obviously. There was a darts match, against Thames Water. Alan – that's Alan where I come from – made me play because he was one short. I had a dress I wanted to wear for the match, so I took it in to be cleaned." She paused. "With me so far?"

"I think so. But—"

Polly held up her hand. "We think," she went on, "that something happened at the cleaners. Don took something in there to be cleaned, and when he got it back there was this brass thing in the pocket."

"Thing?"

"It was a pencil sharpener, but it may not have been. It's complicated. But the point is, that's when all the screwy stuff started. We think it got in the pocket of his coat by mistake. Anyhow, it was after that that things started coming apart. For one thing, the dry cleaners vanished. Then Don started having these –" she winced "– powers. Magic. That was when he vanished your brother."

"He vanished..."

Polly nodded. "Apparently, your brother annoyed him and Don wished he'd just go away, and he did. At the time we both assumed it was something Don had actually done, but now I'm not so sure. Not after what just happened to Alan. Anyway, we thought we'd better find someone we could ask about what's going on, an expert, so we looked on Google and found this man Gogerty, and he—"

"Who?"

"He's a weirdness expert," Polly said. "Don't ask. Anyway, he came round to see us earlier today, and he was really interested in the pencil sharpener, but he seemed to think it should've been in a little wooden box. But there wasn't a box. Only now it's turned up," she added, "in Don's fridge. Is this making any sense to you?"

"No."

"Nor me." Polly nodded to convey approval of a correct answer. "But I was just thinking," she went on, "about what Alan said, just before he vanished."

Ms Briggs frowned. "He said '*Star Trek*,'" she said.

"Yes."

"That doesn't make sense."

Polly smiled and told her about the episode where the matter and antimatter universes collide. She got the impression that Ms Briggs wasn't a Trekkie, but never mind. "I think that's what's happened," she concluded. "I think there're at least two different universes, and you belong in one and I belong in another, but somehow Alan belongs in both." She paused to draw breath. "I think that when these two universes sort of bump into each other, where there's an exact match, one of them gets cancelled out. They overlap, if you see what I mean. Don's my brother and what's-his-name, Kevin, he's your brother. Two brothers of a sister who works in the conveyancing department of Blue Remembered Hills bump into each other – both of them musicians, come to think of it. They're an exact match, so one of them gets cancelled out. *Ping*," she added, then wished she hadn't. "But we can't be an exact match, because we're both still here, and Alan's gone, so I'm guessing that when two almost-the-same-but-not-quites meet and there's a shared factor from both universes present at the same time, it's the shared factor that gets vanished. Alan," she explained. "Of course, it was different with Don and Mr Gogerty, because they went inside the fridge."

"Ah," said Ms Briggs.

"Exactly," Polly said. "I think the fridge is the container, you see, the thing the other stuff goes in. The box. That's why Mr

Gogerty couldn't find the box, because it was already here. The box must *be* the fridge, a bit like the chicken and the egg. So when Mr Gogerty took the pencil sharpener back inside the box, where it belonged, I'm guessing everything started putting itself back how it ought to be. Which isn't necessarily how it ought to be for us, you understand, because we're just innocent bystanders caught up in it all. Well?" she asked eagerly. "What do you think?"

Ms Briggs looked at her for a very long time, as though formulating a considered opinion. "I think you're a witch," she said. "Get away from me, you evil—"

Polly sighed and folded her arms. "Now that's not very constructive, is it? I really don't—"

"*Evil!*" screamed Ms Briggs, crossing her index fingers in front of her face, in the manner of a Labour backbencher heckling Michael Howard. "Get away, get *away*."

She was getting quite impossible, and it was probably just as well that she vanished a moment later. Even so, Polly couldn't help feeling vexed. True, she was glad she wasn't being yelled at and having the sign of the cross stuck up her nose. On the other hand, that was her beautiful hypothesis down the toilet. She mourned its passing with a shake of her head then, much to her own surprise, burst into tears.

Stupid, she thought, and really not helping. She fumbled for a tissue, found none and headed to the kitchen for some paper towel. No such thing (she winced as she passed the fridge), so she went to the bathroom for some toilet paper. Trust Don not to have a single Kleenex in the flat.

She was all alone. Everybody else had vanished. She had no explanation for what had happened and absolutely no idea what to do about it, if there was anything that could be done. Basically, then, she had two choices. She could think hard and try and figure it out from the few scraps of evidence at her disposal, or she could curl up in a ball on the floor and start sobbing again.

She thought. Suppose, she thought, the universe is like one of those coats they sell in camping shops: reversible, so if you turn it inside out there's a completely different coat on the other side. Suppose that, and then suppose it's a coat you can inside-out not just once but lots of times, one coat you can hang on one hanger, but also loads and loads of different coats at the same time. A feature of the camping-shop reversible coat is that the two different coats share the same pockets; you just get into them from different sides. Suppose the reason she hadn't vanished when the coat of reality got turned inside out was that she was a pocket, a fixed point shared by all the various different versions.

Well, you could suppose that, if you wanted to, but it wasn't a great deal of practical use. Besides, shouldn't Alan Stevens have been the pocket? Or maybe he was something inside the pocket (hanky, biro cap, small copper coin, bit of fluff), whereas she was the pocket itself. Eew, she thought, and cast around for a rather less revolting analogy. Suppose the universe was a set of concentric spherical Russian dolls. No, that was just silly.

Out of the corner of her eye she caught sight of the rosewood box. She'd forgotten about it in all the excitement, but Mr Gogerty had been very interested in it, so it had to be important. It lay on the table, looking remarkably like a small rosewood box, the sort of thing they make in India by the million and sell in gift and craft shops. She watched it for a moment or so but it didn't do anything. Just a box. Something tickled the back of her mind, but she couldn't get hold of it to find out what it was. She picked it up.

Well, she'd opened it once before, and nothing bad had happened. Which meant, of course, that there was no point opening it again, was there? Just a box. She put it back on the table, then picked it up again. Why would Gogerty be so concerned about an empty wooden box? Or was it because the brass thing had somehow managed to get out of it, presumably at some point while it was at the dry cleaners? Total waste of time opening it again.

She realised she'd slid one fingernail under the lid. Well, she thought, it really can't hurt, and carried on opening it, remembering as she did so, in the split second before the box grew huge and ate her, that the thing she'd been trying to call to mind a moment ago was her mother once telling her that before she was born, they'd seriously considered calling her Pandora.

# CHAPTER SIXTEEN

"As a matter of interest," Don asked mildly, "why is it the chicken?"

The voice didn't answer, and from the depth and quality of the silence, he knew it would never speak again. A cloud must have passed in front of the sun, because the light no longer streamed through the stained glass window. He thought about trying to find the monk but decided not to waste his time. Game over, he said to himself. And presumably I won.

He got up and walked slowly and wearily to the door. On the threshold he stopped and turned round for one last look, but there was nothing to see. Some old church, its purpose long since obsolete. He supposed someone from English Heritage would be along sooner or later to lock up.

He walked out into the sunlight, reflecting that this was the weirdest time he'd ever spent in a toilet. Even the grass was different now. It wasn't nearly so smooth and regular; there were dandelions and docks in it, and here and there it had been nibbled at, so the ends of the blades were square, not pointed. A crow flew slowly past, wallowing in the still air. That cheered him up, a bit. OK, so it was still the countryside, but he was morally certain it was now real, not gamespace. What he wanted most of all, he decided, was a bus stop.

If he was honest with himself he wasn't really all that bothered, but since he had nothing else to think about that wasn't depressing or annoying, he thought about what he'd just been through, rationalising, order out of chaos and stuff like that. It had, he was pretty sure, been a competition, hence all the terms and conditions, a competition to solve the unanswerable and fundamentally stupid question of which came first. The voice had mentioned a date in the fourteenth century, round about the time (he was no expert) the abbey was built. Guessing here, but presumably the abbey was someone's idea of a games console, a gadget designed to choose the winner. Only there couldn't be a winner, because there was no right answer to the question, not a real answer, at any rate. He shunted that train of thought into a siding, and rejoined the main line.

Obviously, whoever designed the competition had access to some pretty high-level technology. Furthermore, at some point in the intervening centuries the secrets of that technology had been lost and forgotten, so that when he, a native of the twenty-first century, happened to stumble across it, he found it completely inexplicable and assumed it must be magic. But it wasn't, no more than electricity or digital information are magic; that had been his first mistake, and it served him right for not having faith in his own scepticism.

He was climbing uphill now, though he had no real idea where he was going. He'd come out of the abbey and started to walk, choosing a direction at random. While the game was still running, of course, there was no such thing as random. He could have chosen any vector he liked, but every compass point would have brought him to where the game wanted him to be. Now, though, he was on his own. He stopped and looked around, but it was still all just empty green desert. Buggery, he thought, and walked on.

So, the game. He wished he knew what the prize had been;

must have been worth picking up, or why would people bother to enter? Mind, he had no evidence that anybody ever had. At any rate, the competition had remained unsolved and unwon, and since the technology still worked and the batteries hadn't run down, six hundred years or so later, here it still was. The pencil sharpener, he decided, must have been some sort of interface that plugged you into the game. The powers must be things you needed to be able to do in order to get here, or to operate the console. At any rate, by sheer bad luck it had come into his possession and forced him to take part, screwing up his life and the lives of those around him. Some people have no consideration for others.

How many other poor bastards had been sucked into competing in the game, he wondered, and what had become of them? He'd never know, so it was pointless to speculate. They'd never have stood a chance, of course. It had been luck, and a twenty-first-century mindset, that had made it possible for him to succeed where they, presumably, had failed. And he'd only tumbled to the game's secret because he'd spent way too much time playing other, less lethal but equally silly games when he should have been out having a life.

Once you figured it out, though, it was simple. You don't win by giving the right answer. You win by winning. Since the question is unanswerable, there is no right answer. Therefore, the only way you can win is by cheating.

In the distance, the very far distance, he saw a tractor. He altered course a degree or so and headed for it.

He knew he couldn't be the only player of the game, because someone had played it before and had figured out the secret, just as he had. At some stage in the past someone had tried to cheat. He didn't know how his anonymous predecessor had gone about it, but for some reason he'd developed a successful cheat, and then something must have happened and he never got the chance to confront the great voice, give his answer and collect the prize. Pity, in a way. But his sympathy was muted

346 • Tom Holt

somewhat by the appalling side effects of the cheat, into which he and his sister and the Briggses and most likely a load of other people had been unwillingly drawn. It was the cheat that had created the weirdness, the transdimensional anomalies and simultaneous lives and all that crap; it was something to do with the cheat, and once he'd recognised it for what it was, he knew that the cheat existed; at which point, since he didn't know the details of how it worked, he'd been left with a straight fifty-fifty guess. Luckily, he'd guessed right. Simple as that.

The tractor was driving up and down, shooting something out onto the ground from a trailer. If only he could get there before it finished and went away again. He could hitch a ride back as far as the nearest road, then walk until he reached a village or a town, and then he could go home. The thought made him catch his breath. Home, a mythical place where all your dreams come true. Untold millions of naive adventurers had come to grief searching for it, and many people reckon it doesn't actually exist. Still, it was worth making an effort. Knowing his luck, though, he'd probably end up discovering America.

After a very long time he got close enough to smell what was coming out of the back of the trailer. It wasn't terribly nice but it was definitely real. Appropriate too, for inside a toilet, except he wasn't any more. That made him walk a bit faster, even though his feet and the calves of his legs were giving him all manner of aggravation.

When he was close enough to be able to read the tractor's number plate, it turned, zoomed through a gateway and disappeared behind a hedge. Don stopped, realising that he was out of breath and pretty much crippled, and for the past five minutes he'd been walking through the stuff that had come off the trailer. It was enough to make him wish he was back in the game.

No, it bloody wasn't. He trudged through the gateway and found himself on a rough, muddy track between two tall hedges. He could hear the tractor rumbling away somewhere in the distance, too far away for him to catch it now. He looked down at his shoes, which, like him, would never quite be the same again. All because he'd been stupid enough to do his sister a favour.

Well, he knew that wasn't true. Quite where the tipping point had been, where he'd lost his footing and slithered into the six-hundred-year-old mess, he couldn't possibly say. Most likely it had been a gradual process, the final slip being something he wouldn't have noticed at the time. Nobody's fault, though, or nobody living. Just one of those things, like floods or lightning.

The lane curved, and in front of him he saw something wonderful: a house (genuine twentieth-century brick-and-breeze-block job, so he wasn't in the game any more), to be precise, a farm, with a regulation farmyard cluttered with block and corrugate-iron buildings, lots of concrete, some large bits of abandoned machinery, a dilapidated horsebox parked in a corner and chickens. Under other circumstances, far too rural for his taste. He felt like someone who doesn't really like dogs being hauled out of a collapsed avalanche by a St Bernard.

"Hello," he called out, as he took his first step on concrete. "Anybody here?"

No answer, but the chickens came running. Naturally, he wasn't scared of a bunch of chickens; far more scared of him than he could ever be of them, that was the whole point of *Homo sapiens* having dominion over the animal kingdom. The reason they were crowding round his feet was just that they were dead tame and expected him to feed him. That was probably why they were pecking at his shoes, mistaking them for pellets of concentrated sorghum, wheat, bran and essential vitamins, the way you do. "Shoo, chickens," he said in a brisk but friendly voice, whereupon one of them flapped its wings, rose up in the air to kneecap level and pecked him so hard he yelped. "Get out of it, you—" he started to say, but got no further than that, because another chicken had flown up and sunk its claws into his shirt, and was trying to get its head into his inside pocket. Stupid bloody creature, he thought, batting frantically at it and missing; there's nothing to eat in there, just my wallet and my phone.

The chicken had his phone clamped in its beak, for crying out loud. It backed away, hummingbird style, for three wing flaps before the weight of the phone overcame its already marginal airworthiness and it sank, still flapping, still holding the phone, to the ground. It landed running and was halfway across the yard before it occurred to Don to do anything about it.

*Fucking chicken just stole my phone!* But the rest of the flock were right under his feet, almost as though they were deliberately obstructing him from chasing the phone thief. Crazy, or maybe someone had trained them. Could you train chickens? No idea. Didn't care. He just wanted his phone back, but that seemed to be an unrealistic aspiration. He kicked out, caught a chicken on its folded wing and sent it sailing up in the air like a beach ball, which paralysed him with guilt until the bird landed, immediately found its feet and rushed back into the scrum, eyes glittering with warlike zeal.

"Don't kick the chickens," a voice said sharply behind him. "They're human."

He knew that voice. Slowly and carefully – What the hell did he mean, the chickens are human? – he turned to see who it was. Then he tried to speak, but his mouth opened and shut goldfish style and no sounds came out.

"Mr Mayer?"

He breathed out, then addressed himself to the tall, shaven-headed man, not the long, thin bugger in the suit. "Mr Gogerty?" he said.

There had been a time when Polly had been seriously, deeply, passionately into ponies. It had lasted about six months, ending just after her fifteenth birthday (the transitional period, the lady at the riding stables had called it, between toys and boys), and now, when she looked back on it, she wondered what on earth had possessed her. Big fierce things with teeth at one end and hooves at the other; falling off; shovelling poo.

But at least she could recognise the interior of a horsebox when she found herself in one. True, it wasn't like the specimens she'd encountered at Mrs Jeffries'. It was dark and dirty and smelt overwhelmingly, not of horse but of something even worse – something, she noted as she moved her feet, with extremely poor personal hygiene and bowel control. Yuck.

Another thing she remembered about horseboxes: when you're inside and the door's shut, you can't get out.

Ridiculous, she thought. A fraction of a second ago she'd been in Don's flat, peering into the little rosewood box she'd found in his fridge. She couldn't be scared because something like this couldn't have happened. Fear needs belief. This was just silly, and silliness only made her irritable.

She pushed against the door, just in case it was loose. Nope.

As well as the main door, which folds down to double as a ramp, there's usually a little side door. She investigated it, found it, saw that there was no handle on the inside. She tried kicking it and hurt her toe.

"Hello?" she shouted. "Anybody there?"

She waited. Polly wasn't very good at just waiting. Restaurants, airports, building societies, government offices, dentists' waiting rooms: not happy places for her. Add another category to the list. "Hey!" she yelled. "Let me out!"

Nothing. Then she heard a rustling noise, as of wings, somewhere outside. Wings, she thought. Angels? Not that she was in any position to be choosy, but angels struck her as excessive. Whatever it was, it was getting louder, and there was also an element of scrabbling. That implied claws, so she could probably dismiss the angels theory. Her views on the shut door softened. She could see that a steel door, tightly closed, might have its advantages.

Then light burst in around her as the door swung down, and suddenly the horsebox was full of chickens. Some of them scuttled around her feet; others flapped up at her face or tried to perch on her arms and shoulders, prodding at her with their beaks, almost as though they were frisking her for something. Naturally she waved her arms, batted at them and made loud shooing noises, but they didn't seem inclined to take her seriously. One of them had got its beak round her mobile phone. She grabbed at it, but the chicken ducked under her hand and flapped away, weighted down with its trophy. Maybe, she thought, they're going to beat me up, and they want the phone to film it with.

But the chickens withdrew, as suddenly as they'd come, and she was left alone in the horsebox with a view of a farmyard through the open door. It wasn't a situation that called for deep introspection. She was out of there like a bullet from a gun.

No sign of the chickens, thankfully. She stopped and looked round. Rickety buildings, rusty old machinery, concrete, the rural idyll bang up to date. At any rate the weirdness quotient appeared to have dropped to an acceptable level. She couldn't have asked for anything more prosaic.

Some people, though, would be nice, provided they weren't dangerous lunatics. "Hello?" she called out. "Excuse me, is anybody about?"

No answer. Sort of creepy. Perhaps all the humans had been killed and eaten by the feral chickens. She could have called for help if she still had her phone. Was that why they'd stolen it? All things considered, and she didn't think she was being too hasty in her judgements here, she rather wished she was somewhere else.

In which case (her rational self asserted itself) why not just leave? Well, quite. There was a gate on the other side of the yard which could reasonably be assumed to lead somewhere. She headed for it, but before she got there someone behind her called out her name. Both parts of it: Polly Mayer.

She spun round, and saw the unmistakable bulk of Mr Gogerty, the weirdness expert, striding towards her. Behind him, struggling to keep up, was Don. Behind him, looking thoroughly confused, was—

She blinked. Fancy meeting you here.

"Mr Huos?" she said.

And behind him, she noticed, the chicken pack, closing on him fast. "Look out," she yelled, but Mr Gogerty shook his head. "It's all right," he assured her. "They're not chickens, they're people."

An odd sentiment, she couldn't help thinking, the sort of thing you'd expect from Jamie Oliver – maybe a little bit extreme even for him. No sign of her phone. Presumably they'd already sold it to buy drugs.

"Mr Huos, be careful," she shouted. "Those chickens are dangerous. They stole my—"

But Mr Gogerty had arrived, taking up a protective stance between her and the flock. "They aren't chickens," he repeated. "As a matter of fact, I believe they're mostly lawyers, like yourself. There's nothing to be afraid of, trust me."

She stared at him. "Lawyers?"

"I think so," he said. "I haven't had a chance to ask them all."

That was a bit too much, even in context. "Don," she complained, "he's not making any sense." (At which point it occurred to her that she was overwhelmed with joy and relief at seeing her brother again after she'd more or less given up hope, but he was her brother, after all, so the cluster of strong emotions surging about inside her could wait.) "Do you have any idea what he's talking about?"

Don looked sheepish, which was nothing to go by, but he nodded once, briefly, and said, "Maybe, I'm not sure. Look, wouldn't it be a good idea if we all sat down and talked about this?"

"Yes," said Mr Huos, in a very loud clear voice which made

the other three turn and look at him. "And since I'm paying Stan's wages, and I have an idea you work for me—"

"Polly Mayer," Polly said, quickly and in a rather small voice. "Assistant solicitor in the—"

"You're fired, by the way," Mr Huos said kindly. "Nothing personal. I've closed down the company. I imagine there'll be a redundancy cheque waiting for you when you get home. Anyhow," Mr Huos went on, "I think sitting down and talking about it would be a very good idea indeed. What do you lot reckon?"

"I think we should wait for Mr and Mrs Williams," Mr Gogerty said firmly. "I don't suppose they'll be very long, and we owe it to them."

"Are you Polly's boss, then?" Don asked.

"Was," Mr Huos replied. "Like I just said, I've shut down the business, and—"

"So my sister's out of a job, just because you take it into your head to—"

"Don," Polly snapped, her face red as beetroot. "Stop it."

"Yes, but—"

"Really," Mr Huos said, "I had no choice. All the houses I sold never really existed."

"And that makes it all all right, does it?"

Mr Gogerty frowned, unsure what to do. He was no stranger to conflict. He bought silver bullets by the case and wooden stakes by the pallet load. A market gardener just outside Cambridge kept back four acres every year to grow a special variety of garlic just for him. Over the years he'd cut his way out of the bellies of sea monsters that had swallowed him whole, reduced the Lithuanian manticore to a Level 6 endangered species and collected enough yards of mummy bandage to lag the dome of St Paul's. There were some fights, however, that he made a practice of steering clear of, and this had all the signs of being one of them. On the other hand, he was impatient to get on, and he needed these people to help him wrap the job up. He cleared his throat politely, but they took no notice. A complex three-cornered snarling match had sprung up between them, and he doubted whether anything short of a power hose would get their attention. Probably best, he decided, to back off and let them resolve their issues, and then talk to the survivors.

From his deepest, most inside pocket, with its unrippable lining and charm-reinforced Velcro closing strip, he took the ring that had once been a pencil sharpener and gave it the full force of his attention. It was rounded rather than flattened in section, so it wasn't a human finger ring. There was a point where the two ends had been butted together, but not brazed or soldered shut. The wear on one side was quite pronounced. He smiled. He knew exactly what it was. That and his knowledge of dead languages gave him at least a third of the answer, but he still wished he had the box.

He sat down on a rusty muck spreader, took another look at the ring, then glanced at his surroundings. It didn't take him long to find what he was looking for; it wasn't small or hidden. He stood up, walked over to it and sat down on a low wall. Low, that is, to a tall human. He leaned forward, lowering his line of sight.

The cockerel who'd indentified himself as Kevin Briggs waddled across the yard to join him. Stan didn't have his phone any more, but he had something just as good – his pocket organiser, by Hauptmann of Wiesbaden, one of only seven the great man made before he disappeared in 1906. He took it out, switched it on and laid it carefully on the ground, so that the keyboard faced Mr Briggs. The head dipped, the beak pecked.

"well?"

Mr Gogerty picked up the organiser and thought for a moment. Then, stabbing at the tiny keys with the edge of his little finger, he wrote, "nearly there. just need a few more details."

Mr Briggs pecked for a long time in reply. "my sister just turned up and her boyfriend. hes a cockerel too of course a bantam. wanted to rip his head off but didn't. cant you hurry it up a bit? mary byron's got another phone shes trying to call nasa oh and theres a whole lot of cars coming over the hill be here soon thought you ought to know big black ones limos."

Mr Gogerty's right eyebrow twitched. "that's interesting," he typed. "it looks like they've finished arguing over there. stay here i'll be back."

He picked up the organiser and put it away, then walked quickly back to join Mr Huos and the Mayers. "Better now?" he asked.

Mr Huos nodded. "I explained it was all my fault," he said. "It is my fault, isn't it?"

"No," Mr Gogerty said. "It's somebody's fault, but he's not here. I think I may have an idea who it is, but—"

"Don here's got something to tell you," Mr Huos interrupted. "I think you ought to listen."

In the sixth limousine from the back of the convoy the CEO of United Petroleum twisted his hands together in his lap. Next to him, the president of Turkmenistan had chewed his pencil almost down to the stub. Opposite, the professor of pure mathematics at Harvard was staring blankly through the window, while the Chinese foreign minister kept looking at his watch. None of them had spoken for a long time. Understandably enough; there was only so much anybody could say about the weather, the food on the plane and George Bush, and there were no other safe topics of conversation.

"That's just stupid," Polly said.

Don sighed. "Fine," he said. "If you can think of a better explanation..."

"Mr Mayer is quite right," Mr Gogerty said, which shut both of them up straight away. "There was a competition. It's quite well documented, though very few details survive. We don't know who organised it, for example, and up till now the rules have been a matter of wild conjecture.

But we do know what the prize was, and that it was never claimed."

"Prize?" Don repeated eagerly. "What is it? What did I win?"

Mr Gogerty looked him in the eyes. "You should bear in mind," he said slowly, "that the competition was set a very long time ago. Also, I have no idea how you'd go about collecting it."

"What is it?" Don snarled. "Well?"

Mr Gogerty broke eye contact. "Five hundred pounds," he said.

"What?" Don looked as though he'd just been kissed by a giant squid. "Is that all? Five hundred rotten bloody—"

"It was a great deal of money back in the fourteenth century," Mr Gogerty said. "You could've bought a large estate or built a castle. Unfortunately—"

Don made a rather vulgar noise and turned away. "I don't suppose there's a second prize, is there?" he said. "A golden throne or fifty acres of prime real estate in the City of London."

Mr Gogerty shook his head. "If you consider the nature of the challenge," he said.

"Ah well." Don shrugged. Then a bolt of lightning lit up the inside of his head. "What about interest?" he said. "Compound interest, seven hundred years..."

"Impossible," Mr Gogerty said. "There were laws against usury in the fourteenth century."

"Oh." Don wilted. "So that's it, then. Five hundred quid."

Mr Gogerty coughed softly. "There's also the matter of my fee," he said. "For the consultation. As a matter of fact, it comes to precisely—"

Don laughed out loud. "Don't tell me," he said. "Five hundred pounds."

"No," Mr Gogerty said. "Five hundred and six pounds and fourteen pence. No hurry," he added pleasantly. "Any time within the next seven days."

Don shook his head. "Fine," he said. "Polly will write you a cheque. Can we get back to...?"

"Of course." Mr Gogerty straightened his back. "There was a competition – you were quite right about that. And it does seem to follow that somebody tried to cheat."

"Which was the whole point," Polly interrupted.

"Agreed. But he didn't succeed." Mr Gogerty looked thoughtful. "Almost, I would suggest, but not quite. And I believe I know what form his attempt took."

He had their undivided attention, so he paused to shuffle his thoughts.

"I believe he used a transdimensional hub. That's a fairly straightforward piece of technology," he added, as three blank stares turned towards him. "It uses multiverse theory. Essentially, it's based on the premise that a universe exists for every possibility. In practice, it can turn things into other things." He stopped and shook his head. "That's actually not true," he said, "but the effect is almost the same. It's to do with the disruption in morphic resonance fields that takes place when time and space are folded along a six-axis seam."

"Turns things into other things," Polly said firmly. "Got you. Do please go on."

Mr Gogerty smiled. "The cheater decided to cheat by creating chickens that were not born from eggs. You can't create life out of nothing – that's not possible – so the only way he could do it was to change some other life forms – humans, because they're easy to transform – into chickens. This isn't as easy as it sounds. In order to do it, you have to fold across the dimensions, so that humans from Reality A are delivered into Reality B, in which it's possible. Sort of like changing the signs in algebra."

"Never got the hang of that," Don muttered. "I think I was off sick the day they did it in class, and I never quite caught up."

Mr Gogerty nodded gravely. "The technology – the transdimensional hub – is clearly the key to the mystery. I believe this is it." He held out his hand and opened it. "The last time you saw this, it was a pencil sharpener. Mr Huos," he went on, "you're sure you recognise this ring?"

Mr Huos grinned sadly. "Oh yes," he said. "I'd know it anywhere." He looked up with spaniel eyes. "I don't suppose there's any chance—"

"No," Mr Gogerty said, not unkindly. "You put me on the right lines when you mentioned that it kept changing shape inside its box. A hub would do that if it was kept isolated in a strong containment field. If the box is a containment capsule, and there's nothing else in there with it, the hub will change itself because there's nothing else for it to work on. Once I knew it was a hub, the fact that you had it with you when you were found was highly significant."

"Was it?"

"Oh yes." Mr Gogerty frowned a little. "It suggested that the shape you are now couldn't be the shape you were originally born with. I had no idea what you might be, but I knew you almost certainly weren't human."

"You keep saying that," Mr Huos said, slightly vexed. "I wish you'd stop beating about the bush and—"

But Mr Gogerty raised his hand. "All in good time," he said. "You had this thing in your possession for quite some time," he went on, "and you made the connection between its habit of changing shape and the extraordinary ability you found you had to bend and shape the world around you. I assume you labelled it 'magic' and left it at that. You're a practical man, Mr Huos, not an intellectual. A magic ring, you thought, how useful, and proceeded to use your superhuman powers to make money – in a remarkably ethical way, I may add. You took care to hurt nobody, as far as you were aware, for which you deserve some credit."

"Thank you so much, you patronising git," Mr Huos growled. "By the way, you're fired too."

"Other men in your position would not have been so conscientious," Mr Gogerty said gravely. "The fact remains that you were using technology you didn't understand, and that's always dangerous. In particular, you never grasped the crucial point that the containment field, the little wooden box you kept the ring in, is in fact the pocket reality in which the cheater's experiment takes place. The two are a set, you see; neither works properly without the other. Inside the box is where you built all those houses. Your office is in there too, which is why you could have people working for you simultaneously, in time and space layered like filo pastry. Things started to go wrong not because you lost the ring-and-box, but because the ring got out of the box." He shook his head. "Forgive me," he said. "I'm jumping ahead again."

He opened his palm and studied the ring for a moment. "The cheater," he said, "set out to turn humans into chickens. Naturally, he had to be discreet. He wouldn't want the competition judges to find out what he was up to, and you can be sure they'd have eyes everywhere. He chose a perfectly ordinary, nondescript farm, just the sort of place where nobody knows from one minute to the next precisely how many chickens are running about the place. He needed some way of installing his technology so it wouldn't be noticed, and proverbially the best place to hide something is in plain sight. The installation would have to look like part of the everyday life of the farm." He turned the ring over, to expose the worn side. "That was what gave me the clue I needed," he went on. "That, and the name you were found with."

Mr Huos raised his eyebrows. "Huos?"

"Greek for pig," Mr Gogerty replied. "And Greek is the mother tongue of my profession, just like Latin and the law. He hid the transdimensional hub in the nose of a pig – either the brood sow or the stud boar, I'd say, because they're what you might call the permanent staff, not likely to be shipped off to be turned into sausages. He'd have taken the precaution of encoding the hub so it wouldn't be activated until it entered the containment field; in other words, the ring wouldn't start working until it was put in the box for the first time. And that, presumably," he added, swinging round and pointing, "is the containment field, right there."

They looked where he was pointing. "What, that?" Polly said. "It's just a—"

Mr Gogerty nodded. "A horsebox," he said. "But it's also a transdimensional portal, as you yourself proved just now, when you came in through it. Thank you, by the way, for clearing that up for me. It makes perfect sense, of course. Think about it. The experiment is set up to begin as soon as the ring enters the horsebox, which will only happen when the brood sow or the boar comes to the end of its working life and gets shipped off to the abattoir. You can call it a built-in timing device. And the joy of it is, the cheater would be miles away when it happened, with a perfect alibi; nothing to connect him to what would subsequently happen here in the eyes of the competition judges." He smiled. "As soon as the ring entered the box, it'd trigger the experiment. A human being somewhere in the world at large would disappear; one extra chicken would materialise in this farmyard, to be collected by the cheater at his leisure. He'd then take it to the judges and say, 'Here's a chicken I took at random from a farmyard. Examine it, and you'll find it's never seen the inside of an eggshell. Therefore, the chicken came first.'"

Don pulled a face. "That'd never work, surely."

"Why not?" Mr Gogerty said with a grin. "The chicken would be totally, absolutely, 100-per-cent authentic. There'd be no way anybody, even the judges, could tell it apart from any other chicken. The judges would use their powers of insight to see into its past. They'd find that its personal history began when it suddenly appeared out of nowhere, fully grown. No eggs were harmed in the making of this rooster. That would be enough. The cheat's won."

Mr Gogerty fell silent for a while, not noticing the way all the chickens in the yard were looking straight at him. Then he snapped out of his reverie and went on: "But it didn't happen like that. Something went wrong."

Nobody spoke for some time. Then Mr Huos said, "Are you saying I'm a pig?"

Mr Gogerty nodded. "My guess is," he said, "that the pig with the hub in its nose must've got out of its pen and into the horsebox, way ahead of time, before the rest of the cheat's preparations were in place. I don't know the details, obviously, but I'd hazard a guess that he hadn't yet chosen a human to be turned into a chicken, and so the hub hadn't been targeted on a particular individual. Before the cheat's had a chance to perform that particular chore, suddenly the hub vanishes and passes beyond his control. The hub enters the containment field and becomes active. The only thing beside itself inside the field is the pig, so it transforms it. The pig vanishes, and at precisely that moment a previously unrecorded human being materialises thousands of miles away on a mountainside in Georgia, a man with no history but in possession of a brass ring, with steel earrings where the galvanised ear tags used to be, and with the Greek word for pig written on the back of his left hand."

Something odd happened to time, but it had nothing to do with magic. Eventually, Mr Huos broke the silence. "Oh," he said.

Mr Gogerty shrugged. "Well," he said, "you did ask me to find out where you came from. I can't help it if you don't like it."

"Hang on," Mr Huos said. "What about the hundred thousand dollars?"

Mr Gogerty nodded eagerly. "That puzzled me too," he said. "But I think I can explain. The pig had a value; all the livestock on a farm has a value, after all. In your case it was how much you were worth to the farm: your weight in sausages, basically. The hub transformed that too. I have no idea how it came up with a hundred thousand US dollars, but that's what you must be worth." He smiled weakly. "In sausages."

Polly shuffled awkwardly. Part of her was in the process of being purged by wonder, pity and terror. The rest of her, the part that was used to turning up for work in the mornings, wanted to explode in a Krakatoa of giggles. She was a humane, compassionate person, but she was also an office worker, and this man, or this pig, was her boss. "So what happened?" she asked.

"Chaos," Mr Gogerty replied succinctly. "Mr Huos started using the hub. It, meanwhile, naturally obeyed its fundamental programming and started turning people into chickens. I imagine the first victim was a female member of Mr Huos' legal department, whose brother just happened to be a musician. Presumably Mr Huos quite innocently did something which led the hub to think she was the chosen transformee. The hub did its work, but wasn't immediately deactivated, which was what should have happened. So it carried on transforming people. The logical explanation is that it stored the template of its first victim – female lawyer with a brother who plays music – and every time it encountered someone who fitted it transformed her. At some stage, by the look of it, the hub broadened the template to include the brothers as well, which is how Mr Briggs got here."

"Kevin Briggs?" Don interrupted sharply. "The man I—"

"No, you didn't," Mr Gogerty said. "You just happened to be on the spot and thinking harsh thoughts about him when he was taken, but it would've happened anyway."

"Thank God for that," Don said. "I was so worried; I thought I'd killed him." Then he frowned and said, "Hold on a moment, though. How come I got caught up in it at all?"

Mr Gogerty looked grave. "My assumption is that Ms Mayer here was to be the hub's next victim. It had, so to speak, already noticed her, and therefore you as well. Before the transformation took place, however, something happened that changed everything. Mr Huos took his coat to be cleaned. He forgot to take the box out of his pocket. The cleaners found the box in his coat and took it out. They must have opened the box and removed the ring from it. Then, as if that wasn't enough, they put the ring and the box in the pocket of someone else's coat." Mr Gogerty shuddered. "Yours."

His mind suddenly flooded with horrible images of what could have happened, but, as if from a long way away, he heard Don saying, "But I never saw the box. It definitely wasn't in my coat when I—"

Mr Gogerty sighed. Why couldn't people ever *listen*? "The hub transformed it," he said. "I have no idea what it turned it into, but whatever it was, it ended up inside your fridge, so I'm guessing you must've put it there. You wouldn't have recognised it as a box, most probably, because the hub would've transformed it."

Don shut his eyes, the way you do when you realise you've forgotten something. "I went food shopping just before I went to the cleaners," he said. "When I got home, I just shoved all the stuff in the fridge."

"Well, there you have it," Mr Gogerty said, with the slightest feather of impatience on the edge of his voice. "Glad we got that sorted out. Do you want to hear the rest of it or not?"

All three of them looked at him, but it was Polly who spoke. "There's more?"

He explained it to them, slowly and patiently. He told them about Mr and Mrs Williams, who ran a small-time dry cleaning business in Clevedon Road. He explained that without the hub inside it the box couldn't function the way it was supposed to. When the Williamses went through the pockets of Mr Huos' coat, as they always did, to make sure nothing had been left in them, they inadvertently separated the hub and the box. In that short interval of separation the box discovered that it was empty and activated its emergency backup procedure, extending the containment field around the building it was in at the time. It must (Mr Gogerty speculated) have proved too much for the box's programming and overloaded its artificial intelligence, causing it to dislocate the entire shop from its native reality – in practice, sending it whirling off unpiloted in both space and *time*. It went *backwards* in time, so that the dislocation effect was backdated, the timeline was violently adjusted, and the Williamses had been living their nomadic life for years and years by the time Don Mayer first walked into their shop.

"I think," Mr Gogerty said, "that Mr or Mrs Williams must have taken the ring out of the box in the downstairs toilet, because that's where the field coalesced to form a temporal wormhole, joining the toilet to the hub's final anticipated destination, the ruined abbey Mr Mayer here told us about, the place where the competition judges were to be found. Hence, at a set time each day, the toilet became a portal back to the abbey. When everything started going wrong..."

He explained about that too. When Mr Huos no longer controlled the hub, everything he'd done with it started to fall apart, gradually at first, but gathering pace as the consequences impacted on each other. Polly started to realise that someone had been drinking her coffee. The chickens began remembering they'd been human. Norton St Edgar, or the part of it Mr Huos had built on, separated from the rest of the world and sealed itself off, so that the only access in and out of it was through the portal. The same effect drew the Williamses' shop there. From the fact that Don had found it deserted, Mr Gogerty deduced that Mr and Mrs Williams had left it and couldn't get back in. It was just as well, he said, that Mr Huos had closed down the office and scrupulously unpicked every deal he'd ever made. That had at least restricted the spread of the chaos brought about by the separation of the ring and the box. It probably meant that no more lady solicitors would be turned into barnyard fowls.

"Probably?" Polly repeated, shocked.

"Probably," Mr Gogerty said. "The fact that you're still human suggests it's stopped. You'll remember, you were the next on the list. Of course, it may have bypassed you and moved on."

"The Briggs woman," Polly remembered with a shiver. "She vanished while I was talking to her."

Mr Huos started. "What, Rachel Briggs, who works for me? Oh," he added, as he remembered who he was talking to. "You won't know her, of course. She's—"

"She's been drinking my coffee," Polly said. "But I did meet her, as it happens. And she disappeared into thin air. Does that mean...?"

Mr Gogerty nodded in the direction of the flock of chickens presently crowded round Polly's mobile trying to send a text message to the Pentagon. "She's probably over there right now," he said.

"You know," Mr Huos said wistfully. "If a fox were to get into this yard right now, it'd save me an absolute fortune in severance pay. But I don't want that to happen," he added firmly. "I want it all sorted out, right now." He shifted a little to face Mr Gogerty, square on like a boxer. "Thanks for explaining," he said, "and I think it was very clever of you to figure all that out, but what exactly are you planning on doing about it?"

"Ah." Mr Gogerty frowned, and a cloud passed over the sun. "That's not going to be quite so straightforward."

The motorcade was lost.

The chauffeur of the car containing the chairman of the Bank of England, the Polish minister of culture, the CEO of Kawaguchiya Integrated Circuits and the patriarch of Alexandria pulled up and wound down his window. "Excuse me," he asked the driver of the car he'd just met, "can you tell me how to get to Norton St Edgar?"

Trevor McPherson scowled back at him. "You trying to be funny?" he said.

The chauffeur said no, he wasn't, and it was a perfectly civil question. Trevor realised that it was, at that. "Sorry," he said. "You're in Norton St Edgar right now. You just need to carry on down the lane, left at the crossroads, then on a hundred yards and turn right, and that'll bring you out by the church. Excuse me," he went on, his heart pounding, "but where've you just come from?"

"Heathrow," said the chauffeur. "Why?"

Trevor held his breath. "And you didn't have any bother getting here? No roads closed or anything?"

"Roadworks on the M5," the chauffeur replied. "That's about all. Why?"

Behind, the Dalai Lama's driver was leaning on his horn. "Sorry," Trevor said quickly. "I'm holding you all up. Take care, now." He wound up his window, crushed his car into the hedge to get past and shot away up the lane towards the main road. He didn't get that far, of course. Two minutes later he was back outside his house, sobbing into his coat sleeve.

The chauffeur shrugged and drove on. His satnav seemed to have given up entirely. It kept warbling, "At the end of the road, phase-shift into an alternative universe," so he switched it off. Clearly the man he'd spoken to was either a practical joker or from out of town, because the lane just wound on and on, with no suggestion of a crossroads or turning. All he needed, he reckoned, was to meet a flock of sheep coming the other way to make this a perfect day.

In the event, it wasn't sheep; it was chickens.

"It's not up to me," Mr Gogerty said.

Mr Huos waited for him to clarify, but he didn't. Then the implications of Mr Gogerty's silence began to spread through Mr Huos' mind like spilt coffee seeping into a keyboard.

"Oh," he said. "Is that...?"

Mr Gogerty nodded. "The hub," he said, "has to be put back in the box. Unfortunately, I have no idea what's going to happen after that, and I'm not prepared to find out by doing it.

It's your ring," he said. "I think you should be the one to put it back where it belongs."

For a very long time nobody spoke or moved or breathed. Then Mr Huos sort of twisted away like a child trying to avoid an injection. "What'll happen to me if I...?" He didn't finish the sentence and Mr Gogerty didn't reply. "No," Mr Huos said. "I won't do it and you can't make me. You said yourself, it's not my fault."

"Fault's got nothing to do with it," Mr Gogerty said sadly. "It's entirely up to you, of course. You can take the hub back into the containment field and find out what happens, or we can all stand around here for the rest of our lives, if that's what you really want. To be honest with you, I can't imagine anything that could happen to you in there that'd be worse than hanging round this farmyard until we all die of old age or starvation, but perhaps you can. Now, if you'll excuse me for a few minutes, there's a few points I want to clear up with the chickens."

Mr Huos opened his mouth to say something, but thought better of it and let him go. A moment or so later Mr Gogerty was sitting on his heels typing into his personal organiser, a tall mountain towering over a sea of huddling poultry.

"Well," Mr Huos said, as Polly tried not to look at him. "I suppose I owe you an apology."

"Oh, that's all right," Polly replied, her voice as brittle as icicles. "No harm done, I guess. Not by you, at any rate. Or at least not on purpose. What I mean is, yes, you would appear to have completely buggered up my life, and you did it so you could make a lot of money, but I don't suppose you ever thought the effects would be quite so disastrous for all concerned. Or if you did, you probably thought the risk wasn't all that great, so you'd probably get away with it. In any case," she concluded, "it's not all your fault, not really."

Mr Huos blinked. "Thank you," he said. "I feel much better about myself now. How about you?" he went on, looking at Don. "What do you think I should do?"

"Me?" Don took a step back. "Not up to me, is it?"

"No," Mr Huos said patiently, "but just pretend it was. What would you do if you were me?"

"Easy," Don said quickly. "Nothing on earth could make me get inside that horsebox thing. You couldn't get me in there at gunpoint. And you know why?"

Mr Huos smiled. "I can probably guess, but tell me anyway."

"Because," Don said, "I'm weak, gutless, self-centred as a gyroscope and completely lacking in conscience and social responsibility. How about you, Mr Huos? Are you all those things too?"

Mr Huos thought for a while. "If I've understood this correctly," he said, "if I go in there, chances are I'll turn into a pig."

"Back into a pig," Polly amended helpfully. "And it's all just Mr Gogerty's theory. He could be completely wrong. I mean, just think about it. It's further-fetched than apples from New Zealand."

Mr Huos nodded. "You reckon," he said.

"Well, of course," Polly said brightly. "Transdimensional hubs, containment fields, people being lost in time and turned into chickens. If you believe that, you'll believe anything. I think it's all complete crap, don't you, Don?"

Don nodded very slowly. "It's a bit short on empirical proof, certainly," he said.

"Wild speculation, I'd call it," Polly said. "Not a shred of evidence to suggest walking into that horsebox would have any bad effects at all. Don't you agree, Don?"

"You know what," Mr Huos said, and his voice seemed to come from somewhere down around his socks. "I think you're right. It's all just a lot of fuss over nothing – Stan Gogerty trying to make out he's solved some great big enormous mystery so he can whack in a great big enormous bill. So," he went on, quietly, almost grimly, but without a trace of either anger or despair, "why don't I go inside that horsebox right now, and show him up for the rip-off merchant he really is? Well, what d'you think?"

Human beings think words are the big deal, the universal tool, the measure of all things, but there are times when words are about as much use as a soda siphon in a firestorm. "Good idea," Polly said in a very small voice, and Don could only nod. Mr Huos smiled at them, and Polly thought, That's my boss, and he's about to walk calmly into the box and get turned into a pig. Heroes are a bit like supermodels. The papers and glossy magazines are full of them, but we're led to believe they're really a different species, not something you or I could ever become just by deciding to. And particularly not someone's boss. The terms "heroism" and "senior management" exist in separate universes. "Bye, then," Polly said, and Mr Huos walked into the box. The ramp that was also a door swung up unaided and closed with a bang. They waited, but nothing much happened.

"He's gone inside then." Mr Gogerty had rejoined them.

They didn't reply; it wasn't as though Mr Gogerty was relying on them for crucial information.

"What did you say to him?" Mr Gogerty asked.

Polly shook her head; Don said, "Oh, nothing." All three of them were too preoccupied to notice that the chickens had left the yard in a flock and gone scurrying up the lane.

"We must've got through after all," Ms Byron said, her eyes fixed on the column of long black cars bumping slowly down the farm track, like women in high heels walking in mud.

"What did you say to them?" asked Charles the Mahler expert, struggling to keep up with her.

"I kept it simple," Ms Byron replied. "I just said, 'norton st edgar, worcs, we aren't really chickens, take us to your leader.' But it looks like they've come to us instead."

Not the form of words that he'd necessarily have chosen, Charles thought, but apparently it had worked just fine. The cars hit a muddy patch and slithered around a bit. A police outrider fell off his bike and landed in a wide brown puddle, spraying muddy water all over the windows of an enormous stretch Mercedes. "They got here very fast," Charles observed.

"It shows they're taking us seriously," Ms Byron replied, and Charles, thinking about it, decided she was the sort of person who would interpret this particular subset of facts in that particular way. Mind, she could be right.

Ms Byron stopped in the exact centre of the track and spread her wings. She took a deep breath, then called out (in a voice that a human could easily mistake for mere clucking) "Welcome. Thank you for coming. Together I feel sure we can solve this mystery and, working together—"

That was as far as she got. The lead car wasn't stopping. Just in time she burst into flight, her wings flapping wildly, and managed to clear the left front tyre of the oncoming limo by the thickness of a cigarette paper. The other chickens scattered, and watched as the motorcade rumbled past.

"We should go and see if he's all right," Polly said.

Don made a furious-scared noise. Mr Gogerty didn't seem to have heard. She couldn't blame either of them, Don in particular. It hadn't been long since she'd said more or less the same thing to him, leading him to his rendezvous with the Big Voice in the ruined abbey. Fair enough, Polly thought. My turn.

She took a few steps towards the horsebox, realised with a certain degree of annoyance that neither Don nor Mr Gogerty was going to stop her, and carried on the rest of the way. There was a handle on the door for pulling it down. It came down easily.

Inside the box was a pig.

She looked at the pig, and the pig looked back at her and made that unique barking noise pigs make. She noticed that it had a ring through its nose.

"Hello," Polly said.

The pig snuffled at her, then advanced, unsure of its footing on the slatted ramp. She wished she had something she could give it: an apple or a swede, or whatever it is pigs like to eat. She stood aside to let it pass and it stepped out onto the concrete, acting a bit dazed, like a released hostage.

Polly rejoined the others, and they watched the pig saunter slowly (pigs' trotters were never designed for walking on concrete) across the yard towards the nearest sty, whose gate was conveniently open. Don tried to remember the quotation about it being a far, far better thing, but Polly said, "After all, he *was* a property developer." He felt she had a point, but that didn't cover it completely.

"Interesting," Mr Gogerty said.

"What?"

"It's a sow," he said.

"So?" Polly snapped. "Why shouldn't a sow be a successful property tycoon?"

Mr Gogerty raised his eyebrows. "No reason, I guess," he said. Then he noticed something out of the corner of his eye and turned to look. At the same moment, Polly said, "Don, who are all those people?"

They advanced in a column like a school crocodile, except they weren't holding hands. They took no notice of Polly or Don, though the Japanese foreign minister nodded slightly to Mr Gogerty. They headed straight for the pigsty as though they were radio controlled.

"Oh," Mr Gogerty said under his breath. "I *see.*"

The old saddleback sow lifted her head and gazed across the yard at the procession of people coming towards her. She felt a trifle confused because the last thing she could remember was climbing inside the horsebox to look for her piglets, all the many litters of piglets who'd disappeared inside and never come out again. And now, by a remarkable coincidence, here they were coming towards her.

A piglet (but my, how he'd grown) stepped up to the sty gate, stopped and stood there awkwardly. He was dimly aware that he was, or had at some point been, the chief executive officer of Kawaguchiya Integrated Circuits, but that wasn't the main thing on his mind at that moment.

"Mother?" he said.

The old saddleback sow grunted and smiled at him. "Hello, dear," she said, as the archbishop of Cologne shuffled up behind him, peered over his shoulder and mumbled, "Hello, Mum." At that moment the old sow was happy, happier than if she'd been given a sackful of apples, and so she wasn't interested in eavesdropping on Mr Gogerty explaining how the transformation field must have acted retrospectively and turned all Mr Huos' offspring into humans too. She was just glad to see them all, and know they were safe, and that the implied covenant with Humankind on which she'd always relied had been proved true in the end. They'd taken her piglets from her, but only for their own good, to give them a better start in life than she could have offered them. So that, she decided, was all right, and silly her for having doubted it for a minute.

"The next minute," a piglet was telling her, "I woke up on this hillside in the Atlas Mountains, with nothing but a suit of clothes and a bundle of cash in my pocket. Luckily some of the local people found me and looked after me, and when I was old enough I used the money to pay my way through college, and now I'm the Sikorsky professor of solid state physics at Kiev University, so it hasn't turned out too bad. So," the piglet went on, after a short pause to draw breath, "how've you been keeping?"

The sow tried to remember. "Oh, can't complain," she replied. "Now mind out of the way and let me say hello to your brother."

As the procession of the great and good turned into something between a greeting line and a book signing, Polly shook her head and said, "That's so weird. All those people..."

Mr Gogerty mumbled something about collateral forces and interdimensional feedback, even contriving to drag in both Newton and Einstein, and Don, who knew enough science to be able to recognise at least one word in ten of what he was hearing, didn't doubt him for a moment. Interstitiary shear combined with temporal z-axis shunts; absolutely, no question about it, that must have been what happened, and it was nice of Mr Gogerty to explain it all in such detail. But it wasn't science; like hell it was science. It wasn't even magic (which, as he now knew, was simply science nobody's got around to writing up for the journals yet). In fact, he hadn't any real idea what it was, though he fancied that if he was a really seriously good mathematician he might be able to describe it in equations. As far as he was concerned, though, it was quite simply the right thing to have happened. If his life was a seven-note jingle, this would be note number five, the one that nobody ever hears but which makes all the difference.

While he was thinking all that, Polly was talking to him. He was so used to tuning her out while he was deep in thought that he only caught the very end of it, namely, "...wants a word with you."

He frowned. "Say again?"

Polly sighed. "I said," she said, "I think that man over there wants a word with you."

"What man?"

Shuffling into his dressing gown and slippers, George Williams slumped downstairs to the kitchen and put the kettle on. Another day, he thought. Another day, in all probability, just like the last one and the one before that. Not that he was one to complain. He liked things neat and tidy and orderly, and he was only too well aware that he had plenty to be grateful for. A nice little business, with plenty of goodwill and regular customers, in a good location. You don't mess about with a winning formula, after all. Even so. He wandered through into the shop and twitched aside the blind so he could take a peek at the quiet street outside. Same view as always: same doors opposite, same cars parked, and he knew most of the early-bird commuters heading for the bus stop and the station either by name or by sight. When you trade from the same premises for fifteen years, you become part of the landscape. No quarrel with that. Good for business.

Even so.

It'll be different, he thought as he poured the hot water into the mugs, when we retire. We can relax a bit more, take it easy. We could travel. That was something he'd always wanted to do – a bit of the Gypsy in him, Eileen always reckoned – but of course, with the shop and everything, that had been pretty much out of the question. It must be fun, he thought, to wake up in the morning and, for those first few seconds of being awake, not to know where you are; to pull back the curtains and see a different view, unfamiliar streets populated with strangers. Best of all (he smiled as he thought about it) not to have to spend the whole day getting the marks and stains out of other people's mucky clothes. Wouldn't that be nice?

*Be careful what you wish for*, his mother had always told him; be careful, or you might just get it. Always coming out with stuff like that, she was, stuff that sounded good but, when you stopped and thought about it, didn't really mean anything. *Take one day at a time* was another of her favourites, and there were others he'd never quite been able to make sense of, like *Things in pockets should stay in pockets* and *Never open little wooden boxes in the downstairs lav.* Of course, she'd got a bit strange near the end, and when that happens, you gradually stop listening.

By the time he unlocked the door for the first customers of the day, he'd put the unsettling thoughts clean out of his mind. Too much to do for one thing, and besides, in the dry cleaning game there were always surprises. The two men who came in bang on the dot of nine, for example: big blokes, a bit red in the face, between them lugging a great big wicker basket.

"Don't suppose you can help us," one of them said, "but we're a couple of knights and we've been asleep for a very long time. You wouldn't happen to be able to get rust spots out of chain mail, would you?"

"There you are," said Kevin Briggs angrily. "I want a word with you."

Don winced. He had it coming, he supposed. It was all very well Mr Gogerty saying it hadn't been his fault, just bad timing and coincidence, but he hadn't really believed a word of it. He was, of course, delighted and overjoyed that the chickens had all become human again about five minutes after Mr Huos went into the box. *No harm done* and *All's well that ends well* weren't, however, cutting it as far as he was concerned. He hadn't killed anybody after all, but he easily could have.

"Look," he said appeasingly, but Kevin Briggs didn't give him a chance. "I've had just about enough of you," he said, as Don wilted under his glare, "making that bloody awful racket at all hours of the day and night. It's making the walls shake. I can't even hear myself practise the bloody guitar. So if I hear so much as a squeak out of you from now on I'm going straight to Environmental Health, and they'll soon wipe the grin off your—"

At which point Don took a good swing and punched him on the nose. The sixth note, he thought. Perfect.

They hitched a lift with a couple of field marshals, who dropped them off at Tewkesbury station. Polly and Don bought tickets to London. Mr Gogerty phoned for a hire car. They parted without any fuss. Polly mumbled, "Well, thanks for everything," and Don wrote out a cheque. He'd decided he couldn't be bothered to collect his prize for guessing which came first. As the train pulled out he was already humming under his breath (seven perfect notes for Radio Tyneside), while Polly opened the magazine she'd bought at the station bookstall.

Mr Gogerty's car took him to a private airstrip.

"Oh shit," said the pilot. "You again."

"Yes," Mr Gogerty said. "You remember how to get there?"

It wasn't something the pilot was ever likely to forget. They flew there in grim silence. Mr Gogerty made a show of checking his messages and doing some routine paperwork, but just for once he couldn't concentrate. He wasn't looking forward to what was going to come next.

"Stan." The old man stepped back to let him in. He stepped out of the blinding glare of the naked sun, and the old man shut the door behind him. Was there a slight edge to the cheery how-nice-to-see-you smile, or was it just his imagination?

"Always pleased to see you, Stan," the old man said, "but twice in one week…" He frowned. "There's nothing wrong, is there, son?"

Mr Gogerty sat down. He tried not to look at the photo of his mother on the mantelpiece. "That's what I was about to ask you," he said. "Listen."

He told the whole story. He kept it to the bare minimum without leaving out anything important. He was good at that sort of thing. As he spoke he tried to read the old man's face, but all he saw there was interest, wonder, concern, all perfectly registered. The old man would have done well in silent movies.

"It was you, wasn't it?" he said.

The old man looked at him for what seemed like a very long time. Then he chuckled, a sound that came welling up from deep inside him, like something long-contained breaking free. "What kind of thing's that to say to an old friend, Stan?" he said. "You got a touch of the sun or something?"

"It was you," Mr Gogerty said. "You tried to cheat the competition."

"No way, Stan."

But Mr Gogerty's face was grim. "You burned down the Carpenter Library," he said, "just to stop me finding out."

And then the old man's face crumpled, like a paper bag

blown up and then burst. "I'd lose my job, Stan," he said, "if they ever found out. You ain't going to tell on me, are you?"

"I don't know," Mr Gogerty said.

"You can't." The old man was pleading with him, and he wasn't sure he was proof against that. "It'd break your mother's heart."

"You shouldn't have burned down the Carpenter, Uncle Theo," Mr Gogerty said. "That was wrong."

The old man nodded slowly. "How'd you figure it out?"

Mr Gogerty shrugged. "You knew all about it," he said. "You told me, everything I know, when I was a kid. You'll have forgotten..."

"I remember," the old man said. "It was on the beach. You were nine years old."

There seemed to be something wrong with Mr Gogerty's throat. "You're the only man in the profession who could've rigged up that hub," he said. "It was a beautiful piece of work."

The old man nodded – no false modesty. "I was a lot younger then," he said. "Still had good eyesight. Couldn't do it now, I don't suppose." He sighed. "The box was the tricky part," he said. "You know how many connections there were in that box? One thousand, six hundred and forty-three. All done by hand," he added with a spark of pride. "Just an eyeglass and a soldering iron was all I had to work with; couldn't afford fancy tools, not then." He shook his head. "So," he said, "that boy you told me about, he solved it."

Mr Gogerty nodded. "He gave the right answer."

"And the prize?" There was a pale glow in the old man's eyes. "He got the prize?"

"No." Mr Gogerty looked away. "He says he can't be bothered to collect it. He's had enough of, well, our stuff. Just wants to forget it ever happened."

"So the prize is still—" The old man stopped short. There was a hungry look in his eyes Mr Gogerty found disturbing.

"Well," he said, "you could say I've got as good a right to it as anybody."

Mr Gogerty frowned. "Uncle Theo," he said, "do you know what the prize is?"

"Actual figures? No, can't say as I do. But it's got to be pretty damn good – enough to pay off all my debts and see me right in my old age. And there'd be something left over for your mother when I'm gone, and you as well, Stan. You know I always—"

"Five hundred pounds sterling," Mr Gogerty said.

The old man's mouth opened, but for a while no sound came out. Then he said, "What?"

"Five hundred pounds," Mr Gogerty repeated.

"Shit."

"And before you ask," Mr Gogerty went on, "there's no compound interest or anything like that. Cash money. I've got the address to write to, if you want it."

Slowly the old man slumped forward, his face sliding between his cupped hands. It was more than Mr Gogerty could bear. "What we could do," he heard himself say, "is take it back in time and invest it in real estate – Manhattan island or something like that – and then—"

"Wouldn't work," the old man snapped. "You know that. Didn't you ever listen to anything I told you?"

"Sorry," Mr Gogerty grumbled, and suddenly he wanted to leave. "Anyway," he said, "I won't tell anybody about the library. I won't say a word about anything, I promise. I'd better be going now. I've got an appointment..."

He didn't bother to finish the lie. He wasn't sure if the old man even registered that he was still there. He stood up, trying to make as little noise as possible. "I'll see myself out," he said. "And I'll give your love to..."

The old man wasn't listening. As Mr Gogerty stepped from the cloud into the helicopter a thought struck him, something the old man had said. Something left over for his mother, and

378 • Tom Holt

hers the only picture on the shelf. Just a friend of the family, she'd always told him. Well, he thought.

He asked the pilot to take a detour and swoop low over the Malverns. Norton St Edgar looked very small: one street, a church, a pub that never seemed to be open. The stretch Mercs had long since gone, but the lanes were clogged with wandering pedestrians – people who'd woken up out of the strangest dream to find themselves standing in a field surrounded by their furniture, and a whole lot of women lawyers, confused, angry and at a total loss as to who they should sue for what. Mr Gogerty smiled faintly and told the pilot to fly him back to London.

Far below, the old saddleback sow lifted her head, saw the helicopter, figured out what it was more or less from first principles, worked out how she'd go about making one if only she had opposable thumbs, and ate a turnip.

# extras

orbit

# meet the author

*Tom Holt*

TOM HOLT was born in London, England, in 1961. At Oxford he studied bar billiards, ancient Greek agriculture, and the care and feeding of small, temperamental Japanese motorcycle engines; interests that led him, perhaps inevitably, to qualify as a solicitor and emigrate to Somerset, where he specialized in death and taxes for seven years before going straight in 1995. Now a full-time writer, he lives in Chard with his wife, one daughter, and the unmistakable scent of blood wafting in on the breeze from the local meat-packing plant. Find out more about the author at http://www.tom-holt.com/.

# introducing

If you enjoyed
LIFE, LIBERTY, AND THE PURSUIT OF SAUSAGES,
look out for

## BLONDE BOMBSHELL

*by Tom Holt*

*The year is 2017. Lucy Pavlov is the CEO of PavSoft Industries, home of a revolutionary operating system that every computer in the world runs on. Her personal wealth is immeasurable, her intelligence is unfathomable, and she's been voted World's Most Beautiful Woman for three years running. To put it simply – she has it all.*

*But not everything is quite right in Lucy's life. For starters, she has no memories prior to 2015. She also keeps having runins with a unicorn. And to make matters even worse, a bomb is hurtling through interstellar space, headed straight for Lucy – and the planet known as Earth.*

\* \* \*

## Interstellar Space

In spite of the director's misgivings, the bomb launched on time. As it bypassed Orion, blasting through the heart of the Lion's Mane nebula at 106 times the speed of light, it composed a violin sonata.

It felt guilty about that. Violin sonatas, after all, were what it had been built to eradicate. But, it argued to itself, it was above all a smart bomb, a very smart bomb indeed. Warhead (powerful enough to reduce any known planet to gravel), engines, guidance system, targeting and defensive arrays only took up a tenth of the volume of its asteroid-sized casing. The rest was pure intellect, the finest synthetic intelligence the Ostar had ever produced.

Know your enemy, it reasoned. Learn to think like them. An alien race capable of building a weapon as subtle, insidious and devastating as a violin sonata mustn't be underestimated. After all, it now seemed certain that the aliens had somehow managed to knock out the Mark One, the bomb's immediate predecessor; they must have done, or they wouldn't still be there. An astounding accomplishment for a planet whose dominant species were primates (Yetch, the bomb muttered to itself) who could think of no better name for their homeworld than Soil, or Dirt, or some such.

The bomb swerved to avoid a comet, and added a coda and a set of variations. The tune was catchy. It hummed a few bars, though of course in the impenetrable silence of space it couldn't hear them.

The bomb had never known the Mark One, which had been built, programmed and launched long before its successor had been envisaged. Indeed, it was to the Mark One's failure that this bomb, the Mark Two, owed its existence. Clearly the Mark One had been flawed, or simply not good enough, because it had failed. Failure was inexcusable. Even so, as the stars dopplered past in thin filaments of light, it couldn't help wondering what the Mark One had been like; whether, under other circumstances, they'd have got on together, whether they'd have been friends.

(It felt the slight gravitational tug of a hitherto unrecorded comet passing by a thousand light-years away. It made the necessary calculations and adjusted its course.)

On balance, Mark Two was inclined to doubt it. They were both, after all, bombs. When you've been built for a purpose, and that purpose is the elimination of an entire planet, the circumstances of your origin tend to colour your worldview. A certain degree of pessimism is inevitable. What does it ultimately matter? you can't help thinking. The beauty of a sunset, the mind-stopping clarity of a cat singing at dawn, the flash of light on a flawless titanium-alloy panel, the sinuous modulations of a violin sonata; with a supercharged artificial intelligence, you can't help but appreciate all these, but deep down you know they're irrelevant, because a day will come when the mission has been accomplished, the target has been reduced to dust floating on the stellar winds, and you with it. The sun, the cat, the panel, quite possibly the violin sonata will all still be there, back on the planet where your frames were first joined, but you won't be.

To which the programmers had instructed the Mark Two to react: Oh well, never mind, omelettes and eggs and all that. It didn't – couldn't – occur to the Mark Two that its programmers may have been wrong, but it also couldn't help detecting a certain frailty about the logic.

Know your enemy, it reminded itself. It was worth repeating, because it constituted the First Law of Sentient Ordnance: *Thou shalt not blow up the wrong planet.* On that point the programmers had been insistent to the point of fussiness. Accordingly, they'd fed into Mark Two's cavernous brain every last scrap of data they had about Dirt and its people, their history, biology, philosophy, culture, art, literature and, of course, music. It wasn't much, a mere $10^{10,000,000}$ scantobytes, but it was enough to get the job done; enough, also, to intrigue the Mark Two as it trudged across the endless parsecs towards its target. Above all, it posed the question that even the programmers had been unable to answer. Why?

Nobody knew. There were theories, of course. The favourite, endorsed by the War Department and the Governing Pack, was that the Dirt-people launched their music into space with a view to neutralising other races as a preliminary to invasion and the formation of a galactic empire. If that was the intention, it was working, at least on the Ostar. From the day when the first Dirt broadcasts, drifting aimlessly through space, had reached the Ostar homeworld, bringing with them the lethally insidious melodies of Dirt music, intellectual life on the planet had practically ground to a halt. After an alarmingly short time, the Ostar could barely think at all. With the fiendishly catchy Dirt melodies looping endlessly round and round in their heads, even the wisest academicians were mentally paralysed. The weapons researchers who'd designed the Mark One had had to have the auditory centres of their brains artificially paralysed before they could settle down to work, and even then it hadn't been uncommon to find one of them slumped at his console, his jowls noiselessly shaping dum, de dum, de dumpty dumpty dum; at which point the kindest thing was to have him taken away and shot. As for the rest of their once mighty civilisation, it had more or less seized up.

Hostile intent certainly seemed to be the only logical explanation. But there were inconsistencies. For example: how could a race descended from tree-rats who hadn't even mastered faster-than-light yet possibly believe they'd be capable of conquering worlds it'd take them tens of thousands of years to reach in their pathetic fire-driven tin-can spaceships? Did they even know there were other inhabited worlds out there? If the inane babble of their public telecasts was to be believed, a large majority of the Dirters sincerely believed they were alone in the universe. A blind, the War Department argued; a fatuous attempt to lure us into a false sense of security. But that hypothesis did suggest an alternative explanation: that the Dirters, unaware that they had neighbours in the cosmos, were mindlessly polluting space with their toxic aural garbage. They didn't know the harm they were doing; or, worse still, they knew and they didn't care.

To which the War Department replied, "If, as is not admitted, this hypothesis is true, all the more reason to blow Dirt into its constituent atoms." With which line of argument it was hard to find fault. On one thing the Ostar were completely agreed: the Dirters had to be stopped, and quickly.

The bomb skirted a red dwarf, slowing down ever so slightly and flipping through ninety degrees to bask in its rich, sensuous heat. There were times when it almost wished it wasn't a bomb. Sure, every sentient machine on Ostar knew that explosive ordnance was the highest calling to which an artificial intelligence could aspire. Bombs were the élite, the elect, the chosen few; you didn't get to be a bomb unless you were something really special. That side of it, Mark Two had no quarrel with. It knew it was extraordinary, outstanding, and that fitting it to an industrial matter resequencer or a washing machine would have been a crime against technology. It was the getting-blown-up part that bothered it, with a small afterthought-grade reservation about taking a whole planet with it when it went. The programmers, needless to say, had an answer to that. Only with the very finest sentient machines, they said, were they prepared to share their species' greatest gift, the defining quality of canine life: mortality. It was the finite nature of Ostar existence that motivated them, gave them goals and objectives, spurred them on to achieve, discover and create. A dishwasher, by contrast, would chunter quietly on for ever, one day pretty much like the last and the next, never knowing the scintillating urgency that came with a limited lifespan. Count yourself lucky, was the moral.

Yes, Mark Two thought. Well.

Something infinitesimally small brushed its forward sensory array. Mark Two decoded it in a fraction of a nanosecond, and felt a deep chill crawling through its circuits. A ray of light from Dirt's sun. That could only mean one thing.

Mark Two engaged its optical-data-acquisition unit and followed the light's trajectory, compensating for entropic drift, the magnetic fields of all known objects in the relevant vicinity, time distortion and the effects of its own hyperspatial shroud. At the end of the line, sure enough, was a small, pale star with a gaggle of unremarkable planets bobbing along in its wake. The third planet out from the star was blue, with green splodges.

Dirt.

Oh, the bomb thought. And then its courage, determination and nobility-of-spirit subroutines cut in, overriding everything else, adrenalising its command functions and bypassing its cyberphrenetic nodes. Here goes, said the bomb to itself. Calibrate navigational pod. Engage primary thrusters. Ready auxiliary drive. It knew, in that moment, that its own doom was near, because it was giving itself orders, and it wasn't putting in any "the"s. That was what you did, apparently, when the moment came. You could also turn on a flashing red beacon and a siren, but mercifully these were optional.

Oh fuck, thought the bomb, and surged on towards Dirt like an avenging angel.

Orbit
Hachette Book Group
237 Park Avenue, New York, NY 10017
www.HachetteBookGroup.com

First Edition: February 2011

Orbit is an imprint of Hachette Book Group, Inc. The Orbit name and logo are trademarks of Little, Brown Book Group Limited.

Library of Congress Control Number: 2010926893
ISBN: 978-0-316-08002-6

10  9  8  7  6  5  4  3  2  1

Printed in the United States of America

# LIFE, LIBERTY, LIBERTY, AND THE PURSUIT of SAUSAGES

# TOM HOLT

orbit

WWW.ORBITBOOKS.NET

**The old sow waited until the daughter had gone
away and seized her chance.**

Nudging the sty door open with her mighty nose, she charged
out into the yard and trundled as fast as her legs could carry
her towards the trailer. As she did so, she realized that she had
no means of lowering the ramp but, incredibly, when she got
there she noticed that the retaining pegs that locked it in place
were loose, practically hanging out of their sockets. One precisely aimed blow of her snout, at just the right angle applied
with just the right degree of force, would be enough to bounce
them out, whereupon gravity would cause the ramp to swivel
on its hinge and fall to the ground.

Feverishly, forcing herself to concentrate, she did the maths,
calculating the angles in two planes, applying Sow's Constant
(mass times velocity squared) to quantify exactly the force
needed. At the last moment she closed her eyes and appealed to
the Supreme Agency itself: *If I am worthy, let the ramp come down.*

She headbutted. The ramp came down. She lifted her head
and, shaken but filled with wonder, walked slowly up the ramp.

Inside the trailer she stopped. For an instant she was flooded
with disappointment, an agony of existential isolation and despair. The trailer was just a box: four metal walls, a metal roof,
a wooden plank floor, a lingering smell of disinfectant. Then, as
she lowered her head, a dazzling blue light exploded all around
her, so that for a moment or so she was bathed from snout
to tail in shimmering blue fire. And then the back wall of the
trailer seemed to melt away, as though its atoms and molecules
were the morning fog over the river, and beyond it she saw a
flickering archway of golden light, and running under it a road
that led to green pastures, softly rolling valleys and the distant
cloud-blurred shape of purple hills.

"Oink," murmured the sow and walked through the arch,
and was never seen in this dimension again.